T0323904

Praise for Abbie Williams

"Williams populates her historical fiction with people nearly broken by their experiences."

— *Foreword Reviews INDIES Finalist (Soul of a Crow)*

* Gold Medalist - 2015

— *Independent Publishers Awards (Heart of a Dove)*

"Perfect for romantic mystery lovers ... a sweet, clever quickstep with characters who feel like longtime friends." — *Foreword Reviews (Wild Flower)*

"Set just after the U.S. Civil War, this passionate opening volume of a projected series successfully melds historical narrative, women's issues, and breathless romance with horsewomanship, trailside deer-gutting, and alluring smidgeons of Celtic ESP."

— *Publishers Weekly (Heart of a Dove)*

"There is a lot I liked about this book. It didn't pull punches, it feels period, it was filled with memorable characters and at times lovely descriptions and language. Even though there is a sequel coming, this book feels complete."

— *Dear Author (Heart of a Dove)*

"With a sweet romance, good natured camaraderie, and a very real element of danger, this book is hard to put down."

— *San Francisco Book Review (Heart of a Dove)*

ALSO BY ABBIE WILLIAMS

 THE SHORE LEAVE CAFE SERIES

SUMMER AT THE SHORE LEAVE CAFE
SECOND CHANCES
A NOTION OF LOVE
WINTER AT THE WHITE OAKS LODGE
WILD FLOWER
THE FIRST LAW OF LOVE
UNTIL TOMORROW
THE WAY BACK
RETURN TO YESTERDAY

FORBIDDEN

 THE DOVE SERIES

HEART OF A DOVE
SOUL OF A CROW
GRACE OF A HAWK

Abbie Williams

central
avenue
publishing

2018

Copyright © 2018 Abbie Williams
Cover and internal design © 2018 Central Avenue Marketing Ltd.
Cover Design: Michelle Halket
Cover Image: Courtesy & Copyright: iStock: RYROLA
Interior Image: Courtesy & Copyright: Abbie Willliams

All rights reserved. No part of this book may be used or reproduced in any manner
whatsoever without written permission from the author except in the case of brief
quotations embodied in critical articles and reviews.

This is a work of fiction. Names, characters, places and incidents either are the
product of the author's imagination or are used fictitiously and any resemblance to
actual persons, living or dead, business establishments, events or locales is entirely
coincidental.

Published by Central Avenue Publishing, an imprint of Central Avenue Marketing Ltd.
www.centralavenuepublishing.com

RETURN TO YESTERDAY

978-1-77168-130-8 (pbk)
978-1-77168-131-5 (epub)
978-1-77168-132-2 (mobi)

Published in Canada

Printed in United States of America

1. FICTION / Romance   2. FICTION / Family Life

TO LIFE, AND ITS SWEET, WILD, COUNTLESS PATHS.

AND TO THE IMMEASURABLE IMPORTANCE OF GOOD FRIENDS,
CLOSE FAMILIES, AND TRUE LOVES. ...

Chapter One

Dakota Territory - June, 1882

MARSHALL SAT ON ONE OF TWO MISMATCHED CHAIRS IN the little soddy where we would spend this night, a dishtowel wrapped around his neck as I shaved away his thick beard. I worked with deliberate care by the light of a single lantern, using a straight-edge razor; he rested his hands around the curve of my hips, watching me as I worked. Despite the fact that I was naked from the waist up, wearing nothing but one of my old underskirts, a well-worn garment once white and now the color of faded daisies, he could not take his eyes from mine.

"Your face," he breathed, trying not to move his jaw until I lifted the razor to swish it through a small bowl of warm water. "I dreamed of your face every night. Your eyes and the shape of your mouth, and the way your forehead crinkles when you're thinking hard." He added, "Your smile," as I did smile, stroking my bare belly with his thumbs. "And the sweet little freckles on your nose and the way you blush when I compliment you. I feel like I haven't stopped dreaming."

I shook my head at his adoring words, cupping his chin. I had successfully shaved half of his face and admonished in a whisper, "You hold still."

"I mean it," he insisted. "Do you know how many nights I lay awake longing for you until I thought I would die? And now you're here with me. I'm afraid to wake up."

I leaned closer and licked his nose. He snorted a laugh and for a second it was as though no time had passed since our first date way back in

2013, when I'd done the same thing. I muttered, "Don't make me flick you."

He smiled, though tears wet his gray eyes. "Angel, you can do anything you want to me. As long as you're here. Just stay with me. Be close to me. That's all I will ask of this life, ever again."

I leaned to kiss nose this time, then his lips, thinking of Miles, who – had fate taken a sharply different turn – might very well be my husband on this muggy June night in what would one day become South Dakota. The thought of Miles Rawley was a wound in my innermost heart which would never altogether heal. Miles had loved me and he'd been killed before my eyes; before he died I'd told him I loved him, and this remained true. I loved him because he shared a soul with Marshall; Miles had *been* Marshall in this place. Marshall and I were the ones displaced here in the nineteenth century. My thoughts of Miles tangled into my love for Marshall, one inextricable from the other; I had no doubt Miles's soul was right here in front of me, fulfilling his promise to find me again. I studied my man's familiar eyes, the long-lashed, smoldering sensuality of them, and whispered, "You."

Marshall understood with no additional explanation; he whispered, "I can't be away from you. I won't be, until I die and death separates us."

"I know," I murmured, tenderly stroking his hair. "I know, love. And even then I'll find you, I promise."

"After I die?" he whispered, tightening his grasp on my hips.

We were both exhausted from days of strenuous travel, riding under the grim cloak of constant worry that Fallon Yancy would find us as we slept; only compounding this daily stress was the fact that I'd divulged the truth about Fallon's role in Marshall's mother's death and his subsequent agonized fury had been titanic, held since only tentatively in check. Further, the pain of our separation, what we'd endured apart from each other, remained at the forefront of both our thoughts. I couldn't bear to think of a time when Marshall would die, even if that time was far in the future, many years from this moment. I stroked the unshaven side of his jaw and whispered, "Let me finish up and then I believe we have a dinner date at the main house."

Marshall gathered my hand and kissed my knuckles. As he settled back against the chair he spoke with his usual wry humor. "I hope you like gray hair, angel. I've gotten used to it now but I must look different to you."

His hair had grown out past his shoulders, a wavy and snarled mess I'd only just combed through, and remained predominantly the rich, glossy brown of polished walnut; the few silver threads lent him a maturity at which I marveled – all traces of boyishness having vanished since we'd last been together, back in Jalesville in 2014.

"*Marsh*," I scolded. "Even if you had no hair, or if it was completely gray, you could never look anything but wonderful to me." I felt a crooked, teasing smile pull at my mouth. "As wonderful as a double vanilla latte and a stack of peanut butter cups, seriously."

He released a soft breath, with a hint of his grin. "That good, huh? Oh God, angel, I felt so old last winter. Way down deep in my bones, I felt old. But now that you're here I feel restored."

I ran my fingers through his hair. "Besides, the silver is sexy."

He lowered his dark eyebrows, regarding me with the skeptical look I remembered well.

"I mean it," I insisted. "It's sexy *and* distinguished. And with this Civil War-style beard shaved away, you look more like yourself already."

"I still can't get over that we're here, in 1882. You know how many people alive today actually fought in the Civil War?"

"I know," I whispered, dunking the shaving brush in the soap and applying it to the right half of his beard, creating a thin layer of foam. I wiped the razor on the towel and began scraping away the thick stubble, starting at the top and pulling downward with small, delicate motions. "I wish I had a can of shave gel, honey, it would be so much easier on your face. But I want you to leave the rest of your hair longer, like it is." I looked up from my focus on the lower half of his face. "You know how much I love your hair."

His eyes caught fire. "I do."

I'll hurry, I replied with no words, anticipation spiking through my veins.

Marshall shifted the heat of his concentration lower on my body, gliding both hands upward, brushing his thumbs over my nipples, cradling the fullness of my breasts against his broad palms. I wrapped the towel around his jaws, patting away any last stray hairs, feeling the warmth of him beneath the damp cloth. His gaze was steady in its regard, leaving no doubt in my mind what he wanted us to do in short order; dinner in the main house would have to wait. I lifted the towel away and my heart thrashed at the sight of his clean-shaven face. My knees began to tremble as he slipped the underskirt from my otherwise naked body with a slow, caressing motion; it became a soft puddle of linen at my ankles.

"Come here," he murmured, drawing me forward by the waist, pressing a kiss between my breasts before opening his lips over a nipple. I threw aside the damp towel and dug my fingers in his hair, intending to clutch him to me this way forever. His questing tongue sent heated pleasure straight down the backs of my legs and outward to my fingertips. Teasing my breast with the soft heat of the words, he whispered, "You taste so good…"

"Don't stop," I begged, head hanging back. "Oh, Marshall…*don't stop*. I can feel that all the way between my legs…"

"I won't stop," he promised, as he had long ago, in our old lives. "Not ever, angel."

He rose and gathered me close; my breasts came up against the hair on his chest, and the lean, hard muscles beneath. I shifted my shoulders, delighting in the textures of his naked body. Marshall moved with purpose, parting my lips with his kiss, carrying me straight to the bed – a feather tick spread over a frame of woven ropes scarcely large enough for an adult – where he deposited me onto my back.

"More," I whispered, rising to my elbows as he knelt between my legs.

He grinned, his freshly-shaved face so familiar, so handsome and sexy and full of wanting as he eased my thighs farther apart and pressed his chest hair at their juncture, rubbing with a slow, sensual motion. My body pulsed in response.

"You feel so good," he breathed, licking the inner curve of my knees, one after the other. "The softness of your skin, the wet, sweet silk between your legs. Oh God, my angel-woman. You are so much more than I deserve…"

"Don't say that," I whispered, each breath becoming a moaning gasp.

"I mean to bring you joy." He shifted to bracket my hips, kissing a path ever higher.

"Yes." My voice was hoarse, neck arched against the rumpled quilt as he traced the flesh between my legs with both his tongue and his long and knowing fingers. "You bring me so much joy, Marsh…*oh God*…"

He spoke with impassioned reverence, his husky voice at my ear. "You are so beautiful it hurts, angel. I couldn't write a song to do justice to you. You can't know how much it means to touch you, when I thought I would never be given this privilege again."

My hands were all over him, seeking and grasping. "You're so hard, *let me taste you*…"

He rolled us to the side, ropes creaking, and I latched to his chest, kissing his collarbones, his sternum, licking a hot trail down his lean belly. He had already come a little; I could taste it as I swept my tongue in voluptuous circles. His fingers dug into my loose curls as I drew him deeply down my throat.

"*C'mere*," he groaned, taking me beneath him with one fluid motion. His desire was so very magnificent – intense, almost predatory, wide shoulders gleaming with sweat, hair hanging down his neck – I moaned, biting his chin, urging with my hips. Resting his forehead to mine, pulse visibly pounding at his throat, he whispered, "Before I lose…all control."

I murmured, with a gasp of fulfillment, "I *like* when you come in my mouth."

Marshall uttered a low laugh, his engorged length buried deep, shuddering at the pleasure of our joined bodies. His eyes crinkled at the corners as he grinned. "But *nothing* beats this spot, angel."

Chapter Two

DAWN FOUND US CURLED TOGETHER ON THE ROPE BED; we'd missed last night's dinner and were well on the way to missing this morning's breakfast, but I didn't care. Marshall was snoring, one arm tucked under his head, the other slung over my waist, just like it had always been back in our cozy apartment in Jalesville. I lay still, reveling in the moment, the gift of waking up beside him; if I squinted, hazing my vision, I could almost believe we were home. I could picture the little town in the Montana foothills with vivid clarity – I knew Jalesville still existed, just as Marshall and I remembered it – and that the Rawleys, Tish and Case, and my family in Landon were all there in the future, awaiting our return.

I found Marshall. I sent this thought to my sisters and Aunt Jilly, for at least the hundredth time; if anyone was capable of hearing me through the long, echoing corridors of time it was them. *We found each other and even if we never make it back to you, I am so happy. Please know this. I miss you all so much, but I have Marshall. I have him and I could not ask for more.*

I turned, with care, to watch him as he slept, rising to an elbow, tenderness and passion beating at my heart. I studied the face that meant more to me than any other, through all of time; I understood this fully now. Dark shadows of strain remained beneath his eyes but I would do everything in my power to erase those. His sensual mouth was relaxed with sleep, charcoal-black lashes fanned upon his angular cheekbones and the crease of worry at the bridge of his nose now invisible; his breathing was deep and even. I saw the pulse at the base of his throat where I'd first tasted his skin; the long nose that dominated his handsome face. His dark hair was spread over the pillow, streaked with silver. I couldn't have imagined being more attracted to him, and yet here I found myself.

I trailed my fingertips along the skin between my legs, dewy from last night's wealth of lovemaking. And then, as suddenly as an unexpected gunshot, Marshall awoke with a muffled cry, jerking to one elbow, eyes wild and frightened.

"I'm here," I said at once, wrapping him in my arms and burrowing close; this was not the first time he'd woken in a panic and I knew what was wrong. He pressed his face to my hair, breathing raggedly, fingers spread wide on my back, as if attempting to contain gushing blood. I latched a leg over his hips and tightened my hold. "I'm here, sweetheart, right here."

"I dreamed I woke up and you were gone." His voice was hoarse. His heart would not slow its pace and concern scalded me.

"Honey," I murmured, and did not release him until his heartbeat had steadied and sunlight stretched across the floor of the little cabin, warming the space with the first light of day. Our naked bodies meshed as seamlessly as rain-soaked leaves; there was no way to tell where I ended and he began.

"I will never let you go again, angel, not ever. I swear this to you."

"I know," I whispered, shifting position so I could see his eyes; they remained tortured and I longed to banish that expression, forever. Though nearly two weeks had passed since we'd found each other here in 1882, I still battled the aching memories our time apart. We'd talked without end since the evening when Cole and Patricia's son was born on the prairie following our escape from the Immaculate Heart of Mary, the convent where we'd been stashed by Dredd Yancy – and though I'd told Marshall in no uncertain terms I forgave him for the fight we'd had that winter night in February of 2014, and that *none* of this was his fault, he still blamed himself, unequivocally.

"I thought you'd been in a car accident," he had told me on the second night of our journey west, as we lay tangled together in our blankets near the fire. "I was sick with fear, Ruthie. I can only speak about it because I have my arms around you. I stayed at Dad's house after you left, tossing and turning in my old bed, picturing you driving to Minnesota. I tried calling you just before dawn. I was already in misery but it wasn't until midday that I started getting sick with fear. At first I thought you weren't answering because you were so angry. I went back to our apartment and realized you hadn't packed anything, and I felt like such shit. I figured you were in Landon telling them what an asshole I was..." His throat closed off; he cleared it before continuing. "By then I felt like such a fucking jerk I avoided calling you for about an hour, because I was terrified. I was so sure you'd tell me that was it, you planned to stay in Minnesota and you'd mail me your ring..."

"I'm so sorry, love," I whispered, my chin on his chest as he laid waste to the terrible memories.

"You have nothing to be sorry for, angel. By that afternoon I'd changed tactics and called your phone at least fifty times. And then I finally pulled myself together enough to call Shore Leave..."

"And of course I wasn't there," I finished, cringing at the thought of my family's pain; to this day they didn't know if I was alive or dead. "They must be so scared, Marsh. If time moves along there at the same pace as here with us, we've been gone so long..."

"I don't know if it does. I left 2014 within twenty-four hours of you, but I arrived here months later. Go figure."

"I *had* to arrive earlier and maybe somehow that factors into it. I don't know for sure, but think about it. If I'd arrived later than in time than I did, Jacob might already have been born and Celia would have sent him east. He'd be..." I gulped, unable to speak the word.

"Lost," Marshall concluded softly. "He'd be gone. My family would never have existed."

"Right," I whispered. "So maybe when we get back home, hardly any time will have passed at all." Or time might have flown; it could be decades later. There was no way to know.

"Tish and Case know where we are, or at least as best as they can approximate," Marshall continued, tightening his hold, sensing the restless fear surfacing under my skin. "I was in a panic but I stopped at their trailer first to tell them what I intended. I didn't prepare near as well as I should have, I just knew I had to move fast. I tried to bring Arrow, I was riding him when I disappeared…"

"And he couldn't cross the time barrier, or whatever the hell it is, because he's something living that isn't capable." We had spent many an hour pondering this conundrum, using our limited theories. "You and I are capable of crossing that barrier, but Tish and Case aren't." I closed my eyes, attempting to reconcile Tish, my sister, with the Patricia I knew and loved here in 1882; sometimes I could not separate their faces.

"That makes sense," Marshall mused, kissing my shoulder. He had glanced toward Axton, whose back was to us as he slept on the opposite side of the banked fire. Both of us loved Axton Douglas as dearly as we loved our own brothers, Axton who had risked everything to save Patricia and me, with nothing to gain for himself; he'd done so because he loved me and was in love with Patricia, desperately so.

"How long will Tish and Case wait before telling everyone where we are?" I asked. Our families were loving and kind and unfailingly open-minded, but I struggled to believe they could accept such a farfetched explanation for our disappearance. "What did Tish say before you left?"

"She'd guessed where you went. State patrol had found your car off the interstate and the driver's side seatbelt was still fastened but there was no sign of you. I went to their trailer right away to get the letters. I told Tish I'd find you or I'd die trying." He kissed my forehead, bracketing the back of my head with one hand. "Tish understood I had to go alone, that she wasn't able to. I said I figured we'd be back within a week, go figure. If not, I asked them to tell Dad and my brothers. And Tish said she would tell your family."

I thought of Mom, Camille and Mathias, Aunt Jilly and Uncle Justin and Clint, Grandma and Aunt Ellen. Of my stepdad, Blythe, and my half-brothers, Matthew and Nathaniel, of all my sweet nieces and nephews, and Dodge and Rich; my entire family in Minnesota attempting to accept such a preposterous story – even one delivered by Tish, a lawyer with a decided ability to refrain from sentimentality. How could they begin to understand, let alone accept, the truth?

Now our journey to Howardsville, a small town deep in Montana Territory, was but a few days from completion; Marshall, Axton, and I had spent the night at the hospitality of a rancher Ax knew peripherally; he'd stayed in the main house with the family, while Marshall and I had been allowed the delectable privacy of their old shanty cabin – or 'soddy,' as they called it – a small dirt-block structure about fifty paces away. I leaned to kiss him in the morning light; he made a soft, throaty sound and my heart jolted with love and the desire to sweep away all lingering agony, to fill him with only joy from this moment forth. "Good morning."

He released a slow breath through his nostrils, having regained control, and a smile lit his eyes before moving to his lips. "Morning, angel. Do you think everyone will be mad that we missed dinner?" I stretched, deliciously lazy, luxuriating in being tucked within an actual bed after weeks of making do on the unforgiving ground. The ropes beneath us were sagging this morning and I giggled, bouncing my hips. "We might be in trouble for more than one reason."

"I'll take all the blame, it was worth it to make love to you in a real bed. It's so goddamn hard to be quiet for Axton's sake," Marshall said, venting even as he rolled me under his warm nude body, nuzzling my neck, running his palms along my ribcage, on either side. "I don't mind him traveling with us, I actually really enjoy his company, but *still…*"

"I know," I murmured, clutching the lean muscles of his ass with both hands, making a cradle of my hips. "I don't want to offend him…oh God, *Marsh…*"

"You're so wet," he breathed, eyelids lowering in pleasure, grasping the thick horizontal wooden pole that made up the headboard, forearms braced on either side of my head. "Aw, Jesus, love, this is such a beautiful way to start the day…"

"You feel so good…*stay still for just a second…*"

He obeyed at once, holding himself deep, as I shuddered and came in a rush, overwhelmed by the solid length, hard as a fence post, filling my body. He grinned in satisfaction, licking my chin, biting my neck as he murmured, "There's plenty more where that came from."

I writhed beneath him, begging with inarticulate sounds as he took up a steady rhythm, his lips brushing mine. "That's it, angel, come again. Come all over me, sweetheart, I love it."

"*Yes*," I moaned, reveling in the beauty, the strength, of the connection we shared. I had never known myself capable of such feelings, those Marshall inspired within me; not just the intensity of the physical, but beyond. No one had ever truly *seen* me the way Marshall did, and in seeing, understood me. There was nothing to hide, no secrets between us, nothing held back.

I was open to him, in every sense of the word – he was the love of my lifetimes and the thought of being severed from him was one of primal despair. And so I refused to think of it, instead exulting in the here and now where we were alive together, and in the singular intimacy of the knowledge of him that I alone owned – the salty taste of his sweating skin, the sleek interior of his mouth; the way his tongue circled mine with each new kiss. The way he buried his nose in my curls and sometimes quietly sang lines of our favorite songs; the sound of his release, a low, shuddering groan which inspired hot, jetting aftershocks in my body. The scent of him that lingered on my skin long after we'd made love.

Later, sweating, our bodies interwoven, he muttered, "*Damnation*, woman."

I giggled, despite my increasing guilt; I knew we needed to get our asses moving and make an appearance at the main house by lunchtime. The concept of sleeping in was a foreign one to most people in the nineteenth century; their days followed the sun's path in a wholly different way. The 'night shift' in this century was reserved for the women I'd known at Rilla Jaymes's saloon in Howardsville, prostitutes who serviced the railroad workers and miners, or any paying customer who came a-calling; most everyone else, even those who spent the night enjoying whiskey and women in the saloons, were required to rise with the dawn to accomplish a full day's work. The idea of dozing until the noon hour or spending the morning in bed – let alone in blissful lovemaking – spoke of unimaginable indulgence here.

"I'm surprised Ax hasn't come to roust us," I murmured, rolling to sit up, scraping snarled hair from my face, wishing we could spend the entire day right here.

"He's too polite," Marshall countered, heaving to a sitting position with a muted growl, cupping my breasts and lightly jiggling them, making me giggle. I swiped at his teasing hands, ready to emerge from bed when I was caught by surprise at the sudden and marked change of expression on his face. He fell still, spreading his long fingers and slowly lifting my breasts as if determining which might weigh more, the way you would in a grocery store with two melons. His gaze became fixed and intent, mouth somber and brows knitted.

I cried, "What is it?"

"Oh, Ruthie," he murmured, in a much-subdued tone. "Oh, sweetheart."

"What?" I yelped, truly terrified now.

His serious eyes flashed to mine, and yet – I was not mistaking it – there was within them a growing hint of exhilaration. He rested his touch on my knees, thumbs making slow circles. "When was your last period?"

If he'd produced a ten-pound hammer and clocked my temple, I could not have been more stunned. My thoughts scattered like thrown sand, streaking through the thousand things I'd been too distracted to realize, even the glaringly obvious – like the fact that my period was overdue.

I started trembling and clutched his shoulders, my nose at his collarbones. I gathered my wits and whispered, "Well over a month ago."

"Oh my God, angel, oh holy shit." But his voice was distinctly excited and gaining steam. "I thought I was imagining that your breasts seemed fuller than normal and then it struck me. I can't believe I didn't realize sooner. What did we expect? We never miss a night!" He paused for breath before whispering, with pure reverence, "*A baby*. You're carrying our baby."

"Our baby," I repeated, sudden fear clogging my throat – the nineteenth century had never before seemed as dangerous, dirty, or full of hazard. How could I bring a baby into this place?

"A boy." Marshall's voice rang with certainty and tears streaked sideways over my face, wetting his chest. "Rawleys make boys."

"That's what I've heard," I managed to whisper.

"I miss Dad and my brothers more right now than I've missed them since I've been here, and that's saying a lot." Marshall was all choked up. "I want to tell them so bad. I want them to know."

I rose to my knees and cupped his jaws, almost tumbling from the sagging bed. Marshall gripped my waist. We were each tearful, sweaty from the exertion of the previous hour; and then, despite everything, I couldn't help but laugh.

"They would be *so* happy," I agreed, as he kissed away my tears. "I'm not sad, honey, I'm just in stun…"

"We should have known, we haven't been using a bit of protection. Talk about irresponsible." He bent down to stomach level and kissed my navel. "I know it's not an excuse to say we've been distracted, but still. I can't think fast enough, sweetheart. What about prenatal vitamins? Oh God, you better not ride Blade anymore. Can we keep traveling? What about the bumps on the trail? And calcium, are you getting enough calcium? Oh, *Jesus*…"

He was on the verge of panicking and there was a knock on the door; seconds later Axton called, "Marsh, Ruthie! You two awake?"

"We'll be right out, Ax!" I turned back to Marshall, threading my arms around his neck. "Honey. *Hey*. We have to take this one day at a time. There's no other way. I can still travel. I'm just fine. People have babies here all the time."

And die grisly deaths in childbirth, I thought immediately, not about to give voice to the inadvertent realization. But the notion clung, all the same. I thought of the long-ago night Marshall and I had discussed the probability of past lives, and my hypothetical example had been along the lines of, *What if I died early and you lived to the end of your natural life?* Marshall had been so upset over this example he'd made me knock on wood, just in case.

Marshall nodded, resting his forehead to mine. Back home, in Jalesville what seemed like a thousand years ago, we'd hoped to have our first baby by the Christmas of 2014. We speculated constantly about what had taken place there in the future, in our *real* lives – the lives we intended to reclaim, if return was possible. We assumed it was not currently possible to return, at least not until we'd determined why we were here in 1882 instead of our original timeline. Had Derrick Yancy been successful in proving ownership of Clark's land? Had his claims been justifiable?

As of this moment, June 1882, Thomas Yancy was still alive, not shot in the back and killed by Cole Spicer, as Derrick had once alleged; perhaps Marshall and I were meant to prevent that death. We already knew our presence ensured the survival of Miles Rawley's son, Jacob, a child he'd fathered with a prostitute named Celia Baker. The baby had not been sent east, as Celia originally intended, and had instead claimed his rightful place as a member of the Rawley family here in the nineteenth century. We believed the boy was meant to carry on the line of descendants which would one day lead to Marshall's family in 2014. If I hadn't arrived in 1881, prior to the boy's birth, Marshall may very well never have existed at all.

It was enough to make my blood freeze; Marshall and I tried our best to take things one catastrophe at a time.

"Can we tell Ax?" Marshall asked, with giddy delight.

I nodded and he planted an exuberant kiss on my lips. We dressed in a hurry and found Axton waiting in the sunshine, leaning against the side of the soddy when we emerged from it, ducking to fit under the doorway. Axton grinned at the sight of us and I threw myself into his arms, squeezing hard; I wished I could give him what he wanted more than all else in life, which was Patricia's undying love. The most wrenching part of it was that Patricia *did* love Ax, which he and I both knew – but the father of her child was one Cole Spicer.

I prayed that Cole, Patricia, and their son, in the company of Malcolm Carter, had reached northern Minnesota by now. When we parted ways, roughly two weeks ago, they were bound for the place where, one day, my own family would found and build the Shore Leave Cafe; just now, in 1882, the Davises were only newly established in Landon. The cafe itself, constructed on the banks of Flickertail Lake, would not exist until the 1930s. The simple remembrance of the familiar lake, and my family's home there, inspired homesickness on a level I could only compare to dozens of tiny blades jammed between my ribs.

Axton laughed at my enthusiastic hug, rocking me side to side. "Well good morning to you too, Ruthie."

"Guess what?" I demanded, drawing back and regarding his familiar face, so dear and handsome, the deep tan of his skin a striking contrast to the clear, dark green of his eyes. He was kind and true, earnest and sincere, a wonderful man I would handpick for any of my sisters. His ruddy brows lifted at my happy tone.

Marshall roughed up Axton's curly hair. "Ruthie and I have some good news this morning."

We trusted Axton implicitly; he was one of a very few who knew the truth about Marshall and I being displaced in time. What we hadn't yet discussed with him was our desire to leave this place, ideally forever, and return home. I dreaded the conversation; the thought of leaving behind the people I'd come to know and love in 1882 filled me with increasing distress. I was dying to get to Montana Territory to see Birdie and Grant Rawley, Celia Baker and baby Jacob. My hands ached to hold Miles's son, to hug him and observe with my own eyes that he was healthy and thriving. Knowing this would take some of the sting out of saying good-bye.

"What's that?" Axton prompted.

Marshall winked, allowing me the floor, so to speak.

"We're having a baby!"

Axton's lips dropped open. "Aw, that's wonderful!" He hugged Marshall next, and then said, with typical nineteenth-century practicality, "Well, we best find you two a preacher all that much sooner."

Chapter Three

Montana Territory - June, 1882

WE ARRIVED AT THE RAWLEYS' HOMESTEAD LATE THE
next afternoon, the place where one day, many decades from now,
Marshall's parents, Clark and Faye, would build a new house and raise
five boys. It was a distinctly incredible and unsettling experience to be
here in another century – existing within the same geographical space,
the same foothills in the foreground and hazy blue mountain peaks in
the distance, but the house Marshall and I knew so well, the steel-pole
barn and the corral and the stone fire pit around which we'd sat and
roasted marshmallows and sang late into so many nights, all absent.

It seemed that at any second Clark, or Sean or Quinn or Wy, or the
horses we had known and loved in a different century, like Banjo and
Arrow, would come loping around the corner of the barn. Perhaps most
astonishing of all was to observe the essence of Marshall's family upon
the faces of those here in 1882. Both of us struggled not to refer to Grant
as 'Garth,' or Birdie as 'Becky.' I'd already called Axton 'Case' on more
than one instance during our journey northwest.

"Oh, Ruthie, I've missed you every day you were away. We prayed for
your safe return every night, without fail. This past winter proved longer
than any I've ever known," Birdie said, all of us gathered about the outdoor hearth for a homecoming celebration that night, the men drinking
whiskey and the kids crawling all over our laps. I had scarcely released
my hold on Miles's nine-month-old son.

Celia, his mother and my dear friend, sat on my other side, smiling as she watched me feather Jacob's dark hair and study his eyes, long-lashed and deep gray in color, just like Celia's – and Marshall's; I'd finally discovered the ancestor who'd gifted Marshall with his beautiful eyes. When we'd arrived, Celia enveloped me in her warm embrace, both of us crying; she'd whispered in my ear, "Thank you for stopping me from sending him away, dear Ruth. I don't know what I would do without my boy."

"I'm so glad to be back," I told Birdie, leaning to rest my cheek on her upper arm.

"And your Marshall has finally found you." Celia nodded in his direction, her voice warm with satisfaction. "His resemblance to Miles is right uncanny, straight down to the way he moves. I'll tell you, sweet Ruth, that there man was fit to be tied when he couldn't go after you last year. Winter had set in, you see. He was near feral. A Rawley through and through."

Marsh sat between Grant and Axton on the opposite side of the fire, the three of them chatting with ease; the bond forged between Grant and Marshall last year, when Marsh spent the winter here, was undeniably strong, and Marshall clearly reminded Grant of his younger brother, Miles, who had died in this very house a year ago. In addition to Ax, Grant and Birdie rounded out the small group of those who knew the truth. I wasn't sure if they fully believed the story – and who could blame them – but they accepted it, and us, for which I was grateful beyond measure. They were careful not to ask too many questions; among our many fears, Marshall and I were afraid we'd already caused too much damage to the timeline, which, in books, film, and television – our only basis for comparison – always seemed irreparably fragile, like damp tissue paper.

I'd visited Miles's grave earlier this afternoon, not long after our arrival; Grant and Birdie had buried him beneath a towering willow tree growing on the banks of the little spring-fed creek which ran through their property; the turned earth was marked with a handmade wooden cross until a proper headstone could be erected.

"Do you want to be alone?" Marshall had asked as we walked out past the house to Miles's resting place. We stood perhaps a dozen yards distant and I could see the silhouette of the cross against the gold dust of late-afternoon sunglow. Behind us, on the other side of a low rise in the foothills, the steep roofline of Grant and Birdie's house was just visible.

"Just for a minute," I whispered, already burning with unshed tears, and he nodded his understanding acceptance of my need to visit Miles with no one else present. As I knelt at the grave, I wished for a bundle of roses to place at the base of the cross. I touched Miles's name, tracing the letters carved into the wood by Grant's hand: *Miles William Rawley, beloved brother, 1857 – 1881*. I struggled with the knowledge that Miles had been only twenty-four years old; his inherently somber nature always made him seem older.

"Miles," I whispered, aching with sorrow, resting my hands flat on the earth beneath which he lay, the man who'd loved me with all his heart and whose death I'd been unable to prevent. I'd loved him – I was honest enough to admit this – even though I relentlessly avoided the thought of what might have happened had Miles lived to become my husband. I consented to marry him last autumn, before I'd regained the memories of who I really was, only to have Marshall appear seeking me here in 1882. I knew, without a doubt, I would have gone to Marshall no matter what the circumstances – but what if I'd already been expecting Miles's baby at that point? What would have been, then?

It was too much for my mind to wrap around, too brutally painful to consider.

"I love you, Miles." Tears fell to my skirt as I knelt there. "You're gone and I miss you. I miss you every day, deep in my heart." The need to confess rose like smoke in my chest, demanding release; I was aware that Marshall remained distant, watching silently. "I know you would have loved me all your life. I am so sorry for so many things. I want you to know I found my husband and that I believe you were him in this life. That the two of you share a soul, or pieces of a soul, somehow. I believe your son is his ancestor and if not for you, Marshall would never have lived."

I pictured Miles's face as I remembered it best, his black mustache lifting with a smile, his eyes, dark as coffee without cream, resting on me with both tenderness and intensity. I remembered the softness of his lips against mine, his sweet words of love, the way he'd held me and would have done anything to protect me; how I'd watched him play his fiddle so many nights, and the overpowering relief I always felt when he returned from being away from me. The last thing I wanted was to make a scene but I could not stop the flood of grieving. I knew Marshall would understand. He jogged to my side, falling to his knees and gathering me in his embrace, where I clung until the comfort of his strength and scent quieted my sobs.

He cupped the back of my head. "I'm here."

"I could never be thankful enough, for that," I whispered, hiccupping, my voice rough. Before we left the creek, Marshall curled a hand around Miles's name on the wooden cross, rubbing with his thumb as he said, with quiet respect, "Thank you, Rawley, from the bottom of my heart. Thank you for loving Ruthann, and for keeping her safe."

"You've told him that before," I recognized as we walked back to the house a little later. I tucked close to his side, my arms locked around his ribcage; I'd almost forgotten Marshall had lived here for the duration of last winter.

"Of course. Every time I sit there." His chest expanded with a breath and his low voice grew confessional. "I can't admit I'm not insanely jealous of the man. I'm not gonna lie." A hint of his usual good nature crept into his tone. "After all, he was *me*. Or, I was him. I can't quite figure it all out, but if he had even one-*tenth* of the same thoughts you inspire in me, angel-woman, then I would have to kick his ass to the future and back, just on principle. *Damnation*."

"*Marsh*," I scolded, unable to keep from smiling; I knew without a doubt that Miles would have found Marshall's comments amusing. I imagined the two of them regarding each other, face to face, and then shook my head to clear it of such bizarre pictures.

Marshall stalled our forward progress, studying the ground near his boots as he muttered, "He never...you two never..."

"We didn't," I said at once, honest enough to admit I would have wanted to know the answer, were the situation reversed – if somehow a past version of *me* was here to interact with Marshall, let alone make love with him; undoubtedly she would be drawn to him the same way I'd been drawn to Miles. The thought was so strange and inspired such a blazing surge of possessive jealousy my hands became fists. And then

I pictured confronting this past self, ripping at her hair and clawing her eyes for thinking she had some hold on Marshall that trumped mine – that is, if she and I could even *exist* in the same physical space without a thunderclap and a ripping apart of the entire cosmic continuum.

Jesus Crimeny, Ruthann.

It wasn't a thought for the fainthearted.

Marshall released a tense breath and his shoulders relaxed. "I didn't really think so and I'm sorry for asking, sweetheart. I told myself I wasn't going to ask, no matter what, and now I feel like an asshole…"

"*Honey,*" I admonished, and flicked his lean belly, just for good measure. "Don't feel that way. And, just so you know, I would have asked, too."

Hours later, at the crackling fire, I felt the subtle heat of Marshall's gaze and met it with a smile, my chin resting on Jacob's head. The little boy was soft and plump, fond of kicking his legs and gurgling spit bubbles, and my entire being, from the inside out, ached with love for Miles's son. I couldn't hug and kiss him enough to satisfy the strength of my feelings; I thought, *Marshall and I will have a baby by next year and it's because of you, sweet little Jacob. It's because you survived and stayed here in Montana that Marshall's family will exist in the twenty-first century, I truly believe this and I could never be thankful enough for you.*

We told everyone about my pregnancy and though they shared Axton's opinion that we needed a preacher to marry us as soon as humanly possible, they were nothing but delighted.

"March," Birdie said knowledgably. "Right in the midst of sap season, that's what I predict. Oh, how very exciting. You'll have staked a homestead claim by then, of course."

"There is still available homestead acreage to be had near ours, dear Ruthann." Una Spicer sat on Birdie's other side, wrapped in her knitted red shawl. I watched the fire's light touch Cole's mother's face as she spoke, marveling anew at the fact that I was interacting with her, when I'd known *about* her for so long, when I'd read her letters in a century long after her death. I thought again of what Marshall had told me about his first glimpse of Una – that she looked very much like Melinda Spicer, Case's mother and the woman who would have been Tish's mother-in-law, had she lived. Marshall remembered Melinda from his childhood; he said it was like seeing a ghost.

I didn't have the heart to admit to these dear women that I hoped and prayed Marshall and I would be gone long before next March; for tonight, at least, I couldn't bear to think so far in advance. I murmured, "The land is gorgeous here, that's for certain."

Una had exclaimed over Axton with maternal affection, announcing that he looked enough like a Spicer to be her own son. Besides her eldest, Cole, Una was the mother of four additional children; two of her girls had remained in Iowa, already married and settled; the youngest son and daughter, Charles and Susanna, had made the journey west. Charles – and how I wanted to ask him if his middle name was Shea, like Case's – was nineteen but appeared much younger, slim and frail; I remembered Cole saying that Charles had been very ill as a child. Susanna, the baby of the family at fourteen, was fair and shy and quiet. They were frequent visitors at the Rawleys' homestead. Axton, who'd never known a mother or siblings of his own, was quite taken with the kind family, I could tell.

The only thing dampening the joy of our arrival was the fact that there had been no word from Malcolm, Cole, and Patricia. And though Henry and Una did not seem unduly concerned, and there were many logical, plausible explanations for this, none of us were comforted, least of all Axton.

"Do you think they've reached Minnesota?" Ax had asked me earlier, shortly after we had arrived at the ranch. "They should be there by now, Ruthie."

I couldn't lie to Ax any more than I could hide my fears. "I hope so. It scares me so much to think that – " I stopped before speaking aloud Fallon Yancy's name, as if to do so would conjure him.

The expression in Axton's eyes was almost unbearable. I knew it destroyed him to admit, but he acknowledged in a low, gruff growl, "Spicer will keep her safe." Immediately he muttered, "Or I'll kill him."

I hated to see Axton this way – maintaining a stubborn, futile hope that somehow Patricia would one day be with him – when it could serve to do nothing but crush him in the end. Marshall's suggestion that we try our best to find the right woman for Ax before we left the past seemed fruitless; I knew Ax well enough to realize he would hold fast to his love for Patricia if it killed him. I would never give voice to the thought but it tortured me, nonetheless.

At last I whispered, "You're right, Cole will keep her safe."

And though I'd fought it, I was unable to prevent an image of Fallon from assaulting my mind, his hollow eyes seeking mine from somewhere out there; I'd been in his company over the course of an hour while a prisoner in his train car en route to Chicago last year. I would never fully erase the memory of that encounter, no matter how hard I tried. Fallon was not just a criminal, he was more dangerous than any of us could have guessed, gifted with the ability to leap through time. His control was much stronger than either Marshall's or mine; Fallon had leaped to the twentieth century many dozens of times.

For all we knew, he could be there at this moment. Or was Fallon *here* just now, in the nineteenth century, tailing Malcolm, Cole, and Patricia on their journey to escape him? At least Cole or Malcolm would kill him on sight, recognizing the threat he presented; our families in the future had no idea. Further, it was not apparent just how much of the truth about Patricia and her illegitimate son Cole's parents knew; Una and Henry had both spoken excitedly of their expectations of Cole returning west to Montana Territory next spring, but if they anticipated him returning with Patricia and the baby in tow they made no mention, leading me to conclude they had no idea.

I wished, for the countless time, I'd been allowed the chance for a final private conversation with Patricia before we'd parted ways on the Cedar River in Iowa. Maybe it was an unfair assumption, but I understood her better than I knew Cole ever would; the darkest of her secrets was her love for Axton.

It's not as though she could have made any choice but the one she did; the baby is Cole's. There was no longer another choice from the moment she realized she was pregnant.

Henry Spicer eventually produced the family fiddle and I could not tear my gaze from it; I *knew* that fiddle, had watched Case play it a hundred times at The Spoke, or around the outdoor fire pit at Clark's;

the gathering spot I remembered so well would someday be located in a different part of the Rawleys' sprawling yard. Cold shivers climbed my spine and I rubbed my upper arms.

To my surprise, Henry offered the instrument to Marshall. "We've missed your music, young fellow."

Marshall accepted both fiddle and bow, nodding agreement. Grant positioned his own fiddle beneath his chin and as they tuned the instruments with easy laughter and banter, an onrushing sense of déjà vu pelted my senses; was I at the fire with Garth and Marshall in 2014, or Grant and Miles in 1882? I knew Miles was gone but it seemed he was here anyway, playing through Marshall's hands and appearing in his expression.

Exhausted and overwhelmed by all that had occurred in the past few weeks, I relinquished Jacob to Celia and skirted the fire to settle beside Axton; he wrapped an arm around my shoulders and planted a kiss on my temple. Birdie's little boys and the cook's small son shared the blanket with us, curling up like three warm puppies; one of them rested his head on my lap and I feathered his soft hair.

"I miss Uncle Branch," Axton confided.

"I miss him too," I whispered, thinking of the kindhearted man who'd found me on a riverbank outside Howardsville well over a year ago. Branch and Axton had been my first friends in the nineteenth century; in those early days I'd had no memory of who I was, or where I might have appeared from, and remained eternally thankful that two such kind and honorable men took me under their wing.

"Birdie said you visited Miles's grave earlier," Axton murmured. I knew he understood, better than almost anyone, my sorrow over Miles.

I nodded, my gaze fixed on Marshall; he stood beside Grant, the two of them bowing out the notes to "Red River Valley," an old favorite of the Rawleys. I supposed the tune wasn't so very old in this place. Marshall played with his eyes closed and I marveled again, *He's here.* Marshall was here in 1882, when I thought I may never see him again. It had been such a wretched year without him – the pain of our separation remained raw in my soul, not easy to set aside, let alone forget. I settled one hand low on my belly.

Listen, baby, to your daddy making music. Music flows in your blood, little one.

"It does my heart good to see Miles's son here, safe and healthy," Axton said.

"Same here," I murmured. The night was clear and fine, the moon a perfect ivory half-circle in the deep sky. There were at least two dozen people crowded around the fire; the ranch hands not on duty with the cattle always gathered for music. The air was so static anyone within a few miles' radius would be able to hear the plaintive notes of the two fiddles. The stars looked like bright, tumbled stones, flung by a child's excited hand.

"Are you doing all right?" I whispered, turning my attention to Ax. There was a tension in his frame even the sweetness of the music could not fully eradicate. Resolute, since that first night apart from her, Axton had refrained from speaking of Patricia during our journey out of Illinois and across the plains of Iowa. But he called for her in his sleep almost every night, as though in his dreams she was just within reach, disappearing as he woke.

Axton's face was cast in gold by the fire's light. He knew what I was truly asking. "No, but not so's anybody but you or Marsh would notice."

"I wish…"

Axton shook his head, effectively interrupting me. "I had to let her go, Ruthie, I know there was no other choice, and it hurts like fucking poison." I could smell whiskey on his breath; Ax didn't normally drink, or curse, and I attributed the subsequent rush of words to this. He passed his free hand over his eyes. "But even if I could escape the pain I wouldn't, because it's all I have of her. I can't give up even that much of what I have left. When I close my eyes, she's all I see. When I sleep, I dream of her. I'm haunted." His shoulders rose with a heaving breath and in his eyes I saw a conviction that frightened me, not because of the strength of feeling it conveyed but that those feelings would work to consume Axton, burning him alive, until there was nothing left but ash.

I couldn't think of one thing to say to ease his pain.

"I'm sorry to go on this way," he muttered, squeezing me in a one-armed version of a hug. "I am truly happy for you and Marsh, I hope you know."

"Thank you, sweetheart. I know you are. I wish I could make things right." I faltered for a second, unwilling to cause Axton additional pain; at last I admitted, "I've always thought Cole was the wrong choice. I think Patricia should be with you, Ax. I care for Cole, I'm not saying I don't, but I think you're the better man all around. Cole is…" I struggled to settle on a tactful adjective, not wanting to be unjust. "He's fickle. And vain. I hope being a father will tame some of that in him, but who knows? I'm afraid he won't be able to sustain their lives together."

"But they've a child now, it's a claim I can't deny. And he loves her. I can't deny that either, much as I wish I could." Axton's voice was dust. I sensed the questions he could not bear to ask, hovering near our heads.

What happened that day? Why didn't she wait for me?

I knew the answers, at least to some extent, and battled the need to protect Patricia's secrets; the urge to tell Ax the truth pressed against my breastbone like an anvil. The fiddle music, the charcoal sky, and the fireglow lent our conversation a depth of confidence it may not have otherwise possessed. I damned it all and said, "Patricia's in love with you, Ax, as you well know. But a part of her loves Cole, too. And she's tortured by it, to her very core. I spent all last winter with her, hearing her talk about you while carrying Cole's baby, and she begged me not to judge her. I assured her I don't but she tortured herself all the same. That day last autumn, with Cole…"

Axton was motionless as a sculpture, watching me with the intensity of a hawk about to strike.

I bit the insides of my cheeks, glancing down at the little boy whose head lay in my lap, finding him sound asleep. Axton and I seemed alone in the crowd, wrapped in a smooth, glassy bubble of intimacy, bound by the gravity of our conversation. No matter what, Ax deserved to know the truth. Patricia owed him an explanation and was not here to deliver it. I hoped she would understand my reasoning; remembering her last stolen moments in the chapel with Axton, I knew she would.

"Tell me, Ruthie." He spoke quietly but the words were a clear demand, and I thought suddenly of the night I'd first met Ax, the hesitant, boyish fellow he'd been, so unsure of himself. And despite the fact that he remained inherently sweet and kind he'd lost his hesitance, had become much more man than boy. In that moment he reminded me more of Case than ever before.

In order to understand, Axton required the necessary background story. I drew a deep breath, keeping my voice low. "Patricia and Dredd did not...make love. Their wedding night was the first and last time he touched her. Dredd wasn't unkind to her, I saw with my own eyes last year when we were in his company, but he wanted little to do with Patricia. She felt rejected. Worse than that, she felt undesirable. When Cole proposed to her that afternoon last fall, she was swept up in the moment of it." I all but gritted my teeth at the expression on Axton's face. "Up to that point, they'd never even kissed. She'd only kissed *you*. But Cole's very persuasive...and she wanted to know what it meant to make love with someone who loved and wanted her."

"That was...the only time?" Had a fist been clutching his windpipe Axton could not have sounded more strangled.

I nodded. "Once is all it takes, sometimes. It wasn't until late last November that Patricia and I began to suspect she was pregnant. And then we had to think fast, to come up with a story Dredd would swallow. Thank God it was only him we needed to convince." I restrained a shudder.

Axton studied the leaping flames; he traced his thumb over my arm as he spoke, almost meditatively. "I came to know Cole this past winter. I wanted to hate him, Ruthie, but I don't. At least, not for the man he is." He closed his eyes. "But if he ever hurts her, I'll run him to ground."

I wisely bit my tongue; I feared for what the future held for the three of them.

But you won't even be here, I thought next, my mind pinwheeling. *You and Marshall will be home in the future and you'll have to leave everyone here behind. You can't let yourself care this much about people you will never see again in this life.*

And it was devastating to admit that the thought of leaving the past behind was almost as painful as the ache of missing our families in the twenty-first century.

Chapter Four

Montana Territory –June, 1882

MARSHALL AND I WERE GIVEN THE LOFT-SIZED ROOM with low, slanting walls which I'd shared with Patricia last summer and where Marshall had slept alone all winter; we stripped to the skin and curled together beneath the covers of the luxurious feather bed. Marshall rested his nose in my curls, our hands joined atop my belly. I threaded one of my legs between both of his and whispered, "It's so strange being here. I never thought I'd see this place again in this century."

"It's strange as *hell*. I keep expecting to see Dad and my brothers coming around the corner of the barn," Marshall acknowledged. Neither of us mentioned we could not stay here at the homestead for long. It was too dangerous. As much as I wished it otherwise, Fallon Yancy would appear someday, looking for us.

"I know. It's *so* fucking weird, honey. Is the future we remember happening right *now*, like in another dimension…what?"

Marshall was laughing, low and soft. "Sorry, I didn't mean to interrupt you. It's just that you said 'fucking' and you never used to swear."

"I used to swear," I argued, and Marshall snorted.

"No, you did not," he countered. "We've both changed since living in Jalesville."

"But…" I struggled to articulate what I wanted to say, overtired and yet oddly alert at the same time, senses sharpened by the late hour; it seemed Marshall and I couldn't talk enough to satisfy the urge to simply tell each other everything, to make up for lost time. I finally said, "But

I wouldn't change this last year, even if I could. It made me realize how strong I can be when I have to, that I can do what needs doing. I would never have known."

I felt him nod against the back of my head. "So few people have the opportunity to test their mettle. Though, I wouldn't wish the agony I felt when you were gone on anyone. I've been so empty, like a fucking chasm of despair took the place of my heart..."

"Marshall Augustus," I murmured, rolling to face him. "Even when I couldn't remember who I was, I longed for you. You were always there, safe in my heart. I don't know how I existed so long without seeing you."

He kissed my lips, lingering there, with a sense of possession. He murmured, "Now that we're here and not forced to move fast on the trail, I can think more clearly. I feel like we can plan now, for whatever the future holds. We haven't had much of a chance to talk about how we'll get back." He paused and inhaled before admitting, "It scares me, Ruthie, to think about one of us just *disappearing*..."

I gritted my teeth; the same thoughts plagued me, the razor-edged fear of being without him again, of the helplessness in the face of our vulnerability. What if he was dragged into the future but I was not? What if one of us remained trapped here, unable to return? And then horror struck an additional killing blow. I choked, "Marsh, *what if the baby*..."

"Shhhh," he said at once. "*No*. Our baby will come with us, no matter what."

"We have to go before he's born," I understood, knowing Marshall could feel the agitated clanking of my heart. "Even if we haven't discovered everything we're supposed to, here."

"But what if we can't return home until we've accomplished those things, whatever the hell they are? I keep waiting to feel that...force field pulling at me, especially now that we're here at the homestead. Remember the night we rode Arrow out this way, near *this* place, I mean..."

"I do. I haven't felt it yet, either," I whispered. "And will we feel it at the same time? There are so many variables, Marsh, I hate this. Like the fact that we left Jalesville, and 2014, only a day apart, but you ended up in 1881 *months* after me. How do you figure?"

"It makes me wonder how the future – the present, I mean, back in Jalesville – is moving while we're here. It seems like it would be moving at the same rate, but maybe not. Maybe no time has passed there at all."

"Do you think…" I couldn't make myself finish.

"That we're destined to stay in the past?" He knew exactly what I meant. "As long as you're in my arms, angel, I don't care where we are." Marshall kissed my eyelids, one after the other, and the scent of his breath was comforting and familiar, serving to calm my rapid pulse.

"We can get by here, if we have to," he went on. "Technically I have the marshal position until the replacement gets here later this month, Grant was saying. It seems like no one was jumping at the chance to take the territory way out here."

"Because it's nothing but dangerous." I rolled to an elbow, further agitated. "I want you to give it up as fast as you can." I knew Marshall was a fast learner and a good shot with a firearm, but I would not allow him to risk himself for a stupid marshal position, not if I could prevent it. I'd always hated how being a lawman continually put Miles in the path of potential harm, made him an unwitting target and took him away so often. His territory had been vast.

"I will, I promise. But there are perks to the job while we're here in 1882. For instance, I could shoot Fallon Yancy dead without any provocation and it would be completely justifiable."

"It would be justifiable anyway. He would kill *us* as soon as look at us. And we both know he'll come looking, sooner or later. We can't stay here."

"I know. And I'll think about that first thing tomorrow, I swear." Marshall uttered a soft groan, knuckling his eyes. "No matter what, I'd shoot the bastard without a second thought. But it doesn't hurt that way out here there's no one looking over my shoulder. Shit, I was sworn in by a judge passing through the Territory late last autumn. No background check, just Grant's recommendation. All I had to do this past winter was ride into Howardsville once every few weeks and check in with the deputy sheriff. I could have lived in that little cabin behind the jail, but I would have gone crazy there."

"I'm so glad you didn't have to be alone," I whispered, nuzzling his chest hair, which smelled pleasantly musky; I stroked my fingers through the soft, thick mass because it was an intimacy I particularly loved and because I'd gone so many nights without being able.

Marshall cupped my face, letting his fingertips play over my chin and jawline. The room around us was shaded as though by strokes of a charcoal pencil, a study in variations of gray, from ash to pewter. His long nose cast a shadow on the right side of his face; his breath held a trace of whiskey as he whispered, "I was more alone than I'd ever been, without you."

I rested both palms on his chest. "When I saw you riding across the prairie…"

"Holy God, I was dying that day. We knew Ax was in the convent as the gardener's replacement, and that you and Patricia were there, but not that he'd spoken with you. I wanted to storm the walls of that place so fucking bad Malcolm nearly tied me to a fencepost. But I knew if I saw you, if we saw *each other*, there'd be no way we could control ourselves. I knew it would blow the cover we'd worked so damn hard to establish. But I was dying, angel, knowing you were so close to me after all that time."

"If I'd known you were out there…Ax was right not to let me know…"

"Seeing you running toward me was the happiest moment of my life, to that point. And every day since has been the newest happiest moment. Especially this morning." His teeth flashed in a grin, his long hair falling around his neck and inviting my touch. "Can you believe we're having a baby?"

I slowly shook my head. "We *shouldn't* be surprised! I'm ashamed to admit it didn't even occur to me we should be using protection. I've just been so happy to be with you, it's overwhelmed everything else in my mind. If only…" I didn't finish the sentence; were too many *if onlys* in our future right now, too many *what ifs*. I'd been about to say, *If only we were safely home*. If only we were secure in the knowledge that we would remain stationary in time – either here or in the future – from this point onward. But, as in all of life, there were no guarantees.

"If only you had your ring," Marshall supplied, attempting to elicit a smile, I knew. He lifted my left hand and kissed the spot where he'd once placed the lovely engagement band custom-made for me, an heirloom diamond from his mother's side of the family, set with garnets, my birthstone. "I miss seeing it on your hand, angel. What do you suppose happened to it?"

I rubbed my thumb across the base of my third finger; it felt unduly bare without the familiar presence of the ring and all it represented, the promise of our future as husband and wife. I whispered, "I don't know. I didn't take it off the night I left Jalesville. I would have been wearing it when I arrived in 1881." Stolen right off my finger, maybe? But when? I had no memory of any such event.

"I'll get you a new ring, angel, don't you worry. And there's a preacher on circuit, Grant was telling me." Marshall shifted position, bringing my palm to his cheek. "I would love for us to have a church service but I have to say I already feel married to you, in every way that counts. You have my heart, my soul, my baby inside of you. I cherish your every breath. I think of you as mine, Ruthie, in every possible way. And I am just as completely yours."

Tears wet my face and I entwined our fingers. "I keep thinking of the night when we ate at that little diner off the interstate, remember?"

"Of course I remember, sweetheart."

"It was the first time I actually stumbled onto the fact that you liked me."

Marshall snorted, shaking his head. "You had *no* idea? Not even a little? And here I figured I was about as subtle as a strobe light. Which, by the way, really sucks when you're onstage. One time at the Coyote's Den they had one and it just about blinded us out." He laughed at the memory; our conversations always shifted between present and future.

"I figured you were just teasing me because I got so flustered," I admitted, gliding my palms over his lean belly. "But that evening, sitting there talking to you with the sunset so pretty out the window, it finally hit me."

"I didn't just *like* you, you realize. I was already head over heels over heart in love with you, woman. Being around you that week only cemented the fact. Just the sight of your sweet face sent me right over the moon…and trying not to stare at your lips whenever you spoke or let my gaze rove south on your luscious body, don't even get me *started*…"

"*Marsh*…" I muffled my laughter against his neck.

"You think I'm kidding, angel? Jesus, come here, let me touch you…" He caught my ass in a firm grasp. "God, *yes*, that's better…"

"Much better," I agreed, rocking against him, letting the juncture of my thighs brush the increasing swelling between his. Before I lost all focus, I said, "But later that night, Tish and Case got married in the hospital room."

Marshall studied my eyes. A beat of deep awareness passed between us. "We could get married right here, right now."

Yes, I said without words, tears filming my vision. Marshall understood; he knew me.

With extreme and tender care, he resituated us to sitting positions, the covers billowing around our knees. He gathered my hands, kissed each, and then brought our joined hands to his heart; he spoke with a husky, formal tone. "I, Marshall Augustus Rawley, take you, Ruthann Marie Gordon, to be my lawfully wedded wife, to love and to cherish, to hold and kiss and keep safe and make passionate, unending love with. In sickness and health, for richer or poorer, for all time that exists, I will be yours."

My throat ached at the beauty of his words; I mustered my voice. "I, Ruthann Marie Gordon, take you, Marshall Augustus Rawley, to be my lawfully wedded husband, to love and to cherish, to make happy and bear your children, and to see our dreams fulfilled. In sickness and health, for richer or poorer, for all the days between now and forever, I am yours."

The air seemed to sigh around our bodies as he whispered tenderly, "That was perfect. I now pronounce us husband and wife."

I invited, "You may kiss the bride," and Marshall rolled atop me for a warm, open-mouthed one.

Later, snuggled together, he whispered, "We have to warn them."

Lulled almost to sleep, it took me seconds to realize what he meant. "You mean about Fallon. How can we make them hear us, from here?"

I could tell he was collecting his exhausted thoughts; it was very late. "We have to leave them a message, one that won't get destroyed in the intervening decades. Something we could…bury."

"You're right. And it has to be here, near this homestead. Case and Tish know the foundation is here, and what's more, they know it's where you first felt the past pulling at you, that night we rode Arrow. If they're going to look anywhere, it's here."

"Good point. It's our best shot."

"Fallon scares me so much. They don't know him and they wouldn't know who to look for. Tish doesn't even know that Fallon and Franklin are the *same person*. What if he's been there all this time, hurting them… *oh God…*"

"It doesn't seem like he's able to stay in the twenty-first century for long periods of time," Marshall quickly reminded me. "But all the same, I'll feel better thinking they have something to go on. We can bury something tomorrow."

"What if they don't find it…"

"We have to trust them," Marshall said, infusing his voice with confidence, for my sake. "If anyone can find it, it's Case and Tish."

Chapter Five

Jalesville, MT – March, 2014

"THEY SHOULD BE HERE ANY MINUTE," I TOLD AL, SETTING aside my pen. A small but potent rush of anticipation momentarily over-rode my otherwise low mood; an hour ago Camille had texted they were ninety miles east of Jalesville. "The whole family is coming. The kids are on spring break."

"I'd also allege your sister knows you need her," Al responded from his desk, pausing in his work to study me over the top of his bifocals, a pair he'd only just acquired. A recent dusting of late-winter snow bleached the outside light filtering through our front windows, a cloudy-bright day easing now toward its demise. Quiet music on the local radio station and the faint ticking of the old wall clock were the only other sounds in the small space we shared this late Friday afternoon.

Since arriving home from Robbie Benson's funeral in Chicago I'd returned to work at Spicer and Howe, Attorneys at Law. The daily famil-iarity of working with Al Howe, of mundane paperwork and the smell of law books and ink and old carpet, soothed my nerves like a sort of balm. Al had hired a new part-time receptionist, one of the Nelson family's daughters, and her cheerful chatter allowed me the ability to lay eyes upon the desk where Ruthann had worked, without falling to shattered bits.

Case kept our music shop open, located a few doors down from the law office; he continued to give guitar lessons and even occasionally played at The Spoke, sometimes with Garth's accompaniment. We ate dinner at Clark's every Friday, the entire Rawley family reliably in attendance, all of us working hard to contend with the dual storm clouds hovering on our collective horizon – that of Marsh and Ruthie's continued failure to return, and the Yancys' lawsuit, currently pending. Our first appearance as defendants before a judge was scheduled for next Wednesday, March nineteenth, a meeting I dreaded. Despite our adherence to as regular a routine as possible, the formidable tension holding all of us in a state of inertia was at times unbearable.

At each work day's end I hurried home to Case, who usually arrived first and had supper waiting in our cramped doublewide; after eating, we spent most evenings designing our new cabin. Both of us wanted to say 'fuck it' and get the foundation dug and the building process rolling, but we realized that if the Yancys prevailed – as I increasingly feared they would – and were awarded the deed to our acreage, we would lose even more to them. Case kept me sane; Charles Shea Spicer, my husband and love of many lifetimes. We'd been together before this life, we knew – but had not been able (*allowed?* I often wondered) to find each other in every subsequent life, for reasons beyond either of us. This knowledge, as strange and improbable as it might seem to anyone with a grain of skepticism, only served to increase our awareness of the gift of having found each other in *this* life.

"You're right, of course," I told Al, with a tired smile. I attributed my exhaustion to stress but found myself unduly drowsy of late; my upper eyelids seemed attached to iron weights by early evening. "I miss Camille so much. I haven't seen her since last summer." I didn't vocalize it, but I recognized my older sister's need to temporarily escape Landon. Our mother grew more despondent by the day; even Aunt Jilly struggled to rouse her of late. Camille, along with our cousin, Clint, kept me well informed via nightly phone calls.

"You'll bring the entire family to dinner," Al said, with gentle insistence. "At least once or twice. Helen Anne and I wouldn't have it any other way."

"They have five kids," I whispered, trying to keep my smile in place; I didn't want to relent to the urge to weep, as I did on an escalating basis. I hated being trapped beneath a constant raincloud. I sat back and rubbed my temples. At least I didn't have to pretend around Al; he knew the whole story. "*Fuck*. If we could just have one sign, *just one*, that they're all right. What if they're trapped there, Al?" Desperation rang in my voice. "What if it's like a fucking one-way ticket to the past?"

"We can't think like that or we're as good as defeated," Al said; beneath everything, I reflected how much I loved him. His kind, paternal presence and even-keel attitude had bolstered me countless times in the past few months.

Unable to rally my spirits, I all but moaned, "We're defeated anyway! No judge is going to dispute the dates on those homestead claims…"

"Patricia. You *must* refocus. I know you better than this. You're not a quitter. Case isn't a quitter, and neither are any of the Rawleys, from the look of them. Let's not forecast disaster just yet."

"But, Al…"

"No buts. Not a one." His shrewd gaze flickered to something beyond my shoulder; the furrows in his brow relaxed just as the bell above the door tinkled. I turned to see Case entering and a beat of pure, simple gladness stirred my heart.

"Hi, baby," he murmured, skirting the counter and coming straight to my desk; I rose to get my arms around him and burrowed close, inhaling his scent through his soft flannel shirt and thick canvas jacket. Even having just emerged from the chill outdoor air, Case radiated warmth. He was hatless; his hair, as rife with tones of burnished red as an autumn forest, and the tops of his wide shoulders were sifted with melting snowflakes. He'd recently shaved his winter beard and mustache but retained a hint of stubble on jaws and chin. He cupped my elbows and scrutinized my face. "You need more rest than you're getting, sweetheart."

"I couldn't agree more," Al said, rising, crossing the room to shake Case's hand.

I saw the concern in Case's eyes, the worry which had not fully dissipated in months, and murmured, "I'm all right, I promise. Just tired."

"Clark said we should head over as soon as you're done with work," Case told me.

"Then Camille just might beat us there," I said, trying for a little enthusiasm.

The Rawleys' sprawling two-story house had been crafted with local wood and stone. Despite the numerous times I'd been a guest in their impressive home, its sheer presence never failed to rouse awe, shivers rippling along my spine. The grand, sweeping structure was lit from eaves to foundation as Case parked our truck, the front windows ablaze, bright golden squares to counteract the gloomy, slate-gray evening. Holding hands, Case and I had not walked more than a dozen steps toward the front door before it opened wide, emitting Wy, the youngest Rawley brother, followed by Millie Jo and her twin brothers, Brantley and Henry.

"Auntie Tish!" Millie Jo screeched, running full-bore. She overtook Wy and crashed into my open arms.

I laughed, spinning her in a circle while Case caught the twins, one over each forearm. Wy wrapped me and Millie Jo, by default, in a bear hug, almost taking us to the snowy ground.

"We miss you!" Millie said, her words muffled by my puffy coat. "It took *forever* to get here!"

"I've missed you, too." I kissed the top of her curly-haired head and Wy released us, stepping back and offering his wide grin. I reached next for my nephews. "You guys are getting so big!"

"Tish!" called another voice, and tears filled my eyes just that fast.

I was at once enfolded in my sister's embrace. Clad in a wool sweater dress the color of ripe raspberries and furry brown boots, Camille's scent inundated me; one part floral, one part warm cinnamon, as if Clark had been baking something sweet and her curls retained the fragrance. The softness of her abundant hair brushed my cheek as I clung, imbibing the comfort of family.

"I'm so glad you're here," I murmured, eyes closed.

"Me too," she whispered, holding fast.

Mathias was right behind Camille, dressed in a heavy wool sweater and jeans; his blue eyes blazed as he grinned, lips framed by a mustache and full beard. "Tish, Case, it's been too damn long!"

My brother-in-law was just as handsome and full of energy as ever, hugging me and then Case; I thought back to the first time I'd ever met Mathias Carter, years ago at Shore Leave during the busy Christmas season. Since that first winter, when he and my sister had fallen hard in love, they'd made a happy, simple life in Landon; they resided in a centuries-old cabin on part of the Carters' massive lakeshore acreage along Flickertail, a home restored with tender care and devotion by Mathias and his father and now bursting at the seams with the addition of five children. Though I didn't want to acknowledge such thoughts right now, I could not help but think of what Camille feared on an increasing basis – the way her nightmares were returning, more aggressively than ever before, of Mathias ripped away from her.

No, please, no. She couldn't bear it.

Vulnerability no longer skulked in the shadows; instead it hovered within view, a trap poised to spring.

Clark appeared in the open door, holding a darling chubby bundle of a baby boy. "There's someone I think you might like to meet!" he called.

The thick, relentless ropes of worry tangling around my heart loosened their grip as we entered the living room, packed to the gills with family. In the old days, before Marshall and Ruthie went missing, it would have been what Clark called a 'full house,' each of his sons and their families in attendance: Garth and Becky and their two little boys; Sean and his girlfriend, Jessie; Quinn, Wy, Case's brother, Gus, and Gus's girlfriend, Lacy. In addition to the usual crowd and counting Case and me, Mathias, Camille, and their five rounded us out to an even twenty for dinner. Everyone called greetings; the air was scented with the warm, rich crackle of roasted chicken, garlic biscuits, and creamy au-gratin potatoes.

I will not think about Marsh and Ruthie for at least five minutes.

But it was a hopeless, worthless effort.

Everywhere I turned I saw their shadows, mocking my every sense. I pictured where they would be sitting just now, exactly how they would look and sound – Marsh would be wearing one of his old flannel shirts, untucked over faded jeans, his longish hair a little messy, as if Ruthie had buried her fingers in it prior to their arrival; his socks would be dirty and wouldn't match. My little sister, whose angelically beautiful face was so deeply imprinted in my memory it was akin to a scar, would be wearing a big, soft sweater over her jeans and fuzzy wool socks, with her dark brown curls loose and swishing past her shoulder blades. She would be wearing gold hoop earrings and her diamond-and-garnet engagement ring.

She and Marshall would be unable to keep their gazes from each other, let alone their hands; they would be on the couch and Marsh would have an arm around her waist, teasing her, tucking her curls aside to whisper something in her ear while she flushed and giggled and pretended to struggle away. Periodically they would steal a quick kiss. They were like two teenagers with their constant, obnoxious flirting and I would have given almost anything to have them here right now; the desire centered behind my breastbone like growing flames, screaming-hot and unimaginably painful.

"Can I hold the baby?" I whispered to Clark.

"Of course." Clark kissed my cheek as he passed James Boyd Carter into my arms. My newest nephew had been born last Halloween and I smiled even as tears leaked from my eyes; my emotions were in constant danger of wreckage these days. The baby's hair was two inches long and stuck straight up, as though he'd been badly startled or was experiencing waves of static electricity, eyes round with wonder as he regarded this new stranger holding him; his irises were as blue as stars, just like Mathias's.

"I've tried combing it down, but it doesn't stay." Camille smoothed two fingertips over her baby's head; the love on her face renewed the twinge in my heart. "Diana said Mathias's hair was just the same when he was little."

"He's so loud, Auntie Tish, you should hear him at night," Millie Jo informed, hovering all-importantly at my elbow; I found myself remembering the night she was born, Valentine's Day over a decade ago now. Sweet, observant Millie Jo resembled Camille to a marked degree with her lustrous hair and the gold-tinted hazel eyes so common to the women in our family. I wouldn't hurry to mention it but I could detect hints of her father, Noah Utley, in Millie's face; the shape of her mouth, the tiny cleft in her chin and her fair complexion, nothing like the olive-toned tan of Camille's. It seemed as though a century had passed since I'd last seen Noah, let alone my family in Landon.

Camille poked her older daughter's ribs. "You weren't exactly a quiet baby yourself, Miss Millie." She sighed, soft as a bird's wing. "But it does seem like yesterday you were this small."

"Yeah, James has got a set of pipes all right," Mathias said, reaching to curl his fingertip under his son's plump, silken chin, making the baby gurgle and smile; Mathias grinned in response, his whole face lighting with joy. I'd never met anyone who had longed to be a father more than Mathias; he and Camille proved a perfect match in that regard, and all others as far as I could tell. Their twins were roughhousing with Wy and Sean while four-year-old Lorie sat primly near Becky on the couch, holding Becky's new baby with complete ease; I reasoned that my little niece probably had ten times more experience handling infants than me.

Dinner was a loud, messy affair; every topic of conversation was purposely kept light and the overall mood was jovial, if slightly forced. There were a hundred things needing discussing but an unspoken and temporary hold was placed on those as we ate; or, I amended, while everyone else ate and I pushed chicken and potatoes around my plate. Clark's cooking was second to none but my stomach felt strange; hard edges seemed to poke outward deep inside my gut, unfurling like small metal flowers, even though I'd hardly touched food all day. I didn't fail to notice Case's concern and was washed in immediate guilt; as though he needed another reason to worry.

I rested my hand on his thigh, beneath the table, and leaned close. "I'm all right, honey, I'm just not hungry."

"You haven't eaten enough to keep a bird alive in days," my husband responded, refusing to be pacified.

A weak smile fluttered across my mouth. "You sound like Gran."

Case had heard me reference my great-grandmother's wisdom on numerous occasions and was as well-acquainted as it's possible to be with a woman who'd passed away many years ago. He murmured, "I can only just imagine what she would have to say about you not eating or sleeping."

Tenderness for him flooded my body, powerful enough it felt like a small blow to the bridge of the nose. His beautiful auburn hair shone like copper treasure in the lantern-style lighting; his irises were the brown of nutmeg beneath red-gold lashes, resting on me with a mix of exasperation and love. His chin and jawline had taken on a familiar stubborn set but his cheekbones seemed more prominent than usual; the skin beneath his eyes was smudged by restless shadows.

"We'll get to bed early tonight, for more than one reason," I whispered, squeezing his thigh, gratified to observe good humor replace some of the concern in his expression.

"Yes, so you can sleep while I hold you close," he murmured, leaning to place a gentle kiss on my temple.

Chapter Six

BUT I SHOULD HAVE KNOWN BETTER; IT WAS APPROACHING dawn by the time we found our way to bed.

"Mom is in terrible shape, Tish." Much later that evening, seated near me on the tattered old couch in my living room with both feet tucked under her and an afghan drawn over her lap, Camille's face was set in somber lines. The only light came from a small table lamp and the fixture above the stove, lending the trailer a quiet intimacy. "Blythe is so worried. Not even Aunt Jilly can get through to her. She can hardly manage to get to the cafe on any given day, not even for breakfast coffee. Grandma and Aunt Ellen have been keeping watch but nothing helps."

"How are the boys?" I asked, referring to my younger half-brothers, Matthew and Nathaniel. It hurt like hell to hear about Mom and I was more grateful than ever for the presence of my stepdad, Blythe Tilson, whose love for my mother was a force to be reckoned with.

"They help as best they can. I'm so glad they have Bly. He's such a patient dad. He and Uncle Justin take them fishing, along with Rae and Riley and Zoe, so Aunt Jilly can be with Mom. But I don't know how much good it does."

My sister and Mathias had returned home with Case and me after dinner; by necessity, the baby accompanied them while Millie Jo, Brantley, Henry, and Lorie stayed behind at Clark's, excited at the prospect of playing video games and eating junk food with Wy, Sean, and Quinn; meanwhile little James was snuggled on his belly in the center of our bed, sleeping while the four of us gathered in the living room.

Mathias sat on a chair adjacent to Camille, forearms on thighs, his powerful shoulders curved forward. It was strange to observe him in a moment of motionlessness; this alone conveyed concern as much as his grim expression, mouth solemn and brows drawn inward. He cupped Camille's bent knee, making a slow circle with one thumb as he said, "Joelle is struggling to believe Ruthie and Marshall are actually where we claim they are. She trusts us, it's not that. She's just having trouble accepting the truth."

"Just like Dad," I murmured. "We told him last month when we were in Chicago but he doesn't fully believe it." I looked upward, seeing the expression on my father's face as I'd last witnessed it, leaving him behind at the airport. "At least he recognizes that something is seriously wrong with Franklin Yancy." I sat straighter, recalling that Dad had left Case and me a message in that particular vein, only last night. "I almost forgot to tell you guys. Dad has been doing some investigating, and get this: Franklin Yancy has a birth certificate but there is no record of a child with that name born when and where the certificate claims."

"A forgery?" Mathias asked. "Maybe he really *doesn't* exist. But who the hell is the man you saw in Chicago, then?"

"Tell us again what happened," Camille requested. "It's always better to hear in person."

I looked at Case, the two of us exchanging several dozen silent sentences in a matter of seconds. He took my right hand, closest to him, and enfolded it within his left, lacing our fingers, offering wordless support. I released a tense breath before replying; the thought of the Yancys left my chest cavity hollow with fear. "We were at Robbie's funeral. Oh God, Milla, it was so horrible. You guys know we think Robbie was killed. He allegedly overdosed, but I know that's a goddamn lie. What we haven't figured out is *why* he was killed. What did Robbie know? More specifically, what did he know about Franklin?"

"But you *saw* Franklin Yancy," Camille interjected. "So whether or not 'Franklin' is his real name, he does actually exist."

Last summer, the night before he'd returned to Chicago from

Montana, my former college classmate Robbie Benson had received an anonymous text reading *Franklin doesn't exist*. He'd shared the information with Case, Marshall, Ruthann and me on his final night here in Jalesville. It was, I suddenly realized, the last time I'd seen Robbie and I shrugged off an uneasy twinge. My gaze loitered on the screen door as if expecting his ghost to appear on the far side of the meshing, his formerly bronzed skin leached of all color, mutely observing with eyes gone cold and empty. Robbie had been my friend all through college. He was so very *alive*, storming through his days with all the confidence afforded by attractiveness and status and his parents' wealth. I still had trouble reconciling my vivid memories of him with the truth that he was never coming back. I would never see him again.

I swallowed a miserable whimper, with effort, refocusing on Camille. Case squeezed my hand and I found the courage to speak above a whisper. "It was the strangest thing that day. Case and I left the chapel because I felt so ill and Derrick followed us outside. No matter what I've thought about Derrick in the past, I truly believe he was attempting to warn us right then. He told us we should go and not a minute later his brother came striding down the sidewalk through the snow. And he *knew* us, Milla. Franklin, I mean. He spoke to us like he'd met us before that moment. He kept calling me Patricia." It was my real name, but no one had addressed me that way since my dad's mother, the grandma I'd been named for, passed away.

"We thought that maybe Derrick could move through time, like Marsh and Ruthie, but now we're not so sure," Case said quietly. I held his hand like a towrope keeping my head above floodwater, icy depths that wished me dead, no longer able to speculate about time travel or investigate powerful Chicago families with more money and influence than I could ever conceive.

Camille's intense gaze moved between Case and me. "You think Franklin is the time traveler. That *he's* the danger Derrick mentioned at Marshall's birthday party, not Ron Turnbull." I kept my sister well informed. She had not been at that particular celebration, which we'd held for Marsh last fall at The Spoke, but she knew about the events of the evening. I could almost see the sparks created by her spinning thoughts. "You know what this means. It means return is possible! It means Ruthann and Marshall can come home, *here*, where they belong." Tears created a glossy sheen in her eyes, immediately mirrored in mine.

"Where is Franklin now? Has he been seen since that day? What about Derrick?" Mathias persisted.

"Derrick hasn't returned to Jalesville and Jackson hasn't seen Franklin in Chicago," Case answered. "He's keeping tabs on the Yancys and Turnbulls, both." As were we, in a slightly different fashion; in addition to Mutt and Tiny and our newest dog, a lean, alert-eyed shepherd mix named Ranger, Case kept his father's double-barrel shotgun positioned near our bed. We assumed the worst when it came to Ron Turnbull and the Yancys, and were taking no chances.

"Dad's made discreet efforts to contact Franklin," I added. "But he's out of the country, apparently."

"So when he travels 'out of the country,' maybe he's really traveling to another century altogether?" Mathias asked.

I nodded. "It's the most plausible theory we have to work with. We know time travel is possible, we know Ruthie and Marsh are capable. For whatever reason, they're both able to move through the…" I faltered, struggling to remember the way Ruthie described the sensation. She had hated to talk about it; I could hardly bear to recall the sight of her fading before my eyes like a scene from a science fiction movie, her long hair and familiar face and limbs growing as transparent as sunbeams. Somehow the barriers, the locks and dams holding most people fixed in a certain time, did not have power over or simply did not apply to Ruthann and Marshall. Or, perhaps, Franklin Yancy.

"The boundaries of time," Case finished for me. His voice was husky with both concern and the late hour.

"But whereas Ruthie and Marsh seemed to have no control over it, it seems Franklin *does*. If what we believe is true and he can return here from the past, it suggests he has some ability to manage the travel. With Ruthie, it was always because a physical object from the past…pulled at her." I struggled not to grit my teeth at the memory.

"Maybe the real question is where does this man passing himself off as Franklin Yancy come from?" Mathias asked. "What time period is he from, originally, if not this one? And what are his motives for pretending to be a Yancy?"

"Derrick *has* to know the truth. He's the key, like I've said before." I chewed my thumbnail. "I'm certain he was the one who texted Robbie that night. There's some part of him that wants the truth known."

Camille appeared to be attempting to peer into my brain, even though we were fairly adept at reading each other's thoughts. Changing the focus just slightly, she whispered, "Do you think Marsh found her? What if he went too far back, or not far enough?"

"I believe he found her." It took effort but I mustered my conviction. "I truly believe that. I've dreamed about them. They were sitting together in the sunshine. I don't know *when* exactly, but long before we were born. I consider it a sign."

"Do you think she's seen Malcolm?" The hope in Camille's voice was apparent even in a whisper.

"Oh God, I hope so. I hope she's found *all* of them, the Spicers and the Rawleys."

"She seems so close, Tish, almost like we could hear her if we really concentrated. I feel it more strongly than ever now that we're here in Montana."

My spine twitched at her words; I felt the same.

"We think we have to pull them back, somehow," Case said, returning to an earlier discussion. "Marshall's presence was able to bring Ruthie back that night in January, right here in our trailer. He was able to stop her from completely disappearing. It's not much to go on, but Tish and I believe there's some way to pull them back here, to us. To the place they belong. And it's up to us to do it."

"Marshall saved her that night," I whispered, recalling Ruthie's twenty-third birthday, two months and about a hundred lifetimes ago. "Marsh was shouting her name and somehow his will was enough to stall the effects of the force field dragging at her. I believe if he'd been there that day in the snowstorm, when she disappeared from her car, that his presence would have kept her stable in time."

"Then what's to prevent them from being stuck in the past?" Camille asked. This was a no-holds-barred conversation and we all knew it. Nothing was to be gained by avoidance. "If Marshall is with Ruthie now, I mean. What if…they're meant to stay there?"

I could not accept this as truth. "*No*. No, we can't think like that. Al and I have already combed through every archive and record book available in the special collections section at the library. There's nothing to go on, no mention of them through all the decades until now. They didn't stay in the nineteenth century, I *know* it." My conviction blazed like acid in my veins, every bit as painful. It was blind faith and I hated being reduced to it, but what was the alternative? Allow the past to swallow my little sister and Marshall? Give up without even trying?

"That brings us to another subject." Case gently released my hand and made a steeple of his fingertips, wishing he did not have to relay this further devastating news.

"The homestead claims," Mathias understood, sitting straighter. "Clark told us some."

Case nodded agreement and explained, "Thomas Yancy was killed in June of 1882, as Derrick revealed in court back in February. He produced an obituary posted in a Chicago newspaper from that month. Cause of death is noted as a gunshot wound. Derrick has no way to prove who pulled the trigger that day but he alleged it was Cole Spicer, a longtime enemy of his ancestor's. To make matters even more complicated, the homestead documents my father and Clark possessed show dates of purchase near the end of August, 1882. More than a month after Thomas Yancy's death, but somehow signed and dated by him. The deed Derrick holds, one he'd been searching for since he arrived in Jalesville, shows Thomas Yancy as the primary landowner, with no record of having sold the acreages in his lifetime. It's a goddamn mess and a half."

Case squared his shoulders in an unconscious gesture of defensiveness before continuing. "I will be the first to admit that my ancestors don't have a solid track record in the character department. The ones I knew were slackers at their best and mean drunks who beat their kids at their worst, so who's to say my great-something grandfather *didn't* kill Thomas Yancy? I may never know the truth. But it doesn't mean I'm going to roll over and let the Yancys take our land in this century. No way in *hell*."

"If Cole Spicer killed him, he had a damn good reason," Mathias said, and I loved him for his confidence in my husband's family; in that moment, a good word from Mathias meant more than anything I could have spoken, which Case would surely interpret as obligatory on my part, as his wife.

I hated how Case's troubled upbringing loomed now and again to broadside his sense of self, to make him question his heritage. Case's father, Owen Spicer, was lucky he'd never met me; I would have given the son of a bitch a piece of my mind. Would have smashed him upside the head for hurting Case in any way, shape, or form; Case hadn't always been the tough, physically-imposing man he was today. Long ago he'd been a despairing little boy who'd lost his beloved mother and was forced into the role of surrogate father to his younger brother, Gus. Just the thought of Case as a small, vulnerable child at the mercy of a cruel father made both my heart and gut clench. The metal flowers expanded yet again, rigid petals digging into my internal flesh.

I issued a sharp intake of breath, stomach acid ricocheting up my esophagus with the suddenness of a geyser. Covering my mouth with one hand I fled for the bathroom, hearing everyone exclaim at my abrupt departure. Case was there in an instant, kneeling to hold my hair as I vomited, gripping the toilet seat with both hands; at the corner of my vision I saw Camille framed in the open doorway. It took me a second to realize the baby I heard wailing in the background was hers and not the one she was talking about…

"Tish, why didn't you tell me?" she implored, advancing into the bathroom. "I suppose I could have guessed, you've been so pale and tired, but I thought it was due to all this stress…"

Case's head jerked toward my sister.

Hanging limp over a porcelain bowl, I struggled to put two and two together.

Mathias appeared next, cuddling little James, all five of us crowded into a space barely large enough for one. I supposed it was only to be expected; in our family there was never much for privacy. We kept nothing from each other.

Mathias pressed a soft kiss to his son's forehead and murmured, "Sounds like you're getting another cousin pretty soon here, buddy."

Chapter Seven

Axton.

Snared in the dark reaches of fevered sleep, his name was a soft exhalation of longing, a need hidden by day but which broiled to life each night, forcing acknowledgment. Watching events unfold on two separate planes of a recurring dream, I saw him from a distance, astride Ranger and riding closer at a galloping pace while I seemed to hover, both on a horizontal axis and a vertical one. Suspended perhaps twelve feet above the prairie I was reduced to nothing but mute observation. I knew he was in danger. Certainty pierced my transparent dream-body and I cried out in warning.

He could not hear my words – or would not heed them. Though damnable distance kept us apart I beheld his face as if only a breath away, cast in the fire of day's end and set in stubborn lines by the force of his will, the force of his love for me. There was no guile in this recognition; that Axton loved me was the one conviction to which I clung. In the wretched, aching chamber of my soul where all secrets were laid bare, I loved him without reservation. Axton Douglas owned my heart as surely as I owned his – but I would go to my grave without him. There was no other choice, not anymore. I recognized this, too.

His gaze darted upward – and in seeing me only a few hundred yards ahead, he heeled Ranger and leaned over the animal's muscular neck. Tears streaked my face and poured down my hovering body, wetting trails along my clothing and rolling from my hem, creating a gray mud-slick of the ground beneath my feet. Lacking control to prevent events from unfolding but knowing exactly how they would play out, I screamed anew for him to stop, both arms extended. Ranger's strong legs were a blur of rippling motion and Axton could not see the depth of the water, now a mass of swirling energy in which he would plunge headlong and drown.

Axton!

Patricia!

Stop! Axton, stop!

"Patricia! Wake up!"

Cole's voice, gritty with trepidation, intruded upon the dream and shredded my view of the darkening prairie and Axton and Ranger upon it. A different prairie smote my senses, this one shrouded by a bleak, predawn gray. My face was sticky with tears and I gripped Cole's elbows, seeking reassurance. I couldn't draw a full breath and therefore tell him I was all right. It was an outright lie, anyway. I was far from all right. I was beside myself with grief and strain, depleted and ill. I had been plagued by the dull ache of a fever for the past twenty-four hours. Cole's concern was nearly palpable and I focused on him, shutting out the remnants of the dream.

You are a mother now, Patricia. You must set aside your despicable selfishness.

Upon seeing my open eyes, Cole exhaled a sigh of relief and lowered his forehead to my neck, gathering me close to his solid strength. He rolled to his right side, tucking me closer, bracketing my nape with one hand. We remained sheltered in the unforgiving wagon bed, over which Cole and Malcolm had stretched a crude canvas top, enough to keep the worst of the weather at bay.

"You're burning up, love," he murmured, resting his cheek to my temple.

I opened my mouth to tell him I was well but could not manage the words. My lips and tongue were too dry.

Just beyond the wagon I heard Malcolm Carter murmuring in a companionable fashion to my son, picturing him crouched near the crackling flames of the breakfast fire with Monty tucked in his arms. Interspersed with these sounds was the low-pitched rumble of another male voice, belonging to a man who had joined our journey only a few days ago; Blythe Tilson had in fact been awaiting our arrival at the homestead of Charley and Fannie Rawley, intending to travel north with Malcolm into Minnesota.

Exhausted and overwhelmed, I had paid little attention to the addition to our party, other than to note the most basic facts – Blythe Tilson was a giant, weathered bear of a man, whose elderly father, Edward Tilson, resided with Malcolm's family in Landon. After many years of wandering, Blythe wished to reunite with his last remaining relative; the two Tilsons, elder and younger, had not been in one another's company since before the War Between the States.

Though Cole and I had intended to make the journey to Minnesota alongside Malcolm, my ill health temporarily overrode those intentions. I'd heard the men discussing the situation last night, a conversation I recalled only in patches as I listened between bouts of restless dozing.

"I wish Uncle Edward was here just now," Malcolm had said, the words undulating in slow waves to reach me in the wagon. "He's a fine physician, one I trust with my life. He would know what was best for Patricia."

"I won't press on with her in this condition," Cole pronounced, grim but resolute. "Once we reach Iowa City, I'll get us a room in a boarding-house. We can make the remainder of the journey when she is recovered. We can rejoin you by late summer."

Malcolm was a long time silent – or perhaps sleep had claimed my mind for a span of time. At last he replied, "I hate to part ways. And to leave you behind in that city, in particular."

"We haven't been followed," Cole said, again after a strange, disorienting lull. "We'll be safe in town, among so many others. You and Blythe can make better time without the wagon."

When I had first clapped eyes upon Cole Spicer last July, shortly after my initial arrival in Montana Territory, I could not drag my enchanted gaze from the magnificent sight of him. Tall and grinning, auburn hair sparking in the sun, he cut a figure such as I had never seen. I supposed my infatuation with his physicality reflected nothing so much as simple conceit, the shallow naiveté of a spoiled young woman only recently, albeit regrettably, married; Cole was Dredd Yancy's opposite in all ways. There had been span of a time during which I would have given anything to claim every precious moment of Cole's attention – my father's fortune, my husband's fortune, my very eyes. No price seemed too great for the privilege.

I was vain; foolhardy to an unforgiveable degree.

Paces away, outside in the gathering dawn, my newborn son issued a small grunt, the sort which inevitably led to full-scale cries. My nipples swelled and prickled in an immediate unspoken response to this demand. Seconds later Malcolm called in a hushed voice, "This little fella's wantin' his breakfast, I'd wager."

"I'll fetch him, love," Cole whispered, planting a soft kiss upon my brow before extricating himself from our makeshift bed and climbing from the wagon with his characteristic grace. He and Malcolm exchanged a few quiet words before Cole reentered bearing the baby and a canteen, from which he helped me to sip.

"Take a bit more, if you're able," he whispered, with gentle insistence.

The reality of my depleted and ragged physical form retreated to a space at the back of my mind as Cole surrendered Monty to my embrace. With only a little difficulty, I freed my left breast from the damp confines of my tattered, sour-smelling blouse; the shock of the baby's hard gums upon my tender nipples had long since receded, becoming tolerable pain. Monty latched hold with no trouble, as he had from the first, and proceeded to gulp with noisy contentment, the side of his small, soft face melting into my overheated skin as though we were one entity rather than two. I lowered my head to an outstretched arm.

"I am so sorry for this hard travel, love. We'll reach the town by tomorrow." Cole eased full-length alongside us, bracketing my waist with one hand. The light had shifted with advancing day, allowing me to perceive his features in the gloom of the wagon. To claim I did not love Cole would be yet another lie. I could not deny my love for him any more than I could deny Axton's presence in my innermost heart. The distinction was something I sensed at a level comparable only to instinct; I loved Cole, had *made* love with him, taken his body within mine and his seed into my womb, and yet the idea of spending the remainder of my life as his wife was a quiet resignation rather than a rejoicing.

No matter; the choice was no longer within my ability to make. I was determined to love Cole Montgomery Spicer as he deserved to be loved. And yet – *dear God, forgive me though I do not deserve forgiveness* – I wanted that sacred, indefinable thing which my dear Ruthann shared with Marshall Rawley. How did one person become the one, the *only* one, for another? To the point that all others, no matter how well-meaning or desirable, fell short, unable to compete with that *one*. It seemed a notion both insensible and childish; a little girl's dream with no basis in reality.

But I knew.

When you know, you just know, Axton had whispered before he rode away from me for the first time, last summer at Grant Rawley's homestead; even then we possessed no certainty regarding when we would next meet. *And I know you are for me, Patricia.*

I would tear myself innards-out to understand. I could not reach a satisfactory explanation; the truth defied logic. The undeniable certainty of Axton Douglas. Deep in the night, awakening from dreams of him, I lay steeped in memories of the moments I had shared with Axton before my own choices separated us. I blamed no one but myself. I had been the one whose desire to understand lovemaking overrode sensibility – and I had wanted Cole that clear, yellow autumn afternoon, only hours before Miles Rawley was shot and killed in the dooryard of his brother's homestead.

Cole had asked me to marry him, both of us knowing full well I was already wed to Dredd Yancy. His eyes burned with sincerity as we stared at one another, our bodies seeming to bob in a wide, silent sea. Before I could formulate a response, Cole anchored my waist in his strong hands and drew me near, bending to tease my lips and neck with his tongue; it seemed only natural when he began unlacing my dress with practiced fingers.

I had offered acquiescence with one small word, clutching his shirt in both fists.

We made love three times in quick succession, as bright day faded to soft gray evening, hidden there in the confines of the bunkhouse on Grant's property. Cole's hands knew where to go; his mouth was hot upon my flesh. My body had responded to his touch in unexpected quickening bursts of both pleasure and keen-edged guilt; for even in those moments when I closed my eyes I could not help but imagine it was Axton whose body I wrapped my limbs around.

Desire became a heavy, complicated knot, its skeins cinching my heart with no regard for mercy. It wasn't until months later I became aware a child was conceived that afternoon, Cole's child, eradicating forever the possibility that Axton would not only continue to want me after I had been with Cole, but would be capable of forgiving me.

Whore, I thought. *You are an unforgivable, shameless whore.*

I refused to shy from the truth. At the very least I could be honest with myself.

In the next second recriminations flooded my mind.

Stop this. Your son is drawing sustenance from your body.

You cannot think such terrible things.

But I am a whore. I am married and have birthed another man's child. And if I could, I would turn my back on both and find Axton.

Even your son?

No.

Oh dear God, no. I would never leave my son.

Unaware of the dark quagmire of my thoughts, Cole stroked hair from my temple as he continued speaking. "I'll find us a room, with a bed and a basin. And I'll see to it that you're cared for by a physician."

Fannie Rawley had cared for me as tenderly as any healer during the time we spent at their home; how I had longed to remain under her reassuring eye, but we could not continue to endanger them any more than we could seek refuge with Cole's married sister, who lived with her husband, Quinlan Rawley, on a homestead near Fannie and Charley. Something not quite human – the only way I could reconcile Fallon

Yancy's existence —was perhaps already on our trail. We could take no chances. Never mind the danger of loathsome criminals such as Aemon Turnbull or the man known simply as Vole; the threat of Fallon's sudden appearance overpowered all others. If not tailing us, he was in pursuit of Ruthann.

Please keep us safe. Watch over Axton, I beg of you, oh dear God, I beg of you. Please keep Ruthie and Marshall from harm's way. Let them return to their lives in the future. They deserve no less. I prayed with silent fervor, resting my lips to Monty's silken hair. *Please deliver Fallon to hell, where he belongs. Let him be there already, and all our fears be for naught.*

But I knew it could not be that simple; I sensed Fallon out there somewhere, far more dangerous than I had formerly believed, and more than ready to destroy all that Ruthann and I held dear, for the simple pleasure it would bring him. He despised us for reasons I was only beginning to understand. We had parted ways from Ruthie, Axton, and Marshall for that very reason, praying it would prove more difficult for Fallon to find any of us. Even if Ruthann and her Marshall returned to their original time period they would not be entirely safe from Fallon, for he could follow them there. And so the only logical conclusion I could reach was that Fallon must be killed; the sooner, the better.

I had reconciled myself to a life without my dearest friend, ready to endure the consequences no matter what the personal cost. I closed my eyes, seeing Ruthann's beautiful face and the warmth of her direct gaze. I would never have survived the past winter if not for her; she was yet another person my heart ached with loving. How did one begin to separate the two emotions? Were love and pain meant to be intertwined, an inevitable pairing of deepest feeling?

You and my sister share a soul, Ruthann had said. *You are my sister, in this place.*

Together we had spoken of the future – *the present,* as Ruthie knew the twenty-first century – and therefore I had learned of a man named Case Spicer to whom her sister, Tish, was blissfully wed. This knowledge stimulated many a discussion, the two of us speaking in hushed voices late into the night hours. Prisoners in a Catholic convent in western

Illinois, we had talked to ease the desperate fear which would have otherwise overwhelmed us.

I know Cole and Case have the same last name but it's Axton who reminds me most of Case, I swear, Patricia. I truly believe that Axton is Case in the future, not Cole.

And so I clung to Ruthann's conviction; the promise that somewhere in time Axton and I would find one another. We could not be together in this life but at least I retained the assurance of a future life together.

Let it be so, dear God, let this come to pass.

I cannot survive this life without the promise of the next.

And the reproaches blazed anew, as painful as if I stood in the center of a roaring fire.

Chapter Eight

The Iowa Plains - June, 1882

I LONGED FOR AN ESCAPE FROM THE CLAUSTROPHOBIC CON-
fines of the wagon bed and so Cole wrapped me in a thick shawl and
we joined Malcolm and Blythe at the breakfast fire, where Malcolm
crouched poking at golden-brown biscuits with an iron cooking tool.
Blythe sat cross-legged on its far side, warming his large, gnarled hands.
Both men hurried to their feet at the sight of me, offering polite greetings and gladness at my appearance.

Despite the shawl and the heat thrown by the fire, to say nothing of
Monty's plump warmth in my arms, I could not contain a shiver. But
I was determined to take the air for a moment's time and restrained
further trembling, with effort. Cole settled a tattered wool blanket over
the ground and then helped me to sit; I sensed the way he withheld
concerned commentary, and was grateful.

"Those look delightful," I told Malcolm; my voice emerged thin and
pale. I was unaccustomed to illness, to personal weakness in general.

"Thank you kindly, ma'am," Malcolm replied, his kind, dark eyes
flashing to my face as he reclaimed his crouch beside the crackling fire.
"I ain't much of a cook but I do have biscuits down to an art, if I do say
so myself."

"And thank you for entertaining Monty. He is quite taken with you."
I smiled at my contented son, whose eyes appeared as bright as gems in
the dawn's light. Despite Malcolm's striking physical stature and out-
going, demonstrative nature, there existed within him a deep well of

tenderness; the baby seemed to sense it and had ceased crying on several occasions after being placed in Malcolm's arms. I acknowledged, with a sharp pang of guilt, that he had likely held my son as often as I on our journey northwest from the convent.

"Young'uns always are," Malcolm affirmed with an air of gentle teasing. "Between my brother and Becky, and Sawyer and Lorie, I have an even dozen nieces and nephews. And it ain't no lie that I'm the favorite among them-all."

"Among the Rawley children, as well," I commented, recalling the way the youthful offspring of Miles's three brothers had clambered all over Malcolm during our brief time in their rowdy company.

Blythe Tilson remained reticent; I'd learned he was an observer rather than a talker. Besides, Malcolm chatted enough for any two people. Though I desired greatly to know, I was hesitant to inquire how my presence would be received by Malcolm's relations in northern Minnesota, whenever fate decreed we should arrive at their home; I thought of them in conjunction with Malcolm rather than Ruthann, though she too possessed a familial connection. Cole had provided for me all the details Ruthann had been unable to supply regarding her ancestors in this century; the Davis family, along with Malcolm's older brother, Boyd Carter, had established and settled homesteads along the wooded lakefront thirteen years ago, in the summer of 1869. One day, many decades from now, their descendants would manage successful businesses in the selfsame area, places with picturesque names to conjure countless striking images in my mind.

Flickertail Lake. Landon. Fisherman's Street. The Shore Leave Cafe. White Oaks Lodge.

Ruthann had been of the opinion that I would be welcomed with love and acceptance by those who resided in her remembered hometown; I attempted to believe this, refusing to point out that her views were based more upon twenty-first century sensibilities than she realized. While descendants of the people living today may very well prove tolerant of an unwed mother – at least, unwed to her son's father – Malcolm's family could just as quickly cast me from their favor. And rightly so. Besides my sinful behavior on several fronts, my very presence was a danger to everyone with whom I came into contact.

I wished to pose these questions to Malcolm, wanting his opinion on the matter, but had not yet found an opportune or appropriate moment. Despite our brief acquaintance, I knew he and Cole shared a long history, and therefore I trusted him. Furthermore, I quite liked Malcolm. There was an effortless amiability in his manner, a wayward sense of good humor, however tempered by a deep, guarded well of sadness. The little I knew of Malcolm's heartache came from Ruthann and Cole, both of whom had mentioned a woman named Cora, Malcolm's lost love. Empathy and curiosity welled within me but I would never stoop to inquiring after her.

"Are you hungry at all?" Malcolm asked, peering at me with a faint crease denting his otherwise smooth brow. "This is a terrible way for a new mama to travel, I do apologize. You look right peaked, poor thing. Eat, if you're able."

Though my stomach sent out mild protests, nursing the baby sapped my energy like nothing I had ever known. I recognized I must retain my strength and let Cole take Monty so I could handle a plate and fork. Cole tucked the baby in the crook of his left arm and cupped my elbow with his free hand. Nodding southward, Cole commented, "It wasn't too very far from here that Malcolm and I first met. We were but sprouts, both farther from home than we'd ever dreamed possible. I'd never seen a sight like the expanse of prairie we traveled over that summer. Land so wide and empty it seemed we'd never reach the end."

Inspired by the storytelling quality of Cole's words, Malcolm's eyes took on a subtle shine. "Ain't that the truth? What a fine dinner your dear mama served the afternoon we met. Remember them fireflies at dusk?"

Cole laughed, nodding. "I don't know that I've ever seen so many at once, since then. How glad we were for your company. And how jealous I was of Aces High! I begged Pa for my own horse from that moment forth, until he was fit to whip my hide for pestering." Addressing me, Cole explained, "I spent most of those days walking alongside the wagon. Walking and walking in the heat of the sun, blisters across my heels every night. I didn't have a fine horse to gallop away from the monotony."

I listened with fascination despite my aching head and the slight haze across my vision.

"Aces High has been with me since the day I rode forth from Cumberland County," Malcolm said, glancing with fond pride in the direction of the picket line where the same horse now grazed, before returning his attention to me. "I'd spent my boyhood in the hollers of Tennessee, you see, where the sun rose late and set early and you couldn't see the horizon unless you climbed to the topmost ridge and *then* shimmied up the tallest pine. I never knew something so big as the prairie existed. I'm not too proud to admit it frightened me no small amount."

Blythe nodded as he listened to Malcolm's descriptions; he wore no hat in the early part of the day and I revised my assumption of his age; he appeared younger in the fire's light, perhaps mid-thirties rather than past two score. Craggy-featured and with unruly hair, he offered an unexpected smile. When Blythe spoke, the sound of the southern lands was predominant in the cadence of his speech, more pronounced than the hint of it in Malcolm's. Almost shyly, Blythe murmured, "We was raised but a stone's throw from one another, young Malcolm, an' we never met 'til now. Ain't that somethin'? I've traveled far an' wide in my time but I never found me a place quite as pretty as the hollers of home."

"It's a funny thing how life sorta comes around full circle," Malcolm replied, nodding agreement. "Later that same summer your father and I met just yonder, in Iowa City." I did not believe I imagined the way his eyes tightened as he added, "It's a town I could do without ever revisiting, if you want the truth."

I should have bitten my tongue. "Why is that?"

Malcolm fixed his gaze on the fire and gone was the sweetness of youthful memories, replaced by the stern, uncompromising regard of a man who had endured depths of pain I was only beginning to understand. I sensed a torrent of anguished words – the heaviness of guilt, the sting of bitterness, the razor of remembered agony – all held in check by his powerful will. He said only, "It was where I disobeyed Lorie."

Blythe politely took up the conversational reins, drawing Malcolm's focus as he inquired, "Lorie, your sister?"

"I love Lorie as well as my own kin, though we are not related by blood. Lorie is wed to my brother's dearest friend, Sawyer."

Blythe persisted, "And your brother is wed to my cousin Rebecca, ain't that right?"

There were too many connections for my tired mind; I set aside my plate and leaned against Cole, thankful beyond measure for his solid strength.

"Yes, Boyd and Becky been wed for many happy years. They was most overjoyed to learn of your intent to rejoin them." A smile elongated Malcolm's mouth, restoring animation to his handsome face. "I can nearly catch the scent of all the baked goods being prepared in your honor, Tilson."

A quiet yellow slice of sun crested the horizon as if to emphasize this statement and a small prickle of hope caught me unaware. In that golden-tinted moment I let myself believe my son and I would be welcomed, that all would be well; we would find sanctuary in Minnesota and then, next summer, we would venture west to Cole's parents, to claim our own homestead acreage.

But I should have known better.

Cole and I had less than a day left together and somewhere, beyond our perception, the timepiece had already begun its rapid ticking toward zero.

I woke with no earthly idea where I was, aware of nothing but the fact that something was dreadfully wrong. Buried alive was my first thought, for I lay prone beneath heavy layers, unable to lift arms or legs. Inundated by blistering heat and dull pain, I turned my head to the side in an attempt to determine a single point of orientation. Met by little but darkness, fear drummed an increasing beat inside my head. A small bundle tucked close to my breasts shifted with small, mewling grunts.

Monty, I realized, groping for facts through the haze in my mind. Outside, the wind had gained in strength, causing the canvas covering stretched over the wagon's ribs to flap like a flag.

Something is wrong.

Cole…

My tongue scraped the backsides of my teeth but no sound materialized. I could not manage the requisite strength to lift to one elbow, disabled by weakness. No way to gauge how many hours had passed since retiring to bed; the fever had gained in severity while I slept. I realized Cole was not in the wagon. Often he slept near the fire, the better to keep watch with the men. Encroaching swiftly now was the recognition of danger, beating like the hooves of cantering horses across the hot, feverish plain of my awareness.

They're coming.

They're coming because of me and I have to warn the men.

Oh dear God, it is my fault.

Cole…Malcolm…

Monty's grunting gained in strength and a small scuffling beyond the wagon met my ears. My shoulders sank with momentary relief. Cole must have heard the baby. Any second he would emerge from the windy predawn and I could warn him that someone was approaching our position, and just as swiftly he would reassure me that no one had followed us these past weeks of travel; no Fallon Yancy on our trail, my agitation nothing more than a nightmare conjured by a fevered mind.

To some extent, this was correct; it was not Fallon or his men closing in on our camp, using the gathering storm as cover.

A single gunshot cracked the air.

Monty shrieked at his highest register and began wailing.

I whimpered, clutching him close to my chest as mounted horses surrounded our camp; buzzing, shouting chaos reached my ears through the wind.

"Stand down, we've got you surrounded!"

"Drop that sidearm! Toss it aside!"

"On your goddamn knees!"

"This man's been shot!"

"I told you to hold your goddamned fire!"

"Where is Patricia? Tell me at once!"

I knew that last voice and whimpered anew, bending as best I could around my baby's soft, vulnerable body, my own a pitiful, fragile shield.

"You will not go near her, *you son of a bitch!*"

No, oh please no, I begged, hearing Cole's roaring shouts followed by a ferocious struggle.

Another gunshot and I lurched as though the bullet had pierced my flesh; Monty's sobbing cries were at once muted as my ears rang from the inside out. *Who had been shot?!* Seconds later Dredd Yancy's head and shoulders appeared at the oval opening to the rear of the wagon. Clad in riding garments, wool cloak, and a wide-brimmed hat, he lofted a lantern and peered inside, containing his shock and disbelief with monumental effort.

His lips moved, forming my name.

I closed my eyes, trying to hide Monty from his sight against my fevered body.

Oh dear God, no…

Dredd disappeared from view. More shouting, cursing, threats. The ringing subsided enough for individual words to penetrate.

"He's bleeding out!" Malcolm growled. "He will die and you will be at fault!"

Did he mean Cole?! Or Blythe?

Dredd raged, "Let him die! My wife appears ill! She requires care!"

Another voice I knew cut through Dredd's anger, that of my father-in-law, Thomas Yancy. Colder than raw steel, exactly as I remembered, Thomas said, "Your wife is a common whore. You realize this, do you not? That bastard squalling in the wagon likely belongs to this fellow."

I imagined Dredd rounding on Cole. Effectively blinded by the wagon's canvas covering, I had only their words to gauge what was occurring outside. My heart throbbed with agony, pulsing through every channel in my body. I strained to hear over the wind gusts.

"Touch them and I will kill you," Cole spit out, hoarse and raw – he was injured, I could tell by the distortion of his words.

Monty's screams pierced the brightening air, now several shades lighter gray.

"Shoot him, son." Thomas Yancy spoke with mockery, the tone he often used when addressing Dredd. I knew he considered his youngest a weakling, a helpless fop. Fallon was Thomas's favorite, a ruthless businessman and killer, a son of which a man like Thomas Yancy could be proud. He goaded, "Shoot your wife's lover right between the eyes and be done with it. You'll never have a cleaner shot." Undiluted contempt swelled in the loathsome man's voice. "Ain't that why we've come all this way?"

"I know you for a better man than that, Dredd." Malcolm spoke with a preternatural calm, belying his fury. "You are not your brother. You are *not* your father."

"Fancy seeing you here, young Carter." Thomas sounded almost giddy and I pictured his pale eyes alighting on Malcolm. "Not so very far from the place where you took a shot at me, all those years ago."

"If I'd've aimed truer that night, you woulda been sent to hell long before now." I envisioned Malcolm's flashing eyes, his elevated chin. "It's one of many regrets but I'm a better shot now, that I promise you, Yancy."

"I've no doubt. But you've been separated from your sidearm and you'll be dead before the sun rises. Which, by my calculation, is in about a minute's time."

"Hitch up this wagon," Dredd instructed; I sensed he was stalling. "Go on now!"

Someone scurried to follow his orders.

"Take your shot, son, it's your *chance*."

Dredd must have hesitated further.

His tone drenched in ridicule and derision, Thomas brayed, "You worthless coward."

"I am no coward." Dredd spoke with more conviction than I had believed him capable. "*You* are the coward, Father. A man was sent last summer to murder my wife in her train car, on your orders, do you deny this?"

Thomas either made no reply or spoke too quietly for my ears to perceive.

The moment balanced on the edge of a blade, precipitous, the slightest action poised to tip the scale toward certain catastrophe.

You were foolish enough to believe escape was possible, Patricia.

It was never possible.

I would never be certain exactly what happened next; my imagination would later recreate the scene a hundred, a thousand times, each remembrance slightly different than the one before, constructed from an incomplete memory of the moment. Eyes closed, the world smeared gray-red with agony, I pictured the anger as it bloated within Dredd, stronger than the gusting wind, an ancient rage at last allowed release. A third gunshot, followed quickly by a fourth. By the time Monty's cries subsided, the wagon was bumping at a brisk pace over the rutted prairie trail, hauling me and my son away.

Chapter Nine

Jalesville, MT - March, 2014

"A GIRL," CASE MURMURED, HIS LIPS BRUSHING MY TEMPLE.

I snuggled closer to his delicious warmth, content but exhausted; dawn was threatening our window shade and we hadn't slept more than an hour. His strong arms held my midsection secure, both of us naked; the bedding beneath our legs was rumpled and Case spread it out with a few dexterous movements of his ankle before I twined my calves around his knee and held fast, burying my nose against his chest.

Mathias had ridden to town with Case last night after I'd requested a pregnancy test from the drugstore; I'd remained on the couch, wrapped in the afghan, stationed beside Camille while she nursed James, stroking his round peach of a cheek. I'd watched in a transfixed stupor, attempting to fathom that soon I would be the one cradling an infant to my breasts.

"I hope it's twins," Camille had joked, stretching a hand to pat my stomach. She added, with glee, "Twin boys!"

"Oh, *Jesus*," I'd muttered, shying away from her teasing touch. "We need a bigger house."

Sunlight cleared the horizon now, hours later, and painted the cramped interior of our bedroom with a warm, dusty gold. Mathias, Camille, and the baby had returned to Clark's, where there was ample sleeping space; Case and I had promised to venture there for breakfast. Thinking of my sister's words about twin boys – if I remembered correctly, Brantley and Henry had experienced terrible colic for the first three months of their infancies – I infused my voice with certainty and whispered, "Yes. A sweet baby girl."

I had been operating for many weeks now with a sense of trepidation at the thought of future events, the notion that if I anticipated too far ahead it was not only futile but dangerous. Next week could bring devastating news, let alone a time two seasons from now. What if Ruthie and Marshall weren't home by next autumn?

What if...

Case spoke with determination, warding off my despairing thoughts. He kissed the top of my head before murmuring, "Everyone will be so excited, sweetheart, think of that." Camille and Mathias had promised not to divulge the news, at least until I had a chance to call Mom, Aunt Jilly, and Grandma and Aunt Ellen. "And you can spend all summer eating for two."

I made a sound somewhere between a snort and a giggle. "Right now that sounds terrible. No wonder I haven't felt hungry."

The best I could figure was that I was roughly eight weeks along; my last period had occurred in January, which gave us a tentative due date of mid-October. Case and I had been in Chicago for Robbie's funeral at the end of February and I vaguely recalled thinking that I was overdue; in the ensuing stress, I'd missed what should have been obvious.

"Do you remember last summer after we made love for the first time, with no protection?" Case's voice was a low, tender rumble. His hands were warm on my bare skin as he caressed my shoulder blades, then swept his touch downward to massage my lower back. I shivered in blissful response, tucking closer.

"Of course I do," I whispered, gliding my hands to capture his ass, smoothing my palms over the sensual familiarity of my husband's body.

"I told you that our baby would come to us when she was ready, remember? And now is that time, my sweet love, for our baby." His voice thickened with emotion and his arms tightened around my torso, hugging me closer. "I'm so happy, sweetheart. You don't know how much I've longed for our family. No matter where we go from here, even if we lose our land, we'll have each other. Nothing means more to me than that in the entire world, Tish."

"I know, honey. I'm so happy, too." Tears seeped from my eyes and wet his skin. "I am, I promise. Even if..." I choked back the words, biting savagely upon my lower lip, restraining sobs.

"We have to believe that they're happy out there, wherever they are." Case knew what I needed to hear. And to a great extent, I recognized he was not just speaking words to comfort me; he also believed what he said. "Even if they never return to us, they're together. Ruthie is the one person Marsh refuses to live without and she would say the same of him, I'm certain."

You're right, I tried to say, but I could do nothing but cry, muffling the sounds against Case. Maybe it was selfish, but I wanted my little sister. I wanted Marshall, who was like the brother I never had; I was not yet ready to let the universe claim them. I refused to accept a reality in which we never saw them again. Because I couldn't manage words, I let my actions speak for me; I needed Case inside of me, our bodies linked as closely as possible. I never ceased to believe that in those moments our souls meshed as intensely as our physical forms.

"I'm right here," he murmured in understanding, rolling me to my back with extreme care, parting my lips with his in order to kiss me deeply; I was ready at once but he eased within in gentle increments, never breaking our kiss, building the pleasure by degrees. Case knew me down to the tiniest detail, knew how to draw out an orgasm until I was panting with need. He continued his unceasing motion, on and on, slowing when I was close, tasting hot, salty paths over my flushed skin – finally, the sun well above the horizon, I could hold back no longer and was wracked by pleasure, crying out as I clung to him for dear life. And it was only then that he allowed his own release, groaning as he filled me with jolting bursts of wet heat.

When I'd returned to my senses, slick with sweat and still trembling, I muttered, "*Show off.*"

His laughter tickled my stimulated skin and he kissed my closed eyes, one after the other. Low and teasing, he rumbled, "That was nothing. Wait 'til tonight."

Breakfast at Clark's led to a day spent at the Rawleys', all of us lounging on the couches in the living room while the kids played, ranging in
and out of the house. Wy, caught somewhere between child and young
adult, pretended exasperation when Camille's girls begged him to play
"monster" but gave in every time, leaping from the couch with a roar as
they shrieked in delight, racing to escape his clutches. It wasn't difficult
to see that Millie Jo was especially infatuated with him, her pretty eyes
bright with joy when he caught and subsequently threw her over his
shoulder, upside-down. Meanwhile, Mathias, Camille, Case and I shared
with Clark, Sean, and Quinn everything we'd discussed last night.

"I thought that from the first," Sean said, pounding an emphatic fist
against the rounded leather arm of the sofa. Marshall's brothers resembled him so much it hurt; it seemed inconceivable that Marsh wasn't
about to lope around the corner from the kitchen, complaining that
there was nothing to eat. "Together we have to pull them back here
where they belong. It's up to *us*."

"But how, exactly? Do we sit in a circle and hold hands, like a séance?"
I was not attempting to sound facetious, only trying to make sense of
something beyond all logic.

"I don't think that seems totally unreasonable," Mathias said, accepting the sleeping bundle of his youngest into his arms. Camille, who'd
just rejoined us after nursing the baby, slid beside him and kissed his jaw
before settling into a more comfortable position. Smoothing a hand over
the length of Camille's thigh, Mathias went on, "Both of us feel closer
than ever to the past now that we're out here. Just like the time we drove
this way together, back in 2006, when we first met you guys."

I sensed Camille's increasing but unspoken concern the way I would
a change in the air; the sudden, inescapable chill that pierces through
summer warmth, warning of a tornado beyond the horizon. She didn't
have to speak a word for me to understand her fear; so quickly could
someone be robbed of another. In a matter of seconds life could change
course. Time plodded onward in a forward march, not back –

But maybe not always. Obviously, under the right circumstances, it moves of its own accord. Fluid rather than fixed.

"Could it work right now? Should we give it a try?" Quinn's forehead wrinkled in a speculative frown.

Case leaned forward earnestly, his face graced by an expression almost stern in its sincerity; his serious gaze held each of us in turn. "We should, but not here. Out by the foundation of the old homestead, that's where I'd put my money." Dressed in faded jeans and an untucked flannel shirt of dark blue plaid, his hair still a little messy from my questing fingers, I wondered if there had ever been a more desirable man to walk the earth since the beginning of time. He elaborated, "Marsh said the first time he ever felt the force field of the past, that's what he called it, it was out by the old foundation."

"You're right." Excitement swelled in my blood. "If Ruthie and Marsh found the Rawleys in the nineteenth century, like we believe, that's where they would be. Here, but not exactly here." It was such a strange thought; I curbed the desire to peer over my shoulder, as if the Rawleys from another century hovered like ghosts near the hearth or along the edges of the spacious room, watching us in silent reflection.

"They seem so close." Camille unconsciously echoed my thoughts, her gaze alighting on the west-facing windows, toward the site of the old homestead; her longing for knowledge of not only Ruthie and Marsh, but of Malcolm Carter, flowed from the very depths of her soul. I saw it and I knew Mathias saw it, and understood. Her voice was very soft, almost as though she was not speaking as much as thinking aloud. "What separates one time from another? What stands between them and us? Is it a physical barrier? A wall? A freaking mist cloud? Why can some people pass through it?"

"Aunt Jilly believes that time is ongoing, all around us," I said, and Case's grip on my ankle, bent toward him on the couch between us, instantly tightened. The memory of Ruthann dissolving before our eyes remained visceral and terrifying; the thought that I might disappear in such a fashion plagued him, even though I assured him I had never felt the bizarre pull of the past. Recognizing that not everyone knew what

I meant, I explained, "Time never stops existing but most people are totally unaware of its presence. Most people are fixed in their original timeline, with no awareness of any other. To most people it would seem like science fiction, certainly not something they would take seriously."

"But that doesn't stop other timelines from existing simultaneously," Mathias said, and I nodded, thinking of my conversations with Aunt Jilly. I wished she was here, too.

"I think it seems more like a river or something," Quinn said, addressing Camille. "Flowing without stopping, I mean. And we're all caught in the current but some people can sort of, you know, bob *out* of the current."

"Right. Like Marsh and Ruthie," Camille said.

"And this Franklin fellow, the imposter," Clark mused. Dear Clark, possibly the sweetest man alive, a kind and quiet soul who had never remarried after the death of his beloved wife, Faye. I wanted to see Clark smiling and jovial again, as he'd been when I first knew him. It seemed the lines of worry and distress carved into his forehead would never again be smoothed away. It was grossly unfair to lose a spouse so young, but another wrong entirely for a father to lose his son. And Clark had now experienced both.

"Derrick has insisted on more than one occasion that Franklin, whoever the hell he really is, is dangerous," I said, gaining steam. "And after having met him, I believe it. He was armed, for Christ's sake, there on the street in Chicago headed for a *funeral*. And Franklin knew us. How could he have known us, unless…" My thoughts whirled, seeking something that defied reason.

"Unless he knows who you *used* to be. That has to be it." Camille's eyes were now intent upon mine. Awareness crackled between us, sending shivers radiating to my fingertips and toes.

"Cole," I whispered. Before I knew I had moved, I was clutching my midsection. "Franklin knows Cole Spicer, I'm sure of it."

"That's who Case used to be, right?" Sean asked. No question seemed too strange these days.

"That's what we believe," I affirmed, unable to look away from Case.

"And Cole is who allegedly shot and killed Derrick and Franklin's ancestor, Thomas Yancy."

"He no doubt deserved killing," Clark said, and I felt another rush of vindication; I could not have loved the Rawleys more if they were my own family. Their loyalty and devotion was unparalleled.

"We planned to head back to Minnesota next weekend," Mathias said, his wide shoulders rising with a deep inhalation. Determination radiated from his posture and his eyes; he made a fist and cupped it within his other hand, knuckles forming ridges. Rarely had I seen him appear so grave, mouth solemn rather than grinning; I'd always associated lighthearted cheer with my brother-in-law. He added, "So I say, let's *do* this."

"No time like the present," Quinn murmured, with a half-smile acknowledging the irony.

"Tomorrow night is the full moon," Clark said, lacing his fingers as though to prevent tense fidgeting. "And it's supposed to be clear."

Case said, "We'll be ready."

The front door burst wide, emitting a blast of chilly air along with Wy, Millie Jo, Lorie, and the twins. Their screaming, laughing presence effectively ended the conversation but something had taken root in my heart as potently as the baby had taken root in my womb.

Hope.

Chapter Ten

Jalesville, MT – March, 2014

UNWILLING TO PART FROM EACH OTHER'S COMPANY, CASE
and I met Mathias and Camille at The Spoke that night; Garth and
Becky intended to join us later in the evening. The Saturday night mood
was raucous, the familiar little bar noisy and crowded, bathed in neon
and good cheer. The Spoke was owned by Clark's younger sister, Julie
Heller, and her husband; their daughters, Pam, Lee, and Netta, ran the
entire show. After hugs and congratulations, (along with a glass of 7UP
for me), Pam made sure we had a constant supply of beer. The band
tonight was a local father and son duet, and within two songs they'd
persuaded Case and Mathias to join them on stage. It didn't exactly take
much arm-twisting; both of our men were at home singing and making
music.

"They look so right up there," Camille said, beaming and clapping as
Mathias sent her a wink as he accepted both a cowboy hat and the mi-
crophone. Clad in a fitted turquoise-blue sweater and faded jeans tucked
into snow boots, the dark cloud of her hair spilling over her shoulders
and down her back, Camille looked all of about seventeen years old,
and determined to enjoy the evening. "I swear it was just yesterday that
Mathias was up there for the first time, singing with Case and Marsh
and Garth." She looked my way, her lips softening into a fond smile.
"Even that night I realized you and Ruthie should be here with me. That
our men were up there, singing, and you guys weren't even here to see it."

"A lot had to happen in the meantime," I whispered, watching Case as he positioned a borrowed fiddle beneath his jaw. My throat ached at the memory of what I'd put Case through before I understood that he was mine, that we belonged together.

When you know, you just know, he'd once said.

And I know you are for me, Patricia.

"Ax," I heard myself whisper.

My hands were in fists.

Camille, seated to my left, leaned closer. "I can't hear over the music. Did you just say 'ax?'" She angled her beer bottle so I could better see the label, which featured a well-built man wielding what appeared to be a battleax. The beer, Warrior's Ale, was from a local brewery.

"I…" Words stuck to my tongue; I slowly shook my head, indicating *never mind.*

The past year I'd spent so much time sitting at this very table along with Ruthie while Marshall and Case performed. I couldn't begin to count the number of times we'd commented how wonderful it would be if Mathias and Camille were also in attendance, and now here I was with my older sister but no Ruthann. No Marshall.

What if we're never all together again…

No. Tish, no. Don't think like that. Stop it.

You have to believe we have the ability to bring them home.

I didn't want Camille, let alone Case, to worry about me and so I forced myself to relax and appreciate the music. Case bowed the fiddle with his eyes closed, as usual, while the father and son gave their guitars a workout and Mathias sang; his voice was as rich and true as always. Old-school country, one song flowing into the next. I rested both palms on my belly, imagining that the baby could hear the notes, admiring the way the stage lights glinted on Case's beautiful auburn hair, already envisioning our daughter with a soft cap of red-gold curls.

Listen to your daddy making music, I thought. *Music is in your blood, my sweet girl.*

Garth and Becky arrived and Garth was pulled onstage to much applause and encouragement from the growing crowd. Perhaps an hour passed; though I had not consumed a drop of alcohol I felt slightly inebriated, my thoughts rippling from one to the next. I kept thinking I saw Ruthann in the crowd of swirling dancers. My vision seemed to blur at increasing intervals. I despised the way something seemed to be holding its breath at the back of my mind, creating a pressure-cooker of increasing tension. Twice I'd felt Camille's concerned gaze alight on me.

Something's wrong. Something is so wrong.

I knew if I asked my sister she would admit to sensing the same thing, and so I kept quiet.

"I'm going to the bathroom," I finally told her and Becky.

"Are you all right? Do you want me to come with?" Camille asked, but I shook my head.

No one else was in the stalls, to my relief. Alone, I bent forward and cupped my face, which was unpleasantly sweaty. I inhaled against my palms, trying to regroup.

It's all right. Nothing is wrong – at least, not anything new.

You're just tired. You're pregnant, for heaven's sake, and you didn't sleep last night.

I tried to recapture the hopeful feeling I'd experienced earlier, at Clark's.

It's all right. Stop this. You have to start taking better care of yourself.

I splashed my face with cold water then patted it dry with a scratchy brown paper towel. Thank goodness I hadn't worn any mascara this evening. I studied my eyes in the mirror; they appeared stark and bloodshot, rimmed with dark shadows.

Think, Tish.

I prided myself on being a problem solver, someone dedicated to her work, to logic and careful research. I'd completed law school in the top ten percent of my class and hated the current haze shrouding my mind. Though I hadn't mentioned it to anyone, the word I'd spoken earlier had taken root. I knew I hadn't been referring to a weapon; all my instincts screamed that Ax was a person.

But who?

Why does that name seem familiar?

My phone, which I'd tucked in the back pocket of my jeans, suddenly vibrated. I fished it out and fumbled through my pin code; someone had just sent a text.

I need to talk to you. It's important.

My heart seized with a violent thrust. I almost dropped the phone. For a horrible second I thought the text was from Robbie; dead Robbie entombed in his expensive coffin for the past two months. Sweat glided down my temples as I examined the words again, seeking the sender's phone number and a rational explanation. I didn't know the owner of the ten-digit sequence but did recognize the area code, 773. Chicago.

Despite my shaking fingers, I composed a response – *Who is this?*

Derrick, came the immediate answer, blunt and without further explanation. *Call me right now if you can.*

My heart convulsed again, this time in alarm. After weeks of hearing nothing from him, Derrick was suddenly ready to talk? I vacillated between the need to immediately dial his number or scurry back to the bar to tell Camille and Case. Before I made a choice either way my phone vibrated again, flashing a new message and communicating a repetitive sense of urgency – *It's important.*

The next thing I knew I was pushing open the front door and striding outside, tense with restless energy. Assaulted by cold darkness I inhaled the thin late-winter air, searching the assemblage of parked cars and trucks as if for a sign of Derrick; I had no idea if he was in Chicago, Jalesville, or someplace else entirely. Since our confrontation with Franklin in Chicago in February, I no longer feared or hated Derrick; he had tried to warn Case and me, had told us we should leave when he knew Franklin's appearance was imminent. And while I would hardly consider Derrick a friend, I felt an undeniable connection with him. If what we believed was true, he and I had once been married. Unhappily married, but still; something existed between us whether I wished it or not and that something could perhaps save the lives of my family.

The lot was at once familiar and alien, a stretch of blacktop I'd parked my car upon hundreds of times – but never before had it felt so menacing. Twenty feet from the safety of the front entrance I stood alone between diagonal rows of mute vehicles, heart clubbing, my breath creating an increasing vapor cloud.

Stop it, Tish, you're imagining things. You're not in any danger.

I pressed the icon to make a call and brought the phone to my ear. Derrick answered on the first ring.

"Tish?" His voice was a hushed demand.

"It's me, what is it?" I scraped hair from my forehead, shivering, my sweat evaporating in the breeze. From a short distance away I eyed The Spoke, its entrance merry with glowing beer signs. The stage was not in view of the front windows but I imagined Case and Mathias up there, playing and singing. I'd been absent from our table long enough to arouse concern; Camille would come looking for me any second.

"It's Franklin, he's done something," were Derrick's next words.

Anger and frustration tangled together in my throat, propelling forth a volley of fury. "What do you mean?! I'm tired of this bullshit! Who the fuck is Franklin? Why is he dangerous?!" I drew a shuddering breath and heard myself wail, "What has he done with Ruthann? Where is my sister?!"

"Listen to me!" Derrick yelled in an attempt to elevate his voice over mine. "I am so sorry I can't even begin to tell you. I should have told you these things a long time ago, but I was fucked up. I didn't know what to do, I didn't want to betray my family…"

"*What things* are you talking about?!"

Derrick spoke in a quaking rush; in my mind bobbed an image of his face, pale and glossy with sweat, one hand gripping his forehead. "Franklin is Fallon, they're the *same person*. His real name is Fallon Corbin Yancy and he was born in 1853, in Pennsylvania, to Thomas Yancy. He can travel through time, Tish, and does often. He's made millions for Father and me, and Ron-fucking-Turnbull, since the nineties. I met him for the first time when I was about ten or so, and he's been in and out of my life since then. My father reveres him, it's like he's a god. Franklin can do no wrong in Father's eyes but he's incredibly dangerous, like I've told you. I've known for a long time but I've never dared to speak out against him."

I absorbed this tirade in semi-shocked silence, finding room to be ashamed that I had not guessed earlier. The truth had been right in front of us many months ago. A picture formed in my memory, blotting out the parking lot of The Spoke – I saw Ruthann sitting at my kitchen table, winding spaghetti noodles around her fork while laughing at something Marshall was saying, her beautiful hazel eyes flashing with love and adoration as they rested on him, seated to her immediate right. Their first date, last August, during which I'd convinced them to come to dinner at our trailer because Case and I were so excited they were finally dating and because we missed them. I ached from the inside out with the desire to return to that particular yesterday, to that very evening, and scream out the knowledge I now possessed.

I collected my voice. "How many people know this? Did Robbie know it? Was that why he was killed?"

Derrick's voice was hoarse with conviction as he ticked off names. "Father, myself, and Ron Turnbull. No one else to my knowledge but I've always suspected Christina. It's our most carefully guarded secret, so it would have been a long shot for Rob Benson to have found out. It's possible, though. I'm not kept in the loop on everything, I assure you. I can't begin to tell you how sorry I am. I tried to get you to leave Jalesville as long ago as last summer. You wouldn't have been entangled in everything there, if you had."

"Why now?" I demanded, astounded by the mass of what he was unloading. "Why didn't you tell me any of this earlier?"

"I couldn't, don't you see? For one thing, I'm afraid for my own safety. But now it's gone too fucking far. Franklin is losing touch with reality. He's obsessed with causing harm. I'm trying to get my father to see the truth."

"Harm to my sister? To Ruthie?! Has he seen her in the past?"

"He has, and he hates her, Tish, with a ferocity I can't explain. It's on par with his hatred of the Rawleys and the Spicers, families whose interests have opposed his since the nineteenth fucking century."

"Where is she? How can she get back here? How the hell can we stop him?" Questions tumbled end over end from my lips.

"Your sister somehow ended up around 1882. Time moves differently between then and now, I can tell you that, but I don't know much else. Not nearly as much as I should. And I have no idea how to stop Franklin. He disappears without warning. He wants to stay here in the twenty-first century more than almost anything, but he always gets…snapped back, I guess, like a rubber band, to his original timeline. To a particular area around Jalesville, which was the first place he jumped through time. Why do you think we've been buying up that land for our own? Franklin thinks he can figure out how to close off the time barrier for good." He heaved a shuddering sigh. "God, I know how insane this all sounds…"

"Derrick, I believe you! Keep talking!" I imagined what Case and everyone else would have to say after I dashed back inside The Spoke and summarized this volcano of a conversation. I was afire with purpose, already envisioning what we could do with such a wealth of information. The phrase 'close off the time barrier for good' set every alarm bell within my head to clanging.

We have to try tonight, I realized, thoughts racing ahead. *We can't wait until tomorrow. We have to drive out to the old homestead and try to bring them home before it's too late.*

"You don't even know how dead I'd be if he knew I was telling you these things," Derrick was saying. "I'm afraid it's already too late…"

I froze, startled anew; he'd spoken the exact phrase I'd just been thinking, 'too late.' I cried, "What are you talking about?"

"He's done something terrible. I don't know what exactly, I haven't seen him in the flesh since Rob's funeral outside St. Helen's. He was ready to kill me that day for knocking him to the sidewalk so you and Case could get away. I haven't heard from him since then. But he called me tonight, only about five minutes ago, and left a message."

"Can you play it for me?" I hardly recognized the high, reedy bleat of my voice.

"Hang on, I'll try." I heard fumbling and Derrick cursed. Slightly away from the phone he said, "Here, listen."

Franklin's recorded voice sounded poised, a man with no cares in the world – "I'm in town. Just arrived, and I'm curious to see what's changed. I hope to hell they remember. *She* does, but it's only a possibility, not a probability. I had such a good idea while I was away, far better than my original one. Fate is with me, brother, as you'll soon see. And it's a beautiful fucking thing." Franklin chuckled and my blood congealed.

Though I knew it was an illusion sparked by my terrorized mind, all light seemed to blink from existence, plunging my body within deep, swirling water. I should have cried out, I should have turned and fled, but instead I was rendered immobile, floundering in watery gray depths.

Fate is with me, brother, as you'll soon see –

As if from a distant shore, much too far away to reach, I heard Derrick saying, "I don't know what it means, only that it's something bad. You can hear how goddamn crazy he sounds." And seconds later, "Hey, are you still there? Tish? Are you there?"

Case's name hung suspended in my throat.

More than I'd ever known anything, I knew I had to get to him in that moment, that everything depended on it –

But a force beyond my power to control liquefied my legs and I sank to the blacktop. The cold ground seeped through my jeans. Instinctively I covered my stomach with both forearms as danger asserted itself with onrushing aggression; bile surged and I gagged. I heard Camille screaming. I heard Case yelling for me, his deep voice wild with fear, but I could not respond.

Tish! Where are you?
Where are you?!

Chapter Eleven

A ROARING FILLED MY EAR CANALS, THE OMINOUS REVER-
beration of tons of water thundering over my flyspeck existence. Crushed
beneath the liquid weight I huddled, sheltering my head, eyes squeezed
shut in abject denial of what was happening; a part of me recognized I
would never withstand such assault. My body swayed and jerked, caught
in a current so far beyond my control I was no longer certain I even retained physical form or possessed an identity.

Later, the silence that followed was almost more deafening.

My eyelids parted to darkness. I blinked, lifting my chin with a slow,
careful motion, black night penetrating my awareness. I lay atop gravel,
curled in a compact fetal ball, clutching my shoulders in the opposite
hands. Single words jabbed like small knives.

Alive.

Dry.

Quiet.

My thoughts gained form and substance.

How can I be dry when there was so much water?

Where's Case? Where's Camille?

Oh my God, where are they?

I lurched to all fours, pebbles rough beneath my palms and knees.
Despite the dizzy undulations in my head I staggered to a standing position, seeking the only center I knew – my husband, who was mere yards
away inside The Spoke. I had no idea what in the fuck had just occurred

here in the parking lot but Case would make everything right again. I knew he would. He never failed to make my world right.

Thoughts were coming fast and hard now; unmerciful.

Wait a second...

I was just talking to Derrick.

He said that Franklin is Fallon Yancy.

And Fallon said –

He said –

My eyes roved across the scene before me, struggling to make sense of it; I hadn't until this second processed the fact that the parking lot in which I stood was different than it had been earlier this evening. My phone was no longer in my hand, though I had no memory of setting it down.

What in the hell is going on?

No blacktop. No sign with a lighted arrow, announcing 'The Spoke.' No bright glint of bar lights or the reverberations of music being played nearby. No rows of cars and trucks, just a single green Toyota with Minnesota plates, silent beneath the streetlight. The basic structure of the wooden building housing the bar remained intact but it was silent and empty as a long-abandoned home. The windows gaped like staring eyes as I flew to the front entrance and yanked at the knob. Locked. Stunned, I turned away from the door and spied a battered For Sale sign pasted on one of the windows, ghostly in the glow of the solo streetlight.

"Case!" I shouted, jogging across the gravel to the curb lining Main Street, frantic for any sign of life, a fixed point by which to orient myself. Wild with fear, my gaze darted up and down Main, which was devoid of cars but otherwise basically the same thoroughfare I'd driven over hundreds of times; there was the single stoplight, and Nelson's Hardware, and the law office...

I ran down the block toward the building where I had worked since last summer, breathing hard, pressing my hands to the cold windows in order to peer inside. Of course I could see nothing but darkness within the confines of the office. Seconds ticked past, along with my accelerating heart. I retreated two steps, scanning the words Al had painted on the window last August to celebrate my joining him in legal practice, gold letters in fancy script proclaiming *Howe and Spicer, Attorneys at Law*.

"What…"

I reached and traced a finger over the surnames, scripted in black, and which had not changed since I'd first seen them, long before I'd decided to make my stay in Jalesville a permanent one.

"Howe and James…" I whispered, releasing a sharp, disbelieving breath, spinning around to confront the deserted street. Frightened confusion blurred my vision. I placed both palms against my cold face, taking stock, seeking reality – seeking what I knew to be true. I was wearing heeled boots, fitted dress pants, and a coat, a long wool one I didn't recognize. When I'd exited The Spoke I'd been wearing jeans, my well-worn snow boots, and Case's blue plaid flannel over a white t-shirt. My hair was much longer than it had been only minutes ago when I'd been talking to Derrick in the parking lot, falling in thick curls over my shoulders like it had all through college. A quick examination of my left hand showed I was not wearing my wedding ring.

This can't be happening.

There is no way you, and everything else, could suddenly change like this.

No way in hell.

Wait, wait, wait, oh God, wait…

A high-pitched keening rose from my throat as I sought my lower belly with a sudden vengeance – no longer did it retain the feeling of a life beyond my own, the small but persistent swelling ache of pregnancy. I was hollow-hipped and empty.

Empty.

Oh, dear God, what is happening?

I sank to a crouch, bringing my folded hands to my lips. Shaking, profoundly terrified, I begged, *Please let this be a nightmare. Let me wake up. Let me wake up right now. Oh God, let me wake up right now.*

Nothing shifted, nothing altered. All but feral now, desperate for answers, I leaped to my feet and tore headlong back to The Spoke. Or, what had been The Spoke only minutes ago.

"Case!" I screamed his name repeatedly, running around to the back entrance where I'd found him once before, pounding my fists on the door, ready to break windows and force an entry. Case had been playing his fiddle on the stage when I'd seen him last and with the tunnel vision of the desperate, that's where I figured I had to find him now. The murky silence released no clues, revealed nothing. Tears dripped from my chin and clogged my throat. In the course of a fairly eventful life, I had never been more frightened. Something chimed in my memory, stilling my frantic movement. This time, I yelled a different name. "Camille! Are you here? Where are you?"

I was certain I'd heard my sister screaming for me just before...

Before *it* happened, whatever it was. Whatever Fallon had done and Derrick had tried to warn me about. I continued my frenzied trek around the building and almost tripped over her huddled form, falling to my knees and wrapping her in both arms. She lay on her right side in exactly the same position in which I'd awakened, limbs drawn inward, chin tucked down. My breath exploded in bursting huffs, intense relief that she was here, that I was not alone in this nightmare.

"Are you all right? Can you hear me?" It took effort to keep my voice at least a few notches below outright panic. I smoothed hair away from her ear. "Milla, can you hear me?"

She groaned and shuddered; the back of her head struck my chin as she jolted to sudden consciousness, catching me off guard. I muffled a cry, releasing her to clutch my jaw.

"Tish," she moaned, staggering to her knees. "Where are we? What's going on?"

"I don't know, Milla, I'm so scared. The last thing I knew I was out here in the parking lot talking to Derrick Yancy." The words emerged from my mouth like small corks bobbing on ocean breakers. "And then I heard you screaming. I heard Case shouting for me...*oh God*..."

We were out of range of the streetlight and her eyes appeared as nothing but two dark sockets, but I knew her features better than my own. I felt her potent fear, her inability to grapple with what was happening. She grabbed my arms and the trembling in her body flowed into mine.

"What happened inside The Spoke? Do you remember?" I persisted, clutching her coat in a two-handed grip, as though she might just melt away if I released hold.

"I…we…"

"Tell me, Milla, *please tell me*. We have to figure out what's happening."

"It was so strange, so fast…the entire room started to fade away, just *disappear*."

"Disappear where?" I stifled the urge to shake answers from her.

"I don't know." Small gasps punctuated her words. "I tried to…stand up…but I couldn't…"

"And then what?!"

"It was like everything just…went gray and static." She gulped but then steadied her voice, with effort. "They knew something was wrong at the last second, Tish, but it was too late. Case jumped from the stage, shouting for you…and Mathias…oh God, *Mathias*…" His name broke her and she covered her mouth, bending forward with the strength of her cries.

Case. Of course he had tried to reach me but I'd been outside. Camille sobbed, clinging to my ribcage, hiding her face against my coat; I held fast, rocking her side to side, my thoughts shrieking and flapping like a thousand panicked birds startled by approaching hunters. Agony would overtake and cripple us if we let it – and I knew we could not let it, not now. We had to figure this out, had to get to the bottom of it. I wanted my husband with an intense, all-consuming ache, but I gritted my teeth and mustered a measure of calm.

"Milla, listen to me." I waited for a second, until I sensed her paying attention. "There have to be some clues as to what happened. Everything around us seems different, like we're in some sort of alternate reality or something, but we can't panic right now. It's the worst fucking thing we could do. Come on, let's get up. Let's find out everything we can, okay?"

She nodded slowly, using her knuckles to scrape tears from her cheeks, looking exactly like her daughters. It had not dawned on me until just then that if everyone else we knew had disappeared, consumed in the roaring vortex of whatever the hell it was that changed the world as we knew it, her children had likely also been casualties.

Oh dear God, oh Jesus Christ, no…

"Come on, let's go around front where it's not so dark," I ordered, helping her to her feet.

Together we rounded the corner of what had been The Spoke, confronted immediately by the only other sign of human habitation, the small green Toyota with Minnesota plates.

"Whose car?" Camille whispered.

"I don't know. Let me look at you," I demanded instead, turning her toward the streetlight. "I want to see if you've changed. Look, my clothes are different." I indicated my body. Camille's outfit had indeed altered and I grasped her left hand to check for the familiar sight of her gold wedding band, an antique ring Mathias had given her, inscribed on the inner rim with the words *I am yours for all time*.

She noticed at the same second. "My ring is gone. It's gone. That means...*that means*..." She began to buckle and I grabbed her elbows, keeping her upright.

"Mine is gone, too," I confirmed. Steeling my nerves against the onslaught of anguish, I looked hard into my sister's stricken eyes. "And I'm not..." I bit back a moan. "I'm not pregnant anymore."

I saw it engulf her face, the absolute need to fall apart, and so I yelled. I hated myself for yelling at her but I could not let her crumble to bits. "*No!* Camille, no! Don't do this, please, don't do this. We have to stick together!"

"It's just like my nightmares...*oh God oh God*..."

"Camille!"

"LET GO OF ME!" Her eyes blazed with unchecked ferocity and I obeyed at once, helpless as she fell to all fours on the gravel, hyperventilating before giving way to a wailing, inhuman crescendo of distress. The hair on my nape stood straight and at last I covered my ears, doubling forward into a crouch and squeezing my eyes shut, as though to do so would block out the sound and sight of my sister beyond all control.

It seemed she would never stop.

I wrapped both arms around my head and pressed my forehead hard against my knees.

I could still hear her screams long after the sound finally ceased.

The town was truly empty this night. No one came running to

investigate, no vehicles scrolled past on Main. Even after falling quiet, Camille remained on all fours, head hanging. Feeling at last able to approach, I crawled to her side and sat on one ankle. I wasn't sure if I should touch her or not; instinct won out and I curled a careful hand around her right shoulder.

I had almost given up hope when she reached up and grasped my fingers.

We took stock to the best of our ability. A quick walk to the sign welcoming visitors to town assured us that this was still indeed Jalesville. The population, however, had fallen slightly. This Jalesville boasted no all-night gas station, no drugstore beaming with the cheerful fluorescent lights to usher us within a space where someone worked and might be able to provide additional information. No matter how unbelievable it seemed, we were walking and breathing and existing in an altered time-frame. The most probable theory was based on the only real clue we possessed, which was that Fallon Yancy had done something in the past to transform what we'd known as reality to the current reality.

But what? And how?

Back in the parking lot of The Spoke and exhaling with exertion from the walk to the road sign in the chilly night air, we stripped from our coats and searched every last pocket. Camille turned up a key ring strung with three keys, one of which worked on the Toyota beneath the street-light. Once inside the car we dug through everything, tearing apart the contents of the glove compartment, then a single suitcase and two purses we found in the backseat, assuming correctly that these items were ours. Our driver's licenses were current; mine identified me as Patricia Gordon and my address was listed as a Chicago residence, not one that I recognized. Camille too possessed our former surname, Gordon, and her address was the same as that of Shore Leave, back home in Landon.

Ripping through a black leather handbag large enough to fit a couple of volleyballs, I felt a hard, familiar shape and cried triumphantly, "A phone!"

I snatched it up and tapped out a pin code – the year I was born – rewarded when the screen blinked to life.

"Thank God I have no imagination," I muttered, scrolling through numbers as quickly as my fingers could move, ignoring the many I did not recognize. "Here's you, Milla, and Clint, and Dad, Mom and Aunt Jilly…here's Shore Leave…"

Camille found a phone tucked in the other purse but was having no luck breaching its security code. She peered over my shoulder; both of us already suspected but it still hurt like hell to confirm that my phone contained no contact information for Case, Mathias, any of the Rawleys, or…Ruthann.

"It's got to be a mistake," I said, hoarse and breathless, trying with little success to keep abject panic at bay. "Where are they?"

"Call Mom," Camille ordered at once. Her voice was raw and harsh, the way Case's had sounded after the fire in our barn, the fire that had burned his lungs.

"I'm scared to," I admitted. My heart seemed to be hacking shallow trenches between my rib bones.

"Who else is missing?"

I examined my contact list a second time, forcing a slower pace, with escalating dread. "Blythe isn't here, or Uncle Justin or Grandma, or Al and Helen Anne…" And then I froze. My heart skittered and missed several beats. "Oh God, here's Robbie. He's…still alive."

"Call him later, we have to talk to Mom," Camille insisted.

Mom didn't answer, nor did Aunt Jilly. It was after eleven, which meant it was after midnight in Minnesota, but I tried Clint anyway, hanging up before leaving a voicemail, just like I'd done with both my mother and aunt. I had no idea where to begin with what I had to say.

"I'll try again first thing in the morning," I whispered.

We scanned the mess we had created in the unfamiliar vehicle that was somehow ours, clothes and shoes and make-up falling all across the floor mats and spilling out into the gravel parking lot. I was so terrified I felt without actual substance, as though constructed of soap bubbles or vacant air. I was near breaking point and my need for Case rose swift and strong, obliterating all logic; I grabbed the key ring from the dashboard and said with authority, "Come on."

Chapter Twelve

Jalesville, MT - March, 2014

MINUTES LATER THE ROAD WEST OUT OF TOWN HUMMED beneath the tires as I drove with a single-minded purpose – that of reaching my home. I refused to conceive of the idea that it would not be there when we arrived. Camille kept silent and I saw nothing but her somber profile from the corner of my right eye as I roared along the narrow gravel strip called Ridge Road, where I had lived since last summer with Case and our animals. Where our old doublewide sat neatly at the base of a soaring, tree-lined ridge, where I fed my horses and chickens and cats and rabbit, where I'd been happier than ever before in life. It would all be there. The cramped, messy, heavenly space I shared with Case; our beautiful brand-new barn, the blueprints for our new cabin sprawled across the kitchen table.

It took no more than five minutes of driving before I spied the familiar silver mailbox that Case's mother, Melinda, had stenciled with their last name when she was still alive. Relief fell like warm rain over my shoulders. I ignored the sharp stabs of gut instinct warning me to hit the brake and turn the car around.

Camille spoke for the first time since I'd started the engine. "Tish, what if…"

But I couldn't listen.

My green and white trailer appeared exactly as I'd left it earlier today but was encased now in darkness, the kitchen light creating a bright square to counteract the night. I saw Case's maroon truck and additional relief all but punctured my lungs – but my Honda was not parked in its usual spot, instead replaced by a vehicle I didn't recognize. I cranked open the door almost before I'd thrown the car in park. Case was only steps away.

"Tish, *wait…*" Camille jumped out of the car in my wake but nothing was going to stop me now.

I jogged up the steps and threw open the screen, then tugged at the inner door, heart thrusting through my breastbone. It was locked. Dogs immediately began barking.

"Case!" I shouted, with increasing alarm. "Are you there? Case, it's me, I'm home!"

Two or more people had been talking inside. I heard my husband's deep, authoritative voice only a few feet from me as he demanded, "What in the hell? Who's there?"

I began crying in earnest, pounding on the scarred wooden surface. "Case!"

I fell inward, straight onto our kitchen floor, as he yanked open the door. Literally at his feet I stared up at the astonished expression on his face. I didn't hear Camille's breathless explanation as she appeared in the doorway on my heels, I didn't hear the startled exclamations of the woman seated at the table or Case ordering the dogs to get back. I heard only the panic coursing through my veins.

Case did not recognize me.

I hardly recognized him.

Leaner than I'd ever seen him, cheekbones knife-edged and prominent, thick scruff on his jaws and brows drawn inward with confusion. His eyes were bordered by deep shadows. He smelled boozy and I realized he was drunk. Or, was two-thirds of the way there. He wore a threadbare long-sleeved t-shirt and dirty jeans, his steel-toed work boots. His hair was cropped close to his head, severely short. He appeared wiry and menacing and stunned.

But none of this mattered. He was my Case, my Charles Shea Spicer, and *he did not recognize me.*

Reality began reasserting itself, pulling no punches.

The woman at the table knocked over her chair as she stormed to her feet and stood with fists planted on her hips, firing her words like missiles. "Who is this? What is this about? Case, I swear if you've been fucking this bitch I will kill you once and for all!"

I realized dumbly that I knew her; her name was Lynnette and she'd once been married to Case. He ignored her angry tirade and instead crouched beside me. His eyes were achingly familiar, his beautiful cinnamon-brown eyes with their red-gold lashes, and I lifted to an elbow, desperate to force recognition. He was confused as hell, I could plainly see, but somehow, some way, he *had* to know me. The awareness between us was too strong to deny. He was studying me intensely, the way a person would a painting that required deciphering to comprehend. His brows drew together, creating a deep furrow between them.

"Case," I begged in a whisper, unable to resist reaching for him. My hand fluttered through empty air and alighted on his right knee, closest to me. He was warm and hard, so very familiar, and I wanted to die in that moment, knowing that to Case, in this particular timeline, I was nothing but a stranger – and a crazy one, at that.

"I knew it!" Lynnette cried, but neither of us looked her way.

"*Please*," I begged, almost soundless, my throat obstructed by pain. I clung to his knee with one hand. "Please, it's me. It's Tish. *I'm your wife...*"

"What..."

"It's *me*. I love you so much, you just have to remember..."

Case stood abruptly and stalked outside, severing our tenuous connection. Camille darted to the side to avoid being trampled by his angry movements while I scrambled after him, dogging his footsteps to the corral, where Cider was nosing the top beam. Behind us, in the trailer, Lynnette was hollering like a tornado siren but I didn't care. She was lucky I hadn't attempted to kill *her* once and for all. Case increased his pace and I ran to catch up, stumbling in my heeled boots.

"Stop!" I pleaded, grabbing for his arm. We had reached the corral and Cider issued a friendly whooshing sound, stepping in our direction. Having reached the extent of his escape route Case turned to face me, running his hands over his shorn hair, elbows pointed at the sky, pinning me with a look that combined both incredulity and anger. The glow from the kitchen window highlighted his features and before I knew I'd moved I took his face between my palms, desperate to touch him, to feel his skin against mine. Surely I could override this horror. I knew I could make him remember me, remember *us*.

"What are you doing?" he demanded, low-voiced and astonished, catching my wrists in both hands. "Who are you? How do you know me?"

"It's me, it's Tish. Patricia Gordon. I know everything about you, sweetheart, I even know your *horse*. That's Cider, right there, and we've ridden double on her dozens of times, out there into the foothills." I indicated eastward with a tilt of my head, observing the way his eyes registered both undiluted shock and increasing fluster. I pratted on, believing I was gaining momentum. "I know this is crazy, it seems crazy to you because something is so wrong, Case. I don't know what's happened, but somehow everything has been changed. I don't know how this happened but I intend to find out. I promise you I will find out. Just earlier tonight we were at The Spoke with Garth and Becky, and Mathias and Camille, and then…and then…"

Despite everything he had not released my wrists. He'd gently removed my hands from his face but held them now between us, our arms bent in tight, acute triangles. His thumbs enclosed my bones, which felt so fragile in the strength of his long fingers. I caught the scent of whiskey on his breath and my heart constricted further; in our normal life he had long since given up drinking hard liquor. I truly did not believe I was imagining that he was currently a man radiating with lonely despair. I longed so deeply to wrap him in my full embrace that it hurt my limbs to remain immobile. His eyes drove into mine and I knew there was a part of him that wanted to believe me.

And so I continued babbling. "Then I talked to Derrick on the phone and he told me that Franklin Yancy is really Fallon Yancy, they're the *same person*, Case, that was the detail we were missing before. Derrick said that Fallon has done something terrible, sweetheart, to hurt us. To hurt Marshall and Ruthie, and everyone we love. You have to trust me."

Lynnette had closed the distance between us and overheard my last few words. "Are you fucking kidding me, Case, you're actually listening to this crazy bitch?" She grabbed my upper arm and yanked me around to face her; under normal circumstances such behavior would have activated a sort of Gran-style offense mode and my normal assertive self would have shrieked to existence, but I had been hollowed out by desperation. Lynnette wasn't quite tall enough to meet my gaze head on, but rage lent her height; I didn't fight her grip.

"Let go!" Case ordered her harshly, coming between us. But instead of sheltering me he hooked an arm around Lynnette's waist and hauled her a few paces away, next grasping her shoulders and speaking with a sincerity that lacerated my breaking heart. "Lynn, come on, please calm down. I do not know this woman, all right? Would you listen to me? I don't know what's going on here. I swear I'm just as surprised as you are."

"Well, she sure knows you!" Lynnette twisted free to confront me yet again. "How do you know my husband? Are you from around here?"

"No," I whispered, staring at Case, who stared right back. The tilt of his wide shoulders told me with no words that he was strung with indecision, but he remained silent. I didn't advance toward him this time as I implored, "Can we drive over to the Rawleys? They'll still be up. Maybe they'll remember, maybe they can help you remember." My tortured mind had missed a detail and I demanded, "Is Marshall home? When was the last time you saw him?"

Maybe I'd already known it was coming as Case asked, "Who's Marshall? Who are the Rawleys?"

Despite the intensifying doom, I could not stop badgering. "What do you mean? Clark and Faye helped raise you! Garth and Marshall are your best friends. They've been your neighbors all your life. Their ranch is only minutes from here."

Case gripped the nape of his neck with both hands, conveying increasing concern. He slowly shook his head, elbows pointed at the sky. "No, you're mistaken. There's never been a family by that name in Jalesville." Having brought Lynnette under partial control of her emotions, he addressed me now with quiet courtesy. "Ma'am, I apologize, I truly do, but I don't know these people. And…" He paused for an eternal second, his gaze holding mine. "And I don't know you."

Had I been summarily gutted with a dull fishing knife it would not have hurt worse.

I could not accept these statements as truth. Maybe it was selfishness, or pure desperation, but in that moment I exercised zero control; I didn't consider how what I was saying could hurt him, or Lynnette, as I cried, "Case, oh God, please listen to me! You *do* know me. Somewhere inside, you *have* to know me. I'm in love with you. Where I just came from, we were married. I was pregnant…*with our little girl.*" Sobs broke through and I covered my mouth with both hands.

"I knew it, Case! You son of a bitch!" Lynnette was at it in full force again.

"Shut the hell up!" I directed my monstrous agony at her, fair or not. "You have absolutely nothing to do with this!"

She rocketed toward me, fury twisting her face, hands fisted. "Case is *my* husband, you bitch. I will *not* shut up. Get the fuck off our property!"

Camille was at my side in an instant, curling me close, the protector now, just as I had been earlier this nightmarish evening. Weeping, devastated, I allowed her to lead me toward the car. Case did not attempt to stop us, though I sensed his shock as he watched us walk away. Both the driver's and passenger's side doors remained wide open and looked like broken wings. Camille was murmuring to me but I derived no sense from her words. I hid my face in my palms and she helped me within the car; she claimed the driver's seat this time. I could not manage the strength to lift my head long enough to look back as she drove away.

The Rawleys were nowhere to be found.

No house, no barns, no corrals or beautiful, stone-ringed fire pit. No horses, no tack room, no Clark or Marshall, Sean, Quinn, or sweet Wyatt. Each and every one gone. The land formerly occupied by their home, which had belonged to the Rawleys for many generations, was in the process of residential development. A work trailer was parked on the street, adorned by the name of an unfamiliar construction company. There was a small billboard proclaiming that this would be the future site of a condominium complex called Mountain Heights. Earth-moving equipment hunched in the darkness like sleeping beasts. The foundations already excavated loomed like gaping wounds.

This time I was the one shrieking my pain to the star-studded black sky, bending to tear clumps from the ground, the dirt cold and thick against my palms. Inane with grief I repeated the motion again and again, grabbing handfuls of earth and hurtling them like tiny, rage-filled bombs at the work trailer and the small billboard until the offending words were all but obscured by exploded muck. Camille sank to the ground, out of range, and did not attempt to stop me.

"Motherfucker!" I bellowed, addressing Fallon Yancy, wherever the hell he existed at this moment. "I will kill you a thousand times, *you fucking bastard*, you goddamn piece of shit! You think you're the puppet master out there, that you can fuck with us like this, but I will find you! *I will motherfucking find you!*"

I howled and screamed until no additional sound would emerge, my clothing smeared in dirt. I had slipped and fallen too many times to count; my ankles ached, along with my tailbone. Several of my fingernails had torn past the quick and bled with silent reproach. And still no pain rivaled that of Case not knowing me. Case married to Lynnette, Case drunk and miserable, trapped in a life he believed he deserved. A life in which we had never met – whether because the Rawleys were not here, or because Mathias and Camille had not traveled to Montana in 2006, or a hundred other possibilities I could not begin to conjure; I had no idea. Not a notion of where to start.

Death seemed a friendly option as I stood on shifting earth at the edge of a huge, square foundation hole, heaving with uneven breaths, staring at the faintly darker line against the western horizon indicating the peaks of the mountains in the distance. I did not hear Camille until she appeared at my side and wrapped her arms around my upper body.

"What should we do?" I whispered, ragged with exhaustion.

"I don't know, God help me, Tish. I don't know."

Chapter Thirteen

Landon, MN - March, 2014

We drove east toward the sunrise, aiming for the home of our teenaged years and our younger hearts, where we had confirmed before dawn our mother still resided. Unwilling to frighten her, I'd throttled my emotions to a level of manageability in order to make the call. Camille likewise had adopted a resolute, dogged mien; both of us focusing now on what we could do other than give up. Other than let Fallon win. I tried not to notice how my sister's hands shook, or the way her skin was pale enough to resemble bare bone. I knew the desolation in her eyes was mirrored in mine; I'd been avoiding my own reflection. By tacit agreement, we shied from any discussion of our virtual helplessness to restore our real lives.

"You're cutting your trip short?" Mom had asked almost immediately and I played along, attempting to learn as much as I could without asking direct questions and arousing her suspicion, mustering all my lawyerly skills.

Clearly our mother belonged to this alternate universe, unwittingly delivering one shocking blow after another as I slumped in the passenger seat while Camille broke the interstate speed limit. We had decided after leaving the Rawleys' property there was no point remaining in Jalesville where no one knew us. Though I realized he too would consider me a stranger, I planned to call Al for any information he might be able to provide but ultimately we had no place to stay and no real idea what to do; we would return to Montana if it proved to be the right choice after we collected our bearings.

When we crossed the border into North Dakota I watched over my shoulder as the state where Case lived receded into the distance. Then I buried my head in my arms and pressed my fingertips against my eye sockets hard enough to leave bruises; not hard enough to keep from weeping.

Based on my sunrise conversation with Mom, we learned that she and Dad had divorced only a few years back, shortly after my graduation from a Chicago high school. In our original timeline this event had taken place well over a decade ago, in the spring of 2003, and during the course of that fateful summer Mom had met and fallen in love with Blythe Tilson, eventually marrying him and remaining in Landon. In this alternate timeline Mom had never heard of someone named Blythe Tilson and we had returned to Chicago after only a short visit that summer, summarily nullifying every event and memory of our lives in Landon thereafter.

Most stupefying of all was that in this timeline, Ruthann had never been born.

The first clue came when Mom prefaced a comment with, "After your grandma and Aunt Ellen died – "

I restrained a hard, tight gasp.

"How long…has it been now?" I could hardly manage to ask, dreading the answer.

Mom sighed, a soft sound rife with sadness. "The car accident was twenty-four years ago, next month. I know, I can hardly believe they've been gone so long. I should have stayed in Landon after that. It's funny, I had a feeling even then that I should stay but I didn't want to take you and Camille away from your father. You two were so little."

"This was 1990?" I whispered, rapidly calculating. "You weren't around Dad that spring or summer?" Ruthann would have been born the next January, in 1991.

"No. You probably wouldn't remember, but we stayed in Landon until that fall."

I knew I shouldn't ask but I couldn't stop the question. "What about

Ruthann?"

"Who, sweetie? I don't think I heard you right."

I disconnected the call and whimpered, "Stop the car..."

Camille veered to the shoulder just in time for me to clamber from the passenger seat and puke up stomach acid in a colorless ditch clogged with the knee-high remnants of dead weeds.

"It's all right," Camille kept saying, as though this phrase had the power to alleviate anything. I knew she was hanging on by the thinnest of threads, same as me, and so I did not beg her to shut up.

"Mom must think we're crazy," I whispered later, after we were back on the road. I sat huddled around my own midsection, focusing on each subsequent breath. "I kept asking all these questions I should have known the answers to. Oh God, Milla, Grandma and Aunt Ellen died in a car accident in 1990. *Twenty-four years ago.*"

My lips were numb, as if I'd been recently injected with an anesthetic. I felt like a cartoon version of myself, picturing a bubble filled with strings of jumbled words each time I spoke. Absurd, insensible words that could not possibly reflect reality.

"Ruthie wasn't born," I croaked for the hundredth time, clutching my ribcage. I was afraid my innards might start spilling out if I released hold too soon. "She wasn't *born*. Does that mean she still exists where we came from? Is she still in the nineteenth century?"

"It means we have to figure this out as quickly as we can." Cartoon bubbles floated from Camille's mouth too; I wondered if she could see them. The day flashing past outside the car was windswept, flat gray in color. The foothills gave way to the plains of North Dakota, the land level as a tabletop in either direction, the ditches congested with endless cordons of dirty snow long since scraped from the roadway. Camille's knuckles stood out like pearls beneath her skin as she gripped the steering wheel. She glanced my way and her eyes were electric with intensity, the only real sign of life on her face. "For whatever reason, you and I remember our original timeline. The *right* timeline, not this sick fucking offshoot, or whatever the fuck it is. The only advantage we have just now is that we remember what's right."

I tried to nod, my head jerking through the movement like a clunky wooden puppet's. I tried not to think of what I'd screamed last night, about Fallon being the puppet master. I could not lose focus in such a way, not anymore. Camille was right; if we had any chance at all, it was because we remembered. Squeezing my torso with both arms, I whispered, "You're right. We have to stay calm. It's just so – *oh God…*"

"I know, Tish, I know. We have to keep picturing them how we remember or we'll go crazy. I've been repeating their names in my head all morning. Millie Joelle, Brantley Malcolm, Henry Mathias, Lorissa Anne, James Boyd…" Her throat bobbed violently, like she was attempting to swallow an unsliced apple. "They're still out there, I believe this. We have to save them. We can't think otherwise."

I sat slightly straighter, rallying my wits, ticking off what we knew on my fingers. "The Rawleys are gone. Case said there has never been a family by that name in Jalesville. Fallon's message to Derrick suggested that he'd had a new, better idea about how to hurt us. And Fallon said…" I struggled to recall those seconds in the parking lot. "He said he hoped we'd remember and that *she did*. He must have meant Ruthann. So whatever he did, he did to her in the nineteenth century, which suggests she *is* still there in…" Again I searched my memory for Derrick's words; he had helped us more than he may ever know and I hadn't even thanked him. "In 1882. If only we could communicate with her somehow. We have to know what she knows. It's critical." I cupped the lower half of my face, staring out the window, envisioning my little sister. I begged, "Ruthie, oh God, hear us reaching out to you. *Hear us.*"

"He wiped out their family," Camille mused softly. "Fallon, I mean, he wiped out the entire Rawley family. There's only one way a person could achieve such a thing…"

"Fallon would need to have known the exact ancestor whose line of descendants led to the family *we* know in the twenty-first century," I said, my thoughts at last flaring to something resembling life, able to problem-solve in the abstract. "Clark's ancestor whose name is on the land deed is Grantley Rawley. Their family was the first to live on that homestead. Remember, Clark only knew the two brothers, Grantley and then the one who died young. Miles was his name."

"Ruthie and Marshall might be there right now, with that family…"

"If we could warn them somehow…but *how?*"

Hours later, once we'd crossed the border into northern Minnesota, our conversation rolled back around to the fact that our mother and Blythe had never married. Overtaken by the odd surge of stimulation that accompanies extreme exhaustion, I drummed my fists on my thighs. "Mom didn't know who I meant, which probably means Blythe never came to Shore Leave for a summer job. And he was the main reason we stayed in Landon instead of going back to Chicago that summer. Well, that and you getting pregnant with Millie Jo."

It was close to noon. We had not eaten, slept, or exited at a rest stop since driving out of Jalesville in the darkness of predawn. Our list of facts had tentatively lengthened; I'd spoken earlier to Robbie, whose voice brought hot tears bursting to my eyes and throat. It was on the tip of my tongue to warn him of the danger to his life, to beg him to be careful; Robbie seemed completely unchanged in this lifetime, dishing out droll sarcasm exactly as I recalled from college.

"Gordon, please hurry back from your trip. This place blows without you around. I fucking hate spring break when I'm not springing or breaking someplace with topless chicks and rivers of booze. I hate being responsible and shit."

"What place?" I had whispered, holding the phone to my ear with both hands.

"What's with you? You sound weird. Are you and your sister fighting or something?"

"No, I'm just…I'm just tired."

"Did you find a hot cowboy to ride, like you were hoping? Maybe two or three?" He cracked what sounded like a piece of gum and I could exactly picture his smirking smile. His words, delivered as one friend relishing the chance to mess with another, pierced the pieces of my already-shredded heart in ways he could not begin to imagine.

"What place?" I repeated, ignoring his taunting.

"Tish, *come on.* Our place of business, Turnbull and Hinckley, or have you forgotten where you work?"

Radiation zizzed through my limbs and I sat arrow-straight, startling Camille. Before I thought I cried, "We work at Turnbull and Hinckley?"

"Did you by any chance partake in drug usage last night? Maybe excessive grain alcohol consumption? Shit, I'm jealous…"

I bit down on my stupidity and conjured an authoritative tone. "Rob, what do you know about the Yancys? Franklin and Derrick, specifically."

"The Brothers Grimm?" He chuckled at his own joke. "Their holdings are affiliated with several of Ron's subsidiaries, as you well know. Don't act like you don't remember how Derrick tried to snag your sweet ass for, like, our entire last year of law school. He had it *bad* for you, Gordon. Probably still does, I don't know. Haven't seen him in a month or so."

Never mind his shit, get more facts, I thought, sickened by Robbie's insinuations about Derrick.

"What about Franklin, when was the last time you saw him in the city?"

"What's with the urgency? You sound like you're interrogating a witness. Which, at our current rung on the corporate ladder, we won't be allowed to do for another decade-plus."

"*When?*"

"Maybe a month or two. Ask your dad, he sees him more often."

"Thanks, Rob. And listen." For only a second hesitation held my tongue. "*Please* listen to what I'm about to say. If you care about our friendship even a tiny bit, trust me right now, okay? You have to trust me." I stopped short of saying *because your life depends on it*. With as much authority as I could muster I ordered, "Quit. Seeing. Christina. Immediately, completely, and no excuses, all right?"

I disconnected before he could respond; ten seconds later I was on the phone with my father, Jackson Gordon.

"Hi, hon, how's your trip? I can't wait to hear." Dad sounded exactly like the man I remembered, as smoothly polished as a collector car.

"Dad, when was the last time you saw Franklin Yancy?" I demanded, dispensing with any form of small talk or pleasantry. "Have you seen him since last night?"

I sensed my father's puzzlement. "Franklin Yancy?" he parroted.

"When, Dad? It's more important than you could realize."

"Tish, what's going on? You sound panicked."

I drew a deliberate breath, thinking fast. "Sorry, it was a long night. I'm fine, just a little hungover. But I'd really like to know."

"Well then, I guess it's been a few weeks. He travels quite extensively, as you know. I believe he's due home for the benefit dinner next weekend. Lanny and I are planning on attending. You should join us, hon, my treat. You've been dying for a new gown and an excuse to wear it, as I recall. You and Lanny can hit the stores."

My soul seemed to fold even more tightly upon itself – I sounded so shallow and callous when confronted with these descriptions of my words and actions. Robbie and Dad were describing the person I'd been in danger of becoming before moving to Jalesville for an externship with Al, last summer; the materialistic, narrow-sighted woman who had never met Case Spicer and therefore learned what it meant to be loved absolutely, equally met and cherished in every way. With my free hand I gouged my fingernails into my thigh, digging through the layer of denim.

"Maybe I will, Dad," I whispered, near the end of my emotional rope. "Listen, right now I've got to go. Milla and I are headed to Landon."

"I'm so glad you two are taking some time for each other. Tell…" Dad paused. When his voice came back on the line it was rougher than it had been before, the polish having scraped away in spots. "Tell your mother hello from me."

"I will, Dad," I whispered and then hung up, tossing the phone to the floor mat and bending forward over my knees.

The road that curved around Flickertail Lake from downtown Landon and out to Shore Leave remained blessedly unchanged. I traded places with Camille for the last two hundred miles and we sat in expectant silence, alone inside both the stuffy interior of the car and the torture chambers of our own thoughts. Plans built to towering heights as I studied the monotony of the interstate beyond the windshield, only to disintegrate in the next second.

I ruffled without letup through the information we'd gleaned this morning, treating it like a mental stack of research documents. Ruthann did not exist in this timeline but we had reason to believe she continued to exist in 1882. Mom and Blythe had never met. Blythe might not exist. The Rawleys did not exist. Robbie was alive and we worked in Chicago, in the very heart of the enemy's stronghold. And I had a tentative idea where and when Franklin – *Fallon* – might next appear.

Unless things changed dramatically between now and next weekend, I planned to be there in Chicago to confront him.

You should have killed us, you arrogant bastard. Just you wait. Your cover is about to be blown to bits like nobody's fucking business. I will tornado through you like nothing you've ever known.

But rage could only sustain me so long; despair pierced the hot wall of anger with its inevitable blades, each sharper than the next.

Case doesn't know who you are.

He didn't recognize you.

He's married to someone else.

Oh God, I can't bear it…

"We're here," Camille murmured, refocusing my attention; lost in thought, I'd almost driven past the cafe. It was late afternoon, the lake already shrouded in the gloom of early twilight, the air static and silent, as if we'd entered a chapel. We stared at the white, L-shaped structure housing our family's business, the cozy space where so very many of our memories were centered, where so much of our lives had taken place; it was currently as dark and silent as a tomb, the lot empty but for a Landon Fire Department work truck and a small Honda.

I leaned forward, flooded anew with dread. "Where are all the beer signs? All the lights are off. Why aren't we open? It's not winter hours anymore." I peered more closely. "Everything looks so rundown."

"This is so fucking scary. What if we can't pretend?" Camille reached for my hand and I gripped it between both of mine. She was shaking so hard her teeth chattered.

"We can do this," I whispered, with false confidence. "There's no one but us, Milla, we *have* to do this. Come on."

We approached as cautiously as if about to stage a robbery, cataloguing the familiar – the white siding, the wide windows that had never been adorned by curtains, the wraparound porch which maximized the lake view and was always packed with crowds in the summer months; and the unfamiliar – no cafe lights blazing with welcome, no dogs running to greet us; no hope of reuniting with our little sister after all this time. The only sign of life was the outside light at the top of the steps leading to Aunt Jilly's apartment above the garage, glowing through the gloom in anticipation of our arrival.

"It's because Grandma and Aunt Ellen aren't here. They *died*, Milla, even before Gran did." I couldn't speak above a whisper, sick at the thought; when had I last hugged my grandma or great aunt? When had I told them how much I loved them and what their influence had meant in my life? Everything around us seemed dead, or in danger of dying; I clung to Camille's hand, squeezing hard as we hurried past the cafe, whose windows gaped like blank, staring eyes. The mucky sludge of late-winter snow clung to most surfaces while intermittent icicles along the rafters resembled a broken mouth missing teeth.

We both jumped when the door to Aunt Jilly's apartment opened.

"Girls! We didn't expect you until tomorrow. Come on up!" Our mother beckoned from the top of the stairs, the door propped against her hip, and I felt like a coward as I let Camille take the lead.

The three of us crowded the narrow entryway as Mom hugged us, one after the other. She wore jeans and a loose sweater, her soft golden hair falling to her collarbones, but she felt shockingly slim in my arms, as though she might snap in two with only minimal pressure. Was she ill? I scrutinized her face as if vital information could be divulged there; her cheekbones created severe angles on her face and her eyes held mine as she offered a smile. But it was a ghost's smile, a thin reproduction of the genuine one to which I was accustomed.

Aunt Jilly and Clint emerged from the kitchen, gathering around for greetings and hugs. The little apartment was no different, at least on the surface, except it appeared that Aunt Jilly still lived here; in our real lives, she hadn't resided in this space for years. We had interrupted an early dinner, hamburgers and fries from the smell. It seemed that Camille and I were about to enter a carnival funhouse, surreal and vaguely threatening, the unknown lurking around every corner; and in one corner a predator crouched, waiting, waiting. Biding his time for the opportune moment to leap forth and strike.

"You look tired, sweeties, you must have partied too hard," Aunt Jilly said, her voice momentarily muffled by my coat as she squeezed me close.

Despite her petite build, Aunt Jilly had always exuded abundant energy and vivacity. She drew away and my gaze was too intense, I could tell, because her eyebrows drew inward, creating a worried crease above her nose. She wore wool socks, jeans, and a thick sweater, her basic winter uniform, but I was not imagining the subtle difference – as if the invisible aura surrounding her had been dimmed or muddied. Rather than sparking with vitality, she appeared subdued. Her golden hair was cut short and spiky, the way she'd kept it ever since her first husband, Christopher Henriksen, had been killed in a snowmobiling accident.

A shiver cut at my spine – what if Chris was alive in this timeline? What if he hadn't died that winter night when Clint was a baby? Though we hadn't confirmed it, mounting evidence suggested that in this life Aunt Jilly was not married to Justin Miller. And that meant no Rae, Riley, or Zoe, their three children. Further, Blythe's absence meant no Matthew and Nathaniel, my younger half-brothers. Clint wrapped me in a bear hug and I clung to my tall, strong cousin, who smelled like cooking oil and this morning's dose of cologne. He squeezed me like an accordion, warding off the worst of my trembling; knuckling my scalp, he said, "Glad I caught you guys. I'm on shift this evening."

I looked up at him, a thousand questions on my tongue.

"At the fire station?" Camille sidestepped me to ask. Her eyes were wide and frightened and I knew she was dying to ask if Mathias was working tonight – he was also a part-time volunteer firefighter. Camille and I both knew she would respond no less intensely to Mathias than I had to Case, were their paths to cross, and we had no real idea in what condition Mathias might exist in this life. If he existed at all; neither of us had been successful at guessing the pin code on the second phone, therefore unable to scroll through Camille's current list of contacts.

I tucked hair behind my ears, shedding my coat, struggling to maintain a casual air as I guided Clint toward the kitchen before he could answer Camille. Keeping my voice low, I asked him, "Does Mathias Carter still work with you, Clinty?"

"Huh?" Clint grabbed a tote bag from the corner, totally oblivious.

"You know, Bull's son…" I gambled on the chance that Clint would indeed know Bull.

"Oh, yeah, right. I don't think he's worked at the fire station since he was a teenager, like way before my time. I haven't seen him since last summer when his family was up here visiting."

Camille, on our heels, had overhead.

Shit, shit, shit. Fuck.

"His family?" she parroted, unmistakable panic riding high in her voice now.

Do something, I thought. But other than knocking her out to avoid hearing Clint's response, no useful ideas sprang to mind.

Camille grabbed Clint's left elbow in a two-handed death grip, preventing his forward motion as she demanded, "His family?"

Clint seemed vaguely startled at her intensity but he answered gamely enough, with a brief shrug. "Yeah, his wife and kids. He lives somewhere in the Twin Cities. Has since college."

Camille turned away and disappeared down the hall leading to the bathroom without another word.

Clint watched her go with surprise rolling from him in waves. "What's with her?"

"You girls want something to eat?" Mom asked, entering the kitchen and gesturing at the table, where three plates of half-eaten food shared the surface with a bowl of salad and bottles of condiments. "I'm sure you're starved. I can fry up a few more burgers."

"No, we already ate." I leaned backward against the counter, radiating anxiety with all the subtly of a radio tower; from what I could gather,

Mom and Aunt Jilly lived here together. "You two go ahead and finish up." I crossed my arms, applying pressure to my leaping innards. Another minute of this and Mom and Aunt Jilly would know something was off. Way, way the hell off.

"I gotta run," Clint said, hefting the tote over his wide shoulder as he headed for the door. "See you guys later!"

Aunt Jilly reclaimed her chair and her drink. "What will it take to get you to stay here permanently, too, Tish?"

I acted as though I knew what she meant, nodding encouragingly.

Mom picked up the conversational ball. "I'm so glad Camille got hired at the high school. I put in a word for her the second I heard there was a position. They've needed a history teacher since Delores Meeker had a stroke last month." She smiled at Aunt Jilly. "Mrs. Meeker was old when *we* had her for history, so it's no wonder..."

Camille taught history? I glanced toward the hall in search of her, but no sign; I'd heard the bathroom door close, but nothing else. I remembered suddenly that she and Mathias had once lived together in this apartment, along with Millie Jo, before their wedding.

"Why isn't the cafe open?" I blurted. "We're not on winter hours anymore, are we?"

Mom and Aunt Jilly both looked my way, with identical expressions of surprise.

"Are we?" I persisted.

"Hon, we haven't kept winter hours in years." Mom searched my eyes and I tried not to cringe at her haggard appearance. Her skin was cast in typical late-winter pallor but it was much more than that – there was no light in her eyes. Extreme thinness had taken a toll on her beautiful face, exaggerating its planes and angles. She murmured, "You must be tired."

I couldn't shut up. "But where does everyone go for coffee all winter? The coffee at Eddie's is a joke. What about Dodge?" I couldn't imagine a winter morning without Dodge Miller, Justin's dad and the closest thing to a true grandfather I'd ever known, stopping out for coffee on the way to his job at the filling station.

I knew immediately I'd said the wrong thing.

Aunt Jilly spoke first, setting aside her glass. "Tish, what's going on? What are you talking about?"

Concern etching her forehead, Mom adopted a tone I hadn't heard since childhood. "Tish, sweetie, Dodge hasn't lived in Landon in years. He left town over twenty years ago."

My stomach acid seemed to be forming clots as they exchanged the sort of sisterly glance I knew down to my bones, the sort that encompasses an entire conversation, a deep, instantaneous communication.

"But what about Justin? Where does he work? What about their service station?" Tears built, stinging my eyes. I wanted to scream, *What about Ruthann? You don't even know Ruthann!*

Footsteps sounded in the hallway and even before she appeared I sensed Camille's intent.

"Tish." Her quiet voice was an unswerving command and I could do nothing but nod. Hushed expectancy swelled between Mom and Aunt Jilly as they waited for Camille to continue speaking. Her eyes burned in her drawn face as she said, "We can't keep this secret."

Chapter Fourteen

Landon, MN - March, 2014

A horrible few days had drifted past, casting us upon the desolate bank of Wednesday, the nineteenth of March.

I sat at booth five in the cafe, chin in hand, staring at the cheerless sight of a parking lot bordered by dirty snow; the streetlight had just blinked out as dawn smeared ashen light across the gray eastern slope of sky. Today was supposed to have been the first time we faced off with Derrick Yancy in court in regards to the land dispute he'd put into play last November. Those events seemed to have occurred more than a century ago, ridiculous, trifling concerns in light of the odds we now faced. I had not eaten since noon yesterday, and retained no real desire to sustain myself; at night I lay huddled near Camille in the bedroom we'd shared with Ruthann in our younger years, the two of us crammed side by side in a twin bed. Feeling each other's warmth was the only way we had survived the past three nights.

Mom and Aunt Jilly – and Clint, later that first night, once he was home and able to hear the story – did not know what to think of Sunday night's unabridged disclosure of information. The shock we'd dumped over their heads like so many tons of scalding water had yet to settle. Aunt Jilly was the most receptive and I thanked all the powers that be for her open-mindedness; at least that detail had not been altered.

"Tell us everything," she insisted.

And we had.

When we spoke of how she was happily wed to Justin Miller in the life we remembered, Aunt Jilly issued a strangled cry, the sound of a sliced throat. She pressed the side of one fist to her pale lips and began sobbing.

"Oh my God." Mom went to her side and bracketed her shoulders. "Jillian, it's like your dreams."

"What do you mean?" I demanded, kneeling before my aunt, resting my touch on her kneecaps. For long moments she could do nothing but weep; when she lifted her face from behind her palms, her blue eyes blazed with awareness. I tightened my hold on her knees.

She whispered. "I thought…I thought I was crazy. Not long after Chris died, I started having dreams about Justin. And later, about our family. It was so real. So very real."

"Where is Justin now? Is he in Landon?"

Aunt Jilly nodded, tears seeping down her cheeks.

Mom answered for her. "Dodge sold the filling station before he left Landon. Justin lives in town but works as a mechanic over in Bemidji. He's still married to Aubrey. They've been married since high school."

"In this other life, Justin and I have children, don't we?" Aunt Jilly whispered.

"Yes, you have two girls and a boy, plus Clint." I studied her stunned, expressive eyes. "This only confirms what we know, that our real lives are *not this one*. Not this timeline. This is some horrible offshoot that we have to reverse. Your intuition has obviously been trying to tell you that, through your dreams."

Other revelations proved just as torturous.

Grandma and Aunt Ellen's car accident.

Ruthann's absence.

The nonexistence of Blythe, Matthew, and Nathaniel; in this life, Blythe's step-grandfather, Rich Mayes, a longtime employee at Shore Leave, had no grandchildren, nor had Rich worked at the cafe since before Grandma and Aunt Ellen died.

Even Shore Leave itself was altered, a deserted shell of the warm, bustling heart of the little town we remembered.

Mom and Aunt Jilly refused to stop asking questions, begging for every detail.

And Camille and I had questions of our own. We learned that the Carter family, headed by Bull and Diana, continued to own and operate White Oaks Lodge, as they had for the past century-plus. Their children still numbered four, three daughters and a son; the daughters remained in Landon while Mathias resided in a suburb of Minneapolis. In this life, he had never returned home after college, instead remaining in the city to work a corporate job. Mom and Aunt Jilly didn't know his wife's name but the fact remained that Mathias was not only married, he was a father.

"Of course he is." Camille bore the expression of someone being eviscerated; I could hardly bear to look at her. "He's wanted babies of his own since he was a little boy."

Even held in my tightest grasp later that night, she could not stop shaking. I feared her bones would break.

While unable to sleep at night, Camille and I were all but unconscious for most of the daylight hours of Monday and Tuesday. Steeped in pain, we had yet to form any sort of attack plan and temporarily relented to exhaustion. Working together, Mom and Aunt Jilly hauled boxes and trunks from the attic and from Gran's closet – dear Gran had passed away around the same time as we remembered, late in the summer of 2003. They proceeded to unearth family photographs, legal documents, letters; anything to provide some scrap of a clue about the past. None of us had any idea what we expected to find but the act of searching provided a welcome sensation of accomplishing *something*, alleviating a fraction of the vulnerability.

Just before midnight last night, Camille had slipped from our twin bed and crept downstairs, wraithlike in a pale nightshirt with her hair hanging loose. When she failed to return I followed, finding her sitting on her heels alongside a small trunk. I realized her intent just before she found the photograph she sought – the old, black and white image of Malcolm Carter and his horse, Aces. The photo, taken in 1876, and which she'd truly discovered many years ago, while pregnant with Millie Jo, had set off a series of events leading her to Mathias. Poised on the staircase above I kept a respectful distance, not wanting to disturb her, watching as she brought the photograph to her face in the dimness of the living room, bending over it like a flower stalk caught in a harsh wind.

At last I could bear her sadness no longer and joined her on the living room carpet, crouching beside her in front of the sagging couch that hadn't been moved since the mid-1950s.

"I have to be stronger than this, I know." Camille's face was wet, swollen from weeping. She had removed the picture from its frame and held it cupped against her breasts, a talisman to ward off fear. "Or I'm no good to anybody."

"*Hey*. Fuck being strong," I whispered, hoping to coax a smile. "You don't have to be strong in front of me, not ever."

A weak specter of humor flitted across her lips. "Thanks, Tish."

I nodded toward the photograph. Thinking aloud, I mused, "If only you could slip back in time, like Ruthie, and warn him."

"Warn Malcolm?"

The idea gained in both appeal and prospect. "According to Derrick, Ruthann is in 1882. And based on Una Spicer's letters, we know Malcolm was in contact with the Spicers and the Rawleys during that time. If you could show up there and warn him…" I paused, considering. "I would if I could, but I've never felt the pull of time the same way Ruthie does. I'm not capable of moving through it."

"But what makes you think *I* am? I've never felt it, either, Tish, and I've held Malcolm's picture, I've read and touched letters and telegrams he wrote, I used to wear the ring I believe belonged to Cora. For the love of God, I *was* Cora in that life. I've held *her skull* in my hands and nothing ever pulled me backward."

I refused to be swayed by negativity, at least for the moment. "Go with me here. Suppose we could find a way to communicate with them. If you and I aren't capable of traveling through time, could we somehow send a message?"

Frustration overtook Camille's delicate features. "But *what* would we warn them about? We don't know what happened back then to cause this. We have no clue what Fallon did to one of the Rawleys, or possibly to one of Blythe's ancestors."

We had searched online for any and all Tilsons residing in Oklahoma without finding a hint of Blythe; broadening the search to include the rest of the country proved just as useless.

"But we know that Fallon did *something*," I argued, determination welling. "What if we could get a message to Malcolm or Ruthie or Marshall to be careful, to be observant? Derrick said that Fallon knows who Ruthie is so chances are she knows who *he* is, too. It would provide them with information and *any* information at this point could prove helpful."

Camille closed her eyes, bringing Malcolm's picture near her nose and inhaling, as if imbibing the essence of the man she believed had been Mathias in an earlier life. "What if it's our destiny to be separated from each other? If what I believe is true, Malcolm spent the rest of his life searching for Cora. And she was already long gone. They lost each other then and I've lost Mathias now. Maybe that's just our fate and I'm a fool to fight it. Oh Jesus, *Tish*..."

"No. *Stop it*. I don't believe that. If that's our fate, why would we remember what used to be?" I battled the memory of Fallon's recorded message to Derrick – *fate is with me, brother, as you'll soon see.*

Not if I can help it, you arrogant fucker, I thought to counteract the panic. I suddenly remembered something else. "When we were driving home from Montana on Sunday, Dad told me Franklin was expected at a benefit dinner this weekend. I can't just sit here in Landon doing nothing, I'll go nuts. What if I head to Chicago and find out what I can about the Yancys? I work for Ron in this timeline, it's so fucked up, but it gives me another way in, a way to get information."

Camille studied me closely; she knew me too well. "You can't confront this Franklin by yourself, it's way too dangerous. What if he actually shows up there? What would you possibly do?"

"Tell everyone what I know about him, for one thing. Whether he's there or not, it's a perfect opportunity to reveal all the Yancys' dirty secrets."

"What makes you think anyone would believe what you said about him? And you were the one who said Franklin was armed, Tish, you told me that yourself! What's to prevent him from killing you on the spot? I won't let you do this."

"I'll be there with Dad and Lanny, and probably Robbie, not to mention about a hundred other guests. It's a *benefit dinner*, for Christ's sake, a total dog-and-pony show, like Dad would say. No one is actually there because they give a shit about whatever the proceeds are going toward, they're attending to see and be seen. What better occasion to let loose with big news like that?" My thoughts stormed, arcing like lightning to another point. "Besides, Derrick said Franklin is obsessed with causing pain. It would be a kindness in his eyes to kill me now, when he's robbed me of the life I was supposed to live. And I want to get a read on Derrick. He doesn't remember the real timeline but I'd bet damn good money he has the exact same chip on his shoulder in this one. I bet I can crack him."

Camille chewed her lower lip, considering the likelihood of my theories proving true; I was heartened to see her coming around to my idea. "What should I do here, in the meantime?"

"Research. Keep looking for any information we could use. I won't stay in Chicago any longer than the weekend," I promised.

"Maybe we really can figure out a way to send a message. I'll talk to Aunt Jilly tomorrow. Maybe it's possible. I have to believe it's possible. You're right, dying would be a kindness right now, wouldn't it?" She drew a shuddering breath. "My body is so different, Tish, it's totally untouched. In this life I've never been pregnant. I've never nursed my babies. I'd rather die than live the rest of my life without Mathias and our children. They are my everything."

"I love you," I gulped, choked by sudden emotion; I hated this talk of dying. "I couldn't have made it through the past few days without you."

Camille threw her arms around me and we rocked sideways as we hugged. Her soft hair bracketed my right cheek, overwhelming me with her floral scent. Against my temple she whispered, "I couldn't have made it through *any* of this without you, little sister."

After speaking briefly over the phone with Dad, I called for a plane ticket and scheduled a flight for late the next morning, March twentieth. Camille would drive me to the airport in Minneapolis.

"Don't look for him here," I insisted as I settled my purse strap over my shoulder at the gate, leaning back into the car to address her. Stupid, inconsequential things flitted across my mind, like a wardrobe and accessories I did not remember purchasing, as if to allay the tension in my head. She didn't at once respond and I infused my tone with severity, fixing her with my best lawyer look. "Promise me, Milla. Don't do that to yourself. He won't be the man you remember."

At last she nodded, hands hanging lax from the steering wheel, eyes steady on mine. "Have a safe trip and call when you get there. Say hi to Dad." Her gaze sharpened, becoming all at once exacting. "Be safe, Tish, I mean it. Don't take any chances. Please. I can't lose you, too."

"I'll be careful." And then, more softly, "Don't do it."

"I won't," she whispered. "I promise."

I didn't believe her for an instant.

Chapter Fifteen

I WATCHED UNTIL TISH DISAPPEARED INTO THE SWIRLING crowd of fellow travelers, then lowered my forehead to my knuckles, momentarily overwhelmed. I battled the urge to fish from my jeans pocket the notes I'd scribbled on the back of an order pad at Shore Leave, those of Mathias's current work and home addresses. It had been easy – a quick search through an online phone directory revealed Mathias and Suzanne Carter, of Minnetonka, a suburb no more than twenty-five minutes west of the airport. My best guess was that this Suzanne was the person I remembered as 'Suzy,' someone he'd dated in college, a girl Bull had often referred to as a high-maintenance poodle; Mathias had later laughed over the description, agreeing that it was apt, if impolite.

Memories clustered, demanding attention, so thick I could have used both hands to bat them away. I recalled the first winter I met Mathias James Carter, when he was fresh home from Minneapolis, having reached the conclusion that he was not cut out for long-term life in the city; he missed his family and the north woods. In the alternate timeline in which I now existed, Landon had never been my permanent home until the last few weeks. Apparently I'd earned an education degree and had been recently hired to replace an elderly, ailing teacher. Noah Utley, Millie's father, had no obvious connections to me in this life. Because we hadn't stuck around Landon back in the summer of 2003, I'd never dated Noah, which meant no Millie Jo. And no Millie Jo meant I'd never lived with Grandma and Aunt Ellen, and had never worked at White Oaks

Lodge and met the Carters.

An irritated driver laid on his horn in the car behind mine, startling me to attention.

There was little choice but to drive forward. I stared once more in the direction Tish had vanished, willing her to stay safe, gripping the steering wheel so tightly its pattern was imprinted on my palms. I hated to let her go but Tish would not be moved from her decision to search for information in Chicago. She was rabid with the desire to confront Franklin Yancy and I understood this conviction, I truly did, but right now the thought of such a confrontation proved too excruciating; I couldn't bear to consider what could go wrong and so I aimed my thoughts toward something I could accomplish in the next few days – collecting information about the past.

And I intended to seek out Bull and Diana Carter for help.

I loved my in-laws dearly. I'd been acquainted with them long before I met Mathias and it was my interest in history, my deep desire to find answers about Malcolm Carter's photograph, which led me to White Oaks in the first place. *Fate*, I'd believed ever since. At least, until now. Was fate a fixed entity? Or something malleable, a river flowing without stopping, the way Quinn Rawley had described time? It had to be the latter, something pliable enough that a single action retained the power to alter countless future events. What had Franklin done? How had he known where to strike? And what sort of unhinged mind took such a chance? Had he even considered the ways his own future could be rendered different?

Mathias, my heart wept. I swallowed a sob, exhausted from too many bouts of brutal weeping. Furthermore, it seemed unproductive. I was a mother, despite my missing children, and a mother did whatever was required to make things right for her offspring. I had never taken them for granted – had I? Fear and sleeplessness punctured holes in my conviction. The life Mathias and I had created together was a gift, a blessing beyond comprehension. I would have argued until out of breath that I had never taken it for granted; the sweet, dear, unhurried life in our cabin a few hundred yards beyond White Oaks Lodge. The beautiful homesteader's cabin in which Malcolm Carter once lived and my husband and his father had since refurbished, creating a home for our family of seven.

No matter how many times I've watched our babies nurse, I still love it more than about anything, Mathias whispered in my memory, shifting closer to trace a gentle fingertip over James's plump cheek.

I shuddered, pain clogging the dark hollow behind my breastbone, but refusing to allow that particular evening to play out in my mind was beyond my ability.

Thias, I heard myself murmur, lazy contentment ripe in my voice; no one other than me called him that particular nickname. Thunder grumbled in the distance, a muted sound only slightly louder than the steady rain at our bedroom window. Insulated in our cozy bed, I slipped one leg between both of his and he smoothed his warm, broad palm along my thigh, bare beneath the old maternity t-shirt I wore. On that rainy November twilight our newest son was only two weeks old.

This is what I longed for all my life, Mathias murmured, stroking hair from my forehead. His voice was husky with sweetness and love. *My woman, our babies. Honey, I love you so much that my heart almost hurts.* He grinned before whispering, *I need a kiss.*

Come here, I murmured in response, reaching to cup my hand around the back of his head. He leaned over our nursing son, with great care, and our mouths met with a soft suckling sound. I opened my lips and he swirled his tongue in voluptuous circles, tasting me from the inside out.

Lingering close, he whispered, *This is my dream, honey. This is it, right here, right now. Thank you for that.*

Mine too, love. You made it come true.

Just below our faces, the baby detached from my nipple with a soft popping sound and Mathias smiled, leaning to kiss his downy forehead.

He smells so good, he whispered. *You think I'd be used to it by now, their sweet baby smell. But it gets me every time.*

We lay in our room tinted by the ashy light of a stormy evening, kissing softly, snuggling James between us, while rain continued to streak the windowpane. When a wall-rattling burst of thunder exploded above our cabin we both startled, then laughed as James's blue eyes sprang wide; immediately he let loose with the chuffing, breathy cries so common to newborns. Seconds later we heard the sudden thumping of little feet down the hallway.

Mathias grinned. *Brace yourself, honey. Incoming!*

Brantley was the first to bolt into our room, hooking his elbows on the mattress and diving for his father's chest, where he was cuddled instantly close. Henry was on his brother's heels, leaping from the end of the bed. I cautioned, *Careful, sweetheart*, as Henry crawled toward me, intent on claiming the spot that James had, out of necessity, overtaken.

C'mere, little one, Mama's nursing the baby, Mathias said, and I heard the amusement in his voice as he caught Henry around the torso and hauled him close, one twin curled in each arm. He resettled the boys against his powerful chest. *Now we just have to wait for the girls.*

Millie Jo isn't scared, Brantley said, hiding his face against Mathias as the next round of thunder detonated.

Don't be too sure, I murmured as she appeared in the room a moment later, holding Lorie by the hand. Lorie began fussing, reaching for me with both plump toddler arms; she had been the youngest for the past three years and was struggling to relinquish the role to her newest brother. Millie lifted Lorie to the bed and climbed up after her, elbowing Henry. He whined while Lorie wiggled as close to me as she was able, wishing to reclaim the spot which had recently been all hers.

I cupped my youngest daughter's head, ruffling her soft curls and staving off her tears, then placed a protective forearm around James, who had latched hold and energetically resumed nursing. Thunder crashed and lightning sizzled blue-white at the windows; the kids all shrieked, simultaneously fighting to get under the covers. Mathias was laughing.

As he did so often, he began to sing one of his favorite songs, feeling this occasion required the John Denver tune about a crowded feather bed. I giggled as he took up the chorus with characteristic gusto. The kids joined in, with merry exuberance, forgetting their fear of the thunderstorm. They knew all the words; Mathias and I had sung to them from birth. There seemed to be about twice as many pointy elbows and knobby knees than actually accounted for. Parenting was all about elbows and knees in your bed. I smiled at my husband, whose lips were pursed as he sang, getting into the song, as always.

Later, after the kids trundled back to their own beds, baby James asleep in his crib no more than arm's length away, I snuggled happily against Mathias's chest, curling my fingers through the thick hair there, burying my nose and inhaling. He kissed my temple, rubbing my shoulder blades, whispering sleepily, *Good-night, honey.*

I latched a thigh over his hip, with utter contentment. *I love you, Thias.*

I know, he whispered. *And it's what makes every day worth living.*

I drove due north, keeping my gaze fixed on the interstate. I did not take the exit ramp which angled west toward Minnetonka, drawing upon every ounce of willpower in my possession. I tried to keep my mind empty but it was a monumentally worthless effort. Memories of our family assaulted like waves against jagged rocks, close enough to touch, to inhale like a drug. I could not conceive of a world in which those years of memories were negated, where my husband and babies had ceased to exist. Of a world in which Mathias was married to someone else, a woman named Suzanne with whom he shared a different family.

To counteract the horror I passed the miles back to Landon reliving the births of all five of my children.

I collected my strength, building small emotional shields in preparation for answering more of Mom's questions about Ruthann and Blythe.

I cried until my eyes burned, until I could not catch my breath.

I listened to the radio even though I was revolted by what seemed like an otherwise normal day out there in the world. Weather reports, two-minute news bits, mundane announcements of local events. I despised all of it just now, hated it to the very center of my being.

I rolled back through Landon just after five that afternoon. A weak setting sun the sickly shade of a jaundiced eye peered from a slit in an otherwise impenetrable layer of clouds. Fisherman's Street was wet from a recent rain, the air thick with humidity. Nothing had changed on Fisherman's, at least, offering a small measure of peace to my aching soul – there was Eddie's Bar, with its cluster of usual vehicles parked at the curb, and the graceful balconies and sweeping porches of Angler's Inn, the old-fashioned streetlamps which were adorned with decorations dictated by the season, and…Uncle Justin on the opposite side of the street, stepping from his work truck, headed for the bar.

Without considering why, I hit the brakes. He'd disappeared inside Eddie's by the time I parked and locked the car, then jogged across the street, purse bumping my hip. I heard the jukebox before I even opened the door. Stepping inside the familiar space I was greeted by the swiveling of every head on every man occupying the stools along the bar counter. Even the guys playing pool were momentarily distracted by the unexpected appearance of a woman. I knew all of them, most well, and yet I was essentially a stranger to them in this life. I reminded myself to keep this in mind when speaking.

"Well if it isn't the new schoolteacher!" Eddie enthused, coming around the bar to offer a hug. "Everyone, this is Jackie and Joelle's girl, Camille Gordon."

Heartfelt greetings were offered all around. I smiled as sincerely as I could manage, unable to keep my eyes from Uncle Justin. From the back he appeared just as I recalled – tall, broad-shouldered, muscular, his black hair longish and messy, as if he'd run grease-covered fingers through it during the work day. When he turned from the bar to say hello, however, I exhaled in a rush. I'd never seen his face without the intense scarring to which we had all grown accustomed. In this life his skin was unmarred but for some heavy five o'clock shadow; his right eye was a perfect match of the left, not drawn downward at the outer corner.

And yet – he looked so *wrong*. He was Uncle Justin without Aunt Jilly and the toll was apparent in the depths of his charcoal-dark irises, if only to me. I thought of how Aunt Jilly had long sensed their connection and wondered if somehow Justin had also been given a glimpse of what the universe had truly intended for him, the happiness and contentment of life with his true love.

Images from all the years I had known this man in his capacity as my aunt's devoted husband and the kind, demonstrative father of my cousins pelted me with new agonies. How many conversations Mathias and I had shared with him and Jilly; how many lazy summer days spent on the lake, lounging on the pontoon or taking turns waterskiing behind Uncle Justin's newest fixer-upper speedboat. Family meals and annual holidays, watching each other's children for date nights, playing cards and taking camping trips; how empty and pointless life must seem to Justin now, in the absence of the family he was supposed to have.

Even if he could not exactly articulate the realization – and who could blame him – a part of him had to sense the loss of Aunt Jilly and their children; his eyes suggested this, in mute volumes. I recalled that his ex-wife, Aubrey, was shallow and petty, a woman who'd cheated on him before taking her leave from Landon many years ago.

But not, it seemed, this time around.

I claimed the stool alongside Justin's, which he acknowledged with a small nod.

"Whatever you'd like, on the house." Eddie stood behind the bar, winking as he gestured toward the array of drink options.

I shrugged from my coat, standing briefly to settle it beneath me on the stool. "Thank you. I'll have –" I stopped short of adding 'the usual.' Of course Eddie had no idea that the usual was a pitcher of tap beer split with Mathias. I didn't think I could bear the taste of something that reminded me of Mathias and so I said, "I'll have a red wine, thanks."

"Here you go, doll," Eddie said, after first digging around behind the bar, locating and then subsequently dusting off a wine glass. He filled it to an inch below the brim, with a flourish.

In the time it took for Eddie to pour my wine, Justin had already polished off two whiskeys. I wondered just what I hoped to accomplish by engaging him in conversation; part of me was simply avoiding returning to Shore Leave, where I'd be confronted with questions to which I had no answer. Mom remained in a state resembling shellshock, unable to process what Tish and I had revealed on Sunday night. Maybe it had been a mistake to tell them everything, but we never kept secrets. Tish and I could never have continued to submerge the level of stress we'd experienced since last weekend. Who were we kidding?

I drained half the wine without thinking.

"You're a teacher?" Justin asked, leaning on his elbows, glancing my way before returning his attention to his booze. Seated to his right I nodded, trying my best not to stare in amazement at his unmarked face. The conversations I'd interrupted resumed all along the bar counter; Jim Olson was applying chalk to his cue while Skid Erickson leaned on his beside the pool table, joking as he waited to take his next shot. Skid was one of Mathias's best friends; we'd spent so many evenings with Skid and his girlfriend in the past decade and right now Skid would not have known my name if not for Eddie's introduction.

I finished my drink in one more swallow.

"How's your dad these days? I haven't seen Jackie in ages," Justin continued, attempting to make polite small talk when I could tell he really just wanted to get drunk. He nodded discreetly at Eddie, who ambled over to pour him another two fingers' worth.

"Good, he's good." My voice was rough from the wine. "How's Dodge?"

"My dad? You remember him?" Justin registered surprise. "He's the same as always. Lives down in the southern part of the state these days. I s'pose you remember him from your summer visits, huh? He always speaks fondly of Joelle's kids."

The ways in which simple words could unknowingly slash and burn; Justin had no idea.

"Do you still stop out to Shore Leave for coffee in the summer?" I asked, picturing this version of Justin interacting with Aunt Jilly.

"My wife prefers I drink my coffee at home." Justin's voice took on a subtle but distinct edge; I watched his shoulders hunch inward, as though defensively, as he glared toward the polished wooden surface of the bar. He swirled the contents of his glass with a deft movement, then drained the amber liquid.

"But not your liquor!" Eddie said with good-natured gaiety. "But hey, if you want to spend your hard-earned money in here, Miller, all the better for me." Without asking, Eddie caught up the wine bottle and refilled my glass. I gulped gratefully.

"Do you and Aubrey have kids?" I asked Justin, louder than I'd intended. *Shit.* I was buzzed from the sudden splash of strong wine on an empty stomach.

His black eyebrows cocked, creating surprised arches. He shook his head in silence while I scrambled for an excuse.

"I wondered because...I'm a teacher," I explained, hearing the way I slurred the word 'teacher.' Good thing I wasn't actually employed as one; what a terrible impression to make, loaded after a glass and a half of free alcohol.

"You have a ride home, there, teacher?" Justin asked, with a faint glimmer of good humor. "You got someone to call?"

"I'm not...done yet." So saying, I emptied the second glass. As terrible as it was to admit, the fuzzy tint brought on by the booze dulled a fraction of my pain. I realized I wanted to continue drinking until I washed away on a murky current of oblivion, where I was no longer plagued by memories that served to slice open my heart.

Millie Joelle, Brantley Malcolm, Henry Mathias, Lorissa Anne, James Boyd...

Oh God, they're gone. My home is gone.

"You sure, kid?" Justin was concerned now, all amusement having vanished; he'd adopted the protective tone I'd heard many a time when he was addressing his children. He set aside his glass and studied me a little more closely. "Is something wrong?"

I couldn't respond to such a stupid question. Every fucking thing was wrong.

I gritted my teeth.

"Another, please," I requested of Eddie, holding out my glass.

"I don't think that's a good idea," Justin said and I resented his presumptuous tone.

"*Another,*" I insisted.

Justin shook his head at Eddie and despair collided with the alcohol in my blood, obliterating my control; I turned on him like a wolverine. I surged to my feet, sending my barstool flying, and hurled my wine glass in the direction of the pool table, dimly aware of everyone diving toward the floor as if I'd chucked a live grenade. It missed the gleaming, stained-glass beer light overhanging the table by mere inches and shattered on the far wall with a gratifying miniature explosion.

"Holy shit!" someone cried over the general uproar.

"Everything is wrong!" I screamed at Justin, fists clenched as though I meant to strike him. "Why don't you see it?! Nothing here is right! Why don't you know what's right?! *What the fuck is wrong with all of you?!*"

Justin moved fast; before I could inflict more damage he shifted behind me, wrapping my torso in a backward hug, effectively pinning my arms.

"Hey, hey, *hey*." He spoke directly in my ear, using a voice reserved for the insane. "Calm down, kid. It's all right."

I struggled against his hold, to no avail. Not only was he much taller than me, he was as strong as a bear. Sobbing, shaking, I couldn't even cover my face with my hands. I was the newest attraction at the carnival freak show; stun and shock were plastered across the features of every man in sight. Some of them were still on their hands and knees near the pool table.

There goes your teaching job, I thought.

I was vaguely conscious of Justin collecting my coat and purse, and then herding me outside and into the cab of his truck. I sagged against the passenger window, my forehead resting on the cold smoothness, numb now, beyond rage or embarrassment. I owed every person in Eddie's an apology, I realized, most especially Justin. But at the moment I couldn't conjure up the wherewithal to give a shit.

"We'll get you home," he said, hooking left on Fisherman's and following Flicker Trail around the lake, toward Shore Leave. "It's all right, kid. You must have had a long day."

I turned his way and my mouth betrayed me yet again, words spilling in a pleading, helpless waterfall of pain. "Listen to me, Uncle Justin. Please listen. You know you're supposed to be with her. With your *family*. I know somewhere in your memory your real life is still there. You remember your kids, don't you? You can't have forgotten them. They *need you.*"

Justin braked hard somewhere in the midst of my diatribe, halting his truck smack in the middle of the road. It didn't matter; there were no other vehicles headed out to Shore Leave.

"What in God's name are you talking about?" he wondered aloud. He didn't sound angry, only astonished. He sat with both hands gripping the wheel, attention fixed unswervingly on me.

"I'm talking about Jillian!" I cried. Tears gushed, falling faster than I could swipe them away. "You and my aunt. All this time, you should have been with her, not Aubrey. Aubrey left you a long time ago. You're supposed to be married to Jillian. You're Clint's dad, and Rae, Riley, and Zoe's. This isn't right, none of this life is right!"

Camille, stop this. Stop it. You're helping nothing and no one.

I'd rendered Justin speechless.

"I'm sorry," I mumbled, sniffling, knuckling my sore, wet eyes.

He didn't budge an inch, continuing to stare at me while I fixed my stubborn gaze on the dashboard. At last he whispered, "Me and...Jilly?"

Heartened by the husky emotion in his voice, I met his eyes and nodded. "In the place I came from, you've been married for many years. You guys live in a cabin in the woods past Shore Leave."

For a second I thought he believed me. I sensed that he *wanted* to believe me. But all at once he grew belligerent, brusque and clipped, connection severed. "I don't know what you're playing at, kid, but I don't appreciate it. Not one goddamn bit." He drove onward, tires spinning over icy slush, and made short work of the last half-mile to the cafe. Once in the parking lot, he pulled up to the porch without another word.

"Thanks for the ride," I mumbled, struggling to manage the door handle.

He slammed the gear shift into neutral and shouldered open the driver's side door; through the front windows I saw Mom and Aunt Jilly seated at one of the booths in the otherwise empty cafe. Their conversation ceased as they stared out at Justin rounding the hood of his truck to help me from it. Despite his obvious impatience his hands were gentle as he led me up the steps. Jilly met us at the porch door, scraping it open over a thin layer of fresh ice. Justin fell still at the sight of her – I couldn't see his expression, since he was behind me, but I saw hers. Her eyes were an electric, glowing blue, bluer than anything I'd ever seen as she searched Justin's face for answers.

"Jillian." He sounded haunted.

"What's happened?" Mom appeared behind Aunt Jilly, reaching to lead me inside. "Camille, what's going on?"

"I'm drunk," I mumbled, avoiding Mom's embrace and sinking to the nearest chair, slumping against the table.

"She had a few too many at Eddie's, so I brought her home," Justin explained. He spoke around a husk in his throat. "Something's really wrong, I'm not sure what." He hesitated, the full intensity of his dark eyes fixed on Jilly, and the pause grew thick and weighty; I waited for him to mention more specific details. But in the end he only said, "She threw a glass at the pool table and kind of...freaked out."

"Thanks for bringing her home," Mom said, putting her hands on my shoulders.

I lowered my head.

"Do you want to come in for a minute?" Jilly's voice was unusually faint, soft with hesitance; she was about two seconds from cracking, tugging him inside and confessing everything she knew.

A hush overtook the dining room, a mushroom cloud of confusion and need. But then Justin said quietly, "No thanks, Jillian. I just..." He cleared his throat. "It's...better if I just go."

The door closed behind him and we listened to his footfalls on the steps.

"I told him," I muttered.

Chapter Sixteen

Chicago, IL - March, 2014

DAD AND LANNY LIVED IN A CONDO ON THE LOOP, AN IM-
peccably-styled set of rooms furnished with designer pieces and graced
by a stunning view of the city's business district. And apparently I lived
with them, a detail I'd been somewhat surprised to discover. I supposed
it figured; rent was high and I was in my first tentative year of employ-
ment in an expensive city. Never mind that I had no memory of this year
– or any others in this particular life.

I'd learned from Mom that her divorce from Dad had followed a similar progression of events; Mom had avoided dealing with Dad's cheating
for many years, until walking in on Dad and Lanny in the act a month
before my high school graduation had forced her hand. How bizarre that
fate seemed to reassert itself even in this sick, offshoot timeline – certain
events twisting back around to what was meant to be, despite an altering
of the past. Radiating with urgency, I had no time to contemplate such
things; my focus had narrowed to a thin corridor of purpose.

Confronting Fallon Yancy – assuming he would indeed appear at the
benefit dinner scheduled for this Saturday – was first on my list, but I
had an additional goal in mind for this evening.

"Can you meet for a drink?" I asked Robbie once I was safely ensconced in my own room, holding the phone between my jaw and shoulder as I changed into unwrinkled pants. I would not think about the
last time I'd been a guest at my father's – less than two months ago,
with Case at my side, for Robbie's funeral. I fought the urge to sweep

all of my alleged belongings to the floor and stomp them to bits; they were trappings of a life I wanted nothing to do with. I'd already spoken with Mom, assuring her I had arrived at Dad's without mishap; when I requested to talk to Camille, Mom said, "She's resting, honey, she had a bad day."

Fuck, I thought.

"Did she try to find Mathias?" I asked quietly, sinking to the edge of my unmade queen-sized bed.

"No, she confronted Justin. She got drunk and threw her glass at Eddie's pool table."

"Oh, boy," I muttered.

"Hurry back here, Tish, I can't bear to have you out of my sight right now," Mom said then, just barely containing the tremor in her voice. "I'm at my wit's end."

"You and me, both," I whispered. Digging the heel of one hand against my left eye, I promised, "I'll be home by Sunday."

Robbie agreed to meet me at the small bar we'd frequented in college, a trendy dive located one floor below sidewalk level and where the atmosphere on a later-winter Thursday night proved every bit as raucous as I recalled. It was within walking distance of the condo so I bundled into a scarf and boots and scurried seven blocks through bustling crowds and heavy, honking traffic, keeping my chin lowered against the brisk wind. My every heartbeat sobbed for Case and our unborn baby, for our trailer in the Montana foothills and the life I needed more than air or water – the one which would never again be mine unless I could change things back.

You're strong enough, I repeated, until the words became a litany to counteract blatant desolation. *You are strong enough to face this.*

"Gordon!" Robbie waved from the bar and I experienced a blast of déjà vu, a rush of unreality so potent I had to brace a hand against a chair to remain upright. I saw the way his expression changed, registering surprise – even more so as I engulfed him in a hug upon reaching him, squeezing with real force and holding on well past the point of normalcy. He couldn't understand; how could he possibly realize?

"What the hell?" He drew away at last to study my face. He was flawlessly tanned, smooth-skinned and spit-shined, same as always. Clad in posh clothing and smelling of some expensive cologne as if he hadn't a care in the world. Feigning overt concern as he examined my face, he concluded, "Gordon, your vacation did zero good. Zippo, *zilcho*. You look like something the cat ate and regurgitated. No offense, baby doll."

"None taken," I muttered wryly. If only he knew how little I cared about my current appearance.

"Sit, talk," he ordered, then leaned immediately closer, positioning his mouth near my left ear. "Tell me the truth, as my friend. How did you know?"

I knew he was referring to Christina and leaned back to search his eyes, wondering how much to trust him with; further, I realized I had to tell him what I knew about his death before I left this place.

Tonight, I decided, and faltered only a little. It was not a conversation one could well prepare for, let alone initiate.

"Tish, come on. My nuts are on the line here. And I'm pretty damn attached to them."

"It doesn't matter how I know. She's bad news, Rob, trust me. *Horrible* news." I shifted on the bar stool, responding to an uncomfortable twinge in my gut. I lowered my voice. "Besides, my dad is screwing her, too."

"Shit, how do you know about that?" Robbie appeared dumbfounded, his spine straightening as if electrocuted.

"I know way more than I wish I did, believe me."

"Such as?"

"Tell me about work," I requested rather than elaborating. "What do you know about Ron or Christina's connection with the Yancys?"

"Can I at least have a drink to accompany this interrogation?"

We ordered our old favorite, gin and tonic; two limes for Robbie. He bypassed the skinny cocktail straw and drained half his glass but I set mine aside without a sip. I could not stop thinking of the way Case had looked at me when we were standing alongside the corral three nights ago. Of how he'd held my wrists and wanted to believe what I was telling him. I bit the insides of my cheeks hard enough to leave wounds, willing myself not to cry. I imagined Camille out of control with grief, throwing a glass at Eddie's pool table, and the urge to weep intensified.

Tish, focus.

I gathered my wits and cut to the chase. "I need any and all available information on Franklin Yancy. I have reason to believe he's dangerous, potentially criminally insane."

"Wait a second. What are you *talking* about?" I was relieved to hear that the level of skepticism in Robbie's tone was middling rather than explicit. He was attempting to remain open-minded out of respect for me.

"Just go with me here. I need information. If possible, I have to find him."

"You 'have' to find a criminally insane man whose family could purchase its own major airline or tropical island?" Robbie searched my eyes with more sincerity than I'd once thought him capable. "What is this about? Why the sudden interest in the Yancys at all? You've always done your best to avoid them, especially Derrick."

It didn't matter that Derrick wouldn't remember anything about our original timeline – or so I hoped. I clung to the knowledge that Derrick had become my recent, unexpected ally; he was also the last person I'd spoken with before everything in my world changed. I calculated the odds of his willingness to join us this evening and actually consider as factual what I would tell him. I recalled his opinion about Franklin/Fallon losing touch with reality and what I'd learned regarding Derrick's motives. Loyalty to his family only went so far; he recognized the threat Fallon presented and had been ready to take action despite the potential danger to himself. In short, Derrick Yancy was a better man than I had once believed. My perception of him had undergone a complete turn-around. But would the Derrick of *this* timeline be of the same opinion about his ancestor?

You have to chance it.

Robbie continued to wait for an explanation, tapping his empty glass atop the bar, ice clinking in conveyance of his growing impatience.

"Here, finish mine," I muttered, stalling.

"You haven't even *started* it." He accepted my glass and drained its contents. But it took a lot more than two gins to get Robbie drunk. His eyes were troubled, tanned forehead creased with concern; of course he couldn't understand my unwillingness to sip booze when I'd been so recently pregnant. Though the baby was no longer a part of my physical being she was safely rooted within my heart and I refused to damage even the essence of her.

Robbie ordered a third round, allowing me a moment to regroup, before insisting quietly, "You can trust me with this. Whatever it is, I swear. It's something huge, isn't it?"

The image of the glossy, expensive coffin his parents had selected for him loomed in my memory and pain blazed along my nerves. The chapel in which his funeral service had been held was only a few blocks from where we currently sat. I winced, gritting my teeth, and surprised him yet again by gripping his wrist, my fingers curled like claws.

"You might not believe me."

"I will, I swear. Jesus, Tish."

I drew a fortifying breath. "The thing is I think you may have already guessed the truth in the place I just came from." The word 'dead' fused to my tongue. "Robbie, do you trust me?"

He nodded, the expression in his baby blue irises a clear combination of bewilderment and anticipation – that of anyone waiting breathlessly for the revelation of a substantial secret.

I held fast to his wrist. No more delaying. "In the life I just came from, you were…dead. I think Franklin Yancy killed you."

Blank shock for several silent seconds.

Then he squinted as though attempting to focus, as if this would lend clarity to what I'd just said. He whispered, "Killed me?"

"I know this seems insane, Robbie, but you said you trusted me. Trust me with this. I've never been more serious."

Robbie's squint only grew more pronounced. "Tish, hang the fuck on. Assuming you're correct, why would Franklin Yancy have *me* killed? I doubt he even knows I exist. I don't have any dealings with him and I never have. He's only about a hundred rungs higher than me on the social ladder."

"I don't have all the answers," I admitted, retaining my hold on his wrist, the better to impress my sincerity upon him. "My best guess is that you discovered the truth about him. Somehow. Your last text to me suggested that you'd unearthed something big regarding Franklin. You were investigating at the time, you were my eyes and ears at the firm." I winced, overcome by regret that I'd ever asked of him such a dangerous thing. "And evidence further suggests that Franklin and Christina are connected, probably intimately. I think you confided in her and that nasty bitch told *him*. Franklin's ability is the Yancys' biggest secret."

"Hold up. What do you mean, his 'ability?' I'm so fucking confused."

"I'll explain."

Thirty minutes later, safely ensconced in a more private booth near the entrance, I'd related to Robbie everything I knew. Despite his initial shock I knew he believed me, agreeing that we should enlist Derrick's immediate help. And so Robbie had messaged Derrick via various social media avenues, requesting his presence at the bar. I restrained any fledgling sense of hope; it was too easy to assume Derrick would either refuse or simply blow us off, but he responded within a few minutes.

"We'd do well to keep our expectations low," Robbie warned, setting aside his phone. "He only agreed to join us out of macabre curiosity. And of course because you're here. He wanted you *bad*. Still does, I'm sure." He tried for a hint of teasing to counteract his stun at the information I'd divulged, eyeing me with a wicked set to his brows. "Fastest way to extract answers from him is to promise the debauchery of his choice in return."

"I'd rather jump from the nearest ledge."

Robbie leaned forward over his forearms, nothing but earnest now. "Whatever it takes, whatever you need, I'm with you. I hope you know that." A grimace crinkled his features as he added, "And not just because I want to avoid being dead."

"I know, I really do. Thank you." Moisture filmed my eyes and I grabbed for a cocktail napkin.

"Dry up those tears, he's here." Robbie sat facing the entrance and therefore commanded a clear view of anyone entering or exiting.

I turned in time to see Derrick removing a scarf as he scanned the crowd. His movements stilled as he caught sight of us but he rapidly regained his composure, chin just slightly elevated as he strode our way. He looked exactly how I remembered from my early days in Jalesville, arrogant and wholly unapproachable, but I was armed with a hundred times the knowledge I'd possessed then. I sat straighter, with a deep inhalation, mentally gathering up every scrap of information at my disposal.

"Gordon, Benson," he pronounced upon reaching our booth. Formal, remote. He didn't articulate the follow-up question but I heard it all the same, hovering near our noses – *what gives?*

"Do you have a few minutes?" I asked, squelching outright discomfort as I gestured at our table, doing my best to keep at bay any thoughts of potential repercussion. Fallon's abilities were the Yancys' most carefully guarded secrets, I knew well.

Robbie scooted over, silently offering him a seat. Derrick remained standing, his intense focus shifting between us, searching for the con, the punchline, the trap.

The sense of time running out beat again at my control; fearful that he would turn on his heel and exit the bar, I grabbed for his sleeve and went right for the jugular. "It's about Fallon."

Derrick could not contain his shock, showing immediate signs of withdrawal.

"Don't go," I begged, half-rising from the booth, not releasing my hold. "Please, sit. Give me five minutes."

As though in a dream, Derrick complied. He didn't remove his coat or sleek leather gloves, just sank to the booth. His gaze was dark and penetrating; he seemed momentarily incapable of speech.

Satisfied he wasn't going to flee, I reclaimed my seat and pinned him with my undivided attention. "I know this seems crazy and I apologize. But I need your help."

Derrick did not shift position. His irises could have been shards chipped from a wedge of granite.

I leaned forward, forcing myself to meet his exacting stare. "You called me last Sunday night. I wasn't here in Chicago, though, I was in Montana. And you told me you were worried about Franklin. You told me you thought he was losing touch with reality, that he was danger-ous." I paused to inhale an anxiety-riddled breath; my heart was clipping along at the pace of my speech. "Furthermore, you told me the truth, which is that he's a time traveler whose real name is Fallon Yancy. Your great-great-grandfather or uncle, I think, I'm honestly not sure which. You called to tell me that he'd just done something terrible, you weren't sure exactly what, and then…" Fork tines seemed to stab the interior of my throat.

Derrick studied me with no hint of expression; no telltale or errant emotion betrayed.

I rushed on. "You and I have a strange relationship, I'm the first to admit, with all sorts of unresolved shit from another time period. It's my belief that we were once married. I know how insane this all sounds, but it's true, Derrick. You have to help me. I have to find your brother. He's the only one who knows what happened because *he* did it. He did something to alter the timeline as we all knew it and only my sister and I can remember what's right."

Derrick blinked in slow motion and the effect was unduly eerie, re-minding me of an old-fashioned celluloid doll with leaded weights in its otherwise hollow skull. I waited, ill and overheated with nerves, second-guessing my intentions. Seated to Derrick's left, Robbie was shooting me warning looks but I ignored him for the time being.

"Derrick," I pleaded.

He reached across the two feet of plastic table separating us and clenched my right forearm; I couldn't restrain a gasp at the sudden movement but didn't dare fight his hold.

"Who else have you told?" The question fell somewhere between threat and entreaty. To think this was anything less than life or death would be a grievous error.

"No one but you and Robbie." Sweat glided down my spine; I was lying through my teeth and prayed he couldn't tell.

Derrick increased the pressure on my arm; his gaze was unfaltering as he spoke with hushed intensity. "You will never mention these things to another living soul. *Never.* You will forget the name 'Fallon' and immediately cease inquiring after someone who doesn't exist. Do you hear me? *Someone who does not exist.*"

I gulped back the instant urge to counter, recognizing both his sincerity and my mistake in trying to pry such hazardous information from him.

Robbie sat in wide-eyed silence.

The long, slender bones in my forearm ached beneath Derrick's grip.

"Never," he repeated.

I nodded acquiescence and he released his hold.

Less than ten seconds later Robbie and I were again alone in the booth, watching as Derrick retreated through the busy crowd without a backward glance.

Chapter Seventeen

Landon, MN - March, 2014

My daughter's name was on my lips as I woke.

Millie Jo...

I'd been dreaming of her just seconds earlier, my oldest as a little girl. Of all my children, Millie was the one I most associated with this space, the bedroom she and I had once shared. As a young mother in 2004 I'd nursed my baby to sleep in this very bed, watching the stars rotate across the dormer windows. Her absence was so profound I might have been missing a limb, or my very heart. My eyelids parted to the white ceiling above my old twin bed, cloaked now in dimness, and I swore the sweet scent of her lingered, hovering nearby. Close – but completely out of reach.

A low, aching moan clogged my throat. I grabbed a pillow and muffled my weeping, picturing her round baby face, her abundant brown curls which I'd often arranged in two pigtails. Her bright hazel eyes and the lisp it had taken her years to shed. I saw her scampering from our bed to hurry down to the kitchen where she knew Grandma and Aunt Ellen would be making pancakes or biscuits. Where coffee would be brewing in preparation for a day spent at the cafe, where the local crowd would appear for breakfast or lunch or evening beers; where the world as I knew it was secure and unchanged and blessedly dull.

I saw Brantley and Henry, my dear, naughty twins, whose resemblance to their father was more evident every day. Our boys, whose conception had occurred on a night in the Montana foothills, beneath a sky blazing with stars, the summer that Mathias and I first met Case and the Rawleys. During that trip to Montana we had, at long last, discovered the remains of a woman named Cora, a woman with whom I believed I shared a soul. Whose skull returned with us to Minnesota for a proper burial, within sight of the homestead cabin which, in life, she meant to inhabit with Malcolm Carter.

I saw my sweet Lorie and my little James, our two youngest. Lorie, named for the woman mentioned in a letter written by Malcolm Carter in 1876, whose exact relationship to Malcolm we'd never discovered. Lorie with her sweet disposition, who followed me as if magnetized, constantly begging to help with the baby. I saw her lower lip tucked between her teeth as she concentrated, attempting to fasten a diaper on her new brother, giggling over his legs that never stopped kicking. I saw her patting her doll's back to "burp" her the same way I burped James. I saw my baby boy's wide blue eyes and hair that stood on end. I saw all five of my children and their faces lent me the strength to sit up, to endure this day. I refused to believe they were lost from me.

And the first step was to contact the couple I'd known as my in-laws for the past eight years.

I spoke to Diana Carter later that morning. She answered their landline on the second ring and I pictured their spacious, farm-style kitchen, a room in which the perennial scents of spice and cloves lingered. Barring illness or the occasional other obligation, we ate dinner there every Sunday, along with Mathias's sisters, and their husbands and children; it was a Carter family tradition. I heard the sink running in the background, along with the radio and the sound of Tina, the oldest sister, asking who was calling.

"It's Joelle's daughter, Camille," Diana explained to Tina before coming back on the line. "Sure, hon, come on over. You're welcome to look through anything in that attic." She giggled, adopting a conspiratorial tone. "Don't tell my husband I said this, but if you were to, you know, *take* anything with you, I would have no complaints. In fact, bring along a box for that very purpose!"

Attempting to converse with Diana as though I didn't know her well required concentration, not to mention acting skills.

"Thank you. I really appreciate this." I wondered if my outburst at Eddie's had already spread its way through the local grapevine, praying it had not; Diana might reconsider allowing a potentially crazy person into her home, no matter how well she knew my mother.

"No problem!" she said. "That old junk has taken up space in my attic for too long. I'll put on some coffee."

I descended the stairs to find Mom and Aunt Jilly sleeping on the couch, one on each end, their legs tangled together atop the middle cushion. They'd still been up when I went to bed last night and I paused on the landing, observing from above; my mother and my auntie, two of the women from whom I'd learned how to love, to find joy in small details, to appreciate life. I sank to the faded carpet, perching on a stair riser, unwilling to disturb them just yet. Mom's straight hair fell like a silk scarf along her right shoulder, rich golden-blond, gorgeous hair I'd always wished I inherited. So thin I could see her collarbones poking through her shirt; her thinness frightened me on an elemental level, suggesting illness, or despair.

How could we have known the significance of what happened that summer, how much Blythe's presence affected the rest of our lives?

I'd never fully comprehended the power of one event to trigger a series of them, to tip the future in one direction or another. At some level, of course, I'd realized, but I'd taken for granted that my life followed a particular path; the path I was meant to walk, I'd so innocently believed.

Did I deserve my life as a married mother of five?

Mathias and I were so happy.

But maybe that's all the time we were meant to have together.

I bent forward, wrapping into my own arms, but no amount of pressure could combat the ache of considering such a possibility.

Maybe this is what I deserve. Separated from Mathias, just like Malcolm was separated from Cora. Maybe this is our fate and I never wanted to accept the truth.

Tish had insisted otherwise. I glanced toward the small leather trunk in which Malcolm's photograph had been stored for many decades, the photograph now propped against the lamp on my nightstand where it belonged. The photo and the letter existed exactly as I remembered them, as did the other items Mom and Aunt Jilly had turned up in the trunks from our attic; another of which was an old tin print contained in a fragile oval frame. The man peering outward from the brown-toned image was young and smooth-cheeked, so handsome he was almost beautiful. He was the first Davis in Minnesota, we believed, and wore a pale military uniform we guessed was from the Civil War era.

There were no other artifacts from the nineteenth century, no hint that Ruthann or Marshall might have been here in Minnesota at that time. The bulk of the documents, photos, and letters were from later decades, after Myrtle Jean Davis built and founded Shore Leave in the 1930s. Myrtle Jean had been my grandmother's maternal grandmother. Despite several marriages, Myrtle Jean never changed her surname from Davis and raised my great-grandmother, Louisa, and another daughter, Minnie, all on her own. Louisa, in turn, grew up to raise two daughters, Ellen and Joan; Joan was Mom and Aunt Jilly's mother, and my grandma. We'd unearthed a marriage certificate for Grandma and her first and only husband, Mick Douglas – the grandfather I'd never known.

But nothing new. No clues or hints as to why some things remained just as I recalled and others had changed so drastically.

It's like unraveling a tapestry someone started weaving at the dawn of time, Aunt Jilly had said last night. *A fucking single skein could change the pattern of the whole thing. How do you trace the altered thread to its source?*

None of us had a good answer.

No sounds came from the kitchen, no scent of perking coffee, but I was glad for the silence; no need to make conversation. Rather than disturb Mom and Jilly I crept back upstairs, forgoing a shower in favor of brushing my teeth and slinging my long hair in a ponytail. I dressed in faded jeans and an old green sweater, still undone by the sight of my high, firm breasts and unlined stomach in the bathroom mirror. It was a stranger's body, youthful and slender. How I had mourned the loss of my taut teenaged figure in the days after Millie Jo was born; I'd been only seventeen, after all, immature and overtired, unaccustomed to the unceasing demands of motherhood.

And what I wouldn't give now for the return of breasts and belly marked by the rigors of pregnancy and nursing, a soft, stretch-marked body which had contained and grown and cherished five new lives.

Clamping down on those thoughts, I hurried across the slushy parking lot, devoid of any cars but our own, and climbed into the green Toyota. I drove slowly around Flickertail to the Carters' house, a gorgeous modern cabin a quarter-mile down the lake road from their family business, White Oaks Lodge. The little homesteader's cabin in which Mathias and I had lived for the past eight years was tucked in the woods beyond White Oaks; I couldn't bear to think of it today, rundown and lonely, devoid of our busy family.

I knocked on the wide front doors of Mathias's childhood home.

Diana answered immediately, a pretty, petite woman with shining auburn hair, offering a polite but impersonal smile; I was all but a stranger to her in this life, not the wife of her beloved only son. It felt unnatural not to hug her. I entered to the scent of baking bread and coffee and something sweet, like melting chocolate; Diana took my coat, making genial small talk, asking about Mom and Aunt Jilly and Clint, offering commentary on the weather and my new job at the high school. Tina appeared behind her mother and I recognized unveiled curiosity in the blue depths of her eyes. I loved each of my sisters-in-law but Tina had long been my favorite, a no-nonsense woman with an outrageous sense of humor.

Be very careful, I reminded myself.

"We're baking this morning, excuse the mess," Diana explained, gesturing at the kitchen. And then she jabbed me hard in the gut, simply by saying, "My youngest is coming home today, should be here in an hour or so, in fact. He took some time off to help us strip out the floors in the ballroom. He's a good boy, always tries to come when we need him."

Breathe. Just keep breathing.

"I don't think I've ever met him." It cost me, but I spoke with a remarkably even tone. The ballroom was where our wedding reception had been held.

"He's lived in the Cities since college." Diana made disapproving clucking sounds. Then she brightened, gesturing at the corner hutch containing family photos. "That's Matty and the twins, my granddaughters…"

Don't look, oh God, don't look.

But it was too late.

Drawn beyond my will, I lifted one of many framed pictures and beheld Mathias standing on the sandy bank of Flickertail with two little girls. Clad in matching bathing suits, the girls had been photographed in the midst of horsing around, pirouetting and posing; one held her own ankle, knee bent at an acute angle, as though about to begin a gymnastics routine. They resembled Mathias with their dark hair and blue eyes, smiley little girls who were so obviously his children. They could have been my children's siblings; they were the female versions of Brantley and Henry.

Oh, dear, dear God…

Never in my most bizarre imaginings could I have conjured such a situation, witnessing my husband in an alternate life, a life without our love, without *us*. I studied him with faltering control, trying to determine what he'd been feeling when the picture was snapped that summer day. Shirtless and tanned, he held the fishing pole his grandpa had given him for his thirteenth birthday and which he'd always cherished; he was smiling, but not the smile to which I was accustomed, his wide, effortless grin that beamed like a ray of July sunshine. I knew this man better than I knew myself and I saw in that smile a lack of true happiness.

The scariest part is I actually thought I was fairly happy.

Mathias's words, spoken in 2006 while we were on vacation in Montana, rang inside my skull. He'd been referring to the year before he moved home to Landon, a year during which he'd dated Suzy and intended to remain in Minneapolis, the year before we had met at Shore Leave one cold December night.

I saw you and I knew you were mine, in every sense of the word, he had said that gorgeous night in the foothills of eastern Montana, the night we'd conceived Brantley and Henry.

The man in the image I cradled in both hands was Mathias without me; he was Malcolm without Cora.

"I love that picture, even though Suzy isn't in it," Diana was saying.

Tina hooked an arm around her mother's waist, with a crooked grin. "I think that may be *why* you love that picture."

I tore my gaze from Mathias and his daughters, heartened to a tiny degree.

Diana released a small huff of laughter, swatting at Tina. "Don't say that! I like Suzy well enough. It's just that she isn't much for the north woods. I don't think she's been up here with him in the last five years, at least. Matty brings Cora and Cammy every summer and stays a couple weeks. I count on that time. I miss them so much, but Suzy won't stand for living outside the city."

My composure withstood another blow.

Cora and Cammy?

Oh, Mathias...

You know, don't you, sweetheart? Somewhere inside you remember.

Just as quickly, I recognized the danger of being here when he arrived. I replaced the picture, engaged in a sudden, intense battle with my own better judgment.

You have to leave.

No. I want to see him. God help me, I want to see him.

It will kill you.

But I miss him so fucking much.

Go. Go now.

What if we can't get back to the life we knew?

What if today is the only time I'll ever lay eyes on him again?!

Resolve turned my insides to iron. Cold, rigid, obstinate.

Whatever it takes, I will get us back to our real life.

Tina led me upstairs a few minutes later, maintaining an easy, steady flow of conversation as I followed her to a small set of creaky steps at the end of the hallway, which led to a narrow wooden trapdoor. Because I knew her so well, I heard in her tone numerous questions she wanted

– but wasn't quite ready – to ask; she'd very cagily offered to help me and I braced for what was coming. She climbed to the third step and reached for the metal handle, tugging at the trapdoor. Running the entire length of the upper floor, the Carters' attic was a space in which their grandchildren loved to play; it boasted a ceiling with sharp peaks and enchanting, cobwebbed nooks, not to mention boxes of old clothes and hats and other assorted jumble. My kids loved the way they could crawl on hands and knees to peer out the dormer windows, spying on the yard far below.

"Here we go," Tina said, grunting as she pulled harder on the door; it always stuck. Dust billowed and we both coughed.

I spoke without thinking. "Remember when Lydia –"

I hurtled to a halt, wanting to bite through my tongue.

Tina looked over her shoulder, the door frozen at half-mast, her eyebrows lofted. Lydia was her youngest daughter and as far as Tina knew there was no way in hell I would possess any remembrances of her. I'd been about to say, *Remember when Lydia fell asleep up here and scared all of us half to death?* Thanksgiving, five years ago; we'd been ready to call Charlie Evans down at the police station. The door creaked as Tina let it slowly close and turned to face me; I knew that expression. Sweat formed along my hairline.

"It's the weirdest thing." Her voice was low and soft, like someone in the process of revealing dire news. She let this sink in for a heartbeat. "But I feel like I know you better than I should. Like, I *remember* things about you. Did you just mean Lydia, my daughter?"

I was at a loss; my mouth was too dry for words.

She crinkled her eyes, conveying confusion rather than alarm. I reflected that Tina was not a woman easily shaken. She was practical and down-to-earth and I teetered on a knife blade; did I dare trust her with what I knew?

"I heard about what happened at Eddie's last night," she went on, sinking to a seat on the middle step, putting our faces at about the same level; I remained standing in the hallway. "About you freaking out on Justin Miller and throwing your glass." Her lips took on a small, ironic tilt, not quite a smile. "Don't get me wrong, I actually think it's hilarious.

Those regulars need a little shot of adrenaline now and then, along with their booze. But it's not that. It's what you said to him. What did you mean that nothing 'here' was right? That no one knew what was right?"

Shit.

I had underestimated the speed of small-town gossip.

And I had absolutely no idea how to answer.

Tina was undeterred, making no attempt to disguise her desire to know more. She searched my eyes. "You may not believe me when I say this, but what you said to Justin reminded me of something. A dream I used to have, back when I was a teenager. I would dream about Mathias, these horrible recurring dreams where he was trapped somewhere just beyond my sight. He'd be crying for me to find him, *begging* me, and I'd be running all over the place, screaming his name. It scared the shit out of me."

My knees gave way almost politely; I sank to a crouch, folding my hands and bringing them to my lips.

Tina whispered, "And he'd be sobbing in those dreams, just a little boy, telling me that none of this was right. He was trapped somewhere and it *wasn't right*." Her eyes stabbed at me. "This means something to you, doesn't it?"

I nodded, a jerking, puppet-like movement.

Tina leaned closer, clutching her knees. "What does it mean?"

I swallowed, summoning my voice. "If I told you, you wouldn't believe me."

"I would, I promise you," she insisted. Tina was the same age as Jilly, and while I'd never known Tina to experience extrasensory perception in the way of Aunt Jilly's Notions, she was possessed of an uncanny sense of intuition. Despite their age difference, Tina and Mathias had always been close; she was the sister in whom he confided. Further, if any of my sisters-in-law was able to believe such an extreme explanation, it was Tina.

I bent my forehead to my knuckles, gaining strength, before lifting my face to confront her adamant gaze. "I know what I'm asking you to accept seems crazy. I really do. But I've known you a long time, Tina, and I trust you to trust *me*." I drew a calming breath and stepped from the high dive. "In the Landon I just came from, you are my sister-in-law. You have been for many years. Mathias is my husband and we have five children."

Tina absorbed this without expression and my lungs compressed. At last she sat straight and I could nearly hear the thoughts winging across her mind. She murmured, "God, this is so weird. I swear I *knew* this already, Camille. I've known this for a long time." Urgency overtook her features and she leaned forward. "Where is Matty trapped? Do you know?"

I could have crumpled flat to the floor with relief; she had taken a chance and believed me. "Oh God, Tina, I don't know. I'm trying to find out. The only other person who remembers what's right is my sister, Tish. The last time I saw Mathias he was singing at The Spoke. We'd gone out to Montana with the kids, to visit my sisters..."

"Wait." Tina could not let this slide. "Your sisters? As in, more than one?"

"I have two sisters, Tish and Ruthann. Somehow Ruthie was never born in this timeline."

Diana called from the kitchen, "Tina, come grab this tray. You girls will work up an appetite digging through all that junk!"

We stared at one another for a beat of weighty silence.

"I'll be right back!" Tina said. "Don't vanish!"

Two hours later Tina and I were dusty and dirt-smudged, our hair adorned with sticky bits of cobweb. Working together, we dug through trunks, suitcases, drawers, shoeboxes. We upset probably over a century of spider habitation. And as we unearthed junk, we talked. Or, I talked and Tina listened, inserting an occasional question or request for greater clarification. I detailed as clear a description as I could, omitting nothing, no longer caring if it was right or not. Much like Aunt Jilly, the more I revealed, the more Tina insisted she had guessed something was wrong – *off*, as she put it – long ago.

"So, some people and events are the same as you remember, but others different," she mused at one point. "I suppose it figures. Everything makes a ripple of its own, things we don't normally take a second to consider. A single choice has a thousand possible outcomes. We can't begin to imagine. It's fucking mind-numbing."

"It seems like *most* things have followed a path similar to what was intended. By that I mean what I remember as 'right,'" I explained, wiping both palms on my thighs, leaving grime smears on my jeans. "Nearly everyone who used to live in Landon still does, and the town is almost exactly like I remember. But my family is so different. Grandma and Aunt Ellen and Ruthie are just gone. Blythe and my brothers, gone." I covered my face, pressing hard against my forehead with eight fingertips.

"If you make things right again, will this timeline just go up in smoke? Will we remember?" Tina used her wrists to push loose hair from her face; her hands were covered in dust. Again, she did not appear apprehensive as much as intrigued.

For the first time since we entered the attic I'd paused in my rummaging; holding still felt wrong on a subterranean level. Movement suggested purpose, direction. Stillness was admitting defeat. I closed my eyes and whispered, "I don't know. All I know is that –"

"Tina! You up here?"

My eyes flew open, electricity flaying my skin from the inside out. Tina had mentioned earlier that Mathias hadn't planned to drive up to Landon until tomorrow but called early this morning to tell them he'd taken an extra day.

Because he's drawn to you, she surmised. *He knew you'd be here, somehow, I'll bet you.*

"Stay here," Tina ordered in an undertone, squeezing my shoulder as she hurried toward the trapdoor, propped open on the far side of the room. "You look like you're about to pass out. I'll distract him."

No, I tried to say.

But it was too late. The steps creaked and Mathias's head and shoulders appeared. Spying his sister, he offered a grin as he climbed the last few risers with his typical grace and entered the attic, collecting her in an affectionate embrace. Half-hidden behind a trunk stacked with folded quilts I devoured the sight of him, noting every detail, every difference.

Clean-shaven, his wavy hair a mess – he'd been wearing a hat on the way here, I could tell – dressed in worn jeans, work boots, and a green flannel unbuttoned over a gray thermal shirt. My longing for him swelled with the force of an avalanche and I rose, drawn beyond any hope of reason, immediately catching his attention. Tina chewed her lower lip, watching quietly as Mathias headed my way, grinning with his usual amiability.

I felt gutted, filleted, ripped stem to stern.

He stopped with about two feet of space separating our bodies.

"You must be the new schoolteacher." He offered his right hand. "Mathias Carter."

Destroyed by our proximity, pummeled by the sight and sound, the scent of this man I had loved all through time, I stood silent and immobile. If I touched him, I would lose my tenuous composure. I saw the teasing glint in his eyes; because I hadn't moved, he leaned a fraction closer and engulfed my right hand within his own. The shock of the contact almost hurt. I watched, helpless, as his grin was replaced by a sudden sense of bewilderment, which he quickly disguised with a genial running commentary.

"You're the new history teacher, Mom was saying. You're taking over for Mrs. Meeker, huh? She was ancient when I had her in junior high so I can't imagine the poor woman now. She always showed us these old black and white movies on the film projector…"

Our hands remained joined in midair and our real lives, the true timeline, seemed so close that a breath could pierce the barrier.

"Yes," I managed to whisper.

"I've always loved history, too." Warming to the subject, Mathias indicated the rest of the attic with his free hand. "And there's a ton of it up here, as you can see." His dimple flashed as he grinned anew. "I don't mean to pry, but you haven't told me your name."

Heat inundated my neck, climbing my face. "Camille –" I choked back the surname that had been mine for many years – *Carter* – and stumbled, "Gordon."

"Camille," he repeated slowly, as though tasting the syllables. "I'm pleased to meet you."

So polite, so courteous, every word he spoke a new puncture wound to my heart. Aching and distraught, I withdrew my hand. I thought of what Tish had endured in Jalesville, seeing Case with Lynnette, and found a measure of space to be grateful that Suzy had not accompanied Mathias.

I had almost forgotten Tina until she stepped into my field of view; I recognized the compassion beneath the statement as she softly hinted, "Matty, we're kinda busy up here."

But he was not to be deterred; radiating enthusiasm, he asked, "Can I help you guys? What are you looking for?" He shed his flannel in one easy motion, tossing it upon a tattered loveseat. "Something in particular?"

It was beyond foolish to be near him this way. I knew I should go but I couldn't bear to leave just yet; besides, there were dozens of unexplored boxes. My chest rose and fell with a deep breath and I drew upon a small reservoir of courage. "We're looking for anything to do with your first ancestors here in Minnesota. I think there's some sort of connection between the Davises and the Carters as far back as the nineteenth century. Your parents were kind enough to let me look through your attic."

"Are you kidding? If Dad was here, he'd be on his knees right beside you." Eager and excited, Mathias resembled our boys. "What have you guys found?"

"Not much from the nineteenth century," I admitted, returning to the trunk I'd abandoned.

The phone in the kitchen rang; seconds later Diana called, "Tina, it's Sam!"

Tina hesitated before heading downstairs; she had sworn herself to secrecy and I had promised not to reveal anything to Mathias – at least, not yet. I tried to send her a silent message that I was all right.

Mathias grabbed an unopened box and hunkered down right beside me. "Dad said we'd get started over at the Lodge after lunch, we're stripping out the floors in the old ballroom, but I'm all yours until then."

Oh God, don't look at him…

Instead of opening the box Mathias leaned closer to me, perusing my hair.

Incorrigible, I thought, slammed backward to the first week we'd known one another. Even though his gaze was nearly palpable I refused to look his way; the inability to touch him was too painful.

"There's cobwebs in your hair," he observed and I almost smiled; he was as forthright as ever.

"I'm sure there's plenty of them." My voice was reedy with tension and need.

He reached and gently grasped a sticky skein, elongating one of my curls like uncoiling a wire. He stretched until it was almost fully extended before letting it spring back, next rubbing together his fingertips to shed the cobweb.

"That was so cool! Is your hair naturally curly?"

Our first winter as a couple and without a place of our own, we had often made love in Bull's ice-fishing shack out on Flickertail Lake. The cramped, chilly space became our blissful private heaven; laughing as we struggled to free ourselves from inhibiting winter garments, the threat of getting caught only stimulating the urgent desire, knocking over coffee mugs and sling chairs in our need to come together. Memories swarmed, overpowering and undeniable; I could kneel here and pretend I didn't know this man but it did not change the truth. To be near him and feign indifference was a cruelty too bizarre to comprehend.

"It is," I muttered, referring to my hair, still refusing to look at him.

He proceeded to pepper me with questions, exactly as he had when we first met. I kept my answers succinct at first but familiarity, the sum total of our years together, began to win out and before I knew it I was outright flirting with him. I was *flirting* with my husband, the father of my children, who was currently married to another woman. I knew he sensed the connection that bound us, even if he couldn't explain why. We kept finding little excuses to briefly touch each other. He'd nudge my arm or touch my wrist to gain my attention; I pretended to find a smudge of dust on his shoulder, just so I could brush it away.

"Your family owns Shore Leave, right? But you're from Chicago?"

"What made you decide to move here from the city?"

"How'd you decide to major in history?"

"Are you planning to live at Shore Leave or in the apartments by the co-op? My friend Skid Erickson lives there with his girlfriend. It's a nice place."

"Have you seen the northern lights up here? They are something else." He made this comment as he extracted yet another cobweb from my hair, completely at ease.

"Do you mind?" I pretended to gripe, ducking away.

"Sorry," he said, dimple flashing, not truly sorry at all. His grin widened. "There's dirt on your cheek."

There was also a pile of newspapers on my lap; I sat cross-legged, facing him as I riffled carefully through a stack of faded newsprint, ancient editions of *The Landon Sentinel*. I looked up at this comment and my heart struck a solid blow to my breastbone.

His smile faded like smoke in a sudden breeze.

"What?" I whispered.

Dispensing with small talk, he spoke with sudden seriousness. "You'll think I'm crazy, but I swear we've met before today."

I returned my attention at once to my lap. "I don't think so."

He resituated, resting one forearm on a bent knee, focusing his full intensity upon me while I tried not to squirm. "Are you sure?"

Goddammit, don't do this to me, Carter.

I refused to look at him. And then something completely different caught my eye – a typewritten name in a slim column.

"Look!" I cried, angling the paper toward him, indicating with my index finger. "Look right there."

"'Edward Tilson,'" he read. "Do you know him?"

"Oh my God," I breathed, blood coursing as I flipped to the front page of the three-page paper, seeking the publication date. Sunday, May 20, 1906.

Mathias used his shoulder to gently nudge mine. "Who is he?"

I had no answer yet, reading intently, with mounting purpose. An obituary, I realized, detailing the life of a ninety-nine year old doctor named Edward Tilson; a man beloved by the entire county according to the subsequent paragraphs beneath a grainy image.

Tilson…

It can't be a coincidence.

"'A resident of the area since 1869, Dr. Tilson, a veteran of the War Between the States, was proceeded in death by his wife, Adeline Tilson, an infant daughter, and four sons, also veterans. Three of Dr. Tilson's sons, Justus, Amon, and Bridger, died in the service of their country, while his eldest, Blythe, was killed in 1882.'" I looked over at Mathias, stunned by this revelation. He waited with eyebrows raised, surprised by my obvious agitation over these long-ago deaths.

Blythe Tilson. Oh, my God…

At least one of Blythe's ancestors had lived in Landon during the nineteenth century.

"Holy shit," I whispered, lightheaded with astonishment, resting my left thumb against my lips as I reread the line about Dr. Tilson's eldest son, killed in 1882. Ruthann was in 1882. I couldn't process this wealth of information quickly enough. It couldn't be a coincidence. "Holy *shit*, do you know what this means?!"

"I'm *dying* to know what this means," Mathias said. "You have no idea."

I read the remainder of the obituary, hawk-eyed for more information. Dr. Tilson was survived by his nephew, Clinton Clemens, his niece, Rebecca Carter, and –

"Look!" I exclaimed again, tears bulging along my lower eyelids without my consent; it was inevitable. Mathias couldn't begin to know the depth of my emotional investment.

"I'm looking, I promise." Mathias scooted even closer; we almost clocked heads.

"It's Malcolm," I breathed, composure crumbling fast. "And Rebecca's husband is Boyd Carter. Oh God, if only we'd found this after we found Malcolm's picture and his Christmas Eve telegram, Thias. To think it's been in your attic this whole time. *Malcolm lived to 1906…*" Tears dripped from my chin, creating a rainstorm of damp dots on the newspaper; I scrubbed at my face, choking back sobs.

"What did you call me, just now?" Mathias spoke with a dead-serious tone and I heard his confusion, the sincerity of his desire to understand more than I was currently telling him.

I froze, unable to dredge up an answer; in our real lives, it was my name for him.

"Who's Malcolm? What does he mean to you?" Mathias persisted, eyes tracking all over my face, seeking answers. "You're crying about this. What am I missing here?"

My choices diminished to one; I had to leave – *now*.

I shifted to stand but Mathias caught my elbow. "Please, Camille," he begged, hoarse with mounting emotion; I was all but done in by the sound of my name on his lips. "Don't go. Tell me what this is about. It's something important, isn't it?"

I pulled away, unable to brave his staggered gaze as I asked, "Can I keep this newspaper?"

He studied me with a pulse pounding in his throat; I restrained the absolute need to collapse against his powerful chest and cling. I despised running away like this but I'd done too much damage already. He said, "Of course. But can you at least tell me what this is about? I don't understand…"

"No," I whispered. "I can't. I'm sorry."

I fled before he could say another word.

Chapter Eighteen

SATURDAY EVENING CREPT AROUND.

I'd existed nearly a week in this repulsive offshoot timeline, a series of days which inched past my nose, creating the sickening sensation that more than a century had actually elapsed. Though I could have ventured to my "office" at Turnbull and Hinckley on Friday I chose instead to hide out at Dad's, feigning illness. Derrick's warning had petrified me in more ways than one; I was simultaneously terrified and, in essence, frozen solid. I made Robbie promise to hold off on any further investigative work and lay low. I told him I would regroup and keep him posted on anything I discovered. He had agreed to escort me to the benefit dinner downtown, much to Dad's delight; he adored Robbie. I had not revealed a thing to my father as of yet.

Emotionally trampled, tripped up by indecision and a maddening lack of choices, I spent Friday huddled in bed, politely declining Lanny's invitation to join her for a manicure, then spending hours scrolling obsessively through every last online image or mention I could find of Case; in this timeline, without the encouraging presence of the Rawleys, he had not spent time pursuing his music. I didn't bathe or eat; I could hardly rally the energy to shuffle to my small, private bathroom, battling an increasing sense of hopelessness. The inevitability of relenting to this timeline hovered so near I could feel its damp breath.

When I saw Camille's name flash across my phone late Friday afternoon, I debated not answering – but I couldn't leave her hanging.

"Hey," I whispered.

"I found something!" Her voice was a strange mixture of strong emotion, wobbling with intensity as she rushed to explain. "I spent this morning in the attic at the Carters' and found an old *Landon Sentinel* with an obituary –"

"Oh God, whose?" I cried, flying from beneath the covers, heartrate spiking.

"No one we know, don't worry. Here, I'll pull over to read it to you." She did, and I leaned forward in my desire to absorb her every word.

"Who wrote it?" I demanded.

"Get this, Tish, a woman named Lorissa *Davis*. I'm almost certain she's the 'Lorie' mentioned in the list of Edward Tilson's survivors and no doubt the same person Malcolm was writing to in 1876. Lorie was our ancestor. And she knew *Blythe's ancestor*."

"Breathe," I ordered, clutching the phone with both hands, startled by the tone of my sister's voice; she sounded about three seconds from hysteria. Something else occurred to me. "You saw Mathias, didn't you? Oh, Milla, I'm sorry..."

Her sudden, abject sobs were the only confirmation I needed.

"Shit, don't try to drive for a minute, okay? Stay where you are. I'm so sorry."

"I couldn't tell him the truth, Tish. Oh God, he has twins...*it hurts so much...*"

"I know, I really do." The bridge of my nose stung just listening to her pain.

After a minute she was able to draw several ragged breaths. "I just left their house, I'm still shaking."

"It's okay. Let's consider this information." For the first time since speaking with Derrick, I experienced a small sense of control. "First, Blythe's ancestor, Edward Tilson, lived in Minnesota. Second, he lived with the Carters and knew the Davises. What's more, none of his children lived beyond him. This doctor was the last Tilson." The excitement of closing in on key details rose like an old friend in my chest. "Edward wasn't *supposed* to be the last Tilson, because otherwise the Blythe we know would never have existed."

"And Edward's son, nineteenth-century Blythe, died in 1882! That can't be a coincidence."

"He didn't just die, he was 'killed' it said," I reminded her, twining a curl around my index finger until it cut off the blood supply at the tip. "Fallon killed him, I'm sure of it." The simple act of speaking Fallon's name aloud set the hairs on my nape standing on end; my gaze spanned the circumference of my bedroom, unpleasantly gloomy in the late-afternoon light. It was too quiet, the air holding its breath, and a shiver blazed over my scalp – driven by instinct I dropped the phone to grab the tall, slender brass lamp on my nightstand, yanking its cord from the wall. Clutching it like a weapon I leaped into the hallway, fully prepared to split Fallon Yancy's head like an overripe watermelon.

The hall was empty but I race-walked room to room anyway, clicking every light fixture into existence.

Camille's voice demanded my attention from the abandoned phone. "Tish, what are you doing?!"

"It's all right, I just had a bad feeling," I explained when I was back on the line, breathless with exertion.

"Are you coming home now?" she asked.

"I have the benefit dinner tomorrow night, remember?"

"Don't go. Talk about bad feelings!"

"I have to. Fallon might show up. I can't lose this chance to confront him."

"Tish, goddammit! He's *dangerous*. Have you told Dad anything?"

"No," I admitted. Thank God I hadn't revealed any of what Derrick said Thursday evening; Camille's next move would include showing up to drag me home by the car.

"Please just come back to Landon."

"Sunday," I promised.

With thirty minutes to spare before Robbie arrived on Saturday evening, I examined my reflection in the full-length mirror on my bedroom closet. The closet contained rows of designer outfits and I recognized that if I was to appear at a gala such as tonight's, an event commanding something like a thousand dollars a plate, suitable attire was required. And so I'd bathed, applied make-up, and fastened diamond studs in my ears. After consulting with Lanny, who would be appalled if our outfits clashed, I chose a simple floor-length gown, so deep a purple it almost appeared black. One of my arms was left bare and I asked Dad to help me with the clasp of a simple tennis bracelet I found on my dresser.

"You look lovely, honey," he said, kissing my temple with paternal pride.

"Are you sure you want to leave your hair down?" Lanny inquired, scanning me from hairline to hem with a critical eye. She was impeccable in a smoky lavender frock with a plunging, crystal-encrusted neckline. Her dark hair was arranged atop her head, likely in part to feature her glittery diamond-and-amethyst chandeliers. I wanted to ask her if she knew her husband spent a fair amount of his work week engaging in illicit sex with another woman.

Dad, you unbelievable asshole, I thought, avoiding his eye as he held Lanny's coat.

Robbie arrived, clad in black tie, somber as a preacher's son but masking it with an air of forced gaiety. The doorman hailed a separate taxi for Robbie and me; Dad and Lanny promised to see us there as we climbed inside for the brief drive to the event center.

"You look nice. *Way* better than the other night." Robbie sat facing me with one knee bent on the seat.

"You look nice, too. I'm glad you're here." And I truly was, even if I appeared distracted, staring out the window at the city flashing past, the beaming blur of lights and cars. Rain clattered on the roof of the cab and created smeary trails along the windows. It had become increasingly difficult to prevent thoughts of home – my *real* home, my trailer in the Jalesville foothills – from entering my head. I wanted Case more with each passing second, until I feared I might rip right out of my skin, burst apart with the strength of my need for him.

"Tish, you wanna have sex quick? I need some relief from this tension." Robbie managed a small, crooked grin when my head snapped his way; he'd succeeded in catching my full attention.

"Thanks, but no thanks," I muttered, lowering my voice to add, "You have to start using your head, Benson. And *not* the smaller of the two." I held his gaze, praying he would listen. "You're my friend and I care about you very much. *Promise me* you'll remember everything that's happened here, in this time. Remember our conversations and stay away from Christina Turnbull at all costs. I don't want to lose you again, do you hear me?"

Robbie took my hand and squeezed, momentarily lowering his forehead to our joined fingers. "I hear you. And I promise. You're the only real friend I have."

We arrived to the usual bustle and mild mania of well-attended social events, checking our coats and offering greetings left and right. The dissembling occurring all around inspired in me an unpleasant, dreamlike sensation; a slow-motion reel of expensive fabric and flashing jewels, insincerity spilling from shiny lips. Laughter, compliments, and silver trays of champagne flutes all floated through the air.

Robbie and I stuck close; for one thing, I relied on him to guide me through potential missteps. The Tish he knew had worked at Turnbull and Hinckley with him since college and would therefore know the names – not to mention – faces of our colleagues. I held his left elbow as we navigated the crowd, taller than him in my heels; the ballroom adjacent to the wide grand entrance was decked out for intimate dining, the floor scattered with dozens of linen-topped foursomes. Tiny white lights flickered along the length of the bar.

"There's Derrick," Robbie murmured, with a discreet tilt of his head. Two seconds later he broke out his most flirtatious smile as a gaggle of twenty-something women approached from the right, fondling drinks and designer clutches.

"I'll find you before dinner," I promised in an undertone, leaving him at their mercy.

"Don't approach him," he murmured in response.

I had no intention of seeking out Derrick's company, though I was not blind; his gaze followed me with ill-disguised scrutiny. I nabbed a drink from a server simply to possess a prop, something to keep me from fidgeting, and slipped casually to the far edge of things, near the foot of the majestic open staircase that dropped from the second floor. I positioned myself just behind the gleaming wooden banister, where I could observe without being obtrusive, literally in the shadows. Derrick stood the length of the room away and necessity forced him to abandon watching me; he pasted on a smile to engage in requisite small talk.

My pulse was erratic as I waited for Fallon to appear – but there continued to be no sign of the slender, fair-haired man I recalled from Robbie's funeral. I watched Ron and Christina Turnbull enter and hot anxiety slithered over my skin. Without realizing it, I ducked farther behind the banister at the sight of them, the champagne flute slipping in my sweaty grasp. Dad and Lanny were next to arrive, Dad with his 'game face' front and center. A pang of guilty discomfort struck; this was one of those times my father seemed like a stranger, in no way connected to the man I once idolized. Standing there watching him schmooze his way around the crowd, I missed Blythe with a sudden, painful intensity, my kind and patient stepdad. Blythe, whose presence in this life had been thwarted.

But now we know when it happened – at least, tentatively. It's a small piece of the larger puzzle.

We have to get a message to Ruthie. She has to know every possible detail.

A stern-faced, imposing older man eventually joined Derrick, impatiently waving aside the offer of a drink. He bent his head toward Derrick and the two conferred.

His father, I thought at once, noting their resemblance, flooded with new terror. I imagined Derrick pointing in my direction and the two of them subsequently striding across the polished marble floor with the intent to drag me outside and extract answers.

I shivered so hard my jaws clacked together.

Stop it, Tish.

They aren't talking about you.

My own father, however, was looking for me. He'd found his way to

Robbie's side and was casting his eyes over the crowd.

Dammit.

Dad would wonder why I wasn't mingling and so I squared my shoulders and joined them.

"We're at table eleven." Dad brandished a palm to allow Robbie and me to lead the way. Lanny held his arm as they followed in our wake, her beautiful, insipid smile firmly in place.

"Chin up," Robbie suddenly muttered, tightening his hold on my elbow.

Ron and Christina were in our path, roughly two dozen feet ahead. No avoiding them.

"Robert, Patricia, wonderful to see you two together this evening," Ron spoke with his usual pompous arrogance; a tall, broad, silver-haired man with eyes like paint chips, whose authority was unchallenged.

I had not been this close to Ron since Robbie's funeral and a vision of grasping his throat and crushing his windpipe with my thumbs swelled with such strength I tasted bile. This man had ordered Robbie killed, had paved the way for the Yancys to hurt people I loved, had glibly practiced dirty business for the duration of his career. The potent desire to harm him overwhelmed my senses, casting a reddish haze over my perception. Ron must have seen something in my eyes because his condescending smile faltered a little.

Has he spoken to Fallon in this offshoot? Does he know about the real timeline? Does he know that Robbie and I were closing in on Fallon's secret?

There were too many unknowns to take action and I was a breath away from playing the game and mustering up a polite response when I saw Christina's lips bend upward in a small, mocking smile. Her eyes were the glacial green of frost-covered leaves and locked on mine.

"Excuse us." Robbie's voice was impressively level, his manner calm. He conveyed a sense of joviality tinged with mild impatience, carting me around them and toward the ballroom.

"Christina knows," I choked, seething with helpless rage. I tried to yank from Robbie's grasp, almost tripping on my hem as I peered over my shoulder, but the crowd had spread out behind us and only the top of

Ron's head remained visible. "I'm going to fucking *kill them*. They know what Fallon did."

"Tish, enough! We can't stay here if you're going to act like this."

People were beginning to trickle into the ballroom; a few couples were already seated, sipping drinks and waiting for dinner. Robbie drew out a chair at our assigned table but I was too distraught to sit and muttered, "I'll be right back."

Robbie clutched my wrist. "Don't make a scene. It's not the time."

I jerked free without responding.

Chapter Nineteen

Chicago, IL - March, 2014

I HAD NEVER ATTENDED AN EVENT AT THIS PARTICULAR venue but restrooms would be nearby; I skirted the flow of guests and hurried across the main entrance, high heels clicking over the marble floor, passing the coat check and taking the first hallway to the left, a space blessedly free of people. I hurried along its carpeted length until I could no longer hear the sounds of the gala; at last I stopped and leaned my spine against the wall, unaware of my surroundings, overwhelmed by stress. Panic loomed close to the surface, hot and oily. I closed my eyes and pressed the back of one hand against my mouth, afraid I might vomit before reaching a toilet.

You can't win. You know this. You're totally and completely fucked.

How can you outwit a man who is capable of traveling through time, who's protected by people in positions of unthinkable power?

Tell me that!

"Lovers' quarrel?"

I gasped, eyes flying open to spy Derrick standing a few paces away, feet widespread and hands buried in his trouser pockets. His onyx cufflinks gleamed in the muted glow of the wall sconces.

"What?" My palms were braced against the plaster on either side of my hips, a position of vulnerability, and I straightened to my full height, attempting to appear unruffled.

"You and Benson. I didn't realize you two were together," he clarified.

I didn't bother to correct this presumption, instead seizing the chance to demand, "Is your brother here? Have you seen Fallon tonight?"

Derrick stepped closer and I held my ground. I wasn't scared of him in most regards but it was beyond foolish to consider dropping my guard. He kept his voice low to ask, "Who told you the truth?"

I ignored his question and continued pressing. "When was the last time you saw Fallon? When was the last time he was here in Chicago, in 2014?"

Consternation rolled from Derrick in waves. "You can't imagine the level of shit you would be in if my father or Fallon knew *any* of this." He all but spit his brother's name, the word drenched in bitterness. So that particular detail proved no different in this timeline.

"How would they know? Do you plan to tattle on me?" I jabbed his chest with an index finger; I had everything to lose but I couldn't stop now. I stabbed the same outstretched finger in the direction of the ball-room. "I will march out there and tell every fucking person here tonight what I know about Fallon *the time-traveling wonder boy* unless you tell me when you saw him last! Do you know what he did to our lives, yours included? Did he tell you?"

"For fuck's sake, keep your voice down! You would be dead in a matter of hours, do you hear me?"

I gulped back my next threat and searched his eyes; he wasn't bluffing.

Derrick lifted a hand. It fluttered through the air like a moth, unsure where to alight now that it had taken flight, falling short of cupping my face. I watched an internal battle play out across his sharp, wolflike features. "Listen to me, Tish, even though I know it goes against the grain for you. I wish I could say that I won't let them hurt you, but I harbor no illusions." He clenched his jaw before asking quietly, "Did you tell me the truth the other night? You and I knew each other in another life? Fallon actually...changed reality as we knew it?"

Hope seized at my throat. "Yes. I know I'm asking you to believe something that seems impossible, even crazy."

"But it's true, isn't it?"

"It is. You have to trust me. *Please* trust me, I have nothing to gain by lying to you. I need to know everything about Fallon. Where is he? Do you think he'll show up here tonight?"

Derrick closed his eyes, the picture of a man torn.

I grabbed his arm. "Please, oh God, please tell me anything you know. Does he have a weakness? Is anything capable of stopping him? So much depends on this information. You could never begin to guess."

His eyes opened and he snaked an arm around my waist, bringing me close to his body before I knew it was coming, before I could step aside or away. "You said we were married in another life…"

"Stop it!" I hissed, shoving his chest with both hands.

"Well, well," a woman murmured, rife with satisfaction, and we turned as one to see Christina Turnbull ambling our direction, one hand in a loose fist around her long necklace, manipulating the chunky, lustrous gem at the bottom in small circles. "Slumming this evening, are we, Derrick?"

Surprise flattened his features before his cheeks hollowed with growing anger but he held himself in check, not responding to her provocation.

Christina wore a fitted gown of palest green, lined with sleek gold threads; I stepped quickly away from Derrick and closer to her. We were no longer surrounded by hundreds of eyes and I felt capable of dismemberment, capable of ripping the shining, highlighted hair straight out of her scalp. I chose my words, however, with great care.

"I'm sure you're aware that my father is only using you. The same way he would a rental car, or a set of golf clubs."

Derrick released a barking huff of astonished laughter before gripping the lower half of his face, as though to contain another outburst.

But Christina betrayed no loss of composure, no hint of shame. She skimmed her gaze down the front of my dress, unhurried and disdainful. "You poor, stupid creature." Her eyes returned to mine with the force of a physical blow. "You can't stop him. No one can."

Her confident scorn rattled me and I tried to hide it; I couldn't let her claim the last word this way. "You're wrong."

"Am I?" she purred, releasing her necklace to scrape one long pink fingernail down Derrick's sleeve. She plucked at his cufflink and he drew away from her touch with calm dignity, gripping his lapels and adjusting his jacket.

"Tish doesn't know half of what she thinks she does," Derrick said and I realized, belatedly, that he was doing his best to offer me what help he could. I was sinking lower in this shitpile and, worse yet, I had been the one to jump into it in the first place, playing my ace card too soon. It had been a mistake to tell Derrick what I knew.

Christina's expression more than confirmed her disbelief in his statement and my bravado leaked rapidly away.

Focus, Tish. It's not like she's armed. She can't prevent you from doing anything.

You can survive this. You can tell everyone the truth about Fallon. It's not too late.

Oh, dear God...

"She's leaving Chicago tomorrow, aren't you, Tish?" Derrick spoke brusquely. "For good. Resigning from the firm to work back home was an apt decision for you. If you'll excuse us, Christina. We'll see you at dinner." He appropriated my arm and towed me away, back toward the ballroom; as soon as we rounded the corner and were out of Christina's sight, Derrick bent to my ear. "Get out of here right now. Leave the city tonight. I'll make an excuse to Jackson."

Fear gouged my heart – for a second I couldn't swallow, let alone reply.

What about Robbie?

He's not safe here, either.

Derrick shifted me so we were face to face and I witnessed the conflict in his eyes, the faltering; a dam crumbling beneath the intense weight of something far beyond his control as he said, "Fallon arrived in Chicago this morning. I don't know if he's still in town, or even this *century*, but you can't chance it. Christina tells him everything. Now *go*."

"Thank you," I gasped. And then I ran for the exit.

Rain gushed from a wet black sky, splattering over awnings and creating miniature hurricanes along the traffic-choked street. I staggered in my heels, cursing, and kicked them aside, lifting my hem knee-high. No longer impeded by footwear I dashed away from the event center, not slowing until I reached a corner three blocks away. Heart thrusting, drenched and barefoot, I was too scared to look over my shoulder. I perched on the curb and scanned the array of vehicles for a taxi.

No one is chasing you. But get the hell out of here!

I would call Robbie and Dad as soon as I could.

"Hey!" I shrieked as a speeding car roared past, sending a cascade of dirty rainwater over my thighs. "Asshole!"

The streetlight rotated through its cycle four times before anyone stopped. I could not draw a full breath until the taxi stopped at Dad's building. Simultaneously I realized I had no money; my purse was back at table eleven. The driver was unamused, then belligerent.

I pleaded, "Give me a second to run upstairs. I'll get your money, I swear."

"You're kidding me, right? You think I was born yesterday?"

"Seriously, I'll be right back!"

He glared at me over the front seat. "Five minutes, lady, then I'm calling the cops." As if I didn't believe him, he held up and wiggled his phone.

"Two minutes," I promised and stepped directly in a cold, murky puddle as I climbed out. "Shit. *Shit!*"

My dress was too long without my shoes and I fumbled with the slippery material, unable to clench a handful to lift my trailing hem. Inundated, my hair swung across my wet face, momentarily obscuring my sight as I stumbled barefoot over the slick sidewalk. And so it was that I thought I was hearing things when someone shouted, "Patricia!"

My heart halted all operations.

It can't be —

Shock would have taken me to my knees if he hadn't been there to slide his arms around my waist.

"Patricia." His voice was low, with a deep husk, and I heard his longing and confusion and sincerity, all tangled together. Rain poured over our bodies as he held me secure, water dripping from his hair and running in rivulets down his lean, sunburned cheeks.

Case, I tried to say but I was crying, clutching his precious face in both hands to receive his ravenous kisses, both of us trying to climb within one another's skin, to devour each other and become one being, never again separated.

But I should have known better.

We had less than five minutes left together and somewhere, beyond our perception, the clock had already begun a rapid countdown toward zero.

"Case, oh God, *Case*," I gasped, forgetting myself in the absolute elation of being near him, kissing his neck, his chin, running my hands over his back as he sought my mouth with the heat of his own, kissing me past all reason, all agony. I knew his taste, knew the blessed feel of this man; he was mine. I was his. Nothing else mattered.

Without breaking the contact of our mouths he hauled us under a nearby awning, allowing for a full aligning of our bodies. He clasped my jaws, studying my eyes with a mixture of amazement and certainty.

"How did...when did..." I clung, knotting my arms around his torso, terrified he would disappear from my embrace.

"Your eyes," he whispered as if in a dream. "I know your eyes, I swear on my life. I knew it the night you showed up at the trailer. I'd never seen you before that night, but I *knew* you. I've hardly slept since you left, or eaten. Your face has haunted me. And all those things you said..." He trailed to silence, thumbs caressing my wet face as if it were constructed of porcelain. With reverence, he bent and kissed my right eye, closing it, then the left. Resting his lips to my forehead and inhaling deeply, he whispered, "You know all these things already, don't you?"

Tears seeped through my lashes. Reality was asserting itself more aggressively now but I fought it, unwilling to move from his embrace. He might not have been the Case who was my husband in our real lives, but he was still Case. And I couldn't bear to lose him so soon, especially when this version of him had been lonely so long, without the gift of the lifelong presence of the Rawleys and their devotion to him; without our love for each other to keep the outside world at bay. "I do know. I love you, Case, *I love you so much*. I've missed you so much, sweetheart, you can't begin to know. Oh God, I don't know how to make you understand what I have to tell you..."

"Then tell me, please tell me everything. I drove straight through from Montana to get here, I couldn't bear it anymore. I looked you up online and tracked down your address. I know it's crazy, it's something a stalker would do, but I'm not a stalker, I promise you. I just had to find you. I've been here maybe fifteen minutes. The doorman wouldn't say where you'd gone, so I was waiting." He noticed my bare feet and concern swept over his features. "You're soaked. Where have you been? Are you all right?"

My thoughts flew, streaking across wide, windswept fields of thought. I had no true idea where to begin; the last thing I expected this evening was for Case to appear in Chicago. Furthermore, I had no intention of remaining in this timeline where neither of us rightly belonged, this alternate horror in which I'd been enmeshed for too long already. Agonized anew, I studied the sincerity in his eyes and felt a razor pass across my soul.

"Let's go upstairs," I insisted. "This is my dad's place and we can clean up. Then we have to leave, we have to get out of Chicago right away. I'll explain everything once we get going…"

But all decisions were suddenly removed from my hands.

The slow-motion, time-stop reel suddenly reasserted itself, each second jolting-jerking-clunking to the next. Sounds retreated. My limbs grew dense. I watched, transfixed by horror, as Fallon Yancy strode toward us through the rain. Teeth exposed. Grinning. Lips moving-flapping-speaking – "This is fucking poetic. You really are a whore, aren't you, Patricia?"

My own voice then, raging-screaming-sobbing – "What did you do to them?! Where are they?! *I will fucking kill you* –"

I tried to launch at Fallon but Case had already moved between us. Swift, fluid, full of purpose. He would never let anyone hurt me.

I should have known, I should have known –

This exact moment had played out in my nightmares dozens of times.

Fallon was ready this time and it happened fast; so fast I would have missed it had I blinked.

But I didn't blink. I saw.

The gun was small, well-hidden between their bodies. The bullet pierced Case's stomach and his hands fell away from Fallon. He stared down at the blood blooming on his wet shirt as though merely surprised, lips parting. And then went almost gracefully to his knees.

Begging-sobbing-screaming, I tried with both hands to staunch the flow of his blood.

Fallon leaned close to my ear. "Don't bother. He's beyond help. It's fate, you see."

"What the fuck?" someone was yelling from behind us, perhaps the cab driver; I had no idea. He bellowed, "Jesus Christ, this man's been shot! Get help!"

Too late, too late...

Fallon was already gone.

You can't stop him, Christina had said. *No one can.*

Chapter Twenty

Montana Territory - June, 1882

I WOKE SHROUDED BY UNEASE, THE REMNANTS OF A BAD dream lingering for a last second before wakefulness swept them away. Our room was veiled in darkness but I sensed the approaching dawn, hunching my knees toward my belly and closing my eyes, attempting to cling to the images so recently playing out in my head – did they seem more ominous than a normal jumble of bad dreams, or was I imagining that? So many worries crowded my mind by day; I had so few solutions to any of them, it only made sense they would find an outlet at night. But I was someone who trusted her instinct, and mine suggested this sequence of dreams contained deeper significance –

I could not shake the feeling that Tish and Camille had been screaming for my attention from the opposite side of a wide chasm. I knew they were out there in actuality, not just trapped within the confines of a nightmare, both terrified for me and made helpless by the longtime lack of news. Had more than a year passed in their lives, as it had here? Marshall and I had reason to believe time flowed differently here in the past, but did it move more swiftly, or less? And who besides Fallon Yancy could answer such a question? Against my will, Fallon's face burned across the screen of my mind, slender and lethal, eye sockets like deep holes; he was laughing and I slammed the door on the image, conjuring instead a picture of my older sisters.

Tish, I thought, first separating her face from Patricia's, trying yet again to reach her through the unimaginable barriers separating us.

Camille's features took form more readily because I had no one here with whom to confuse her. *Camille. I'm here. What were you trying to tell me?*

Marshall and I had spent an afternoon last week writing a note, selecting an appropriate location we prayed would contain the metal lockbox until its intended twenty-first century discovery, and then digging a deep, narrow hole in which to bury both. A sense of foreboding had crept in as we worked, stealthy as a predator, but I'd refused to acknowledge its presence. Because I was pregnant, Marshall would not allow me to help him with either the initial digging or the replacing of turned earth atop the lockbox and so I sat in silence, watching him work with quiet efficiency; thoughts of gravedigging kept intruding. I'd reminded myself countless times that Marshall was not shoveling dirt onto a coffin.

"It's the best we can do, for now," he'd said afterward. Though we didn't speak a word of it, I knew both of us harbored doubts. But the very act of doing something lent us a sense, however fleeting, of accomplishment.

Now, just over an uneventful week later, I rolled to the opposite side and latched an arm and leg around Marshall's naked body, seeking the only security I knew; he was still snoring but responded to my touch by clasping a protective hand around my thigh. I nuzzled the warm skin between his shoulder blades, hoping to claim a little more sleep, when he surprised me by murmuring, "I was dreaming about Garth and Case and Mathias, just now."

Adrenaline erupted in my blood, eradicating any urge to continue resting. I lifted to an elbow, hooking my chin over his shoulder. "I dreamed about my sisters."

Marshall shifted to his back; his eyes were troubled.

"What did you dream?" I insisted, cupping his stubbled jaw.

"They were singing at The Spoke, which isn't so strange, I suppose. I mean, I dream pretty often about us all being there together. But this time…I don't know, it was eerie, Ruthie. Behind them, almost like I could see through the wall to what was happening outside, there was this huge ocean wave. Like something in a disaster movie, a huge gray breaker swelling over Jalesville, higher than the entire town. If I hadn't woken up just now it would have swept over everything in its path. Swept them all away."

My spine ached at this description.

Marshall drew me closer to his warmth. "It was a big crowd, like they were playing a weekend show or something. There were a couple other guys on stage with them but I couldn't tell who they were…"

"Did you see my sisters in the crowd?"

"I didn't. Shit, this scares me. I hate to admit it." He searched my eyes. "What did you dream, angel?"

"I can't remember exactly. Tish and Camille were screaming for my attention. More than usual, though. They were frantic. Oh God, they're trying to tell us something, Marsh. Something maybe even worse than us being trapped here."

Awareness descended, drowning us in momentary silence.

When I could bear it no longer I sat straight, throwing off the covers, furious at the level of our vulnerability, our inability to know what was happening to our families.

"I agree." Marshall spoke with quiet resignation and I was glad he hadn't tried to tell me everything was all right. "I'm goddamn sick of having no answers." His tone softened. "I know you are too, love."

Angry moisture blurred my vision; the last thing I wanted to do was cry, but these were not tears of sadness. I was hot with fury. I wished something constructed of glass or china was within arm's reach, if only so I could hurl it against the wall and hear the satisfying sounds of demolition. "I hate feeling so helpless. We have *no way* of communicating with them. We can't just sit here at Grant's and do nothing. We'll go crazy."

Marshall sat up, the sheet draping his hips, and engulfed me in his embrace. Compounding our stress was the continued lack of word from Malcolm, Cole, and Patricia. Even allowing for a generous margin of time they should have reached Landon by now, and therefore been able to send a letter. Something had happened to prevent this, it was growing harder to deny. Tomorrow was the first day of July and we'd parted ways in Iowa weeks ago; the only confirmation of their progress we'd received had been a letter tucked in a package mailed to Birdie and Grant by

Grant's mother, Fannie Rawley; they had spent one night in the company of the Rawley family.

Somewhere in the depths of my mind, where dark what-ifs and restless memories and aching guilt hunkered, I considered how this selfsame woman, Fannie, might have been my mother-in-law; had fate taken a different direction and I'd become Miles's wife. I bit down on my lower lip. I did my best not to think about Miles in that context; Miles, who had spent his last night of life holding me close in the very bed I now shared with Marshall.

"I know we can't just stay here at Grant's indefinitely, but for now it's the safest place." Marshall roughed up his hair, then passed a hand over his unshaven face. "I'll telegraph the Rawleys once we get to Howardsville later today, tomorrow at the latest. Ax said we'd be there by evening if we set out pretty quick here. I best get my ass in gear..." So saying, he swung his legs over the side of the bed and sat forward, knuckling sleep from his eyes.

The reminder of his trip to Howardsville sent a shard of fear through my heart. To an increasingly obsessive degree I hated letting him out of my sight.

"Let me come," I begged, knowing it was a futile request. Howardsville was a hard day's ride by horseback, a journey made considerably longer in the ponderous wagon; and I'd be forced to ride as a passenger in the flatbed, I knew. A pregnant woman couldn't very well be saddling up and withstanding a horse's cantering gait across dozens of miles. But I pleaded my case nonetheless. "Please, Marsh, *please* don't make me stay here without you."

We hadn't been apart for more than a few minutes since being reunited here in 1882 and I knew it pained him to consider it, even when the separation was brief and necessary; at my insistence, Marshall had agreed to relinquish the marshal position he'd assumed last fall. A new candidate had been found and was due in Howardsville in the next day; word had arrived in the form of a telegram, along with a request that Marshall be there to greet him and offer a tour of town and the law offices. A separate and official document had arrived for Marshall, releasing him from the position, much to my overwhelming relief. In the month since we'd found each other there had been no hint or sign of the Yancys' presence in town, and I attempted to derive a measure of relief from this fact.

"Aw, angel, don't do this to me. You know I hate to leave you here but you can't make a long trip like that on Blade, not anymore. Not in your condition." He remained sitting on the edge of the bed, palms braced against the mattress, regarding me over his left shoulder. His back was lean and muscular, darkly tanned and so very familiar; I knew by heart the pattern of moles along his skin, and could have traced the paths between them with my eyes closed.

"I'll ride in the wagon," I insisted, already losing ground, frustrated by my lack of choice. We'd already hashed out this line of conversation a few days ago, when it became clear that Marshall would be required to travel to Howardsville. Part of the discussion included the fact that if we were, indeed, fated to remain in this century we both had to accept certain duties and conform to certain expectations; for example, as the rational part of me understood, we could not hope to get by forever without interacting with the greater world. And this meant perhaps an occasional parting.

"Angel." The single word was infused with an entire host of tones, running the full gamut between endearment and exasperation.

I wrapped both arms around my bent knees and glared at him.

Marshall knew there was no point arguing and took the lofty ground; rather than lock horns with his pregnant wife he calmly stood, bending his arms, fists near his ears as he engaged in a quivering, all-over stretch, with an elongated, growling groan.

"You know what that does to me," I complained, instantly wet and aroused, which only further infuriated me this early morning. He was so gorgeous, pretending innocence as our gazes held; all innocence dissolved as he grinned, wide and wicked.

"Then my evil plan worked."

I rolled to my knees, unable to resist reaching for him, and he issued another low groan, this one of pure appreciation. He closed the distance between us in less than a heartbeat, scooping my heavy, tangled hair upward from my nape in one lithe hand, tilting my head to close his teeth over my earlobe. A shiver electrocuted the entire left side of my bare body.

He nipped a second time, his hands everywhere at once, lips brushing my skin as he whispered, "I didn't kiss you good morning yet, angel." And without another word he pressed my shoulder blades gently to the mattress and knelt alongside the bed, as if about to pray, spreading my thighs in one effortless motion before lowering his head.

No matter how much we rebelled against it, occasional leave-taking could not be avoided. I clung to the knowledge that Marshall, accompanied by Axton, rode a strong, capable horse accustomed to swift travel over many miles and that both men were not only cautious and careful, they were armed to the teeth, each with two pistols, a hunting knife, and a shotgun. Birdie prepared bundles of food suited for travel, they had full canteens; warm coats and wool blankets were tied in neat bundles behind their saddles; they were as well prepared as possible. I squelched the urge to beg Marshall not to ride away; a serrated chunk of ice had been growing in my gut with each second that ticked past.

"C'mere, sweetheart, it's all right," he murmured, gruff with emotion, gathering me in the shelter of his arms as we stood alongside Blade. The sun had just cleared the horizon and cast us in the rose-petal flush of a summer morning. The day promised fair skies, which heartened me; at least they wouldn't be riding in a downpour. Ax was still inside the house, chatting with Birdie and Grant, allowing us a moment of privacy for farewell.

Marshall, Marshall, Marshall. God, how I love you. I can't live without you. I can't even think about it.

I buried my face in the scent of his neck, gripping the material of his shirt with both hands. "Hurry back to me."

"I will, angel. We'll be careful." He drew apart just enough for our eyes to meet, imparting his strength and love upon me. "We'll be home by the day after next. Don't stay too long on your feet and don't lift anything heavy," he went on, cupping my belly, making small warm circles with his hand horizontal to the earth. "Take good care of our boy."

I forced my trembling lips to smile. "I will, I promise."

"Give me your sweet mouth," was his final order.

We were summarily joined by Axton, Grant, Birdie, and Celia, who held Jacob on her ample hip. The baby was bright-eyed in the morning's rosy light, his irises the deep, rich gray of his mother's. Marshall bent down to the baby and planted a kiss on Jacob's downy cheek. The baby was his great-something grandfather and while Celia and Jacob would likely never be aware of the fact, I had not forgotten for a moment.

"Take care of the womenfolk, little guy," Marshall murmured. He rose and tipped his hat at Celia, who beamed her wide, attractive smile, angling her impressive breasts in his direction in a gesture too deeply ingrained to ever overcome; she had worked for many years as a prostitute before leaving the profession altogether. I loved Celia dearly and considered her one of the noblest people I'd ever known. How amazing to be allowed the gift of looking upon the actual flesh-and-blood faces of Marshall's ancestors. My thoughts skittered, taking an unexpected detour eastward, toward Minnesota. The Davises were alive in Landon at this very moment.

Imagine seeing them in real life.

I shivered; the notion seemed to possess weight, a premonition rather than simple speculation.

Axton hugged me next and I squeezed hard in return, this man I loved as much as a brother. "Keep safe," I said in his ear. "Please, keep each other safe."

"We will, I swear, Ruthie." Ax drew away and my gut knotted at the haunted look in his green eyes, the daily strain of missing Patricia compounded by the increasing intensity of his fear for her safety.

I wanted to whisper that she was all right, that everything would be fine, but I refused to patronize. Instead I insisted, "Hurry back."

There was a final flurry of hugs and admonitions to be safe – Marshall swept me close for one last kiss – and then he and Axton mounted Blade and Ranger, respectively. I shaded my eyes against the expanding glow of the bright June sun, my heart beating too fast. Marshall's face grew stern with love, his eyes steady on mine as he angled Blade toward Howardsville, many miles east of the ranch.

Be safe.

I will, angel.

He and Ax paused to look back and wave before they were out of sight.

I watched until they rode out of view over the horizon.

After supper Celia and I walked down to the creek to visit Miles's grave, arm in arm, taking our time through the knee-high grass and abundant wildflowers blooming in riots of color as summer advanced. I eyed the mountain peaks bordering the western horizon, attempting to focus on this moment rather than allowing my thoughts to scurry across the distance separating me from Marshall. I couldn't bear to think about the coming night hours, when terrible images would swarm – stealthy figures stalking him and Axton, bullets flying from the darkness to pierce their bodies. Axton had already survived three gunshot wounds; I had assisted Birdie in stitching his first two. It had proven harrowing enough to witness Ax in pain; I refused to imagine Marshall enduring the same.

"They'll have reached Howardsville by now, I'm certain." Celia infused her voice with confidence, for my sake. "Don't you fret, little Ruth, not in your condition."

"I'm fine," I murmured, squeezing her elbow more securely to my side, I hoped conveying my sincerity.

"I know a lie when I hear one. I promised your man I'd watch out for you, so don't you go getting me in any trouble," she warned, with a subtle air of good humor. "I know enough about the Rawley temper to avoid stepping straight into it."

I couldn't quite manage a laugh, muttering, "Damn right."

"Besides, that man loves you like I never seen. He'll hurry on back here, be home before you know it."

I stretched to tiptoes and kissed her soft cheek, catching the scent of her warm skin, a lingering essence of lavender oil. Strands of hair had escaped the heavy knot at the crown of her head to drift around her flushed face.

She bestowed her soft smile. "If you're too lonely tonight, you come right on downstairs. You can bunk in with me and the baby, if you'd like."

"Thank you," I murmured. "I just might. I hate sleeping alone. I never did. My sisters and I shared a room forever. Sleeping alone feels like…I don't know…being contagious or something."

Later I would wonder, tearing my heart out, if things might have been different, had I joined them.

"It does me a good turn to see you remembering things," Celia said. "I hated to see you suffering so last summer, when you didn't know your people."

Hesitation cut a quick, inadvertent path across my forehead. I knew she sensed I was withholding information; her shrewd gray eyes missed nothing.

But if anyone understood the necessity of keeping secrets, it was Celia. Instead of further comment she gently released my arm, making her way toward the tree beneath which Miles lay buried; the creek flowed only a few yards beyond his grave. The afternoon air had grown hot and stifling, a wide, deep oven spanning the foothills. Inspired by the sight of the creek, its surface speckled with golden drops of sunlight, I sat in the tall grass, with care, to remove my shoes.

"You ain't planning to swim, are you?" Celia asked over her shoulder.

"No, just wade. I don't think the water's deep enough for swimming." Flickertail Lake loomed in my memory, clear and lovely, a hundred shades of blue. I knew my family was absent from its shores in this time period, but homesickness swelled within my chest cavity nonetheless. I cupped my lower belly, blindsided by missing the womenfolk. Tears stung the bridge of my nose and I closed my eyes.

Mom, Tish, Milla. I'm pregnant.

Do you hear me? I'm having a baby.

I want Aunt Jilly to tell me she knows he's a boy. I want Grandma to smooth my hair and call me 'little one.' I want Aunt Ellen to hug me close and make me hot chocolate and blueberry pancakes. I want to see Blythe and my brothers, and Clint and Dodge and Rich. I want the Rawleys to know Marshall is going to be a father.

I pretended to dally over my shoes until Celia knelt near the wooden cross bearing Miles's name; I didn't want her to notice my distress any more than I wished to intrude upon her weekly conversation with Miles. Half-hidden in long, scratchy grass, I knuckled my eye sockets, tears seeping. My chest bounced with quiet, aching sobs.

Oh God, Mom. I miss you. I need to feel your arms around me. It's been so long.

I want to turn around and see Clark's house instead of Grant and Birdie's.

I want to see Garth and Becky, Sean and Quinn and Wy.

I want to go home to the Jalesville I know.

Her back to me, Celia spoke to Miles in low tones, a continuous, one-sided dialogue. I knew she was telling him about their son, a ritual she observed without fail. At last I gathered my wits and swiped the last of the moisture from my cheeks; there was no point in kneeling in the dirt, crying, and I stood and headed for the creek, cautious in my bare feet. I lifted my hem, toes sinking into the gooey mud on the bank, and imagined Marshall and me bringing our son here in a few years, each of us holding one of his chubby hands as he giggled and splashed. With a secret smile, I fit a palm against the smooth roundness of my abdomen, thinking of Patricia's baby, named Cole Montgomery Spicer after his father.

Marshall Augustus, Junior, I thought, indulging in my vision of wading in the creek with Marshall and our son. *Your daddy and I already love you so. Someday you'll meet your whole family, every last one of them. You have so many cousins already, baby. So many people to love you. Mathias and Camille have Millie Jo, Brantley, Henry, Lorie, and James. Garth and Becky have Tommy, and Becky was pregnant when I left, and I bet Case and Tish are going to have a baby any time now...*

My twenty-first century family claimed the upper hand in my thoughts, seeming close enough to touch. Just beyond the limits of my perception the earth tilted and the sun shifted, its lower curve bisected by a rocky peak; brilliant orange light seared my retinas.

I recognized what was happening a second too late.

No!

My arms flew outward, palms extended. As though I exerted any control over it – I never had. And there it was all at once, backhanding me to awareness, the deep, insistent pull of time. A pull so powerful my cells buzzed, my skull rang.

No, oh God, no! Not without Marshall!

Fighting it, I scrambled for the bank and dropped to my knees, grabbing stalks of grass with both hands, holding for all I was worth.

I should have known, I should have known…

It had been this same location that Marshall and I once felt the pull of the past, the star-bright night we'd ridden Arrow to this very creek bank. And, just now, my awareness had been consumed by thoughts of our families in the future.

NO!

"Ruthie!" Celia's voice cut through the buzzing nonsense. She flew to my side, slipping in the mud in her hurry to kneel and clutch hold of my upper arms. "What in God's name? What's wrong?!"

Shaking, wet from hips to hem, I clung to the security of her warmth, her solidity, concentrating for all I was worth on her immediate presence.

"Don't let me go," I begged, numb with fear. "Don't let me go until it stops."

"I got you. Hold to me, girl, hold fast."

And I did until the pull receded, a long, undulating wave drawn back to the endless, infinite expanse of liquid called time.

Chapter Twenty-One

Montana Territory –June, 1882

CELIA DID NOT ATTEMPT TO ASK QUESTIONS ON OUR RE-
turn walk. I didn't even thank her, a mistake I regretted in the aftermath.
So many necessary things left unsaid.

The what-ifs would not assault until later that night – and every night
thereafter, a torture so excruciating I would have died to end it, if only
Axton would have let me.

What if I'd returned to 2014 in that moment?

What if I hadn't resisted the pull?

Would he have survived then?

Too shaken, I declined Birdie's invitation to join everyone at the fire
and retreated upstairs, curling up atop the blankets of my unmade bed,
listening as Grant and several of his ranch hands made music for many
long hours. A spectacularly full moon began a slow ascent; one elbow
bent beneath my right temple, I watched it rise across my narrow window in a perfect diagonal pattern.

I kept thoughts of what had happened at the creek firmly from my
mind, instead imagining Marshall and Axton in Howardsville. A new
jailhouse and marshal's quarters had been constructed since last summer,
when Aemon Turnbull and the man called Vole burned down the original structures, and I pictured Marshall and Ax safely ensconced therein,
laughing and talking over plates of biscuits and gravy from one of the
nearby saloons.

He'll be home tomorrow evening at the latest.

Hurry back to me, Marshall, I'm so scared, sweetheart.

In this era, until this evening I had not once experienced the sensation of displacement, of being literally yanked through time, and did not know what to make of today's occurrence. Marshall and I had spent many hours near the creek in this century, to no avail. Nothing. Not so much as a glimmer, a breath, a hint, of our twenty-first century lives. And I was almost too scared to tell him the truth – that the door or the current, or whatever it was, still very much existed. If we returned to the creek together and I felt the same pull but Marshall did not –

I won't chance it.

Hours ticked past. The hands on duty rode out for their night shift. Grant, Birdie, Celia, and the boys retired to bed, their muted voices drifting to my ears before quiet settled over the house. The moon vanished above the peak of the roof. I shifted from one side to the other probably a hundred times, hot and restive, utterly unable to sleep. At some point after midnight I could no longer deny the need to use the outhouse. Though there was a small porcelain bedpan tucked beneath the bed, I felt clumsy using it; maybe a brief walk through fresh air would do me some good.

I slipped through the sleeping household, tracing my fingers along the wooden banister, taking care to avoid the creaky step third from the top. I didn't normally ghost about the house at this time of night and squelched a surge of painful remembrance; a year ago Miles had been shot and killed in the front yard. Earlier that same evening, despite qualms, I'd accepted his marriage proposal. My feet stalled on the last stair and I paused there, grimly studying the empty space where we'd stood when Miles kissed me for the last time. I wrapped both arms about my waist, suddenly uneasy to venture another step.

Forgive me, dear Miles, I thought, and swore for an instant he hovered close enough to touch. My eyes darted around the dimness of the large living space, seeking his reassuring presence; the bright moon had long since set, leaving the earth swathed in darkness. Despite my better judgment, I whispered, "Is that you? Can you hear me?"

I imagined Miles appearing at the foot of the stairs and taking my hand; just as swiftly, urgency filled the air. I swore I heard his voice.

Sweet Ruthann, how I have missed you.

Shivers erupted along my limbs.

Stop it, I reprimanded with my next exhalation. *Go to the bathroom and get back to bed. You're all right. It's all right.*

I crept outside, feeling the night's immediate encroachment on my body. I knew my way and hadn't bothered to tote along a lantern, having long since grown accustomed to the absence of artificial light; no streetlamps, no batteries or flashlights or electric bulbs connected to wires and transmitters. I'd come to regard the darkness as a natural, even friendly, presence and tried to scrounge up that particular feeling as I hurried to the closest outhouse. The enormous barn loomed to my right, the bunkhouses beyond; it was just my imagination that it seemed too quiet…

Stop it. It's all right.

He moved without sound, catching me from behind just as my fingertips made contact with the rough wooden handle on the outhouse door. An inflexible palm covered my mouth, blocking any attempt to scream for help, and a body jammed up against my spine as I tried to buck the hold. He was wiry and strong, inevitable as death, and I knew a fraction of a second before he pressed his mouth to my ear to whisper, "*Ruthann.* I've missed you."

I went limp in his grasp, strangled by shock and fear; the words were almost exactly the ones I'd just imagined Miles speaking.

Another word rotated on a slow axis through my mind, repeating until it became nonsensical.

Stupid. Stupid, stupid, stupid.

Of course Fallon would reappear. He was always going to reappear. How could we have thought otherwise?

You can't stop me, he'd once told me in a nightmare. *No one can.*

He walked backward at what seemed a leisurely pace, in this way keeping our gazes directed toward the main house where the Rawleys slept; he spoke into my left ear, narrating in a low, mocking whisper as together we made a slow, deliberate retreat.

"I've been waiting for you to come outside. I knew you would. It's been quite a year, hasn't it, *dearest* Ruthann? I meant to kill you the very moment I next laid eyes upon you, as you may know. You broke my forearm, after all, but something occurred to me while I was away. You see, death brings a certain measure of peace. No more chance for suffering once you're dead, at least to my knowledge." His sigh ruffled my loose hair. "I once told Boyd Carter the same thing." He lowered his left hand – the one not locked over my mouth – and cupped my right breast.

A growl of vicious loathing rose from my throat and he increased the pressure to a painful level. I bit back all sound.

"Good girl. Fate is with me, as you will soon be unable to deny. I realized something quite profound yesterday. You see, Dredd did something useful for the first time in his miserable life. He took *action*. Just as I am now taking *action*."

I had recognized Fallon's ruthless arrogance the last time I'd been in his company, on a train bound for Chicago, but he hadn't sounded insane that evening. Tonight he did, blatantly so. There was an agitated, unhinged quality to his voice not present during our previous interaction. My thoughts spun, fixating on one-syllable words in the extremity of my fear.

Bad.

This is badbadbadbadbad.

Help me.

Oh God, helpmehelpmehelpmehelpme.

"You and Dredd's whore wife thought you could escape with her bastard, didn't you?" He issued a clucking noise of reprimand and the ice chunks in my gut multiplied. "She didn't escape and neither will you. But I am not going to kill you quite yet. There's something I'd like you to watch, first. They should be ready any second. I told them to give me five minutes…"

He halted. We were over fifty paces from the main house but close enough for a clear view as flames leaped to existence around the entire structure. My eyes bulged, unable to process the sight. I screamed behind his palm, struggling and thrashing, with fewer odds of escape than a rabbit in the jaws of a steel trap.

"Gasoline would be preferable, of course, but that won't be in widespread use until 1913. Fortunately, alcohol burns almost as well. The structure is wooden, a further advantage, as is the dry air. They'll be engulfed in less than two minutes by my best estimation."

He released my mouth and wailing cries tore free.

Celia – Jacob – Birdie – Grant –

Every one of Marshall's ancestors in Montana lay sleeping inside that house.

Every last Rawley in Montana.

Fallon let me scream, keeping me tightly restrained, my arms pinned; he knew I was no threat to his plans at this point. No one could hear me from this distance. I watched black stick figures swarm the house, men on foot and horseback – Grant's ranch hands trying to tame an inferno already blazing beyond control. Drained, destroyed, I finally fell silent and Fallon's hold on my torso relaxed ever so slightly. The second he did I jutted my head backward in the vain hope I would connect with his face. He grunted, stumbling sideways, and flung me to the ground; I had underestimated his strength once again.

"You're a fighter," he whispered, pinning me supine with one knee on my chest; his head and shoulders created a silhouette darker than the night sky. Stars turned cartwheels at the edges of my vision. "And probably a hell of a fuck. I don't have time just now but I'll teach you a thing or two when we meet again." He bent and licked my cheek, his breath rough and elevated; he was excited by all of this. "We'll meet again, I promise you."

And then he struck my temple with a small, blunt object.

Axton found me in the gray light of dawn. It was almost surreal, regaining painful consciousness to the sight of his face just as I had a year earlier, when I'd first arrived in the nineteenth century; only this time I wasn't numbed by the anesthesia of amnesia and disbelief. I blinked at the bits of char and ash drifting and twirling in the air around his head. There was a beat of deep silence between us, a speck of eternity during which our gazes held fast.

I saw his eyes and I knew.

"*Ax...*" I moaned.

I knew.

He bent and collected me to his chest, which heaved with deep, choking sobs. I clamped my teeth around the material of his canvas jacket; I wanted to cover my ears, to block out everything he would proceed to tell me in the next minute. I wanted to scream at him to shut the fuck up; I wanted to run out into the foothills and never return. Axton rocked us side to side, gripping the back of my head the way he would an infant's fragile skull.

"Ruthie, oh Jesus Christ, Marshall disappeared." Choking over the words, wishing he did not have to speak them. "He just up and disappeared and there was nothing I could do..."

Shut up, shut up, shut the fuck up...

Later, I would not remember the brief span of time during which I knelt with Axton in the tall grass, the charred shell of the Rawleys' house visible in the distance, smoke drifting in lazy blue-gray curls from the ruins. I would not remember struggling to my feet and running headlong for the creek, sobbing as I fell to my knees, begging time to sweep me away. I would not remember my vicious struggle to remain there in the cold water when Axton tried to haul me out, I would not recall his words or mine – I only knew later because I made Ax tell me everything.

Marshall disappeared because Jacob died in the fire, the baby I came to the past to save.

Jacob is gone.

The Rawleys are gone.

My baby is gone.

OhGodohGodohGodohGod...

I wished I was able to forget the journey on horseback to Howardsville and the subsequent endless train ride, with its multiple connections, to St. Paul, Minnesota. Hollow and iced-over, my insides echoing with despair, I was aware of little but clinging to Axton, the only security left to me in this world. I slept most of the way as the train cars rolled east. When he whispered, "We're here," I refused to open my eyes and behold the depot of the St. Paul railroad station, where Malcolm Carter awaited our arrival. Midmorning sunshine glared on my eyelids and I hated its brilliant light; I wanted to scream the sun out of the sky, to watch it plummet toward the horizon in a fiery plume of destruction.

"C'mon, Ruthie, we can't stay here." Axton spoke gently and I marveled at the depth of courage he had shown, the resolve and determination, the refusal to bow beneath the weight of despair.

By contrast I was a coward of immense proportions, unable to tell him Patricia was lost for good. Axton would never get close enough to find her; Dredd Yancy had found her first. Dredd had killed his own father, Thomas Yancy, the same day that Fallon had ordered the Rawleys' homestead burned, and had blamed Cole for the murder. Cole was now in jail in Iowa City, awaiting trial. Malcolm had witnessed the entire spectacle as it played out on the prairie; a man named Blythe Tilson had also been killed in the ambush. Only hours before Marshall disappeared for good, he and Axton had received the telegram Malcolm sent to Howardsville, instructing them to pass the word of Cole's arrest on to the Spicers.

Blythe Tilson.

The familiar name rotated around the inside of my head. He couldn't possibly be the Blythe Tilson wed to my mother in the twenty-first century. An ancestor, then? A connection forged between my family and the Tilsons long before 2003?

Dredd killed Blythe's ancestor.

Dredd killed Thomas Yancy, his own father.

And he took Patricia and the baby.

Patricia, my sweet, dear friend.

I couldn't bear to imagine in what condition she and Monty currently existed. I tried to find comfort in the fact that Dredd had shown us compassion last year, when Patricia and I lived in the Yancy estate.

We should never have parted ways. You could never know how sorry I am, Patricia…

Axton supported me down the clanging metal steps and through a noisy, bustling crowd. I squinted at the brightness, overwhelmed, tucked to Axton's warm side. He kissed the top of my head and murmured, "Come on, we gotta find Malcolm."

I moved obediently along with Ax, flinching when I heard someone call, "Axton! Ruthann!" I spied Malcolm Carter standing in bright sun on a dusty boardwalk flanking the depot, waving his arms in wide arcs, hat in his left hand. He hollered, "Over here!"

It took only seconds to observe that others waited with Malcolm, two women and three men, and the urge to shy away, to retreat and avoid all contact, swept over me. But then one of the women stepped forward to meet us and my heart – dead in my chest cavity these hundreds of miles – issued a small, unexpected thump. She hurried to us, letting her bonnet tumble down her back, and a whimper choked my throat as she appropriated me from Axton's arms.

"My dear, dear girl," she whispered, stroking my loose hair. "I am Lorie Davis."

"Axton Douglas," Ax was saying to those who crowded near but I saw none of them, holding fast to the woman who so closely resembled my mother. Introductions flew and danced in the air above my head.

Sawyer and Lorie Davis, Boyd and Rebecca Carter, Edward Tilson.

"You two look like you just seen a ghost," Malcolm was saying as Lorie released her embrace, taking care to keep me close. I huddled against her side, seeing for the first time the others standing with Malcolm. Simply because of the obvious surprise on their faces, I focused on two of the men – one of whom wore a patch over his left eye – each studying Axton with unblinking gazes. With almost comical unison the men looked at one another, wearing identical expressions of stun, before returning their amazement to Axton.

"Boyd, honey, you've confused this young man in addition to the rest of us," commented a lovely woman with a glossy topknot of dark hair, nudging his ribs with her elbow.

"I apologize, young fella, it's just that I can't quite believe my eyes," said the man named Boyd, whose strong resemblance to Malcolm suggested an older brother. "You are the goddamn *spittin' image* of –"

"My brother, Ethan." The man named Sawyer completed the sentence in a hoarse whisper, peering at Axton with a feature I suddenly realized I knew. Despite one being hidden beneath a patch, I knew his eyes; I staggered slowly to awareness.

The Davis family eyes. This man is my ancestor.

"I know this ain't seemly and for that I do apologize," Boyd Carter continued. "But what was your father's name, young Douglas?"

Axton stammered, "My pa was killed before I was born. His name was Aaron Douglas."

"You were born in Cumberland County?" Sawyer leaned closer, forehead knitted. Tall, wide-shouldered, solid with muscle and missing an eye, he was altogether imposing, focused intently on Axton. "Near the town of Suttonville, is that correct?"

"And your pa died in the War Between the States?" Boyd persisted.

"Was your mama named Mary?" Sawyer asked.

"Boys!" commanded the oldest of the bunch, a man with silver, shoulder-length hair and skin like wrinkled leather. "Cough up what you-all mean before we bust apart with curiosity!"

Axton held his hat to his chest. Perplexed but too polite to deny information, he addressed Sawyer as he confirmed, "Yessir, my mama's name was Mary."

Sawyer gripped the lower half of his face and his throat bobbed as he swallowed hard.

Boyd clapped a hand around Axton's bicep. "I'll explain for my oldest friend, as he is overcome just now. Long ago I had me some tact, but I've lived too long and seen too much to beat around the bush." He paused, sympathetic dark eyes fixed on Axton. "Young man, I do believe your real daddy was Sawyer's brother, Ethan. I know it's a goddamn shock but I promise to tell the whole story first chance we get."

In the morning another train would take us as far north as a city called Fairfield. From there it seemed we would complete the last five miles of the journey to Landon by wagon; in the meantime we were booked for the night at a hotel near the train station. Axton relinquished me to Lorie and Rebecca with promises to return to say good-bye before he collected Ranger from the stock cars, resupplied for the journey south, and subsequently rode out; Malcolm intended to accompany him to Iowa, in order to do whatever they could to help Cole.

Ax held me close and hard for a long moment in the steep shadow of the sharply-pitched depot roof. The strength of his need to continue moving radiated like lightning from his lean, tense body; remaining stationary when Patricia was in danger gouged deeply into his already-wounded heart.

"Be careful," I begged, burying my face against his sweat-stained shirt, gulping with restrained sobs. "Please, Ax."

"I'll keep in touch as best I can, I swear to you, Ruthie. I got you here but now I have to go." He drew away, lifting my chin so I could no longer hide my eyes. "They will care for you. These are good and decent people. I would never leave you here if I thought otherwise."

"I pray you'll find Patricia," I whispered. He never would; he had no chance. I knew I would never see Axton Douglas again after today and my only comfort was the notion that soon I would be dead. Lorie said we would reach Landon by tomorrow evening; once there, I intended to slip away and take a midnight swim in Flickertail Lake. What I did not intend was to come out alive. The promise of drowning was all that kept the pain at bay moment to moment. I knew Marshall and our unborn son would be waiting for me on the other side.

"I'll find her," Axton vowed, looking south. He didn't have to say, *Or I'll die trying.*

"Your middle name is Ethan," I whispered; the fact had just occurred to me. "Like the man they believe is your real father."

Axton returned his gaze to mine, slowly shaking his head as a meditative expression replaced a fraction of his stress. "Ain't that something else? Boyd promised to tell me the whole story when we get supplies." A hint of a smile graced his mouth. "It would mean I still have kin, Ruthie, imagine that. I never would have guessed such in a hundred years."

"Remember that day I washed your hair for you? Branch said neither of your parents was redheaded, remember? Maybe your mother named you for your real father, after all." Inundated by tenderness and love I stretched on tiptoe to kiss his cheek, gripping his head with both hands, my palms bracketing his ears. "I don't care who your parents were, I love them for making you. You are more special to me than you could know, Axton Douglas. I love you." Tears jammed my nose and throat, gliding in hot trickles down my cheeks; I was glad he could not read my mind, and was therefore unaware of my intent to die. "Never forget me, okay? Promise me."

Tears swept his cheeks. Unashamed, he let them fall. "I love you too, Ruthie. And you won't have time to forget me. I'll be back with Patricia before you know it."

I nodded, pretending I believed him.

The noon hour came and went, and along with it Axton and Malcolm. The St. Paul streets were noisy, crowded with wagons, buggies, horses, mules, and foot traffic; I watched them until I could see nothing of Axton but his hat, before that too was gobbled from view. We had gathered on the hotel steps to bid them farewell and I meant to retain my composure, failing utterly as Axton disappeared from my life; the universe had already swallowed whole my reason for living. Vision blurring, I would have gone to my knees if not for Lorie's quick movement, catching me around the waist. Despite her delicate build her arms were strong, holding me secure.

"It seems Malcolm is always riding away from us," she said softly. "I hate it so."

I locked my knees, praying I could stave off the shaking until I was alone. I found a measure of comfort in Lorie's presence, touched that she would confide in me.

She drew a fortifying breath, patting me twice as she gently ordered, "Come, Ruthann, I promised Axton I would see to it that you ate a proper dinner."

Chapter Twenty-Two

Landon, MN - March, 2014

THE FIRST NIGHT, TISH WOULD ONLY ALLOW CLINT AND
me near her. We lay on either side, bracketing her body, holding fast,
but our strength was not enough to overpower the shaking. I spoke not
a word, nor did Clint after his first attempt to offer comfort. Mom and
Aunt Jilly stayed near in case we called for something. Tish's friend,
Robbie Benson, had flown home with her from Chicago and was stationed in the living room; I heard the quiet murmur of his deeper male
voice conversing with the womenfolk when Tish wasn't weeping or
vomiting. There was nothing to say to change what had happened; I
refused to pacify her with promises that everything would be all right.

Nothing was all right.

Case had died in my sister's arms.

Force had been required to remove her from the crime scene in
Chicago; she wouldn't let the police take his body away.

I only allowed my thoughts to stray a few minutes ahead at a time; to
consider any farther into the future of our current reality was too terrifying. I had to believe, now more than ever, that we could change things.

"Thank you for being here," Tish whispered near dawn, startling me
from a light, troubled doze.

"I'm not going anywhere." I brushed hair from her wet, tear-sticky
face, relieved to hear her voice. She lay facing me with knees bent to
her chest and hadn't spoken since yesterday evening. Flat on his back on
her far side, Clint rumbled with snores. A grayish tint lent the bedroom

an eerie, otherworldly feeling; Tish's features seemed shaded by pencil strokes. I drew the quilt higher over her shoulders.

"Is Robbie still here?" she croaked.

"He's sleeping downstairs. Dad called twice last night but I didn't talk to him."

"*Camille*," she moaned and I curved around her at once, bracing for another onslaught of anguish. Her words were self-inflicted punishment. "I thought nothing could be worse than seeing Case with Lynnette… but this…*this…oh God…*"

Clint released a loud, grunting snore and rolled toward us without waking up, slinging an arm and inadvertently striking my cheekbone.

"Ow!"

"Sorry," he mumbled.

Tish shoved aside the blankets and tumbled over me, falling to the carpet. She rose and dashed for the bathroom while I braced on one elbow and slogged a hand through my tangled hair.

"Shit," muttered Clint, both forearms crossed over his eyes as we listened to Tish throw up for probably the tenth time since midnight.

Resolve – or desperate foolishness – propelled me to my feet. "I can't take this anymore. It's time to fucking fix this."

"Ruthie needs to know everything we know." Aunt Jilly curled her fingers around mine as she spoke; seven of us crowded around table three. "We have to find a way to reach her."

The more we talked about Ruthann, the more Mom and Aunt Jilly remembered her; as with Mathias's sister, Tina, there was ample evidence to suggest the real timeline existed just beyond reach, *there* and very much alive, but shrouded as though behind heavy cloud cover. Determination burned anew in my veins; I would tap into the sunshine that would pierce and annihilate those clouds. I would accomplish this if it was the last thing I ever did. Shore Leave smelled of perking coffee; we were closed to customers but the interior lights created a warm glow to counteract the sobbing, steel-gray sky. It seemed only natural to gather here in times of stress, as we'd always done.

"But if Fallon already killed the Rawleys and Blythe's ancestor in the nineteenth century, if those things already happened *then*, how could Ruthie hope to change anything?" Possibilities swam in endless circles around my head; one problem seemed barely solved when another five rose to take its place. Frustration struggled to gain the upper hand.

"What if we could get a message to her *before* those things happened?" Aunt Jilly sat with both hands wrapped around her coffee mug to keep from wringing them, I knew. "We have a tentative idea, after all. We could warn her."

"If we could reach her before 1882, you mean," Mom said.

"We're assuming more time has passed there than here," I explained to Robbie, who sat to Clint's right, an untouched cup of coffee on the tabletop before him. Robbie wore an old Shore Leave sweatshirt Mom had lent him and a serious, troubled expression. "Derrick Yancy told Tish that time moves differently in the past, faster somehow."

"You're referring to Derrick from the correct timeline, right?" Robbie asked the question with an air of deferential politeness I sensed was somewhat foreign to him.

"Yes."

"What if..." Robbie pursed his lips, frowning at the ceiling as he considered. "What if your sister could return here? Like this very minute, I mean. She can travel through time, right? What's the possibility that she could *then* travel backward far enough to prevent the deviation from the original timeline?"

It was an angle I hadn't yet considered. "You know, that's close to what we were talking about at the Rawleys' before everything changed. Bringing Marshall and Ruthann back by force, so to speak."

Mom shook her head. "How could I let Ruthie go if she showed up here?"

Before anyone could respond, Clint's face registered sudden concern; he sat facing the windows and I looked over my shoulder to see Tish shuffling across the porch. She wore a tattered bathrobe over jeans and a sweatshirt, her hair hanging in tangled loops; she made no attempt to shield her head from the downpour, as though sleepwalking.

Mom leaped from her chair, overturning it, and raced outside. She hurried Tish inside and wrapped her in a coat from the rack near the door,

"You should be resting," Mom admonished, helping her to a chair.

The skin around Tish's eyes appeared painfully fragile, bruised beyond repair. She made an X of her forearms atop the table and rested her head on her wrists.

"Let her stay," Aunt Jilly said softly.

"Are you warm enough?" Mom hovered near her chair. "Oh, sweetheart, I'm so sorry…"

"Don't call me that," Tish begged, barely audible. "Please, don't call me that…"

I knew 'sweetheart' was Case's favorite endearment for her.

Robbie leaned forward, pinning Mom with an earnest expression. "Not all that long ago Fallon Yancy had me killed. Tish attended my *funeral*. Even though I don't remember any life but this one, I trust what your daughter has told me in the past week. I feel like I've been given a second chance here, to reverse what happened. I'm willing to risk my life to get back to the real timeline, that's how goddamn serious I am."

I took up the gauntlet, intuiting what he meant. "Robbie's right, Mom. Ruthie would be willing to do whatever was required, just like any of us. Whatever events changed things now, in the twenty-first century, happened *to* Ruthie in the nineteenth. Fallon said she 'remembered' and that he hoped Tish would, too. If I could, I would go back. I wouldn't think twice." Tears wet my eyes but I blinked them away, too impatient to cry.

"Camille, tell us what you talked about with the Rawleys," Aunt Jilly requested. "How did you plan to bring Marshall and Ruthann back?"

"One of the places where the past seemed strongest was the foundation of the Rawleys' original homestead. Ruthie and Marsh both felt the pull of time there. Marshall called it a 'force field.' We intended to gather there, all of us, and *will* them back. There was no reason to assume it would work, we just hoped. We decided this the Saturday we were last in

Jalesville. Clark said there would be a full moon the next night, Sunday, and we'd try then."

"But then everything disappeared." Tish did not lift her face. Flat and monotone, her voice was all but lifeless. "Gone, just like that."

Clint suddenly indicated the parking lot. "Whose car?"

The rain blurred all outlines and it wasn't possible to discern who climbed from behind the wheel under the protection of a black umbrella; at first I thought the man emerging into the rain was my father, but Robbie said, "Shit. I don't believe it."

"Who is it?" I demanded.

All of us except Tish rose to confront him; somewhere in a shadowy corner of my mind lingered the memory of the day another stranger entered the cafe, a man named Zack Dixon. But Zack was not part of this timeline; Aunt Jilly had not been attacked that summer, back in 2006.

Robbie said, "It's Derrick Yancy."

Tish lifted her head, leaning on the table for support.

I opened the screen door as Derrick climbed the porch steps, noting his obvious discomfort at finding himself the focal point of everyone's attention. He closed and shook off his umbrella before entering, gaze leaping straight to Tish.

"I am so sorry, Tish," he said with quiet sincerity, and whatever negative opinions I'd harbored about this man were at once dashed.

Her voice was as jagged as broken glass. "Case is *gone*..."

Ignoring everyone else for the time being Derrick strode to her side, wet shoes squeaking across the floor, and knelt. "I couldn't get away until now. No one knows I'm here. I didn't even chance an airline ticket. I drove straight through. Fallon has not reappeared since Saturday night. Father refuses to believe Fallon was responsible for anything. He thinks you were mugged, for Christ's sake." Derrick cupped Tish's upper arm and squeezed. "I know otherwise. Fallon has lost all touch with reality. He has to be stopped. And...I may know how."

Two hours later no one was hungry even though it was well past the dinner hour. Icy rain continued to fall, drumming on the roof; the wide front windows resembled distraught, weeping eyes. The conversation had deteriorated from its earlier animated progress; everyone was talking and no one was listening. I slipped outside for a moment to collect my thoughts, keeping under the eaves to avoid the drizzle as I paced. The wind had died. Flickertail no longer roiled with whitecaps, its silver surface pockmarked now by less-violent droplets. I paused at the far end of the porch, stalling, trying to process what Derrick had revealed.

So the Yancys' ability to jump through time is not exclusive to Fallon.

But Derrick is too scared to try.

The back of Derrick's head was visible from my vantage point as I peered through the front windows, hidden in the shadows of the eaves. He sat facing Tish, elbows widespread on the table; I couldn't discern their words through the glass, only muted sounds. At age thirteen, Derrick woke one morning in a bed not his own. More bewildered than afraid, he wandered long hallways and peered into opulent rooms, at last coming across a newspaper abandoned on a desk. The date on the paper, a *Chicago Tribune*, was Sunday, April 10, 1910. As if touching the newsprint triggered a mechanism operated by someone out of sight, he was abruptly whisked back to his own bedroom in 1998.

"I've done everything in my power to forget that day," were his exact words. "I knew enough about Fallon by then to realize he would kill me if I told him what had happened. He would have viewed my ability as a threat. I was terrified to sleep for months after that but it never happened again. To this day, I don't know if I caused the jump to occur or if it was simply a fluke. I've never tried again."

The jump.

"You have to try now." Tish was gritty dead-serious, her bruised eyes fixed on his with the intensity of a cornered animal.

"I have no control over it. What if I can't get back again? It's not like there's a guarantee for return."

And so on.

I felt utterly disconnected, free-floating, all strings clipped as I peered through the front windows of my family's longtime business. If returning to our real lives proved impossible, nothing else mattered – not even Derrick's ability. So what if everyone believed this timeline was a horrible deviation from what was meant to be? Justin couldn't very well leave Aubrey and start having babies with Jilly; Tish couldn't bring Case back any more than Blythe and their sons could be restored to Mom, or Mathias and our children to me. Grandma and Aunt Ellen were gone. Ruthann and Marshall might as well have been stranded on distant planets. I turned away from the window, grinding my teeth, and descended the porch steps, lifting my face to the damp black sky.

The name on my lips was one I'd called upon many times in past years, connected to the man whose photograph once led me to Mathias. Whether he knew it or not, Malcolm Carter had sustained me for a long time. Clasping my hands as though praying – and, in a way, I truly was praying, hoping that somehow he would hear me through the barriers of time – I brought my intertwined fingers to my lips. "*Malcolm.* I know you're out there. I can *feel* you out there. I always have. I believe that my sister Ruthann is with you and I need you both to hear me. I need you to know what's happening to us here. Please, oh please, Malcolm, *hear me…*"

Nothing but the deep, repetitive pulse of falling rain met my ears. I inhaled a slow breath, concentrating for all I was worth. I pictured Malcolm's face on the black and white photograph, the only tangible image of him I possessed, filling in the colors of his hair and eyes and skin, the mellow sunset sky behind him. I imagined the scent of him and the way his shoulders would feel beneath my hands. I remembered how often I'd kissed the two-dimensional image of his face; the face of a man I had loved through all time. And then I tried again.

"I know you're out there, Malcolm. I forgive you, do you hear me? I know you never found Cora. Me, I mean, because I used to *be* Cora. Mathias and I brought her home to Minnesota almost eight years ago and buried her near the cabin where you meant to live after you were married. She's safe now. I'm so sorry you couldn't be together in your lives. It scares me so much because I'm afraid it means…" I gulped, clenching my jaw. "I'm afraid it means fate wants us to be kept apart in this life, too. And I can't bear it."

Headlights swept over my closed eyes; I opened them in time to see an unfamiliar truck park beside Derrick Yancy's car. I heard the driver's side door open, then close, before a man rounded the hood.

It was Mathias.

Joy burst through my blood, stronger than reason, stronger than instinct.

Malcolm sent him here…

But joy could only override sense for so long. Truth stared me down, an uncompromising force I could not deny. In this life Mathias was not mine. He was married; far worse, I knew he was a father to two children. I stood with both hands clasped at my chin, watching him approach Shore Leave. When he caught sight of me, immobile in the rainy darkness, he halted.

The next thing I knew I was in his arms.

"Camille." He spoke against my hair, holding me so tightly I couldn't draw a full breath. "I had to find you, I had to see you…"

Trembling and overwhelmed, I clung to him, pressing my lips to his neck, inhaling his scent the way I would inhale air after being trapped underwater. I knew I should shut my stupid mouth but I didn't have the strength. "*You're here*. I've missed you so much, Thias, oh God, I've missed you every second we've been apart…"

He dug his hands in my wet hair, rocking us side to side, his jaw against my temple. "I've dreamed about you every night since you left my parents' attic. I'm not crazy, I swear to you, but I know I belong with you. We belong *together*. I've never known anything more right. It's like I've been living in a dream world and I just woke up to the real one." He drew back, clasping my face, thumbs tracing my lips. His voice was low and tortured, rasping over the words. "How is this possible?"

Hot tears seeped over my face, mixing with the cold rain. I knew what I had to do and I wasn't sure I possessed enough will; I had to let him go. This version of Mathias was not mine and we could not remain in this horrible timeline in which we'd never met until now. It was my worst nightmare realized; every terrible what-if I'd ever asked, every moment

I'd taken for granted. Every path that had led us to one another uprooted in this place, overturned and upended. Destroyed beyond repair.

"How?" he whispered a second time, agonized and intense. "Tell me everything. Please, trust me with this. Tell me what you told Tina."

"I won't do that to you." My voice shook. "You're a husband, *a father*. I know you would never do anything to hurt your children...or their mother."

I felt his muscles tense and knew I'd struck a nerve. At last he said, "You don't know her." Gruff now, with strain. "We're not happy."

"But she's still your wife."

"Not in my memories. I only see you. I see *us*."

"But it's not us in this life. This life was never meant to be!" My control was crumbling and I broke away, heading for the dock.

"I don't understand!" He followed right behind me, not about to let this go.

"Dammit, Mathias, you need to leave. I love you too much to do this to you!" I increased my pace, unable to bear looking at him.

"I *knew* it! I knew I wasn't wrong." He caught my elbow, halting my forward motion, and spun me around to face him in the wet darkness.

"Let go!" I cried, battling the image of Case dying in Tish's arms.

"Not a chance. I love you too, don't you hear me? I'm *in love* with you."

"Don't do this to me..." Crying now, I tried again to yank from his firm grasp.

"Who is Malcolm?" he demanded. "What does he mean to you?"

"He's you!" I screamed, hands in fists at my sides. "You are *him*! Our souls have been connected through a hundred different lives and I have loved you in *every last one!*"

There was a sudden, tremendous commotion in the lake.

Chapter Twenty-Three

Landon, MN - July, 1882

WE REACHED LANDON THE DAY AFTER AXTON AND I HAD arrived in St. Paul.

"We're home, dear one, come and see." Lorie peered over her shoulder from the wagon seat as she offered this invitation. Her green-checked bonnet trailed down her back and her smile pierced my side all over again; it was my mother's beautiful smile, warm and effortless, rife with love. Late-afternoon sun slanted against the west side of the wagon, creating a bright, oblong patch on the canvas. I lay in a restless doze, my body jostling to the rhythm of the grinding wheels, but climbed to the front of the wagon at her kind request.

I squinted as sunlight bathed my cold face, just in time to spy a wooden, hand-painted sign reading *Welcome to Landon*. Flowering vines bursting with blossoms climbed the sign, not to mention every fencepost in sight.

Oh –

My lips dropped open as the wagon, driven by Sawyer, rolled and creaked over Fisherman's Street in my hometown. It was the nineteenth-century version of Fisherman's Street, a narrow dirt track instead of smooth pavement bordered by concrete sidewalks, but I would have known it anywhere. The pine trees that guarded the south end of the road were only saplings but Flickertail glimmered wide and blue just a few hundred yards north, totally unchanged. My eyes darted left and right, conjuring up the buildings I remembered which had not yet been constructed – Anglers Inn, Eddie's Bar, the post office, the hardware store…there was the exact spot where my family sat to watch the annual Fourth of July parade.

The only manmade structures in sight were wood-framed buildings housing a livery stable and a blacksmith shop, these to the left, while a general store with a square false front stood to the right. The general store was called Sorenson's Dry Goods. The afternoon air shone hot and bright, sun spangling the dust stirred up by our passage along the street; two men sat on a wooden bench beneath an awning stretching from the storefront and there was an exchange of greetings. Horses were tethered to hitching rails along the street.

"Our homestead is around the lake, but minutes away," Lorie explained.

I could only nod in response, too overcome as the wagon approached Flicker Trail, the path that forked at the beach and curved east and west around the lake. It seemed impossible that Shore Leave would not appear within the next mile on the eastern bank; I couldn't fathom its nonexistence. Surely Mom and Grandma would be standing on the porch to welcome me home. The lake lapped a reedy shore inhabited by high-stepping white herons; rather than the wide, sandy expanse I remembered, the beach was a shallow strip of small granite stones. Boats dotted the blue surface, tranquil beneath the July sun. I'd never heard such a variety of birdsong in all my life.

How incredible that I'm seeing this.

Flickertail Lake, glimmering like cerulean satin, upon whose banks I had sunbathed for countless summer hours, in whose water I had splashed and dove, floated and tubed and skinny-dipped with my sisters and our friends.

Full circle, I thought, agony replaced by a sudden, unnatural calm.

It seemed right that I would die in this lake.

Soon I'll be with Marshall and our baby.

At the fork we parted ways with Boyd, Rebecca, and Edward, whose homestead, White Oaks, lay to the west, the very same acreage upon which Mathias's family would one day build their family business, where my sister and Mathias lived with their children in the homesteader's cabin. I could picture it all so perfectly, my family in the twenty-first century. The womenfolk had remained at the forefront of my thoughts as we traveled north from St. Paul but I supposed that only made sense; their faces and voices were vividly alive in my memory because I would never see them again, at least not in life.

Please, let them be safe in their twenty-first century lives.

Let them be happy.

At all costs I shut out the sharp, intrusive voice that pleaded with me to listen, that warned I was making a terrible mistake.

Don't do this, Ruthann.

The Rawleys are gone. You know what that means.

Fallon is still out there, he's still a threat.

Not to me, not after tonight.

Exhaustion weighted my limbs; I had slept as though drugged in the hotel room last night, grateful that no one other than Axton knew I had lost my pregnancy. We'd told everyone that I was widowed; they were all well acquainted with the Rawley family in Iowa and believed Marshall had been a cousin to Miles, as close to the truth as I dared venture. The conversation at yesterday's dinner in the hotel dining room had swayed between sorrow over Edward Tilson's lost son and anger over the Yancy family causing yet more destruction in their lives. I recalled listening to Cole and Miles speak of the Yancys in Howardsville, the very night Patricia and I first met. It seemed more than a hundred years had passed since then.

A dizzying sense of disorientation settled over me yesterday as everyone crowded in a haphazard fashion around a large table in the dining room; exactly like the two families I had loved best in my old life, my own and the Rawleys, these people spoke and interacted with the ease of longtime companionship and abiding love. They *were* my family, to a certain extent, my Davis ancestors, flush with life and vitality and color. It was surreal to catch fleeting glimpses of Mom or Aunt Jilly in Lorie's expressions, to watch the animation in Sawyer's remaining eye as he spoke; golden-hazel, with a darker ring surrounding the iris, the exact same eyes I beheld when I looked in a mirror.

If Axton is Sawyer's nephew, like they believe, then Ax and I are related after all.

I thought of the words he'd spoken at the depot.

It would mean I still have kin, Ruthie, imagine that.

"Who in the goddamn hell would believe what we had to say in defense of Spicer? Compared to the Yancys, we're nobodies. Poor farmers from a remote corner of Minnesota. And former Rebs, to boot! I told Malcolm there wasn't a thing he could do for Spicer but he's stubborn as hell, always has been. He won't let a friend down and I admire him for it, I do." Boyd's energy seemed almost visible in the air around him, unable to be contained. I figured him to be in his middle thirties, roughly ten years older than Malcolm, a huge man bristling with muscle and black curly hair. A thick mustache obscured his upper lip and he was tanner than saddle leather; it was his eyes that reminded me most of Malcolm, pecan-brown and deep with feeling.

"It destroys me to know my boy was only a few hundred miles from me when he was kilt," Edward Tilson said. "He was the last of my boys. If I wasn't so damn old and frail, I'd have ridden south with Malcolm and young Axton."

The last of my boys...

Lorie and Rebecca sat to either side of the elderly physician; Edward was Rebecca's uncle and lived in her and Boyd's home. Lorie leaned her head on his arm, tears in her eyes; he bent his elbow to rest a hand on her cheek.

"I am goddamn sorry, Edward," Boyd reached across the tabletop to grip the older man's hand. "Goddamn sorry."

"As we all are." Sawyer spoke quietly, wide shoulders lifting with a deep sigh.

"We shall bury Blythe in the apple grove," Rebecca decided. "So that we might visit him often. Lorie and the girls and I shall plant flowers near his stone, what say you, Uncle Edward?"

"I'll help you, love, and I thank you," he said, eyes crinkling in a web of wrinkles as he managed a smile.

"To think Thomas Yancy is dead at last, after all these years." Sawyer stared into the middle distance as he spoke. "And killed by his own son's hand. I recall Dredd. I would never have figured him for such an action. Fallon, for certain, but not Dredd."

"Fallon is more dangerous than you could know." My voice rasped over the words. All attention swung my direction.

"We know, believe me," Boyd said. "I've had that bastard in my gunsights. I've regretted not killing him many a time." His observant eyes missed nothing; his voice softened as he said, "He's the one burned up the Rawleys' homestead, ain't he?"

Lorie saw in my eyes that I could not handle speaking of it; without drama, she rose from her chair and skirted the table.

"You have traveled far and endured much. Never mind eating just now," she murmured, leading me up a flight of steps to the hotel room where I had earlier bathed and changed clothes. This time, however, she remained behind. "I'll sit with you a spell, dear one, if you've a mind to let me."

I curled around my belly on the narrow, squeaky bed and panic assaulted, hard and merciless. I suddenly couldn't remember what Marshall had been wearing when I saw him last – for a few horrible seconds I could not even conjure up his face. I sobbed, "He's gone, he's gone, oh God, *he's gone*…this time he won't be back and *I can't bear it*…"

Lorie lay beside me and wrapped an arm over my ribs; she did not try to offer words of comfort as I wept, my body wracked by tremors, but she did not release her hold. At long last my breathing slowed, my blood calmed; the sun had shifted, tinting the white curtains the color of weak tea. She smoothed hair from my wet face and I pretended that she was Mom, somehow here to take care of me, her youngest; her lost daughter. It had been so long since I'd seen my mother. Lorie even smelled like her, just faintly of peaches.

"Stay," I begged, even though she had not moved.

"Of course I will," she whispered, and when I woke the next morning she was still holding me.

At least half a dozen people met the wagon as it rolled up to a massive wooden barn and a smaller, wood-framed house. I stared with wonder, despite everything, at the structures in the same clearing where my family's cafe would one day exist. The shoreline was unchanged, though the barn and house had been constructed much further from the lake than Shore Leave would one day perch to face Flickertail with both porches. I let my gaze trace the imaginary path of the steps leading from the cafe to the water and then out over the dock, steps I had raced down a hundred thousand times to jump into the lake. No dock at the moment, only a floating, raft-like platform anchored about ten feet from shore.

Childish voices, high with excitement, rang through the air. Sawyer jumped down from the wagon seat and was mobbed by his children. He picked up a small boy and tossed him in the air, grinning widely. Upon catching his son, he tipped the boy forward and planted a kiss on his cheek.

"Daddy, who's here?"

"Hi, Mama!"

"Daddy, can I ride into the barn with you?"

"Mama, Jemmy hit me!"

"I did not!"

Introductions were made, Lorie taking care to repeat each child's name so that I retained a small hope of remembering them. Rose was the eldest, a somber girl of about fourteen with gossamer hair and golden-green eyes, just like Sawyer's; she could have been a young version of my mother. Next in line were rowdy, blue-eyed twin boys, James and William, followed by a second fair-haired daughter, Ellie, and the youngest, a son also named Sawyer. I marveled at their faces and voices, these youngsters whose descendents would one day become my family. And just as quickly, horror assaulted; how vulnerable they were, how easily destroyed if Fallon should appear here to harm them.

No. It's not up to you.

You failed Celia and Jacob.

You failed Marshall and your baby.

It's time now to go.

The young woman in charge in Lorie's absence was named Libby Miller, grown daughter of Jacob and Hannah Miller, whose family lived a few miles around the lake.

Miller...

As in, Dodge and Justin Miller?

Libby wore her long black hair in a single braid hanging nearly to her waist; tanned to a deep brown and with large, expressive dark eyes, her speech carried the sound of someone raised speaking more than one language.

"I brought everyone over after lunch, when they could wait no longer," Libby informed Lorie, brandishing a hand at the excited brood of children. "They have been begging since sunrise to come home!"

"Did you behave for your aunt and uncle?" Lorie asked her children, hands on hips.

"Of course we did, Mama!"

Rose touched her mother's elbow, a quiet request for attention; only because I was close enough did I hear her soft, beseeching question. "Did Malcolm come home with you, Mama?" The girl's beautiful eyes contained an agony of hope, and certainty resounded in my head, a deep awareness of something beyond all of us; I recognized, *She's in love with him.*

Lorie shook her head, resting a hand lightly to her daughter's cheek.

I would wish, later, I remembered more about that evening. Awash in grief, I strayed to the periphery, caught up in studying the familiar lakeshore and imagining my childhood home more than seeking company or conversation. I had been introduced as Ruthann Rawley and the children, other than perhaps Rose, were young enough not to speculate too deeply about my presence. The assumption was that I would live with the Davises indefinitely, which Malcolm had arranged. And it was obvious Lorie and Sawyer loved and trusted Malcolm, and did not question his opinion, even regarding something as substantial as a widowed woman arriving to make her home with them for the foreseeable future.

The wagon was unloaded and horses cared for. Dinner was prepared, eaten, cleaned up. The sun eventually sank over Flickertail in a rosy wash of orange and peach. As though mesmerized, I watched it melt and sizzle into the shimmering blue water; it was not lost on me that this sunset was my last. I listened to the others discuss the trip to St. Paul, Malcolm's potential whereabouts, and the upcoming funeral for Blythe Tilson. The world grew increasingly surreal. I felt as if I sat watching a muted television screen, attempting to make sense by lip-reading. With each incremental darkening of the air, I grew colder.

Soon.

But wait until they've gone to bed.

It's horrible, what you're doing. It's not the answer.

I don't care anymore…

And so I waited until the household sank to quiet, all lanterns extinguished, all whispered voices hushed. I had been given a bed in the girls' room; Rose and Ellie talked in quiet murmurs, interspersed with giggles, shifting around their shared bed as I lay flat on my spine in a narrow trundle bed nearby, whispering a response only if addressed. All of my belongings had burned in the fire and both Lorie and Rebecca lent me clothing until new items could be made; and so it was that I would sneak outside to drown myself in a borrowed white nightgown embroidered with daffodils and lilies.

If I thought too much about what I intended to do, I grew frightened.

So I kept all thoughts submerged, save one; I gave over to the memories of Marshall's face and voice and body, his scent and every last feeling he had ever conjured and inspired and wrought forth from me.

Forgive me, I thought as I slipped from the house with the illumination of nothing but a three-quarters moon. Silver-white light pooling around my shoulders and toes as I crept down the bank toward Flickertail, its windless surface otherworldly in the moonglow, I clung to my image of Marshall. I knew just where the dock would someday jut over the water and stood exactly there, small, jagged pebbles and larger, smoother stones pressing up against my bare feet. The lake was cold around my toes, then my calves. I sucked a sharp breath and kept walking.

Once submerged to my neck, mosquitoes whining around my ears, I retracted my feet from the marshy bottom and kicked forward, toes pointed, angling for the center. It had been a long time since I'd pumped my arms and fluttered my ankles but my limbs had not forgotten the motion of swimming. The nightgown became transparent immediately and I felt a surge of embarrassment over it; I should have dressed to die in something opaque. I swam faster, spurred by the chill water and a notion that I needed to get this over.

It's time.

Dead center from either shore I ceased my crawl stroke and hung suspended, treading water with legs no longer accustomed to this kind of exertion. The lake might have been suspended on a distant planet, as alien to me as anything I'd ever experienced; the black water continued to ripple in the wake of my passage, shattering apart the moon's reflection, leading back to the point of no return. I turned in a slow circle, eyes wide, absorbing these last moments of life before whispering, "Forgive me."

I lifted my arms in a rush, the splash echoing across the silent water, and plunged beneath the surface.

Soon…

It took effort to force my body down when nature insisted I float, but I made sawing motions with each forearm, aiding gravity in this case rather than fighting it, and so I sank, eyes closed, the water temperature dropping along with my body. I opened my mouth and prepared to inhale –

No!

NO!

It happened just as I would have filled my lungs with lakewater. A shift, a pull – and then shrieking, hurtling passage along a space devoid of color and sound and light. I knew this feeling; I'd been sucked through this abyss before. Aware it was happening but helpless to fight it I simply gave up, surrendering to the flow of time that I, for reasons unfathomable and beyond my control, was allowed to traverse. Barriers which kept most people stationary in the timeline to which they were born.

Take me. Go on, take me.

Kill me this time. You almost did the first time.

The motionless motion slammed to a halt with enough force that I was almost knocked unconscious, tumbled end over end. This time, my mouth truly filled with water.

Underwater –

I was still beneath dark, icy water. I thrashed, unable to scream, clumsy in my disorientation. Instinct asserted itself and I kicked, then kicked again, propelling my body toward the murky light wavering in the distance. It may have been up, down, or sideways; I had lost all sense of direction. I rolled and heaved, like a rock in a tumbler.

Air – I need air –

Lungs blazing, I kicked and fought the heavy water, straining for the surface; I broke through with a gasp, thrashing to remain above. A shrill gasping noise, not quite a scream, burst from my lips. Muted voices grew sharp. Frantic and coming closer. A man splashed through the water and grasped my armpits, dragging me from the lake. My unbalanced weight took us both down before we cleared the bank but there was no longer any danger of sinking beneath; we were in the shallows now, close to shore. He braced on both elbows, gasping at the cold, while I tumbled over his chest and fell sideways. A woman splashed to our sides, crying, bending to us and speaking my name, over and over.

She knew me.

I knew her.

Adrenaline pierced my heart.

I tried to speak her name but my teeth were chattering too hard; I reached both hands toward her instead, realizing that Mathias had been the one to charge into Flickertail. He slogged to all fours before regaining his footing, and together he and Camille helped me stand up.

"Ruthie! Oh God, Ruthie, *it's you...*" Camille crushed me against her warmth; I clung, wracked by shuddering cold, reeling with disbelief, unable to process what this meant.

Milla…

My lips moved but no sound emerged.

"She's freezing, help me get her up there, hurry!" Camille wrapped me in her coat as she issued instructions, bundling it around my shivering body.

Mathias gathered me in his arms without another word and carried me up the bank toward the glowing lights of Shore Leave. *My home.* My family's home, which I thought I would never see again. Quivering with shock and cold I huddled close to the warmth radiating from Mathias; he shouted for help as he jogged over the snow-slushy yard.

"Mom!" Camille raced ahead, slipping on the porch steps.

My chest heaved and stuttered, cracking apart with the force of my emotions. Mom, Aunt Jilly, Tish, Clint – all of them streamed outside, a river of love and life to surround me. *To sustain me.* I had returned to them. I had tried to die and was instead returned to them. My lips were blue and numb, my skin a sheet of thin ice, but deep in my chest my heart had started beating again.

Chapter Twenty-Four

Landon, MN - March, 2014

"WE HAVE TO GO BACK."

"I can't let you leave yet." Mom wrapped both hands around one of mine when I insisted that returning to the past was the only option. "My baby. My Ruthann. You've already been taken from me and I can't let it happen again. Not yet."

I interlaced our fingers, unable to argue with her. "I know. I'm not going anywhere tonight." At that point the conversation had been so intense a pause seemed overdue, and entirely necessary, and I stood to wrap my arms, and the quilt, around my mother.

The big, classroom-style clock over the pass-through door had now edged past midnight. I was dry and blessedly warm but still required a blanket over my shoulders to ward off the chills. Rather than retreat to the house we stayed in the cafe; the amount of caffeine pumping through my veins would probably prevent sleep until next week. But I had no intention of sleeping. Explanations had blown around us like miniature tornadoes for the past two hours. Absorbing everything which had occurred in my absence was impossible but the most crucial information had been exchanged. We were now armed with information to reverse what Fallon had done to the timeline. Or, so I prayed.

Table three, our perpetual gathering spot, was surrounded by chairs, coffee rings decorating the ivory plastic surface beneath our elbows and forearms. Mom and Aunt Jilly left to traverse the slippery path leading to the main house; I hated to see them retire to bed, craving the security of their faces and voices, but it was late. Sleep deprivation would help no one. Tish, Clint, Robbie Benson, Derrick, and I crowded around table three while Mathias and Camille sat together at the booth a few feet away; they could not bear to stop touching.

Derrick Yancy, the least sentimental of anyone present, was positioned straight across from me; I found I appreciated his blunt, almost cynical, attitude. He leaned forward once again. "How certain are you that we can reach the correct moment in time?"

I hesitated and his eyebrows lowered; there was no point lying. "I'm not certain at all. But if what I believe is true, we can come close. I've never had a particular date or year in mind when I've…traveled. I've always been pulled. But I believe that pull exists for a reason. I would never attempt this if I didn't think we had a chance of reaching the right destination. If we focus on a particular moment, it's my hope we can be pulled there."

"And that moment is June thirtieth, 1882?" Tish pressed. "The day Blythe Tilson was killed and the night of the fire at the Rawleys' homestead, right?"

I nodded. "But that's cutting it way too close. If we jump from Minnesota, we'll land in Minnesota. We have to give ourselves enough time to get where we need to go. For me, that's Montana, and for you," I indicated Derrick, "that's Iowa City."

He exhaled slowly through his nostrils, reabsorbing what he had agreed to do.

Please, oh God, please, don't back out on us, I thought.

"Two weeks, you think? Will you be able to find them?" Camille's intensity escalated another few notches. I knew she really meant 'Will you be able to find Malcolm?' I had told her everything I could about him but she wanted more. Despite unfathomable circumstances, including his marriage to another woman, Camille had not moved an inch from her position on Mathias's lap; he kept his arms locked around her waist. Their need for physical contact only intensified my desperate longing for Marshall but I refused to let aching thoughts chisel away my self-control.

I'm coming for you, Marsh. I will find you, I swear to you. I will make this work.

"Wouldn't it make more sense to start from those locations in the first place, rather than the other way around?" Robbie asked, lightly tapping his empty coffee mug on the table. "I mean, isn't it like a hundred times easier to travel by car or plane than by, like, I don't know, donkey cart? How did people travel around then? It sounds fucking horrible."

"I don't know about you, but I'd rather we went together," Derrick admitted, focusing again on me. "I'd prefer a traveling companion who knows the time period."

"If we left from different places, we'd have no way to know whether the other one made it there," I agreed. "Robbie's right about the inconvenience of travel, but two weeks should be plenty of time. Trains run east to west in 1882."

"Will you be safe, Ruthie?" Concern furrowed Clint's brow.

"I'll be as safe as I can," I assured my cousin, submerging all guilt over omitting certain events I'd lived through in the 1880s. My own safety was lower on my list of priorities than I would ever admit. "And there are plenty of people to help me once I get back to 1882. Our own family, for one, the Davises."

"Besides, how safe are any of us? Jesus, it gives me the fucking heebie-jeebies to think of Fallon just appearing here, right this minute. What's to stop that insane motherfucker from killing all of us like he killed Case?" Robbie shot a belated apologetic look toward Tish, wrapping an arm around her slumped shoulders before muttering to Derrick, "Sorry, I know he's your brother."

"He's no brother of mine," Derrick said, with quiet sincerity. "He is insane. And I'm tired of fearing him." And then he surprised me, resting his fingertips lightly on my forearm. "I'll protect you, Ruthann, to the best of my abilities. I feel responsible for much of what has happened. I've known for years that Fallon should be stopped, and I've done nothing."

"Thank you," I whispered. I hesitated for only a second. "I think you should know I intend to kill him." I kept my gaze steady on Derrick's as I made this vow.

There was a beat of silence before Derrick made a steeple of his fingertips and then nodded. "I intend the same."

The air felt expectant and fragile, as if a wrong word or thought could shatter its integrity to jagged pieces, and I fought a wave of seizure-like shivers. What if I'd succeeded in drowning myself in Flickertail in 1882? What would have become of my family here in 2014? They would have been doomed to a life in this altered world, a place without Grandma and Aunt Ellen, Mom and Blythe, Aunt Jilly and Uncle Justin, without my sisters and their men. *Without Marshall.* No nieces or nephews or little brothers. In this timeline Case was dead and the Rawleys vanished. It was hell on Earth as we knew it and I had almost condemned them to this reality. I brought a fist to my lips and pressed against my teeth.

At last Tish broke the silence; when I'd last been in my sister's company, we'd lived in Jalesville and worked together at the law office on Main Street. We'd been so blissfully happy with Marshall and Case at our sides and I couldn't bear her ravaged eyes, the mirror image of my own. It took effort to keep her voice steady. "Love brought you back to us, Ruthie, and love will bring you home again. To the home we all remember, I mean, the *right* one. We have to believe that. There's nothing stronger than love, not through all of time."

Conviction swelled in my soul, a tiny flicker of hope, repairing some of the damage inflicted therein. I reached across the table and her hand met mine halfway. Throat thick with tears, I managed, "You're right. We can fix this, Tish, I know we can."

"I wish I could go with you," she whispered.

"Same here," Clint added.

"Jesus, not me." Robbie shuddered. "No offense. I'll keep watch here."

Derrick's shoulders squared with a deep sigh. "Tell us again what must be done."

As promised, we waited until morning for our initial attempt. The clouds had shredded apart at some point during the night hours and sun rimmed the eastern edge of Flickertail as I crept outside for a moment alone, clicking off the overhead lights in the cafe. I hadn't begun to re-acquaint myself with electricity and running water, flushing toilets, telephones, and refrigeration; modern conveniences I had learned to do without. I let my thoughts return to the place I'd left yesterday, when this land belonged to Sawyer and Lorie and their children. What must they think of what happened to me last night in the lake? Of course they would assume I had perished there. How long would they search for my body?

I shuddered, hating the thought of their suffering. Besides that, I may see them again later this same morning. If – *when*, I corrected – Derrick and I succeeded in arriving in the past, I believed we would arrive in this geographic location. I rested my hips against the porch railing, attempt-ing to view the sunlight as a good sign. I hadn't slept but felt replenished nonetheless, restored by the presence of my family; I'd been returned here by the force of their love, just as Tish said last night, and I let this certainty shatter the fearful *what-ifs* clamoring for attention at the back of my mind. I'd been pulled to the nineteenth century originally to save both Jacob Rawley and Patricia – both of them survived because I'd been there. Jacob would never have known his true family and Patricia would have been killed in her train car.

Fallon's interference had thwarted what was meant to be; somehow he'd pinpointed the exact moments in time to strike for maximum dam-age. He had claimed twice that fate aided his efforts and if I considered events from Fallon's perspective, as I must if we were to beat him, those words made a twisted sort of sense. Dredd's ambush on the Iowa plains had resulted in Blythe Tilson's death – which would not have occurred without Patricia – it was her presence which drew Dredd to pursue them. Five men, Malcolm had said, including Dredd's father, Thomas Yancy. And Patricia, I further reasoned, had only been alive there on the prairie with her baby because *I'd* saved her from certain death the sum-mer before.

It was enough to make a sane person crazy.

Blythe Tilson's death effectively ended the Tilson family line, just as Jacob Rawley's death in the fire created a gaping hole which should have been filled by the Rawleys in Montana, whose descendants would eventually become Marshall's family. And Fallon had used this knowledge to his extreme advantage; he must have figured there was nothing I could do once those catastrophic actions had been put into play. We were placing all our bets on this presumption – and the fact that Derrick's ability to jump through time was unknown to Fallon. Derrick's help was immeasurable but not entirely altruistic; besides his obvious infatuation with Tish, there was surely a part of his soul still connected in some small way to Dredd. I prayed that Fallon had underestimated these men for the final time.

What if this doesn't work?

Stop. It will. You survived.

And you've come too goddamn far to turn back now.

I let the first rays of morning sun rim my eyelids with gold dust; thousands of crystals spangled to life on the crunchy remains of snow across the yard, dazzling my vision. The screen door squeaked on its hinges behind me; seconds later Tish slipped her arms around my waist. She'd told me about her recent pregnancy and I understood more than anyone the ache of that loss.

"Oh God, Ruthie," she whispered, anchoring her chin on my shoulder. I felt her trembling and lined my forearms over hers, pressing them more closely to my body.

"I know."

"*Case...*"

"I know," I repeated, squeezing harder. "He's still out there, I swear to you."

She shook with quiet sobs.

"They're all still out there, everyone who was stolen from us." I stared just to the side of the rising sun, greedy for its warmth and light. "I can feel them."

"Yes," she gulped, gaining partial control.

"Then we can't give up."

"I love you, Ruthie, you don't know how much."

"I do, because I love you the same."

"Can you believe Derrick is helping us like this?"

"He has his own reasons."

"I'm scared," she admitted at last. "So scared. What if..."

The sun cleared the horizon and spilled red-gold fire over the last of the ice on Flickertail.

"No. No more what-ifs."

Preparations took mere minutes but my impatience grew beyond reason. I wasn't the least hungry but forced myself to choke down eggs and bacon in the cafe. Derrick and I dressed in warm clothing and snow boots, and packed our coat pockets with granola bars, raisin boxes, and matches.

"Shouldn't we bring additional items? Weapons? Tents? Water?" Derrick roamed between tables with restless energy, unable to remain still.

"Only what's touching our bodies will come with us. If we tried to carry anything in our arms, or bring a backpack, it wouldn't cross through."

Everyone gathered near and I almost couldn't bear the collective expectant fear. I focused on Aunt Jilly, who appeared the most calm.

"How long do we allow for your return?" she asked quietly. Over a year had passed in the nineteenth century during my absence but only a matter of months here.

"Give us four weeks, to be safe. If we're not back by then, you'll have to pull us back." We had discussed this possibility last night. We'd long since passed the point of no return, relying completely on faith at this point.

"Ruthie..." Mom cupped my face, tear-streaked but determined to get through this. "You are the bravest woman I know."

"You are," Tish agreed, and she, Mom, and Camille enclosed me in a four-way hug.

Shore Leave glowed with sun. I moved from one pair of arms to the next, gaining strength.

"Hurry back to us," Aunt Jilly said.

"Keep safe." Mathias held my shoulders, searching my eyes; he'd remained through the night, unwilling to leave Camille's side, and none of us had slept. Malcolm's soul inhabited the man before me and now that I'd known Malcolm, I could see him so clearly in Mathias – in his movements, his energy; the deep wells of feeling in his eyes. Just like Miles and Marshall; different men, but the same soul. The recognition was too strong to deny.

"I will," I promised.

"No point delaying." Derrick cleared his throat.

"Thank you for this, from the bottom of my heart." Tish hugged him, hard and fast, and summoned a small piece of her usual attitude. "I never thought I would be saying this to you, Yancy, but take care of yourself. Please."

Derrick echoed my words. "I will."

My heartrate had increased, my palms were sweating. Derrick was right; there was nothing to be gained by dallying. Either this would work – or it wouldn't.

"Should we stay here?" Mom asked, her voice a ghost of its normal self. She and Aunt Jilly were all but leaning on one another for support.

"Yes. Please stay. I want everyone to concentrate on the past along with Derrick and me." I held out my hands, acting on instinct, and Derrick grasped them, facing me a few feet away from everyone else. He was tall and fit, with sharp features that tended toward arrogant; he bore little resemblance to Fallon or Dredd, despite their shared ancestry. My heart stuttered at the flicker of true fear I witnessed in his eyes, which he quickly, admirably, submerged; I filled my lungs and held the breath.

"What happens now?" he whispered.

"Concentrate." I squeezed his hands.

He returned the pressure and I closed my eyes, picturing the original homestead that had occupied this space. I envisioned Lorie and Sawyer and their children. I let the date we had chosen – June tenth, 1882 – emblazon itself across my mind. Bright red, flashing and glowing on the backs of my eyelids, I willed us toward that date.

Derrick's hands began to lose substance. I felt it in the same exact moment, the void of soundless screaming, the passage from one time to another, like a door waiting to be opened by the correct key. Shore Leave, and my family within it, faded to gray static.

Concentrate!

My fingers closed around nothing – Derrick was no longer in the same space.

I felt the pull of time but something was wrong –

When I'd traveled before my body was submerged within seconds, swept beyond my own control into the powerful current that existed outside the usual flow of time. The past was *there*, close enough to inhale, just behind a layer so thin and gauzy light passed through its transparent sides to pierce my eye sockets – but I was forbidden. I knew without words. I already existed there and I could not exist twice in the same space. I went to my knees, certain I would snap in two but maintaining the connection all the same. I had to reach 1882.

A scream rose in my throat –

No – oh God, no –

I have to go! Let me go!

He needs me!

Screaming full-scale now, the force exerted on my body so intense I flopped like a hooked fish.

Let me go!

Someone rushed near, crying out my name.

And then, in a flicker of light, she disappeared.

Chapter Twenty-Five

The Iowa Plains - June, 1882

I REGAINED CONSCIOUSNESS FLAT ON MY BACK, STARING UP at a sky so bright I flung a shielding forearm over my eyes. Sense returned more slowly, in fits and starts; it took seconds for my mind to catch up with my body as I struggled to recall my last memory, the one just prior to this brilliant blue sky edged with a tall fringe of grass stalks.

Shore Leave.

Ruthie and Derrick.

They were trying to get back to the nineteenth century –

Oh God –

I sat up too fast, only to be blasted by a rush of dizziness; I hung my head until the blotchy colors receded from my vision, rolling next to all fours on the scratchy, uneven ground. I tried to grasp handfuls of grass to gain my footing but fell instead, as wobbly as a toddler.

This is not the time to freak out, Camille.

Think.

The last I knew I'd been standing in Shore Leave, thinking for all I was worth of Malcolm Carter, concentrating on his existence in June, 1882, picturing his face and his horse, and the prairie...and me at his side.

Oh, my God –

"Ruthie..." I cleared my throat, heart flapping, panic mounting like a storm surge, and tried again. "Ruthann! Derrick!"

"Over here," came a faint reply and my shoulders sank with relief.

"Can you speak up? I don't know which direction you're in!" My voice echoed over what seemed an endless expanse of prairie. Flickertail Lake was not in sight; we were nowhere near Shore Leave, I knew that much. I inhaled for three counts and exhaled for six.

"You're on my left," Derrick called. "I think, anyway."

"Are you all right? Do you see Ruthie?" Successful at my second attempt to stand, I hurried toward the sound of his voice, parting waist-high grass with both hands, keeping an eye out for snakes or other creatures. My back felt bruised, but that was the least of my worries. "Where in the hell are we?!"

"Iowa," said someone only a few yards behind me. I hadn't heard anyone approach and spun around so quickly I fell again, this time flat on my ass.

A man riding a horse sat watching me, a beautiful chestnut-brown horse, holding the reins in one hand while the other rested on the saddle horn. He wore a cowboy hat and dirty jeans and at the sight of me, his expression changed swiftly to one of abject disbelief – I felt the same thing happening to my face. My heart delivered a hard, hammering punch to my breastbone before taking abrupt wing, disappearing in the cloudless blue sky. Both hands flew to my lips as I stared, open-mouthed.

He dismounted with such effortless grace he was on the ground before I knew he'd moved. He would have crossed the meager distance between us with two strides except that I was already there to meet him.

"Malcolm," I gasped, threading my arms about his neck, unable to restrain this elemental instinct. He was damp with sweat, exhaling in a rush against my loose hair and returning my exuberant embrace as I imbibed the physical reality of him, the immediacy of Malcolm Carter at long last close enough to touch. His hat fell off and I laughed with the pure delight of a child, running my fingers through his dark curls, over his eyebrows and cheekbones and lips. He was tall, bending forward in order to receive my touches upon his skin. His muscles curved like lean bands of steel; he might have been carved from warm hardwood. But his hands were gentle, fingers twining deep into my tangled curls, cradling my face.

Amazement radiated between us as we traced paths over one another, but no unease; our touching was the most natural thing in the world. Of course it was – his soul was the other half of mine. He was Mathias in another version of himself, my husband, my lover, the very essence of my true love.

"You're here!" My smile was wider than the horizon, all agony, all fear, momentarily annihilated. "You're actually here."

"I know you." He spoke the words slowly, bracketing my ribs with both hands. "You aren't Cora, but I *know* you…"

By contrast, words flew from my lips. "Of course you do. I'm Camille, Ruthann's sister! She told you all about me. And I've known about you for years. Do you know how long I've wanted to do this?" Before he could respond – or I could think twice – I drew his head closer and kissed his mouth, a soft, quick, elated stamp of possession, giddy with the bliss of finding him, of actually setting eyes and hands upon him, when for so long I'd had nothing but a cold, flat, black and white photograph. His lips were so very familiar; he smelled just like Mathias.

He grinned as I drew away, wide and warm. A grin to rival the sun, one I would have known anywhere. Betraying no lack of composure over the fact that I'd just kissed him, he murmured, "Holy God," speaking the words as though praying, crushing me closer, resting his cheek to my hair while I buried my face against his chest, trembling and overcome; an intermingling of pain and joy unlike anything I'd ever known. We may have continued holding each other until time ran out if the sounds of Derrick's clumsy approach through the tall grass had not reached our ears.

Malcolm shifted us at once, a fluid, effortless motion, positioning in front of me, gun drawn from a holster on his hip before I could blink.

"No, I know him, it's all right. Derrick, freeze!" I yelled, darting forward. "I've found Malcolm!"

I recognized the need to gather my wits; there wasn't time to speculate why I'd been pulled through time and Ruthann had not. I crashed through the grass and intercepted Derrick, who was puffing and sweating with exertion; he'd tied the arms of his heavy winter coat around his waist.

"Where's Ruthann?" he asked. "What in the hell happened?"

"I don't know. We'll have to figure it out later."

Malcolm was right behind me; he had holstered his gun, to my relief, but he demanded of Derrick, "Who are you?" His tone bristled with authority and threat; Derrick stepped back a pace, speechless, not removing his eyes from Malcolm.

I babbled, "He's with me, it's all right. I'll explain everything, I promise." Urgency reasserted itself, swarming like hornets. "Oh God, what day is it? Where are we? You said Iowa...how did we end up here instead of Minnesota?" I clutched Malcolm's left arm. "Are you with Cole Spicer and Blythe Tilson?"

In short order Malcolm helped me atop his horse, whose full name, I was delighted to learn, was Aces High – nicknamed Aces, as Malcolm explained – but not before I hugged the beautiful animal's solid neck and kissed the white blaze on his long nose.

"Hi, boy," I murmured, bestowing another kiss, this time between the horse's velvety nostrils. Aces issued a soft whooshing sound, watching me with his head cocked to the right, left eye fixed on me with intense curiosity. "You remember me, don't you?"

Malcolm, explaining that he'd ridden ahead this morning in order to hunt, led Aces back to the slower-moving wagon in which Patricia and her son were contained. Cole Spicer and Blythe Tilson were also accounted for on this journey, according to Malcolm; he, Cole, Patricia, and the baby had parted ways from Ruthann, Marshall, and a man named Axton Douglas earlier this month. My relief over these facts, however, was quickly submerged – today's date was June twenty-ninth, 1882, and we were most definitely not in Minnesota, but instead a day's hard ride south of Iowa City. Derrick, walking alongside Aces, looked up at me, his expression communicating more clearly than any words that we were totally and completely fucked.

Dismay became outright fear. "How did this happen?! We were supposed to arrive weeks ago. *Fuck.* We have to get word to Marshall and Ruthie in Montana...assuming Ruthie's still out there right now." My thoughts whirled. "She *must* be. I bet that's why she couldn't return this time, since she's already here." Distraught, I cried, "We'll never make it there in time! We're too late. Oh, my God…" I sat clutching Aces High's dark mane in both hands, terrorized. There was no way we could travel hundreds of miles in a single day, let alone hope to get word to them. We were in the middle of a prairie in Iowa, in the middle of fucking nowhere.

Malcolm halted Aces and stepped close to the saddle. He reached for my right hand, cradling it between both of his as he said, "Tell me what we need to do."

The wagon rolled along a mile behind; as we gained ground I saw the sun glint off a man's auburn hair.

Cole Spicer, I thought, and a deep thrill spiked through my gut. Though I'd barely had time to process the fact, I was indeed here in the nineteenth century, in the presence of people I had never imagined meeting. The deep-seated ache in my heart throbbed. *Mathias, oh God, I wish you were with me. I miss you so fucking much. You would be amazed at what I'm seeing. Tish, you should be here too. I'm looking at Case's ancestor.*

I refused to consider what was occurring at Shore Leave in the wake of my departure rather than Ruthann's; I had two goals here in this place and if I wanted my real life back, I sure as hell better keep focused. There was no other option. I could break down like nobody's business some other day. A second man rode a gorgeous pinto mare on the other side of the wagon and while he didn't much resemble the man I knew as my stepfather many generations from now, I recognized Blythe Tilson.

Cole drew the wagon to a halt. To describe his expression as staggered was something of an understatement.

Malcolm took charge. "Plans have changed, fellas. There's no time to lose."

Cole peered at me with amazement curling his reddish-gold eyebrows. His gaze flickered to Malcolm and then returned to my face. He didn't have to speak the words aloud for me to understand; I knew how much I resembled Cora – Malcolm's lost love, the woman with whom I shared a soul.

Blythe heeled his mount and rode closer, addressing Malcolm. "What do you mean?"

"We're in danger," Malcolm said succinctly. "The Yancys are on our trail. They'll catch up with us by tomorrow morning if we don't take immediate action."

"Fallon?" Cole asked, shoulders squaring in immediate offense. "He's back?"

Malcolm shook his head. "No, Dredd and his father are in pursuit. This is Ruthann's sister, Camille, and she's traveled a long distance to get to us." His gaze flickered to Blythe. "This-all is gonna seem a mite strange to you, but I pray you'll trust me. This man here," indicating Derrick, "is a descendent of the Yancys. He and Camille have come to warn us. They're from the twenty-first century."

Blythe's lips twitched with either disbelief or amusement, I couldn't tell which. But he was clearly a man able to take things in stride; he nodded politely at me as he said, "I wondered why them clothes looked so odd." His voice rumbled like thunder.

I knew Cole was already aware of many truths, including Ruthann's abilities; he wasted no time on additional questions. "If the Yancys are already on our trail, we can't lose more time. What's your plan, Malcolm?"

"We have to get to a town with a telegraph in an all-fired hurry. On horseback we can make it before nightfall. But not with the wagon."

Cole stowed the reins and jumped from the wagon seat, calling for Patricia. Malcolm reached to help me from Aces; his touch on my waist blazed all across my skin, there was no denying. Flustered, I avoided his gaze, instead hurrying around to the back of the wagon, following Cole.

"Ruthann's sister is here?" a woman inside asked, her voice low and rough.

"Darlin', come here." Cole climbed on the tailgate to assist her and Patricia's face appeared in the oval opening. I gasped, I couldn't help it – she looked so much like Tish that my spine prickled. Pale and drawn, shadows deep beneath her electric-blue eyes, exactly the way Tish had looked earlier this very morning, at Shore Leave.

"Oh, dear God. You are Camille, are you not? I would know you anywhere."

Tears glided over my cheeks; the second she was on the ground, supported by Cole, she flung her arms around me, squeezing as tightly as was able in her weakened state. Her skin burned with fever and there was a faint tremble in her limbs, and I took care to keep my hug gentle. We drew apart but I cupped her elbows, afraid she might tumble over.

"What must we do?" she whispered. "Where is this descendent of the Yancys?"

Derrick approached and Patricia assessed him with the imperious nature of a queen. Of course he noticed how much she looked like Tish; I could see it all over his face. "Ma'am," he stumbled.

"You do not look like a Yancy." Her tone was an exact replica of Tish's, the way my sister sounded when employing her lawyer voice.

I almost expected Derrick to drop to one knee but he straightened his spine instead.

"Your eyes," she whispered, before he could reply. "There is no ruthlessness in them."

Reclaiming Patricia's attention, I said, "I apologize for all of this, I know it's a shock. But we have no time to waste." Names and facts spun through my head. "By this time tomorrow, Dredd will shoot Thomas Yancy and then blame Cole for the murder. Cole will go to jail. Someone in Dredd's group will shoot and kill Blythe." I paused for a quick, gulping breath, ignoring everything but the need to impart facts, including Blythe's obvious shock at this news. "Fallon is here in 1882, but he's in Montana. Tomorrow night he will burn the Rawleys' home to the ground, killing Miles's son, Jacob, and destroying that branch of the Rawley family. We have to get word to them."

Patricia's skin drained of all color, leaving her so ashen she appeared lifeless. "Ruthie…where is Ruthie? How do you come to be here with this information?"

"She was returned to the future about a week after the fire, but it isn't the future she remembers. Fallon's actions created an offshoot in our timeline, an alternate reality. A nightmare I can't even describe. Ruthie knew we had to warn you and she tried to return here this morning, but she couldn't. It's like she was blocked." I struggled to recall those moments – Derrick had vanished almost at once while Ruthann's body jerked and flopped, as though caught in a violent current. I had rushed forward, mere steps ahead of Tish – and woke here.

It was your connection to Malcolm. The strength of what binds your two souls drew you here to this place in time. There is no other explanation.

"She is safe? What of Marshall? What of…Axton?" Pain cut a trench across Patricia's face.

"I left Ruthie behind in 2014. But I think she's still here too, in this time." I looked to Derrick for help.

"As far as we know they are all still in Howardsville, Montana," he supplied. "Ruthann and I intended to arrive here two weeks ago in order to reach them with time to spare. We know that Marshall and Axton will be in Howardsville by tomorrow evening, but obviously they would be unable to return in time to prevent the fire at the Rawley homestead."

I witnessed the play of thoughts across Malcolm's mind as he considered our options at lightning speeds; I marveled again, struck to my very core, how much he reminded me of Mathias. Despite physical differences, most notably the shade of his eyes, Malcolm's every movement, his mannerisms, his mouth and eyebrows and posture were achingly familiar.

Be very, very careful, Camille.

To claim I was not in love with Malcolm Carter would be a lie of immense proportions; I had loved Malcolm since the first winter I held his picture in my hands. I loved him to his very soul, my own crying out with recognition of our connection. But the fact remained that he was a different man; Malcolm was not my husband. I could not find room for guilt over imagining making love with the man standing before me, making love until our souls were fully sated and all sadness, all pain, vanquished forever.

Stop. There is no way you can let that happen.

"Cole, listen up good," Malcolm ordered. "Get Patricia and the baby out of here. The Yancys are coming from Chicago, that we know, and expect us to be on a northern route. They are still a day from our current position, so that gives us time to flee."

"West," Cole said at once. "We'll head due west, aim for the nearest settlement. Windham can't be more than twenty miles." He gathered Patricia to his side and kissed her tangled hair. "I am so sorry, love, to ask this of you. I know you're ill."

"I am well," she assured. "Hard travel could never be worse than what Camille has just described."

"Go as fast as you're able," Malcolm said. "Waste no time." He paused, briefly considering. "Blythe, if you would accompany them and help keep watch. Meanwhile we'll backtrack to Muscatine and telegraph Howardsville. We can make it by nightfall, it ain't more than thirty miles, give or take." His eyes met mine.

"I'm up for it," I announced at once, understanding what he was about to ask. "I'll be fine."

"Good, since I wasn't planning to let you from my sight," Malcolm said, just serious enough I couldn't discern if there was a hint of humor in his words, or not. My heart throbbed fiercely. He looked next to Derrick. "Yancy, what of you? Can you handle a firearm?"

Derrick shifted uncomfortably, tugging his gaze from Patricia. "I've never shot a gun in my life."

"Well, there ain't time for lessons anyway." Malcolm's observant eyes flickered over the wagon, then back to Derrick. "You'll stay and help keep watch."

Derrick struggled to submerge his unease. "I'd rather we stuck to-gether if it's all the same to you, Camille."

I knew he feared losing what he considered his only connection to the future and I couldn't blame him, but the decision was out of my hands.

"There ain't enough horses." There was zero room for argument in Malcolm's tone. "We'll catch up once we've sent a message. Give us until tomorrow night, Cole. We'll look for you in Windham."

And so, less than ten minutes after our first meeting, I was hugging Patricia good-bye. "Be safe," I begged in a whisper, closing my eyes against the softness of her hair. "Please, be safe."

"You have already saved us, dear Camille." She drew back and studied my eyes. "I could never thank you enough. I pray you are able to warn Ruthann. I shall pray every moment until we meet again."

Derrick masked his fear with admirable effort, cupping my upper arm as he ordered, "Watch out for yourself. Jesus Christ, Tish will kill me if you get hurt."

"You'll be safe with me, I swear on my life." Malcolm held Aces by the horse's lead line, eyes steady on mine as he spoke. Fate enclosed my heart in a merciless grip – how many times had I stood facing this man, this horse, with the sun beating down on my head and the prairie grasses rippling to the horizon on all sides? The exact number was lost to me – only Malcolm and Cora would ever know for certain – but it didn't matter.

One last time, I thought, aching from the inside out. *Give me this one last time.*

Chapter Twenty-Six

The Iowa Plains - June, 1882

ACES HIGH CANTERED OVER THE PRAIRIE WITH US ON HIS back, the miles disappearing beneath his long, graceful legs. Malcolm slowed him to a walk roughly every twenty minutes and the animal's ribcage expanded and contracted as his powerful lungs drew huge breaths, preparing for another bout of running. I buried both hands in the coarse hair of the horse's thick brown mane while Malcolm held the reins, his arms encircling my waist from behind, his thighs aligned with mine. I tried at first to pretend his proximity didn't affect me but it was absolutely no use. An agony of need and desire battered me with full force. And love. I loved this man so much it hurt.

My hair was tucked beneath Malcolm's bandana, which he'd been kind enough to lend me, a tattered rectangle of indigo cloth which I tied over my loose hair so it wouldn't blow in his face, knotting it at the nape of my neck. At first he'd offered his cowboy hat but it was too big, slipping down to cover my eyes. My clothing was what I'd left Shore Leave wearing – a pair of faded jeans, wool socks, and snow boots with rounded toes never intended for fitting in stirrups; a ragged gray t-shirt under an old green sweater. Clothes meant for chilly, slushy, late-winter Minnesota, not a prairie in Iowa under a hot June sun. Even with the wind created by Aces High's fast pace, sweat trickled in slippery paths beneath my double layer of shirts.

Malcolm's forearms rippled with lean muscle, exposed by the rolled-up sleeves of his threadbare shirt, a garment that might once have been white. His fingers were long, with blunt square nails, his hands calloused and hard and more capable-looking than any man's I'd ever seen. I'd noticed almost immediately the braided leather band on his right wrist, with Cora's name carved upon its surface; one winter night long ago I'd used a magnifying glass to read the word on the surface of a photograph. And again the unreality of this situation beat at my senses; after all this time, I was in the same physical space as Malcolm Carter.

"What was her last name? I've wondered for so long." I touched the band on his wrist as I asked, rubbing a thumb over the single word carved upon the smooth leather. I felt an undeniable connection with this woman, not only because she had loved Malcolm as much as I loved him, but because she was also part of me. In this century, Cora had *been* me.

"Lawson. Cora Elizabeth Lawson." He spoke her name with a quiet reverence that tore at my heart.

"Who was she? How did you meet? *When* did you meet?" I was dying with curiosity.

"I was a boy of thirteen, green as sawgrass. It's a long tale, but we have a long ride."

"Tell me everything," I demanded, smiling as I sensed him grin.

"Only if you promise the same." He tightened his elbows around my waist, just slightly.

"I promise."

He was a talker. But I already knew that, basking in the warm flow of his words.

And I listened, peppering him with questions, as he told me of his first sight of eleven-year-old Cora Lawson in the late summer of 1868, on a cattle drive toward Montana Territory. He backtracked, at my request, relating memories of his boyhood in Tennessee with descriptions so vivid I felt I'd been there with him. He spoke of running wild in the holler, trying to keep up with his older brothers, of mealtimes at dusk and his father's fiddle singing through the early hours of the night. The Davises – my own family – lived on the opposite end of the holler. I learned of Sawyer Davis and his twin brothers, Ethan and Jeremiah, dear friends of the Carter boys. Then the advent of The War Between the States, when darkness blotted out the bright happiness of youth and robbed Malcolm of two of his three brothers.

His parents, Bainbridge and Clairee, survived until 1864 only to die within an hour of one another.

"Daddy loved Mama so." Malcolm's drawl grew more pronounced the more he spoke of his long-lost Tennessee home. "He couldn't bear to go on without her. She was the very light of his life."

The back of my head rested on his left shoulder as Aces walked for a brief spell, and I turned my nose toward his chest, eyes closed as I breathed his scent, lulled by exhaustion and the beat of hooves, by Malcolm's stories and the security of his arms.

I felt his chest rise as he inhaled; his words rumbled against my spine as he continued the story. "Boyd and Sawyer came for me a few months later, after I'd given up all hope. I figured I was an orphan through and through, but by the grace of God they returned to me."

"When did you meet Lorie?" I asked when he next paused for a breath.

"My first sight of her was just outside of St. Louis, the summer of 'sixty-eight. I was but twelve years old and I figured she was an angel straight from heaven. My brother and Sawyer, and our old friend, Angus Warfield, rescued her that very night."

"Rescued her?"

"She worked as a prostitute, was forced into it when she was no more than fifteen. She'd been raised but miles from our hometown back in Tennessee and Angus recognized her. He took her away from the place where she worked, where she lived no better than a prisoner."

I thought of the way Grandma and Aunt Ellen had always claimed there was a 'saloon girl' in our family tree; Ruthie, Tish, and I always assumed they were just trying to spice up our ancestors.

Hours passed while Aces cantered southeast; I'd never realized nor appreciated a horse's true stamina. Though Malcolm asked several times if I was all right, we kept an overall breakneck pace, not stopping for food or water until late afternoon. He lifted me to the ground a few feet from a small creek and I sank to the ground with my first step, my legs stiff as plywood planks. Despite the gravity of the situation and the weight of urgent stress like a yoke across my shoulders, laughter bubbled from my belly as I ended up cross-legged on the warm earth.

"I'm so sweaty and dirty," I moaned, laughing harder still, grinding my fingertips against my grimy forehead. "I smell awful."

Malcolm's grin – *Mathias's grin* – lit up his entire face. "You don't smell anything but wonderful, believe me. And I would know, as your hair's been tickling my face for the past twenty-five miles."

I hooked my chin on my left shoulder, looking up at him as he stood nearby, hands latched on his lean hips. He'd let his hat fall down his back; his hair was wild with disarray, plastered to his temples with sweat as he grinned. He was so handsome, and so very familiar, and a hot, vibrating pulse ricocheted like an electric charge through my center. I mustered a teasing tone to cover my nerves. "Well, you could have said something."

"I didn't say I minded, did I?" His grin widened.

"No, but…" I faltered, smile dissipating like dandelion seeds in a rush of air. Increasingly flustered I turned away and rose to both feet, summoning every ounce of willpower to keep steady.

Malcolm sensed my agitation and was intuitive enough not to tease further, leading Aces to the creek; he crouched near his horse and filled his canteen while I knelt a few yards downstream and splashed water over my blistering face. Taking care not to simultaneously peel off my t-shirt I stripped from my sweater, tossing it well away from the water, and then splashed my face again. Malcolm kept his attention pointedly focused on the tasks at hand, while I self-consciously swiped at the sweat rings decorating my collar and armpits. I did smell terrible, even if he was too kind to admit it.

"How much farther?" I asked.

He straightened and offered me the canteen; I gulped gratefully, water trickling over my chin.

"Muscatine isn't more than five miles. Half an hour, at most." He nodded at the canteen in my hand. "Have another sip, you've lost fluid this day."

"And you think someone will be willing to ride out to the Rawleys' place tonight and warn them?" I asked after another swallow of the icy creek water. I pictured Ruthie and Marshall, hundreds of miles west in Montana, unaware of the danger headed their way.

"I pray so. A good rider with a solid horse can make it to their ranch by tomorrow morning if they leave immediately." Our gazes held for a beat, then longer; my heart thrust with such force I was sure he could hear it. He drew a slow breath, accepting his canteen as I handed it over, bringing it to his lips to swallow two large gulps before saying, "As should we."

Muscatine appeared on the horizon twenty minutes later, a small town on the Mississippi River. I stared with wide eyes at the sights, at horses and buggies and wagons, men and women moving through their day with no idea whatsoever that someone born in the twentieth century gawked at them. These people had never watched television, listened to the radio, or heard of plastic; stupid thoughts took precedence, keeping distress at bay. I hadn't slept in over forty-eight hours at this point and the fear of failing to accomplish our goal of getting word to Ruthie and Marshall was stalking my self-control.

You saved Patricia and Cole. They're no longer in Dredd Yancy's path. And Blythe, he's safe now too. And Patricia's baby, don't forget about him!

I hadn't even set eyes on the baby.

Malcolm made a low clucking sound to Aces, tightening his right knee, and Aces responded at once, slowing to a graceful walk. I'd noticed many times throughout the day how effortlessly the horse responded to Malcolm, almost as if they were one being. After Malcolm's teasing about my hair in his face I'd braided its length, tucking it over my right shoulder. The immediacy of his strong, lean body behind mine proved torturous; constant reminders that I couldn't want him this way were of no use. I wanted him in every way.

We had covered an entire gamut of conversational topics over the hours of riding but still managed to sidestep the story of Cora's disappearance. I'd told him of Mathias and our children, of living in the homesteader's cabin that he and his brother, Boyd, had indeed built. He was full of questions and demanded lengthy descriptions of everything and everyone, which I was happy to deliver; Mathias and I had been correct in our assumption that Cora and Malcolm intended to live together in the little cabin. I was further stunned to discover that Cora's mother's name had been Millie. Aces continued along the town's dusty main street until Malcolm drew him to a halt in front of a general store; a small, hand-lettered sign propped in the window read 'Telegraph Station.'

"How can you stand upright?" I groaned as he dismounted with ease. "My legs feel like two-by-fours."

"Years of practice." He helped me from Aces, keeping a gentle grip on my waist until certain I was steady. The sun sprawled low on the horizon, visible between two false-fronted buildings, amber light spilling in bright beams to spangle my vision. I fought dizziness and hunger, disorientation and low-grade panic. Malcolm held my gaze, concern creasing his brow.

"You need food and rest," he said softly. "Come. We'll send word and then find a bite to eat."

The telegraph operator wrote out the message as we dictated, debating over exact wording with every sentence; the operator was a patient man. I thought of the telegram Malcolm had sent on Christmas Day, 1876, in which he'd described missing home so much he hurt. Watching him now, six and a half years later, a man whose bearing was one of admirable strength, who carried himself with an abundance of grace and capability, I was overcome with pride and happiness and love and lust, a complex knot of emotion. Tears flecked my lashes and I turned away so the telegraph operator, already clicking out our message on his small device, wouldn't think I was crazy. Malcolm rested a hand on my lower back, warm and reassuring, as we waited.

The telegram read, CAMILLE ARRIVED THIS MORNING. PLEASE GET IMMEDIATE WORD TO GRANT AND MARSHALL RAWLEY. TELL THEM FALLON IS ON HIS WAY. WILL REACH YOU BY TOMORROW. BE PREPARED. DO NOT LEAVE FOR HOWARDSVILLE. C&P SAFE. REQUEST WORD WHEN RIDER IS SENT. MALCOLM A. CARTER.

"What if someone doesn't ride out there tonight?" I worried as we descended the wooden steps out front in the rich copper glow of sunset. "Because they don't understand how serious this is! What if Fallon is already in Howardsville? What if he showed up early?"

Malcolm stopped midstride and turned to face me, gently grasping my upper arms. "Hey. We'll check back here as soon as we've found a place to stay the night, don't you worry. We've done all we can for now. Think of what you've accomplished today. You oughta be proud of yourself."

"You're right," I whispered. "Thank you."

He offered his right arm, with a sweet half-grin lifting the right side of his mouth. "May I escort you to dinner? If I remember correctly, they serve a fine plate of fried chicken at the hotel, yonder."

We crossed the street, anonymous in this little town other than a few curious glances at my strange modern outfit. I did not allow my thoughts to stray beyond each passing second; I felt almost as though we walked together through a dream sequence, through the warm balm of the tail end of a hot afternoon, candle lanterns blinking to life in establishments remaining open for the evening hours. Too much had happened today, far too much to deal with; right now there was only Malcolm Carter, holding my arm and asking what I liked best to eat.

"Best of all?" I asked, squeezing his elbow closer to my side. "It would have to be the fried fish we serve at Shore Leave. The only times I couldn't eat it was when I was pregnant. My morning sickness was always too bad in the first few months."

Just like Mathias, Malcolm was an expert at maintaining easygoing conversation; talking, storytelling, yarn-spinning, all came naturally to the Carters. "Lorie is a midwife. I remember her saying many a time that morning sickness is a good sign."

"I've always heard the same. I went through it five times and my babies were all healthy." My throat tightened at the mention of my children, as it had each time we'd discussed them today. I couldn't explain it – the ache of missing Mathias and our children was a long, double-sided blade jammed through my heart, existing simultaneously alongside the buoyant joy of being near Malcolm. There were no words to describe this paradox of feelings and so I did not attempt to understand. I simply felt – and in feeling, somehow understood.

His soul is Mathias's soul. And yours is Cora's. You belong with both of them in this way. And they belong to you. What is fate if not the force that pulled you to him this very morning?

"Millie Jo, Brantley, Henry…which of them has my name as his second?" he demanded.

"Brantley," I whispered around a lump. "He's about the sweetest of my babies."

"And then comes Lorie, and little James Boyd. Aw, Lorie and Boyd would be proud to know your babes bear their names. I have a dozen nieces and nephews, two of which are named for me."

"Ruthie met them, in Landon. She told us all about them. Or wait…I guess she hasn't yet. Not in this timeline. It's so confusing."

We'd reached the hotel, a white clapboard building with a deep front porch and a balcony running the entire length of the second floor. Malcolm paused with one boot on the bottom step, abruptly realizing, "You'd prefer a moment to yourself, I'd wager." He adjusted his hat brim in a gesture both endearing and self-conscious. Keeping his gaze directed at the steps, he murmured, "I'll inquire after our rooms for the evening."

Sawdust coated my tongue; it took courage, but I stuttered, "You needn't get…two rooms."

His eyes lifted at once, burning into mine with such powerful certainty that a sharp thrill pulsed in my belly, undeniable as tomorrow's sunrise.

Had I known how this day would end?

Of course I had; there was no other way, not from the second we first laid eyes upon each other many hours and miles ago. All paths circled back to this exact moment, facing each other on a dusty set of steps with evening light creating a golden nimbus around his upper body, his wide shoulders and lean arms, his cowboy hat. Without a word he lifted my right hand to his lips and tenderly kissed my knuckles, then my palm, before lacing our fingers and bringing our joined hands to his fast-thudding heart.

"I was hoping you might say that," he whispered.

Chapter Twenty-Seven

Muscatine, IA - June, 1882

OUR ROOM FACED THE MAIN STREET AND I PROPPED OPEN the window to the pleasant evening air, alone for the moment while Malcolm returned downstairs to ask after dinner and a pitcher of hot water for the basin. Elated and terrified in almost equal parts, feeling like a bride on her wedding night – and an ignoramus at that, one who had no earthly idea what occurred between a man and a woman – I fluttered around the cramped space, the narrow wooden floorboards creaking underfoot. The mirror revealed my sunburned face, cheeks and eyes blazing as brightly as if I'd spent the past two minutes guzzling a jug of wine. My heart was no longer only in my chest but hammering at every pulse point.

A knock sounded and I jumped as if prodded by an iron poker, almost too afraid to answer the door. I needn't have worried; it was only the woman from behind the front desk, carrying a steaming teakettle, which she emptied into a porcelain basin on the dresser.

"There, my dear, you take a moment to wash up. Your husband said to tell you he would return with a plate of food, not to worry. And I've taken the liberty of bringing you a nightgown, as he said yours was ruined." She handed me a length of white material I'd thought was a towel, trying not to wince at my unkempt appearance, and then bustled around the room, lighting both lanterns, clucking with maternal concern. "Poor dear. You wash up and rest, you'll be right as rain in the morning. Soap's in the top drawer."

"Thank you," I stammered as she took her leave.

Steam rose from the water in small curls; the basin was exactly like the one stationed on Gran's dresser, back home. While grateful for the hot water I couldn't help but wonder how in the hell a person was supposed to wash up with what amounted to about six cups of liquid. But it was better than nothing and so I drew the curtains at the window. The candlelight created golden ripples on the water as I brought the basin to the floor, small agitated waves. I stripped from my t-shirt and bra, cringing at the thought of putting them back on tomorrow, and left my hair in a braid as I scrubbed my face and armpits, in that order, using the small yellow-brown chunk of soap that lathered about as well as a stone.

Fumbling, cursing, dripping water everywhere, I knelt over the basin in a state of nervous anticipation so heightened my stomach seemed to be floating in a hot air balloon somewhere near the stratosphere.

Hurry, Malcolm. Oh God, hurry back to me.

I'm afraid I might die before you get back.

I peeled off my socks and jeans and panties, breathless, shaking hard now. There was less water in the basin than on the wooden floor at this point; the soap stung the skin between my legs, prompting another spill as I scrambled to rinse. Because I couldn't get my clothes wet, I used the nightgown to mop up the mess on the floor, about halfway done and completely naked when a second knock sounded. I swallowed a shriek as Malcolm said, "It's just me. If you're ready, I brought us dinner."

He sounded as if there was a large, fibrous husk lodged in his windpipe.

"Hang on!" I gasped, tearing the sheet from the bed and wrapping it toga-fashion around my damp body. I could hardly force air from my lungs, let alone words, but I managed to invite, "Come in."

He opened the door and I saw immediately he had two plates piled with chicken and mashed potatoes balanced on his right forearm. I hurried to help him and he caught sight of me – and my lack of clothing – at the same instant. Heated tension flared between us with more impact than a lightning bolt. We almost bumped heads as I stumbled forward to take the plates from his arm, both of us talking at once, a rush of nervous babbling.

"I know this sheet looks stupid…my clothes are so dirty…"

"No, no, it's not stupid at all…I shoulda given you more time up here…"

"Watch out, the floor's all wet, I'm so sorry…"

"No, it's all right…"

"I should have saved you some water…"

"There's no need, I washed up downstairs…"

A flush blazing across his cheekbones, Malcolm watched me set the plates on the dresser and then grab for the sheet as it threatened to slip from my breasts. And then a grin spread slowly across his lips, one hand at his mouth as if to hide the evidence of his amusement, shoulders shaking with restrained laughter. I giggled too, trying with no luck to latch the sheet around my torso; the bottom of it sprawled across the wet floor like the train of a filmy dress, well past my toes.

"C'mere," he muttered, laughing, advancing to offer his assistance, removing his hat and setting it aside. Without another word he stepped behind me and tucked my long braid over my right shoulder. I was afraid I might pass out – or my heart would just plain burst – as he gathered the sheet and neatly, efficiently, tied it between my shoulder blades, creating what amounted to a threadbare strapless dress, complete with soggy hem. Once finished he murmured, "There," and turned me gently around.

I tried to thank him but I couldn't speak past the force field in my chest. His dark hair was damp, curling along the nape of his neck, his shirt undone past two buttons at the collar.

His smile vanished; his hands remained on my bare shoulders. He whispered hoarsely, "You are so beautiful, I can't hardly breathe."

"*Malcolm…*" His name scraped my throat, at the crest of a merciless storm of emotion, a storm from which we could no longer run or hide. The press of Cora's memories, her desperate longing for this man, were at once intertwined with my own; no separating the two.

The time had come.

I dove into his arms, seeking refuge, seeking something for which no words existed. He crushed me to his chest as I sobbed in huge, messy gulps; I feared I would never stop, that the grief, at long last given release, would never fully abate.

"I'm so sorry, Malcolm...*I'm so sorry...*" The words burst from all the shadowy, boarded-over chambers in my soul, places where no light had ever shattered the darkness. "Oh God, please forgive Cora. *Forgive me...*"

He spoke in my ear, rough with tears. "I have prayed for so many years for your forgiveness, my love, my sweet love, and to beg forgiveness of Cora. And of you. I would turn my soul inside out to be returned to that night in the foothills, when I left you behind. I thought you were safe, I would never have left if I thought otherwise..." Pain throttled him to silence; his chest heaved.

I took his face between my palms, desperate to see his eyes; to look upon one another in this moment was both an exquisite gift and excruciating punishment. "I know, Malcolm, I truly know. Don't be sorry anymore, promise me, sweetheart. If I could grant you one wish, it would be absolution from your pain." My breath caught on a sharp sob. "I love you. I've loved you since I first knew who you were. I've loved you through all of time, even the times we never found each other."

His eyes cut straight to my soul. "I have never loved anyone more than you. I never will. Nothing can change what you mean to me, not time or separation, not even death. You are the reason I live."

Holding each other close was no longer close enough and we both knew it.

Slow, deliberate, never removing the heat of his gaze from mine, he lifted my braid and unraveled it, next burying his hands in the wild length of my loose hair. His face grew almost stern with the depth of emotion I'd tapped and I made a small, inadvertent sound, pleading for more, and only more. For everything. He stroked my curls with slow, sensual movements, spreading them over my shoulders, letting his knuckles softly brush my nipples in passing.

I let the sheet fall to the floor.

He inhaled deeply, eyes darkening with overpowering arousal as he claimed my mouth, parting my lips and tasting me with deep strokes of his tongue. I moaned, knees buckling, and he swept me into his arms with an effortless motion, carrying me straight to the little brass bed which, for this one night, would become our heaven on earth; the fulfillment of over a century of waiting. He took me backward with a fluid, predatory grace as we kissed open-mouthed, gliding his warm hands in a path down my ribs, circling to cup my breasts, my hips.

Desire slammed me against jagged rocks, shook me in its teeth, until I was trembling and gasping, lifting into his touch with a violence of need. He broke the contact of our mouths to kiss my neck, opening his lips over my nipples, gently latching my right knee around his waist to stroke between my thighs, exploring each soft fold, inside and out.

"*Your shirt...*" I yanked at it, wanting it gone. No further barriers between us.

He grinned at my demand and I shivered hard, feverish with heat and slippery-wet at the sight of that grin. He drew back to tug the shirt over his head, his chest with its hard, wiry muscles and clear demarcations where clothing protected him from the sun.

"Pants," I ordered breathlessly and he obeyed at once, exposing his lean hips and the huge, swollen evidence of his desire. I begged, "Oh God, come here, come here *now...*"

He lunged and I shrieked, giggling, as he growled against my neck, pinning my shoulder blades to the mattress. And then the flood came on, stamping out all amusement as rampant hunger flared anew between us. I took him firmly in hand, my bare thighs gliding around his waist, and he convulsed with a shuddering gasp as I guided him straight to the tight, wet cleft between my legs. He groaned as if I'd torn out his heart, thrusting deeply as I clutched his shoulders. My hair spilled all over us when I rolled on top, riding him until we hung off the opposite side of the bed.

Malcolm took control once more, clutching my hips and shifting me full-length beneath him, there pausing for the space of several frantic heartbeats. Breathing hard, he smoothed hair from my sweaty forehead, cupping my cheek, bracketing my lower back to anchor me against the hard length buried fully within my body. He smiled so sweetly I came all over him yet again, quivering and gasping as he grasped my right ankle from his lower back and drew it gently higher, latching it around his neck as he resumed our rhythm. Kisses deep and deeper still, on and on, an eternity of living and loving, enclosed within the barriers of this one precious, stolen night.

Much later we lay entangled, utterly sated and lax in each other's arms, unwilling to release hold; dawn could not be more than an hour away. I didn't want to waste one second sleeping, my forehead against his neck, my right arm and thigh draped possessively over his torso.

Ending, I kept thinking. *You're coming to the ending.*

Devastation hovered close, ominous and unavoidable.

Malcolm rolled to an elbow, bracing above me; his eyes told me with no words he knew my thoughts. His beautiful, sensual lips appeared slightly swollen, his dark hair standing on end; bite marks decorated his shoulder muscles and thick stubble covered his jaws and chin. The only illumination in the little room came from the guttering candle on the dresser; we hadn't touched our dinner. In the dimness, which masked exact eye color, he could have been Mathias. There had been moments last night in which I had confused the two of them – Malcolm became Mathias in my mind, and back again – my husband and my lover, their passionate, sensitive souls one and the same. My love for them was inextricably braided together in my heart, no separating one from the other.

"You're thinking of him, aren't you?" he whispered, fingertips trailing along my flushed cheek.

"You *are* him," I whispered. "And he is you, just like Cora is *me*."

"If I had any less honor, I would beg you to forget him and stay here with me."

I cupped his jaws, tears rolling down my temples. The words cut at my throat. "I can't stay…"

"I know, love, I truly do." He kept his voice steady but the torture in his eyes could not be so easily hidden. His expression grew all the more intense, his arms tightening hold. "How much time?"

"I don't know." I pressed closer to his naked warmth; I harbored the notion that once we'd succeeded in preventing Fallon from altering the timeline, I would be returned to 2014. But I assumed, using my severely limited experience in the matter, the moment of return would occur without warning – a few seconds from now, or much longer.

"They'll have received word by now, out in Howardsville. The station operator there wired back last night that a rider was sent to Grant's. I forgot to tell you I checked. And Cole will have taken Patricia far from our original route by this time." Malcolm searched my eyes. "This Yancy from your own time, he is to be trusted?"

"He wants Fallon dead as much as we do. My sister trusts him."

Malcolm's gaze went suddenly to the middle distance, sending a spike of pure foreboding down my spine. His voice came from far away; he sounded like a stranger, a man full of menace and dark purpose, a man who had seen things I couldn't imagine. "Ain't no one alive wants Fallon dead the way I do."

"Tell me why. There's so much I don't understand…"

And so he spoke, low and quiet, explaining the hatred between the Yancys, Carters, and Davises. Of an ancient wound never healed, of vicious loathing between men who fought on opposite sides of the conflict I knew as the Civil War. Of Fallon's intent to enact vengeance, to drive the blade of pain so deeply within our families it could never be removed.

"He tried to hang you?!" I cried at one point. How had I ever imagined understanding what Malcolm had lived through, what horrors he'd faced in his life?

"Fallon would never have been able to hang me on his own. He was no older than me. But he had others to help disable us, including Virgil Turnbull, the rotten bastard. Ruthann told me of an association that yet exists between the Yancys and the Turnbulls, even in her own time. I suppose it ain't no surprise. There was a rumor I heard once, of a child Virgil had fathered with Isobel Faucon…" He drifted to silence, overcome by an onslaught of memories. I held fast, listening with all my attention, and at last he whispered, "Boyd and Cora saved me from hanging that night. There's been many a time I wished they hadn't, if only to kill the pain that came later, after Cora was lost."

"Cora forgave you long ago, sweetheart. Never forget that." Tears built in my eyes at the expression in his; dawn threatened the window by now, our time leaking away. Rebelling against its encroaching expiration, I gripped his strong hands and threaded our fingers.

"Once more," he whispered, a command and a plea, both at once.

Yes – the word lost between our mouths as I rolled atop his chest, taking him back inside the sleek wetness in which he had spilled over countless times since yesterday evening. Urgency tinted everything now, each kiss, each touch – no longer secure in the night with the promise of another hour to follow. We both knew it, clinging, coupling with the desperation of those who understand how little control they truly possess. He cried out, low and harsh, as he came, and I wrapped arms and legs around his body, unable now to restrain sobs.

"I love you, Malcolm, *my sweet Malcolm…*" Crying hard, gasping between each breath.

"Don't cry, sweetheart, it breaks my heart. I love you more than my next breath, more than my own life. I'll never stop." He rested his forehead to mine, our bodies linked as closely as our souls for one final moment in this place in time. And it was enough and never enough, both at once.

Chapter Twenty-Eight

Montana Territory - June, 1882

I WOKE SHROUDED BY UNEASE, THE REMNANTS OF A BAD dream lingering for a last second before wakefulness swept them away. Sweat plastered my nightgown to my skin. Our room was veiled in the darkness of deep night, morning still hours away, but awareness pulsed at the base of my neck and I sat straight, the covers falling to my hips.

Camille...

I hear you…

"What's wrong, love?" Marshall murmured, rolling over, wakened by the sound of my voice.

"I don't know exactly. I was having a nightmare…" I threw off the quilt and hurried from our bed, drawn to the single window to peer out at the black night, plagued by the sense that my oldest sister had just called my name. I'd been restored to full consciousness for a reason – something out there demanded my attention and Camille wanted me to know. *But what?* I shivered so hard I would have pitched forward out the window if not for the glass.

Marshall was on my heels, clutching my upper arms in a gesture both concerned and protective. He drew me from the window – and potential harm's way – sheltering me against his nude body. "Same here. I was dreaming about Garth and Case and Mathias, just now. They were singing at The Spoke and something was really wrong. Something was about to happen, I don't know what exactly, I just knew they were in danger."

Shivers rippled over every inch of my flesh; my voice emerged as a terrified, high-pitched bleat. "Camille was trying to tell me something, just now. Marsh, something's happening…"

"Stay away from the window," he ordered, grabbing clothes from the floor, scurrying into them before opening our bedroom door and yelling, "Grant!"

It was more than I could bear – far too similar to the night last summer when Miles was shot and killed. "No," I choked, watching Marshall buckle his gun belt into place around his hips. "No, don't go down there."

He crossed the room in three strides to gather me close, understanding the reason behind my distress. Harsh, unyielding in his conviction, he said, "Angel, listen to me. I'm not Miles. I will not die and leave you alone, do you hear me?"

Raised voices in the rooms below, the household roused to action. I heard Grant and Birdie, then Celia; baby Jacob began crying. Thunking clatters met our ears as rifles were pulled from the rack and boxes of bullets retrieved from the top drawer of the hutch. No chances would be taken this time.

"Do you think Miles *thought* he was going to die?" I cried, not about to release my hold on Marshall. "He had no control over what happened, just like we have no control!"

"I can't argue with that, Ruthie, it's not fair."

"Don't tell me what's fair!" Pregnancy robbed me of what little emotional control stress had not; tears painted wet tracks over my face. "And don't you dare mention dying! Knock on wood, right now!"

Grant hollered up the stairs. "Marsh! Rider!"

Holding my gaze, Marshall reached and rapped his knuckles firmly on the doorframe, then planted a kiss flush on my lips and tucked me close to his side. "I love you, Ruthann Rawley. C'mon. Stay beside me."

The rooms below remained shrouded in darkness as we descended the stairs; lighted candles would obscure the view outdoors. Grant, armed with a rifle, waited to the left of the front windows. Birdie and Celia had herded the boys into the pantry, a small, windowless space in which Birdie had once stitched Axton's gunshot wounds.

"Ruthie, come join us," she ordered in a hushed whisper.

Marshall kissed me once more, quick and possessive. "I'll be right here."

He took up a position to the right of the windows, opposite Grant, as we all strained to listen. Celia, sitting on the floor with her back braced on the pantry wall, nursed Jacob so he would keep quiet while Birdie knelt, holding her boys around their waists. I crouched beside Birdie and her sons, pressing both fists to my lips.

Shouting voices outside – I heard Axton's among them.

"Grant! Marsh! Rider from Howardsville!" Ax yelled, and Grant lowered his rifle barrel from a position of direct threat, flinging open the outer door.

Axton, who slept in the bunkhouse, entered in the company of three other men, two of them ranch hands, the third unknown to me. Axton carried a lantern and everyone spoke at once. The pantry allowed for a slanted view of the action; behind Birdie and me, Celia murmured, "That's Pete Darnell's boy, from the telegraph office in town."

Grant ordered, "Hush up, you-all! Darnell, what's this about?"

Darnell pulled a slip of paper from inside his shirt, which he thrust at Grant. "Telegram for you, from Iowa. Sender requested immediate delivery, so I told Pa I'd ride out." He was young, probably no more than seventeen or eighteen; excitement radiated from him at the privilege of such an important and urgent errand.

"From Iowa?" Axton spoke roughly and I knew, like me, his first thought was of Patricia.

I refused to stay put in the pantry and scrambled to my feet. Marshall reached with his free arm and gathered me close to his side while Grant unfolded the tattered paper containing the message; rifle propped against his hip, Grant cleared his throat and began reading.

"'Camille arrived this morning…'"

My heart slammed to a halt; Marshall and I stared at each other with flat-out stun.

Grant read on, "'Please get immediate word to Grant and Marshall Rawley. Tell them Fallon is on his way. Will reach you by tomorrow. Be prepared. Do not leave for Howardsville.'" He paused for a split second, rereading a line. "Cole and Patricia are safe. Request word when rider is sent. Malcolm A. Carter.'"

"Holy shit. Holy fucking *shit*." Marshall's eyebrows were lofted almost to his hairline.

"When was this sent?" Axton demanded.

"Around dinnertime, last night," Darnell said. "From Muscatine, Iowa."

"Oh, my God..." I couldn't think fast enough to make sense of what this meant. Camille was here in 1882? In Iowa? *And she had found Malcolm.* Reeling, I clung to Marshall, seeking a single point of orientation upon which to focus. How had she known when and where to come? For that matter, how had she arrived in the nineteenth century in the first place?

"Yancy." Grant spoke the name like a curse. "It's time to finish this, once and for all. Time to send that bastard straight to hell." He looked to his ranch hands. "Fellas, we got a situation here. Shit, we have to spread the word quick, it's nearly tomorrow already."

The hows and whys would have to come later; Grant was right – it was time to finish this.

A fair morning bloomed on the eastern horizon; June thirtieth, the last day of the month. Marsh and Axton were due in Howardsville later this day to greet the new marshal, a man sent to Montana Territory to replace Marshall's post, but Malcolm's telegram ordered to stay put and we were not about to question the warning, let alone disobey it. Word had been spread to Grant's men of the approaching danger; they were armed at all times but most rode in at some point to gather additional rifles, bullets, and pistols. Morning passed in a tense haze, bright sun shining down as a benign, windless day unfolded outside.

Despite my anger over it, Marshall rode Blade to the summit of the ridge opposite the house, along with Axton and Grant, who toted along a telescoping brass spyglass. From the ridgeline, the spyglass allowed observation of the foothills for dozens of miles. I stalked the front window, feeling like an animal in a too-small cage, not removing my gaze from the specks of their mounted figures up on the distant ridge.

"*Men.* They ain't no better than little boys when they get a notion in their damn heads," Celia said as she joined me. "And the Rawleys are about the worst, stubborn as hell, the entire lot of them." She rubbed a comforting hand between my shoulder blades, muttering, "Don't we know?"

I cupped the roundness of my lower belly, where Marshall's son grew daily; Celia knew just how to coax a smile, albeit a grim one. I muttered, "Damn right. Don't they know it's dangerous to be out there, exposed like that?"

Birdie, who alleviated her worry best by keeping busy, looked over her shoulder at us. She stood at the table, a smooth, perfect oval of pale dough rolled out before her. Using a small water glass, she cut biscuits with the deft movements of an action completed thousands of times before. "Grant said he won't be kept like a rabbit in a cage in his own house." She sighed. "Danger and excitement tend to blend together in their man-minds."

I smiled at Birdie's words, which reminded me of something my sisters would say. I'd spent so much of the day imagining Camille somewhere in Iowa, both of us existing in the same century for the first time in over a year. It killed me that I couldn't make contact; riddled with questions I had no hope of answering short of a conversation with her, the foremost of which being *how*. How in God's name had she known, with such specific timing, where Fallon would appear? How had she reached 1882 and found Malcolm Carter? I was dying to know. And I wanted so badly to tell her my news. I wanted so much for the women-folk to know I was pregnant.

Celia snorted at Birdie's words; Celia knew her own sense of humor was far more ribald, winking at her dear friend as she muttered, "Most every man's got but two things on his man-mind, himself and his pecker."

"And his pecker's likely higher on the list," Birdie said, giggling, the three of us craving a little relief from the tension.

"In my experience, that's God's truth." Celia grinned, that wide, knowing Rawley smile I'd seen so many times on the faces of her many descendants. Love for her swelled in my chest. Nodding toward the ridge, Celia murmured, "Aw, them fellers are good men, as men go. Even if they are stubborn creatures the Rawleys know how to treat a lady, and Axton is as sweet as a man can be. Sweet to the bone, that one." She clucked her tongue. "It's a shame he's so dead-set on a woman he can't ever have. I hate to see it."

"Me too," I whispered. "I worry about him so much. And I miss Patricia all the time, not a night goes by when I don't think about her. I can't imagine what Ax is feeling. I pray she's safe with Cole, like Malcolm said." Even as I spoke, I kept my eyes fixed on Marshall and Blade, the two of them no larger than the top joint of my index finger at such a distance, Blade's gorgeous hide catching the sun like a silver coin – and making a clear target for anyone looking, damn him.

Birdie balled up and then kneaded the remaining dough, flour dusting her nose, fingers, and wrists. She spoke with quiet reassurance. "Cole can handle himself. We have to trust in that. I wonder where they are as we speak. Are they still so far south, in Muscatine along with Malcolm? They'd have backtracked in that case, because we know they reached Fannie and Charley's homestead weeks ago, which is much closer to Iowa City."

I sifted again through the limited information available to me, imagining circumstances that would culminate in Camille appearing in the nineteenth century. 'Arrived this morning' the telegram stated, meaning she had been here for at least twenty-four hours. Had she arrived from 2014? Was she alone? As close as I could figure, her passage backward through time was probably inadvertent, just as mine had been; I found it very difficult to imagine Mathias allowing her to leave the safety of the twenty-first century without his protection.

Unless...

Unless something of magnitude had happened in our absence.

My lungs compressed at the thought; my every instinct screamed that this was true.

And whatever Fallon did must have been catastrophic.

But what?!

I imagined the worst, ill at the thought that he had killed someone in my family or Marshall's; I could envision nothing more devastating. When last in Fallon's presence, I had been a prisoner in his train car, rolling toward Chicago. There, he'd detailed an account of his own abilities, taking great pride in the fact that he could leap across centuries to harm those Marshall and I loved, including Marshall's beloved mother, Faye. Horror further drained my self-control as I reconsidered what Camille's presence in 1882 meant.

Whatever Fallon did, your family knew about it before you. Somehow Camille knew where to show up to deliver a message. Even if she was swept back in time without her control, she knew when and where Fallon would appear.

But how?!

"I hate waiting. I fucking hate not knowing what's happening!" The words flew like darts from my mouth, startling both Celia and Birdie to silence. I rarely cursed in front of them.

Celia hooked an arm around my waist. "You and everyone else drawing breath at this moment, honey-love."

The afternoon sun inched along the sky's western curve. Marshall, Axton, and Grant returned and gathered around the table in the kitchen – now free of biscuit dough – occupying their time by taking apart and cleaning their firearms, talking in low voices. I knew they chafed at the necessity of remaining all but hidden indoors, but Miles had died only a few yards from the front door of the house; to this day, despite several suspects, we didn't know exactly who had fired the rifle that terrible morning. Grant's men bristled with armaments, every last one of them on high alert; inside and out, the atmosphere was one of heightening tension but I couldn't shake the feeling that we were all balanced on the edge of a blade, waiting for something that wasn't going to happen.

I sensed Fallon out there.

I knew I wasn't just imagining it.

He knows.

He knows Camille is here, he knows we've been warned.

Enmeshed as we were in the midst of the longest days of the year, each hour lasted a tiny eternity, chipping away at our sanity. A rich purple dusk eventually settled over the land, the sun melting in a magenta river behind the mountains. Birdie and Celia served supper but no one was hungry. I paced the floor in our bedroom, drawn time and again to the window even though there was nothing to see. Marshall lay on the bed with both arms folded beneath his head, eyes closed though I knew he wasn't really sleeping. Afraid, restless, and emotionally drained, I wanted to pick a fight if only to crack the tension in the air.

"Sweetheart, come lay down for a minute. You're gonna wear a hole in the floor." Marshall chose his words with care, sensitive to my volatile state; I knew he was really saying something along the lines of, *Quit pacing before I go fucking insane, woman!*

"Camille is in this century, Marsh. Right *now*. I can't believe she's really here." I rested my forehead to the window glass, which retained the day's heat. "How did she get here? What happened to cause it?" Of course we had already exhausted every conceivable possibility; Marshall was every bit as terrified that someone we loved was already gone – that a death had spurred Camille's journey to the nineteenth century. Speculation reached a point at which it became unproductive, if not outright maddening, and we were well past that point.

Marshall dropped all pretense of resting, propping on his left elbow. The last of the daylight bathed his lean, handsome face with a bronze tint, gilding his features and highlighting his lips. A pulse of pure desire caught me unaware; this was hardly the time for lovemaking. I thought of how, under other circumstances, he and Axton would have been in Howardsville at this moment, to meet the new marshal. Another pulse – but this one of prickling awareness. My thoughts spun in a completely different direction.

"What is it, angel?" Marshall studied me with a familiar crease of worry between his brows. "What did you think of?"

I moved to sit on the bed, bending my left knee toward him, which he immediately cupped. "You and Ax weren't supposed to be here tonight. If not for Malcolm's telegram, you would have been in Howardsville."

Marshall sat straighter, nodding. "Leaving only Grant to protect the house."

"And there's only ever two, maybe three, ranch hands not on duty at any one time. Most of them are out with the cattle, nowhere near the house," I added. My thoughts flew back to the hour in Fallon's train car. Parts of that encounter had since blurred; self-defense against the terror of the memory. But I recalled enough to know Fallon wanted me dead. I'd broken his arm, I'd sent him flying through the channels of time to God only knew what destination. Over a year ago now – and other than in the dark spaces of nightmares, I had not seen him since.

But he had seen *me*, I was certain. Camille's arrival and Malcolm's telegram had altered events, had somehow thwarted Fallon's intentions.

A knifepoint scoured the length of my spine.

I stood in a rush, thrusting aside the urge to cower instead. "He's out there, Marsh, right now." Breathless, agitated, I returned to the window. Awash now in crimson light, the rippled glass appeared to glow with fire.

"I know it. I can sense him waiting like a fucking ambush predator. I've felt it all day but he's biding his time." Marshall slid from the bed with his typical grace, joining me at the window and enclosing my waist in his arms. I wilted backward against the security of his chest, so grateful he was here with me tonight and not miles away in Howardsville; for whatever unfathomable reason, that journey was not meant to occur.

"Where could he hide that we wouldn't see him watching?" I shuddered and Marshall tightened his embrace, bending to hook his chin over my left shoulder, linking his fingers protectively over my lower belly. "Grant's men are everywhere out there, Marsh. They checked the bunkhouse and the stables…even the outhouses."

"Fallon knows this area probably better than anyone, and that's to his advantage. He knows Grant and I won't leave the house unguarded, so we can't go looking for him." He inhaled, slow and meditative. "I keep thinking of the foothill caves where Garth and Case and I used to play. They'd be a perfect spot to hide out and wait."

"But *what* is he waiting for? Malcolm's telegram said Fallon would reach us today but he has to know by now that we've been forewarned.

He may not know how we were warned, but he knows." Relying purely on gut instinct, I whispered, "Something was supposed to happen today, and it didn't. I don't know how I know this, but I do." The upper curve of the sun sank from view as I spoke and I shuddered violently at the vanishing of the light. "Marsh...we can't beat him. How can we beat someone who can jump through time?"

"We can jump through time too, angel. I've been wondering all day if we should try to get back to 2014. No more delaying." Marshall turned me around to receive the full impact of his serious gray eyes, his expression adamant. "This has gone too far. You're carrying our baby. I want us *home*."

"But we can't jump the way Fallon can. He has more control. And even if we could return home right this second" – and the thought of home, our *real* home, filled me with sharp, torturous longing – "Camille would still be in 1882. We have no idea how or why she's here. We have to find her before we go. We can't leave her behind. There's too much we don't understand."

And there was little else to do but continue to wait.

Chapter Twenty-Nine

Montana Territory - June, 1882

HOURS PASSED. WE VENTURED DOWNSTAIRS TO EAT, AT Marshall's insistence, where I choked down a biscuit, dunking each subsequent bite in a cup of warm tea, recalling the months when Camille was pregnant with Millie Jo, many years ago. I'd been twelve at the time and hadn't even gotten my first period, but clearly remembered the terrible morning sickness Camille had suffered through, the way she couldn't bear the lingering scent of fried fish in the cafe; perking coffee incited her gag reflex. I understood much better now, fighting waves of nausea as I studied the darkness pressing against the window glass, imagining my sister out there somewhere.

Camille, I'm going crazy. Are you all right? Are you with Malcolm? I need to talk to you. I would give almost anything for a cell phone.

The clock hands eventually swung around to midnight, taking us past the 'tomorrow' Malcolm mentioned in the telegram. Still nothing. Birdie, Celia, and the boys went to bed; Grant and Marshall stood talking with several of the ranch hands in the kitchen while Axton sat with me in the cramped living room at the back of the house; we hadn't found a moment alone all day, and I was glad for his company.

"Where do you think they are?" Ax sat facing me on the narrow sofa. The curtains were drawn and only one small lamp lit, but we avoided the windows all the same.

I knew he meant Patricia and Cole. "I don't know. Oh God, Ax, I wish I had a better guess. The telegram was sent from a city they'd already traveled through, according to Birdie, which suggests they'd backtracked. But why?"

"It might be only Malcolm who backtracked," Axton speculated.

"That's true. He wrote that they were 'safe,' which doesn't necessarily mean they were still in his company." I tried again to imagine Camille interacting with Patricia and Cole. But most especially with Malcolm. I pictured the photograph of him Camille had kept on her nightstand for many years, the one she routinely kissed and held, cherishing it like a talisman.

Camille, I understand more than you could know. Malcolm is Mathias, just like Miles was Marshall. But I didn't realize until it was too late. You already know.

I could only imagine what might have happened if I'd recognized my true connection to Miles – but it was best not to let my thoughts stray in that direction.

Axton lowered his voice. "Did you know your sister could travel through time, same as you?"

I grasped his hands and squeezed; they were hard and warm and he returned the pressure. "No, I had no idea. I can't believe she's here, Ax. It makes me wonder what else I don't know. What happened in the future that caused Camille to come *here*, looking for Marshall and me?"

"I wish I knew." Ax studied my face for a heartbeat. "Ruthie, you're exhausted. You have shadows like big pools under your eyes. And besides that, you're expecting."

"I'm not ready for bed," I argued, glancing toward the kitchen, reassured by the sight of Marshall's right shoulder and arm, all I could see of him around the corner of the wall. He clutched his rifle by the barrel, the stock resting on the floor.

"Just try to rest a spell. I promised Marsh I'd try to coax you up to bed," Ax tattled, with a hint of his natural good humor.

"Is that so?" I muttered. I didn't want to interrupt the conversation in the kitchen, conceding that Axton was right; I was helping no one by staying up well past the point of fatigue. Maybe I could claim a few hours of sleep before morning. Maybe by morning there would be additional word from Malcolm and my sister.

I hugged Axton. "I love you so much."

Axton kissed the top of my head. "I love you too, Ruthie. Try to get some sleep, all right?"

I climbed the back steps, avoiding memories of the night I'd skulked up the back staircase at Rilla's, the whorehouse where I'd lived after arriving in Howardsville. I'd been on a mission that night, along with Axton and Cole, to save Patricia from the Yancys; we hadn't saved her that particular night and I prayed that this time was different, that she and Cole were indeed safely away from harm. My vision swam with dizzy fatigue as I closed the bedroom door, not bothering to light a lantern.

None of you are safe from harm, not so long as Fallon is alive.

In the gray gloom I unbuttoned my blouse and shed my corset, skirt, and underskirts with disturbing realizations undulating across my mind. A full moon had long since set, drawing its bright radiance behind the horizon. Nude, I leaned over my side of the bed in search of my nightgown and clunked my shin on its wooden frame.

"*Ouch.* Dammit."

"Not a sound." He materialized from the shadows, closing in behind me before I could draw my next breath, let alone scream for help. "I'll cut you from ear to ear."

I believed his every word, blinking rapidly, adrenaline sharpening my senses before panic could obliterate them. Fallon wrapped his left arm below my breasts, maintaining an unbreakable hold; he clutched a knife in the opposite hand, its blade poised under my left ear, just where my jawbone met my skull. The metal felt obscenely warm against my skin, as if he'd already used it to spill blood tonight. His breath thundered hot against the side of my face; he stayed close so I couldn't buck his hold, his hips against my backside. He was hard. I could feel it through his pants and my stomach lurched; I tasted bile, sour and acidic.

"Ruthann. I told you we'd meet again. You knew I was here waiting, didn't you? Your heart is beating so fast." He spoke with a lover's tone and my horror multiplied, scattering my focus. Did he intend rape before killing me? I heard the muted voices of the men in the kitchen downstairs. I couldn't risk calling out but maybe I could knock something over…a crash to draw their attention. My wide eyes darted in a frantic circuit of the room, seeking options; no weapons, the door on the far side of the bed.

"You make one sound before I order it and your blood will *paint this floor*. Do you hear me, you little fucking whore?" He shifted almost seamlessly between an unnatural calm and seething rage, far more frightening than one versus the other. When I didn't at once respond, Fallon rotated the knife so the pointed tip created a burning pinprick in the flesh beneath my ear. He spared a second to sweep his thumb down the side of my neck, showing me the dark smear of my own blood before swiping the wetness across my lower lip. "Nod if you understand."

I nodded, once, twice; two jerking bobs of my head.

Mouth at my ear, he hissed, "Tell me how Malcolm Carter knew to warn you. I know it was him, I saw the bastard's message from Muscatine. Who is the woman?"

I tried to shake my head, to indicate I didn't know what he meant.

"*Tell me*."

I could not force sound past the boulder of fear in my chest.

"How the fuck did he know? *Who is the woman?* Tell me or I will kill you and everyone in this fucking house."

If I die, my baby dies…

Oh God, don't let him hurt the baby…

Fallon gripped my right breast as he spoke softly in my ear, the pendulum of his voice swinging back to eerie calm, a man boasting his own accomplishments. "No matter. Malcolm and his whore are as good as dead by now. By my reckoning, Vole and Turnbull caught up with him earlier this very day. I told them to kill the woman but hold off killing Carter, if they could manage it. He's a slippery bastard, you see, and I want the privilege of killing him."

Something overrode the sound of my panicked breaths – that of Marshall's footsteps advancing on the stairs. Fallon felt my muscles go rigid with agony and whispered, "Make a sound and he dies first." Swift and effortless, an action completed a thousand times, Fallon sheathed his knife and drew his gun, pressing the small barrel to my temple just as the door swung inward.

"Are you awake, sweetheart? Ax said you came to bed." Having come from the lantern-lighted kitchen, Marshall's eyes hadn't yet adjusted; he propped his rifle on the floor, letting it lean against the dresser as he spoke.

A choking whimper wrenched free of my lips and Fallon increased the pressure at all points of contact on my body.

Marshall froze, eyes locked on the unimaginable – his naked, pregnant wife with a gun to her head.

"Not a word. Shut the door, Rawley."

Marshall obeyed, not removing his gaze from us. He was in what amounted to his calm before the storm – calculating, honing, preparing. If Fallon made even the slightest wrong move there would be nothing left to identify as human once Marshall finished with him. I held perfectly still, watching Marshall. If Fallon's life was directly threatened I knew he would vanish, a sort of self-defense mechanism with which he was equipped. Part of me expected to feel the pull of time at any second, dragging me out of this moment just as it had the winter night when my Buick crashed on I94 – but perhaps the threat was not yet pronounced enough.

"Toss that piece to the bed," Fallon commanded. "*Slow*, or she's dead. You go for that rifle and she's dead."

I watched as Marshall unbuckled his gun belt and pitched it gently to the surface of the mattress. "Let Ruthann go and I'll do anything you want."

I heard the rampant distress just under the surface of Marshall's voice and prayed Fallon did not.

But of course he did; I sensed his lips part in a smile as he whispered, "You'll do whatever I want or you'll watch me bend her over the bed while I fuck her. Tell me how Malcolm knew to warn you. Who is the woman with him?"

"She's Ruthann's sister, from Minnesota. She came from the future to warn him you were on the way. Malcolm sent a telegram last night, from Muscatine, Iowa." Marshall spoke without hesitation, advancing a step toward the bed.

"That's far enough. How did the sister know?"

"We don't know. We haven't talked to her."

Fallon removed his left hand from my breast and slid it down my belly, clutching my pelvis in an unrelenting grip. A growling protest rose from my throat even as I dared not struggle. Marshall hissed a low, enraged breath, hands fisted. The surge of violent energy radiating from him was nearly visible in the air.

"You're lying," Fallon said calmly.

"*I will break every fucking bone in your body.*"

"You'll tell me the truth."

"*You fucking son of a bitch, I will kill you...*" Teeth bared, feral with rage, Marshall was at breaking point and Fallon knew it.

His pleasure heightening with each subsequent taunting word, Fallon said, "Ruthann wants me to fuck her. I can feel it, right here between her legs. And then I'll kill her before your eyes, Rawley, just like I once killed your mother, what do you think of that?"

I acted without thinking, terrified by the loss of control on Marshall's face. Fallon's left arm, pointed downward as he gripped my pelvis, no longer restrained me against his chest and I twisted sideways, grabbing his right wrist with both hands, using my weight and momentum to drag his hand – and the gun – toward the floor. The gun discharged, a bright orange flame exploding from the barrel, and annihilated all other sound.

Fallon's vicious punch caught me between the shoulder blades, propelling all breath from my lungs; I sprawled flat on my belly, unable to break the fall, as Marshall lunged over the bed and took Fallon backward. I would have scrambled away if I could breathe. Straddling Fallon, Marshall seized his neck with both hands and slammed Fallon's head repeatedly against the floorboards before bearing down with all his strength. From my vantage point I saw Fallon's boots scraping the floor as he tried to heave upward and buck Marshall's hold. And as I watched, mouth flopping like that of a hooked fish in an effort to draw air into my chest cavity, Fallon began fading.

No! He's getting away...

Just before he vanished from view, Fallon lifted the gun and fired pointblank at Marshall.

Chapter Thirty

The Iowa Plains - June, 1882

MALCOLM AND I DRESSED IN YESTERDAY'S CLOTHES, GATH-
ered our belongings, and left behind our room at the hotel before the
day was an hour old. We checked in at the telegraph office, discovering
no additional news, and then collected Aces High from the livery stable.
Once Aces was headed northwest at a cantering clip we ate a breakfast
of corn muffins the woman at the hotel had been kind enough to send
with us, perplexed by our early, rapid departure. We shared water from
Malcolm's canteen when Aces slowed to a walk, the proximity of our
bodies torturous in a way it hadn't yet been yesterday. Yesterday we hadn't
fully realized, let alone tested, the depth of our connection. Today, we
knew just how powerfully it bound us.

Yesterday, we hadn't yet spent the entire night making love.

Rain loomed on the western horizon within the first five miles. I
smelled it almost immediately, Malcolm and I watching as heavy pewter clouds released silvery sheets of water in the distance. There was no
avoiding the downpour.

"At least we'll be clean," I said, trying to make a joke. I was shaky and
distracted and overwhelmed, even sheltered as I was against his chest
and within the circle of his arms. I'd braided my hair and slung the braid
over my shoulder so my hair wouldn't be in the way when I turned my
face toward Malcolm's neck, inhaling, sometimes resting my lips upon
the skin his open shirt collar exposed. In turn, he pressed soft kisses to
my temple, gliding his free hand – the one not holding the reins – in

gentle, sensual patterns over my belly, my arm, my thigh.

"What if we started a child, last night?" he quietly asked at one point, resting the length of his hand flat on my stomach.

This had occurred to me as well. I had no earthly idea how to respond; he sensed this and didn't push further.

But awareness of the possibility burned between us.

We rode toward the sheeting rain for perhaps thirty minutes before struck by the first sting of cold droplets; I couldn't shake the ominous metaphors infiltrating my mind as we approached an inescapable storm. Malcolm reined Aces to a halt and quickly dismounted, rooting in his saddle bag, extracting and then shaking out a rain blanket. He paused for a second, resting a warm hand on my calf. In the ashy sheen cast by thick clouds he looked up at me, his dark eyes so full of feeling I realized I would never recover from loving him.

"We have hard riding ahead, love. I am sorry, I wish it wasn't so."

I held his gaze, aching and overcome. "I can do it."

Once again in the saddle, he situated the blanket like a shawl around us and I tucked the ends near my breasts, creating as much protection as possible.

"Keep close, we're in for a soaking," he murmured, kissing the top of my head, shifting his hips to urge Aces into forward motion. The horse snorted and whooshed, tossing his long brown head, clearly communicating his displeasure at the crying sky. Malcolm leaned to pat his horse's neck, murmuring, "We been through worse, ain't we, boy? C'mon now, we gotta catch up with Cole."

"How far ahead are they, do you think?"

"If we figure that Cole got them to Windham, as he intended, we should reach them by early evening."

"I'm sorry to put you through all this."

The rain swiftly obliterated all chance of further conversation, but Malcolm put his lips to my ear so I would hear over the pounding assault. "Don't be sorry, Camille, not for a thing. Having you here in my arms means more to me than any heaven I could imagine."

Tears surged, mixing with the rain, and I closed my eyes, huddling as close to him as I could; his hat offered some shelter but the onslaught of water grew brutal. Aces was forced to a walk, shying from the incessant deluge striking us at a slanted angle. No lightning accompanied the storm and we could have sought shelter beneath a cover of trees, if any were in sight. At last Malcolm tugged Aces to a standstill, angling him sideways so our heads, all three, were offered some meager protection. Yesterday's unrelenting sun became a distant memory. Malcolm rewrapped the rain blanket, tucking my head to his chest. Despite our combined warmth, shivers overtook my limbs.

"Hang on, love, it'll soon pass," he murmured in my ear, and within fifteen minutes the worst of it blew over, hauling the rain westward, leaving behind a soggy but manageable drizzle. Malcolm removed his hat, shaking excess moisture from its brim before doing the same thing with the blanket. He dismounted to resituate it behind him on the saddle, patting Aces on the neck and speaking to the animal in low tones while I squeezed out my braid and willed my muscles to stop quivering.

Standing beside Aces, rubbing his horse's damp hide, Malcolm sent me a grin and the fault lines along my heart throbbed; tenderness came so naturally to him. He observed, "Aw, sweetheart, your lips are blue."

"Yours…too," I mumbled, hard-pressed to speak through my numb, discolored mouth. "Come back…up here…please."

He took the saddle in a hurry, curling me close. "C'mere, I've got you. Put your face against my neck."

The clouds remained thick and inhibiting, intermittently weeping over the prairie as we rode without letup through tall, dripping grasses, along a bumpy road carved into the earth by wagon tracks and hooves. To my relief the air warmed as the hidden sun rose, growing humid; combined with the heat of Malcolm's body, the chills eventually receded. I decided it was best not to dwell on the state of my hair and clothing. Open prairie dominated the landscape, though from time to time we passed split-rail fences separating the road from cropland, at least some evidence of human habitation. No towns, very few trees. I conjured up an image of Iowa as it appeared on a road map, attempting to guess our exact position. I had no idea, trusting completely in Malcolm's sense of direction.

"Where are we?" I asked at one point, when Malcolm slowed Aces to a walk, conserving the horse's energy. While clouds continued to shadow our route, the rain had finally ceased. The trail was bordered to the right by a trickling creek edged with cottonwoods and willows; it flowed along in a friendly, gurgling rush. "I'm trying to picture where I think we are in the state."

"We're about centered, and I pray a good deal farther south than Dredd and his father aim to travel this day. We've a stretch yet to cover, likely eighteen or twenty miles to Windham. How are you holding up?"

"I'll make it. I can't pretend I'm not sore, but I'll survive."

"This sort of travel must seem all-fired strange to you, coming from another century." His voice took on a faraway quality, as he was attempting to conjure images of vehicles racing along concrete roadways. How strange that world would seem to his eyes; the image of him and Aces among the clamoring, fast-paced chaos of a city street was so blatantly wrong as to evoke tragedy.

"It's slower," I allowed, lacing the fingers of our left hands. "If we had a car, we could cover that distance in about fifteen minutes. But..." I brought his knuckles to my lips. "We can sit much closer on Aces than we could in any car."

"I've been thanking God all darn day for that very thing." I sensed his grin, its warmth enveloping me like a bright, errant sunbeam. He squeezed my fingers, our hands still interlocked and resting between my breasts, and inhaled, about to speak. But I would never know what he intended to say just then, because his bearing snapped alert with such suddenness I gasped.

"What is it?!" I searched the road stretching before us, seeing nothing but the cloudy-bright landscape through which we'd traveled all day. But something had changed, I knew without being told.

In the space of a breath Malcolm became the man who had spent much of his life stalked by danger, who had endured perilous conditions I was only beginning to understand; a man whose survival depended on his instinct, his senses, his weapons, and the knowledge of when to fight and when to run. And right now, it was time to run.

Severe and intense, he ordered, "Lean forward, hold tight to his mane. Don't let go. Don't lift your head."

I felt Malcolm's posture shift, every muscle tensing like a sprinter poised on starting blocks, and he heeled Aces with a double kick; the animal snorted an immediate response and rippled into a canter.

"*Gidd'up*, c'mon now, boy," Malcolm urged, keeping low, bracing over me as best he could. Tension and trepidation resonated in his voice and I followed his instructions without question, starkly aware of the difference in the horse's rapid passage; we were not hurrying in effort to deliver a message or flee a rainstorm.

We were being pursued.

"Run, *c'mon!*" Malcolm growled, heeling Aces a second time, taking us to a full-out gallop.

I pressed my forehead to the rough bristle of hair lining the animal's neck, my bones clacking with the pounding of his powerful hooves, clutching hold until my fists ached. True flight now, the prairie a rippling blur on either side, choice stripped away from one second to the next. I knew without being told that my presence impeded our flight; two riders hindered even the strongest horse's abilities. A strange popping sound, like that of ice cracking in quick bursts, met our ears; Malcolm hissed a low breath and pressed me lower.

Guns, I realized, my twenty-first century mind sorting the sounds into sense. *Oh, holy shit…*

Malcolm was behind me, his back exposed to flying bullets. And there was exactly nothing I could do.

"*C'mon, boy…*" But Aces was charging at full capacity, ribs heaving, hooves thundering.

I felt Malcolm shifting position; though I couldn't see what was happening I knew he had extracted his own pistol, twisting sideways to fire – once, twice, three times. My ears throbbed, the rapid shots echoing my bursting heart. Aces lost ground and Malcolm spun back around, holding the gun at his right thigh, angling protectively over me. Our pursuer fired again, bullets fracturing the air with sharp cracks; he was much closer to us now.

Malcolm exhaled a hissing breath, his right elbow jerking.

Was he shot?!

Frantic, I couldn't even turn around to see if he was hurt.

The world narrowed to a thin, jolting corridor.

After two days of hard riding, Aces was flagging.

As though outside my own body and watching from a short distance away, I realized, *He's going to catch us.*

I became suddenly aware that two horses flanked Aces, one to either side; my peripheral vision picked out the looming shapes. Numb and horrified, unable to blink or move or utter a sound, I could do nothing but watch as one of the men aimed a gun at us, his mouth flapping. Yelling, ordering us to stop.

Malcolm shouted in my ear, "Hold on!"

He yanked on the reins, slowing Aces enough that the other horses flew past us; my head jerked so hard I saw stars. With an unyielding forearm across my shoulder blades Malcolm held me down, leaning around me to fire repeatedly. Aces brayed a high-pitched whinny and Malcolm circled him sharply to the right, as though to make a U-turn, but it wasn't enough; we had no chance. I opened my eyes in time to see two mounted horses charging us, one man aiming a pistol while the second raced near with a long, slender rifle held lengthwise; I screamed then, sharp and piercing, as he struck Malcolm's head with its stock, knocking him backward from the saddle.

Men shouting and cursing. Horses wheeling around, Aces rearing and squealing, reins dangling. I couldn't stop screaming, even as I was summarily dragged from Aces, straight to the back of another horse. Fury burned across my vision, tinting everything red. I fought my captor's one-armed hold, kicking, elbowing, breathing with fast, enraged breaths – no thought in mind except to reach Malcolm, who lay on the ground perhaps twenty feet away.

"Hold still, you little bitch!" raged the man restraining me; he shifted, cursing, trying to hold the reins and the rifle in one hand. He bellowed to his companion, "Get to Carter 'fore he gets his piece!"

"*Malcolm!*" I shouted as the second man charged toward him on horseback, gun drawn.

Malcolm rolled sideways before leaping to a crouch and I saw the deep gash on his forehead and the wound on his arm, blood flowing at both points. My heart sank like a stone in a lake – he was hurt, separated from his gun. The man yanked his horse to a halt, the animal dancing in a tight circle with the motion; he aimed square at Malcolm's chest and ordered, "Stay put." Only then did he turn in his saddle to deliver orders. "Shut up that little hellcat and fetch that mount before he runs straight to Missouri!"

I'd never experienced true brutality, stunned by the level of aggression with which I was backhanded across the jaw, plummeting from horseback to earth. I heard Malcolm's rage as I fell, the world pitching and tilting, rising to meet my left side with a dull thud. Small black spots danced, colliding in the air before my eyes. The sky gleamed like polished tin; from my position flat on the ground, I watched as the man who'd struck me heeled his horse and took off at a clip, presumably to round up Aces High.

The man holding a gun on Malcolm bellowed, "Not a move, Carter! I'll shoot you dead!" He spared a glance in my direction and decided, "She ain't hurt bad." He chuckled, a raw, grating sound, as he added, "Yet."

"I'll split your skull, Vole, I'll gut you like a *fucking hog*." Vicious with fury, I imagined how Malcolm's eyes appeared; from my current position, I couldn't see his face.

I heard Ruthann's voice in my head, the hushed, painful information she had related to us that night at Shore Leave, and thought, *Vole. This is the man who shot Miles.*

Vole ignored Malcolm's anger, addressing him with a taunting lilt. "It's been a spell, ain't it, Carter? You're still fulla piss and hot air. Last I saw you, you was emptying your pistol into poor old Bill Little's dead carcass. I been busy since then, as I'd wager you heard. Shot Miles Rawley last summer, killed the bastard clean dead with two rounds." He paused before issuing a snorting sound of pure derision. "Got yourself another woman, looks like. I don't s'pose you'd much like to watch while we stick it to the little hellcat once Turnbull fetches your horse."

Turnbull, I thought, able to place this name in context as well. *Aemon Turnbull, who once tried to rape Ruthann.*

I found the strength to lift to my elbows, a metallic taste on my tongue. Malcolm knelt on the ground before Vole's horse; at last able to make eye contact he assessed me as best he could. I wanted to speak but hadn't regained enough breath. Something rolled across my tongue like a chipped marble; I spit and watched a molar land on the ground in a spatter of blood droplets. Before it could register that I'd lost a tooth, a dull gleam of silver on the ground caught my attention and then Malcolm's; his gun, dropped in the fall, was perhaps a body length away from my position.

Our eyes held for an agonized heartbeat before Malcolm, with a measured lack of speed, returned his attention to Vole; from this point forward it was up to him to retain Vole's focus and it was up to me to fetch that gun.

Malcolm squared his shoulders, studying Vole with open defiance. "I heard how you shot Miles from a distance of a good half-mile. Ain't a bit of cowardice in that, is there? Never mind that he'd have sent you straight to hell before you could draw, you ugly rodent."

Vole spit a thick plug of saliva toward Malcolm, who did not flinch.

Keeping my belly on the ground, edging perhaps an inch, I made the first small move in the direction of the gun. Malcolm did not dare look my way. Vole was positioned with his back to me and the second man, Turnbull, had ridden after Aces; no way to judge how long Turnbull would be out of sight but I had to assume only minutes. Probably less. I crept forward another inch; I could have grabbed the gun with one good lunge, but I didn't dare draw attention to my intent.

"Get your sorry self on your feet, Carter. Much as I'd like to see the light fade from your eyes this very day, I got orders. Fallon wants to hang you. Said he intends to see to it you're hung proper this time."

Malcolm stood, clutching his right arm near the elbow, applying pressure to his wound. I kept belly-crawling and he kept talking. "Fallon tried to hang me once before. No dice. But I figure he'll be in hell before too long. Devil has a spot reserved, special-like, for the Yancys, I'd bet my last dollar. And one for you, Vole. You know you two'll rendezvous there before long."

"Shut your *goddamn mouth*. You'll be dangling from a tree by tomorrow morning and I'll be the first to piss on your sorry corpse."

I was maybe eighteen inches from Malcolm's gun. One good stretch with my right arm and it would be in my grasp; sweat burned my eyes and I spared a flickering glance toward Malcolm and Vole. In the distance, fast approaching, was the sudden vibrating thud of hoof beats.

Turnbull.

Fuck!

And just that fast Vole, alerted by the sound of the returning horses, turned my way; I watched shock flatten his broad, sunburned face. Without warning he swung his gun my direction, aiming at my spine – granting Malcolm the necessary distraction to lunge, grabbing Vole's right wrist and dragging him straight to the ground. Vole's horse whinnied and sidestepped, kicking its back legs as the men grappled almost beneath its hooves.

I scrambled forward, clutching the pistol in a two-handed grip. It was long-barreled and heavy and somewhere in the tiny, non-panicking part of my mind I realized I had no idea how to fire it – there was more to it than a simple trigger pull, right?

Isn't there a hammer? Something needs to be cocked!

Frantic thoughts, a whirlwind of desperate decisions and no time to consider any of them.

Shit, shit, shit! Camille, do something!

I flew to my feet in time to spy Malcolm roll atop Vole and straddle his waist to deliver rapid-fire punches, one fist after the other, directly to Vole's head. Teeth bared, blood flowing from his forehead and grunting with the extremity of his effort to destroy, Malcolm was a far cry from the tender, passionate lover of last night; I understood at a deep, visceral level there were parts of this man I had no hope of fully understanding, depths I could sense but never touch. Only Cora Lawson was capable of meeting him equally, of filling the chasm in his heart.

But Cora isn't here. You are.

And no matter what else happened, I refused to let violence claim my life as it had Cora's and further destroy Malcolm. It was the least I could do for the man both she and I loved with the entirety of our souls.

Vole bucked upward with a hard, vicious movement, throwing Malcolm sideways; I saw the gun still clenched in Vole's right hand and there was nothing else to do but scream, "Freeze!"

I aimed at Vole's head with both arms outstretched, sweating and shaking but resolute with purpose.

It happened in the flicker of an eyelid, the beat of a bird's wing; the soft expulsion of a held breath – the last thing I expected in that instant.

Vole twisted to the left and fired his gun at me.

I saw the spark of fire in the barrel and the round passed so close to my head I heard its whine, felt the energy of a bullet that, had it flown another inch to the right, would have split my forehead.

So fast it was almost a blur, Malcolm extracted a knife from his boot and sliced open Vole's throat. Blood bloomed like an exotic flower, a bright scarlet waterfall of draining life. Vole's limbs twitched and danced like a wooden puppet's. I heard nothing but my own frantic breath, watching in a stupor as Malcolm grabbed Vole's gun, leaped over his body, flew to my side and clenched my arm, hauling me backward with the force of a steam engine. He shouted something but I couldn't hear – I could hardly will my legs to hold my weight. Malcolm dragged me with him, catching hold of Vole's horse's abandoned reins. The animal kicked, wild-eyed with distress at the chaos, but Malcolm held fast.

He's using the horse as cover, I realized.

Oh God – because –

Turnbull rode in hard, firing at us from horseback. Vole's horse jerked and bucked, fighting Malcolm's death-grip. Malcolm put his body in front of mine and leaned over the animal's back, both clenching its halter and returning fire on Turnbull with Vole's gun. Images loomed before my terrorized gaze – the ashy sky, now spitting small pellets of rain; the shiny brown hide of Vole's horse; Vole's gaping neck and wide, dead eyes. And Malcolm, protecting me with his life. He had taken stock of our situation, analyzed every possible angle, and utilized all available defenses, acting faster than I could even think. Turnbull doubled back, galloping momentarily out of range; he'd lost his grip on Aces High's lead line and Malcolm whistled shrilly, calling the horse back to us.

Aces cantered our way.

Malcolm turned to face me, keeping hold of the horse's halter, his panic under strictest control; his dark eyes burned as he commanded, "Turnbull's riding out to reload that rifle. If anything happens to me, you ride hell-for-leather due east, back the way we've come. Do you hear me?"

"What are you going to do?" Wild-eyed, scalded with fear and concern, I wasn't about to leave his side.

Aces reached us and Malcolm grabbed his lead line. "Thank God for you, boy, you damn good horse." Not about to be disobeyed, he ordered harshly, "Camille!"

"No! I'm not leaving you here!" Tears gushed, infuriating me.

"We'll run for those cottonwoods beyond the creek, there ain't a second to spare. Keep close to me between the horses!" Malcolm latched a solid grip on the lead lines of both animals and yanked their heads forward, roaring, "*Gidd-up!*" and then we ran, using their heavy bodies as cover, angling for the creek and away from the threat of Turnbull's long-distance rifle. Not five seconds later a deep, echoing boom split the air and I cried out; both sounds were muted in my ringing ear canals. We made it to the water before another shot shattered the stillness, splitting the slim trunk of a nearby willow. We splashed through the rocky creek, sending water cascading over our feet and calves.

"Keep low!" Malcolm shouted.

We cleared the opposite bank, dodging branches, and positioned behind a stand of towering cottonwoods. Breathing hard, Malcolm wasted no time slinging the horse's lines around a tree branch and slipping his rifle from Aces High's saddle.

"Get down!" he ordered, cocking the weapon, and I dropped to a crouch against the middle tree's massive trunk, gasping for breath, pressing my forehead to the rough bark as Malcolm stood to my left, his upper body exposed, to aim his rifle. He shot, cocked a second round, and shot again.

Turnbull returned fire.

Malcolm ducked to a crouch to slip two more bullets in his rifle; he was a foot away from me but in grave danger, with little protection between his body and the path of a flying bullet. Bleeding from two wounds, his lower lip split, he clenched his jaws and rose with a roar, taking aim and firing. I flinched, digging my nails in the bark. I could hear nothing but intense, high-pitched ringing.

I finally realized Malcolm was speaking.

I got him.

Even in triumph he moved with caution and care, edging closer, his rifle trained on Turnbull – in whatever state the man now existed. I didn't dare move from behind the trees, watching with hawk eyes as Malcolm crept forward, assessing the situation. And at last, he lowered the rifle.

We resumed our course, aiming northwest toward Cole and Patricia's last known destination, together again on Aces. Malcolm had untied Vole's horse and let the animal run free.

"I'm not about to be taken for a horse thief," he'd explained.

I did not break down until we'd ridden perhaps two miles; once we'd put distance between ourselves and the dead bodies of two vicious criminals, Malcolm reined Aces to a walk, then a complete halt. He dismounted and lifted me down; able at last to embrace full-length, we crushed each other close and clung. He cupped the back of my head, holding fast, letting me weep; I wrapped my arms around his torso, holding like I never meant to let go, sobbing out all the fear I'd restrained in the past terrifying hour.

"I was so scared, Malcolm, oh my God. You're hurt, *they hurt you*, and I couldn't do anything but watch…" I hid my face against his chest, his shirt flecked with blood and wet with a mixture of rain and sweat.

He rested his lips to my temple, scraping aside flyaway tangles of my hair. "You are a brave woman, Camille Carter. I can't think about what might have happened back there or I'll go crazy, but that doesn't change the fact that you're a damn brave woman."

I wanted to tell Malcolm I thought he was braver than anyone I'd ever known. In the span of an hour we'd been pursued and attacked; we'd been shot at and Malcolm had killed two men who intended to kill us first. But none of that seemed real; all I could consider just now was the fact that Malcolm bore injuries, one of which I was certain was a gunshot wound.

I looked up at him, scalded anew with concern. "You're hurt, Malcolm. You were shot in the arm, weren't you...*oh God...*"

"I been hurt plenty worse, sweetheart, I swear." He drew away to show me his arm, which I inspected with the diligence of a field nurse – or someone deeply in love with him. Although bloody and raw-looking, the wound didn't appear as dire as I'd imagined; the bullet had scored only a shallow path along the muscle and skin above his elbow.

I ran my fingertips over his face, his forehead with a lumping purple bruise and the blood dried on his split lower lip. I stood on tiptoe to gently kiss both injuries. "I love you," I whispered. "You saved us."

"My heart breaks with loving you," he said in return, cradling my face between his hands. "And as much as I hate to admit it, we aren't safe yet. Not 'til Fallon's dead."

Chapter Thirty-One

Windham, IA - June, 1882

IT TOOK ANOTHER TWO HOURS OF HARD RIDING TO REACH
the small settlement, a rainy twilight looming from the west in a wash
of dark purple and gray clouds, the sky behind them a chilly violet blue.
Thunder grumbled and lightning threatened as we rode into Windham;
a hand-lettered wooden sign announced its unincorporated status.

"They'll have waited for us here. Patricia was ill and Cole will have
found a place for them to spend the night." Malcolm slowed Aces to a
walk, rewrapping the rain blanket around my huddled, shivering form.
I was a mess, physically and emotionally drained; any part of me not
touching Malcolm's warmth seemed coated in ice crystals. I needed a
hot shower. I needed a heaping plate of fried fish and mashed potatoes,
Shore Leave-style. I needed my twenty-first century life, my children
and Mathias, and our cabin in the woods beyond White Oaks. I could
hardly shift my head to nod in response to Malcolm's words.

"Hold on, love, it ain't much longer now," he murmured.

Backlit by the gloom of fading dusk, the settlement appeared as little
more than a handful of false-fronted structures. No streetlamps burning,
no horses tethered along the street, the drizzle keeping all signs of life
to a minimum. Only one set of windows shone with evidence of inner
light and Malcolm headed straight for this place – a nondescript wooden
building two stories high. Behind it loomed another, larger structure,
ringed by a corral, in the second floor of which I spied a haymow as
Malcolm helped me from Aces. I struggled to find my footing, overcome

by a dizzy rush, but Malcolm kept an arm locked around my waist. He patted his horse's neck, promising, "We'll find you a dry place to spend the night, old friend, and get that saddle off."

The rain blanket bundled over my shoulders like a shawl, I rested my forehead on Aces High; his damp hide bristled against my skin and he made a soft, snorting sound, an acknowledgment of our affection. I whispered, "Thank you, boy. You're such a good horse."

"He's carried me through a fair amount of the worst times in my life," Malcolm acknowledged quietly. "He's the best horse I know. I love him as much as Sawyer loved Whistler in her day."

We climbed wooden steps and Malcolm knocked on the deep-set door. Moments later a man inquired sharply, "Who's there?" The tone of the question suggested he was aiming a rifle in our direction.

Malcolm's shoulders slumped with relief as he muttered, "*Thank you, Jesus.*" And then, louder, "Cole, open up!"

An hour later our physical circumstances had drastically improved. Clean and dry, I sat in a rocking chair near Patricia's bed, snuggling a sleeping Monty to the rhythmic creak of our gentle motion. Patricia lay facing us, both hands tucked under her cheek, blue eyes tender with love and, by turns, tearful. Pale and much too thin, she appeared ill despite her insistence that she felt worlds better. The room was one of two in a boardinghouse belonging to the same couple who owned the adjacent general store and livery stable. They had promised help and, later, discretion when Cole appeared on their doorstep yesterday, begging for a place for his ailing wife and newborn son to rest.

"We arrived here in the evening hours," Patricia had explained. "We pushed hard once we parted ways from you and Malcolm and I was in a state of fatigue so pronounced I could not walk of my own accord. But we did not encounter Dredd or his father on our flight westward, nor did Fallon darken our path, and so I care little for my current physical state. Monty and I may have been Dredd's prisoners at this time had you not found us, dear Camille."

Shortly after Malcolm and I left them to ride for Muscatine, the decision was made for Blythe to continue northward to Minnesota. Alone, he would not be a potential target for the Yancys; they had no idea who he was in relation to Cole and Patricia, and he was anxious to arrive at his father's home, not only to set eyes upon him, but to deliver word of all that had transpired. Patricia said Blythe had been initially reluctant to leave them with one less person to offer protection, but Derrick was given a gun and Cole insisted there was no additional reason for Blythe to detour so far west when he was headed north.

Derrick, without a horse, had been left with the choice of either walking alongside the wagon or riding with Cole on the wagon seat. The two men ended up taking turns driving the wagon, neither any too eager to chitchat; Patricia mentioned the mild animosity bubbling between them, almost beyond their control.

"Perhaps I was fortunate to be in a state of immobile exhaustion. At least I was not required to participate in such awkward conversation as that which transpired between them. When they spoke at all, that is." A wan smile lifted her lips as she related this detail.

Derrick had gathered me in a tight, intense hug upon my appearance at the boardinghouse, pure relief overpowering his usual aloof arrogance; his first question was, "How soon can we return?"

But I had no answer for him.

Derrick was currently downstairs, along with Cole, Malcolm, and the proprietors, an elderly couple named Lund. Aces High was bedded for the night in the Lunds' nearby barn. Not a moment too soon; the downpour let loose only minutes after our arrival. The scents of beef stew, bread, and coffee wafted up the narrow staircase, sending hunger pangs on the attack. The smell of a hearty dinner, not to mention the rich aroma of coffee, brought to mind Grandma and Aunt Ellen, and the cheerful home in which I'd lived as a pregnant teenager and new mother.

Millie Jo spent the first few years of her life in their house, making pancakes and biscuits, pies and pan sauces along with her great-grandma and great-aunt in the bright, comfortably cluttered kitchen. Tears sprang to my eyes, accompanied by the sharp slice of homesickness; missing my children was a constant torture. I bent my face to Monty, kissing the silken wisps of hair covering his downy head, but not before Patricia observed my sadness.

She lifted to one elbow, the quilt sliding to her waist. "How much you remind me of Ruthann. Not only are you similar in appearance, but your mannerisms are quite alike." She sighed as I lifted my eyes to hers, holding my gaze with sympathy and sorrow. Thunder rumbled over the crying of the rain, followed seconds later by a burst of lightning; the window momentarily glowed bright blue. "I miss Ruthann every day. I pray, for all our sakes, that your actions have restored your future lives to that which you recall."

"She loves you very much," I told Patricia. "For *you*, not just because you're so much like our sister, Tish. And I pray the same, that what we've accomplished today will change things. But how will we know? I thought once that happened, Derrick and I would immediately be returned to the future." A shiver clawed at my nape and I fought the urge to look over my shoulder, toward the shadows gathered in the corners of the room. "It must mean we have to finish things here, first."

"And by that, of course, you are referring to Fallon." Patricia was equally frightened by his name, her eyes following a similar path along the dark edges around us. "Malcolm has dispatched two of Fallon's associates this day, which shall infuriate him. He counted upon Vole, especially, to carry out his orders in this century. I am glad to hear of their deaths. I wish only that they would have suffered, prior." She shuddered, drawing the quilt back to her shoulders. "Filthy bastards. Turnbull attempted to rape Ruthann, the selfsame night she and I met. I am proud to say I struck his head with a stick of firewood. If only I had killed him then! And if not for Vole, Miles Rawley would be alive this very day."

"And Ruthie would be his wife," I whispered, marveling at the strangeness of the thought. What would Marshall have done, had he arrived in the nineteenth century to find Ruthann married to another man? It was, of course, no stranger than the fact that I'd made love with a man other than my husband – but who *was* my husband, here in this place.

A hard knot of longing grew in my heart, interrupting its continuous beat.

Mathias. Oh God, I miss you. I know you're here, in Malcolm, but I still miss you. I need you to be there when I get back home, the you I remember, the life we both remember. I have no place in the future, not without you.

"Miles loved her with all his heart, that is true. I believe Ruthie would have been happy with him, had fate taken that particular path." Patricia was perceptive and blunt; she was Tish, after all. She whispered, "Malcolm is quite desperately in love with you. He is your husband in this life, is he not?"

I tried to swallow the massive lump in my throat so I could respond.

Patricia saw I was beyond words, continuing softly, "Surely it is your resemblance and connection to Ruthann that inspires my trust. She spoke so often of you, and Tish, and the men with whom you share your lives. The love you share." She paused, inhaling a short breath. "I love two men, Camille, and though I am ashamed to acknowledge it because it is far less than either deserve, it is no less true."

I looked up. Her eyes were like blue spears.

"Axton," she whispered, bringing her folded hands to her lips. "I love Axton Douglas, very deeply. And yet, I also love Cole. I have chosen to share my life with Cole, and sworn to myself I would forget Axton, but to do so I've suffered a cleaving. Here." She rested a hand to her heart. "And I fear it will never fully heal. I would never dishonor Cole by confessing to my love for another man, and I trust you to keep my dreadful secret, as did Ruthann, but the fact remains."

"Axton, who's out west with Ruthie and Marsh right now?"

Tears rimmed her lower lids. "I ache with missing him. I am a selfish beast."

"But..." I sifted through the enormous amount of information Ruthann had divulged the night she reappeared at Shore Leave, searching for the relevant detail. "Wait. Axton is who Ruthie believes Case is, in the future. Right?"

Patricia nodded slowly, unable to staunch the flow of tears; she used the quilt to blot her eyes, speaking in a strangled voice. "Derrick spoke of...what happened to Case Spicer, your sister's husband."

"Tish was destroyed," I whispered, flinching at the memory. "And it's all the more reason we have to stop every possibility of that timeline ever existing." No sooner had the words cleared my lips than I sat straight as if jabbed in the ribs, eyes leaping to the west-facing windows. The curtains were drawn on the stormy night but it was not the violent clap of thunder that commanded my sudden attention. Jolted by both the noise and my abrupt motion, Monty stiffened and began to fuss.

"What is it?" Patricia gasped.

Alerted to danger but unable yet to answer, I stretched outward with my mind, toward Ruthann, all senses firing. In light of today's chaos I'd been allowed no time to imagine my little sister's reaction to the news that I was here in 1882. The Ruthann out there in Montana tonight had not experienced the fire and its horrible aftermath; she was roughly a week behind the Ruthie who had surfaced in Flickertail Lake burdened with the knowledge of those events. But tonight was when Fallon had intended to burn the Rawleys' homestead.

"*Ruthie…*" I gritted my teeth, straining to reach her.

"Something has happened? Something is wrong?" Patricia's voice was high with fright.

"I don't know," I admitted miserably. I stood, with care, and handed Monty to her before scurrying to the window. I parted the curtains to find the view obscured by the downpour, struck by a sudden, horrible vision of Fallon standing below me on the wet street, impervious to the rain and aiming a gun at the bright square of this lighted window, with my body dead center.

I dropped to a crouch.

"Dear God, is he out there?" Patricia cried.

I shook my head, lips numb. The bone-deep cold returned, rendering my limbs all but useless. I rocked back on my heels and found my voice. "I don't think so, but something is wrong. I felt Ruthie just now, really strong. I think…I think Fallon found her."

"You are certain they received your telegram? That they have been made aware he was headed their way?"

Booted feet thundered up the stairs; I knew it was Malcolm before he appeared in the doorway, hatless and wild-eyed, scanning the little room as he entered. Spying me crouched at the window he flew to my side and helped me to my feet. He brought me against his chest and I cinched his waist with both arms, holding fast.

"What's wrong? Are you hurt?" His rapid heartbeat thudded against my right cheek.

"Camille felt Ruthann, just now," Patricia explained. "Something is the matter."

"I think Fallon found her," I repeated, my words muffled by Malcolm's shirt. His forehead was bandaged, his dry, clean clothes borrowed from Cole. He drew back to look at me, his thumbs tracing careful paths along my cheekbones. The left side of my body was bruised from my fall, never mind the ache of a lost molar; my tongue had been unable to leave the small concavity alone. But my wounds were minor compared to Malcolm's.

Malcolm wasted no time questioning why we believed something was wrong; he saw the desperation in my eyes and spoke adamantly. "They are prepared this time around, remember that. They know he's coming. Marshall and Axton will be there, along with Grant."

"But he's so dangerous." I clenched my thigh muscles to keep them from trembling. "I'm so scared…"

Malcolm held my gaze; the white of his right eye was redder than blood, a result of being struck in the forehead. I cupped my hand on that side of his face, wishing I could reverse the damage done to him today. Wishing we were back in the little hotel room in Muscatine with the whole night ahead of us. He admitted quietly, "I'm scared too. But if we give in, we're as good as lost. Fallon ain't undefeatable. Remember that."

"But he…he's…" I couldn't finish; Fallon was so many terrible things it seemed beyond words.

"Come downstairs with me, we'll keep watch together. I don't much like having you out of my sight as it is, I can't pretend otherwise." His lips curved with a hint of his sweet smile before he turned toward Patricia and Monty. "And I'll send Cole straightaway to you and the little one, dear lady."

The Lunds had retired to their personal rooms above the general store, located in the building across the street. Probably so that eye contact was not required, Cole and Derrick sat at right angles to one another at a small dining table in the downstairs gathering space, the only other people in the boardinghouse. A fire crackled in the belly of a squatty iron stove, filling the room with warm orange light. They both looked up at the sound of our descent on the steps, their features highlighted with odd slants of light and shadow, elongating their noses. Though I didn't know Derrick well, I realized he was reaching the end of his patience with all of this.

"Patricia requests your company," Malcolm said to Cole, who nodded, gathered up his rifle, and disappeared upstairs.

Derrick shifted position like a restless cat, pinning me with a direct, irritated gaze. Eyes flickering between my hand – intertwined with Malcolm's – and my face, he asked brusquely, "How much longer, Camille? And don't pacify me, please. I'll implode."

I studied Derrick for a beat of silence, noting his rumpled appearance, including wrinkled clothing and heavy five o'clock shadow, his hair in disarray; this man was severely unaccustomed to living rough and I was not unsympathetic. But that didn't change the fact that I had no answers, appeasing or otherwise. I took the seat Malcolm withdrew for me; he rested a hand on my shoulder for a moment before claiming the chair to my left. Rain lashed the single window at the front of the room while lightning continued to backlight the curtains.

"I don't know," I admitted, clearing the thickness from my throat. "I don't know if it will be instantaneous once we've…once we've…" I skittered to a halt.

"Once Fallon is gone, you mean?" Derrick finished for me, leaning forward with his forearms lining the table's edge, lacing his fingers and fitting his thumbnails together.

"Yeah," I whispered, scooting my chair closer to Malcolm's just as he scooted his closer to mine.

A perplexed frown beetled Derrick's brow as he observed this, but to his credit he made no mention. He lifted his left hand, fingers splayed as he counted off events. "We've saved the man named Blythe, we've rescued Patricia and the baby, and we've sent word to your sister in

Montana. Is that enough to reverse the timeline? What are we missing?"

Irked by his assumption that I possessed all the answers, I snapped, "How the hell should I know? I know exactly as much as you do right now."

Derrick's lips thinned. "I am not attempting to aggravate you. I'm fucking scared out of my wits, if you must know the truth. I've already jeopardized myself by helping your family. My father would kill me. *Fallon* would kill me, on sight." Derrick's tone was outright hostile and I sensed more than saw the way Malcolm's shoulders squared. I rested a hand on Malcolm's thigh, beneath the table.

Derrick continued, with slightly less steam, "We're trapped here, for all I know. What guarantee do we have that Fallon will show up any time in the next few years? He despises this century even though he's always drawn back. Against his will, I might add. This is his natural timeline, so I suppose it makes sense."

"When did he first travel?" Malcolm asked, fitting his hand over mine, interlocking our fingers atop his leg.

Derrick stifled a sigh, forced down a new conversational path. "I don't know for sure. His early teens, I think. By the time I met him, when I was about nine, he had established himself as his twentieth-century persona, 'Franklin' Yancy. My father went along with everything he said because Fallon knew things. Not only about our lives – our *future* lives, I might add – but about money. Our family achieved its status and wealth only because of him, as Father is always quick to remind me. And I've always taken that wealth for granted. I've lived a shallow little life and I've never regretted it until this past week."

"Even if your life has been shallow to this point, what you did to help us negates all of that," I insisted, conviction blazing in my chest. "It was completely unselfish. I can never thank you enough."

"Oh, it wasn't unselfish, I assure you." Derrick inhaled through his nostrils, fixing his gaze straight ahead. "You realize I'm in love with your sister, don't you?" He issued a short, self-deprecating chuckle. "Not that she'd ever notice."

I chose my words carefully. "I think what you believe is love is really unfinished business between the two of you. You were married, but unhappy, in this life. And, on top of that, Dredd's father attempted to have Patricia murdered. Of course you still have strong feelings. But Tish isn't the woman for you. It's time to let go of all that ancient anger and bitterness. Maybe that's part of why you realized you had to help us…to also help yourself."

Derrick glared at me. "Spare me the goddamned psyche analysis."

"Do not speak to Camille in that tone." Malcolm's voice stayed even but there was no room for doubt in his words.

"*Seriously*, this century," Derrick muttered, plunging both hands through his uncombed hair. He pushed back his chair. "I'm going to lie down."

"Oh God, I wish I had a cell phone," I muttered as Derrick retreated, his footsteps echoing on the stairs. "I hate not knowing what's going on. I know Ruthie tried to reach me earlier, I *felt* her, Malcolm."

"Waiting is worse than about all else," he agreed. "As bad as living in constant fear."

I moved to sit on his lap, needing to be closer to him. He latched his arms around my waist and rested his face between my breasts, inhaling slow and deliberate as I twined my fingers in the thick waves of his hair, taking care not to bump the bandage tied around his battered forehead.

"You were so brave today. You saved our lives in a dozen ways and they hurt you so much. You've been in harm's way hundreds of times, haven't you?" I kissed his temple, lingering there against his warm skin. "I can't bear to think about anyone hurting you, ever again."

What about you, my heart demanded. *Your leaving will hurt him more than anything.*

Malcolm met my eyes, not quite able to manage a smile, as if discerning the direction of my thoughts. But he spoke with unquestionable sincerity. "I'll heal, don't you worry. I don't want to cause you a moment's worry, Camille. This time that we've shared is a gift I could never have imagined. A gift I'll be grateful for until the day I die."

Tears blurred my vision. "Me too. Oh Malcolm, me too."

"And once you've returned home to the life you remember, your *real* life, I want you to live it without a single regret. And know that I'm living mine the same way. All regrets washed away, washed clean. I swear to you, love, my sweet love, they've washed away."

"Do you promise?" My voice shook.

"I swear," he repeated, kissing my lips with utmost tenderness. "I'm no saint. I won't pretend to be. But I would never ask a mama to be apart from her babies. You go back to those little ones, your Millie and Brantley and Henry, your little Lorie and James." He clenched his jaws, as if gaining strength. "And to Mathias. I'm frightful jealous of him, I can't lie, but you need him. You spoke his name, last night. You spoke *both* our names, but he's who you need, I ain't fool enough to pretend I can't see it."

My heart throbbed with love and pain, in equal parts. "Promise me the same, Malcolm. I want you to be happy. *Truly* happy, here in this place and time. But it hurts so much to think of…" The sentence fractured around the depth of emotion clogging my chest. "Of never seeing you again. I don't want you to be alone here…I can't bear it…"

Tears wet his dark eyes as he whispered gently, "Now, that's enough." He stroked my hair, slowly, both hands sinking deep into my curls. "I want to tell you something I believe. Something I've been thinking about for a long time now. Last autumn, when I met Marshall Rawley and heard his story of traveling through time, it was hard to swallow the tale, at least at first. But there must have been a part of me that had always known, somehow, that souls returned to the earth for another go-round. When Marshall told me of your family – *of you* – I wanted nothing more than to set eyes on you, to know that my Cora was alive again, thriving and happy, with children of her own. She wanted so much to be a mama. You have given me that knowledge, Camille, and I couldn't ask for more."

"But she's not *here*," I whispered, aching and overcome. "And I want you to be happy here, Malcolm. You belong in this place; I couldn't imagine you anywhere else. And you have so much life ahead of you."

His eyes shone with an earnest light, an intense desire for me to understand. "There's no life without its share of pain. This whole past winter I thought on it, on the reasons a soul would return for another life, knowing ahead of time that life means suffering, no exceptions. But then I realized it's not for pain that souls return. It's for love. Maybe…" He paused to inhale a soft breath. "Maybe it's because this is the only place where love is fully felt. Where love exists in its truest form, as something you would risk everything for, even the loss of it. And that's why souls keep on coming back. And you know what? It's worth it. In the end, I believe it's worth it."

Malcolm carried me to the wide rocking chair near the stove, so we could sit together more comfortably; for a long time he kept the rocker at a slow, steady pace while I sat with both knees drawn up, my head on his chest until I could breathe without crying. Our hands stayed linked, resting upon my belly. Since this morning, neither of us had mentioned the possibility of a baby nine months from now. Eyes closed, inundated by Malcolm's words and presence, I silently vowed, *I'll name him for you.*

Chapter Thirty-Two

THE WINDOWS SHOULD HAVE SHATTERED WITH THE FORCE of my wailing shrieks but the sound snagged on my damaged lungs. Wide-eyed with horror, nude and flat on my stomach, I was able only to watch as Fallon's gunshot sent Marshall flying backward. Not a second later Fallon's body lost substance, fading to misty nothingness, and I scrabbled toward it, fingers like claws, hissing with the furious need to destroy. Desperate huffs of air burst from my lips as I grabbed for Fallon's boot. I thought I had him but my hands fisted around empty air...

And – minutes later, maybe more, I had no sense of time – my eyes opened upon a bright, silent, vacant space. No distinguishing characteristics to offer a clue, no hint as to where I was or how I'd come to be here. Precious seconds ticked past as I attempted to collect my bearings before the memory of Fallon's attack rushed back to the forefront of my consciousness. Still naked and short of breath, I struggled to maneuver into a sitting position, my eyes leaping in wide, wild arcs, trying to make sense of the surroundings.

"Marshall!" I cried, my voice sliding through an octave of pure fear. "Where are you?"

I stood, reaching outward as if answers hovered in the lukewarm air, terrified down to a cellular level. I wasn't outside. But the space around me didn't seem contained within a building, either. When I tried to peer farther ahead than about six feet, a gray fog, the sort that hung over Flickertail on muggy summer mornings, obscured the view. I stepped forward only to find that the fog parted to allow passage through it; my bare feet touched solid ground and I could walk in any direction without reaching a limit, other than the fog. The ability to inhale and exhale returned, but too rapidly; panic beat a tattoo against my breastbone.

"Where am I?" I begged, turning in tight circles. I covered my belly with both palms, protecting the firm melon-curve of my baby. Louder now, terror swelling. "*Marshall!* Where are you? What's happening?!"

Was I dead? Or had I come to some sort of standstill in the flow of time?

"Can anyone hear me?" I shouted. "Where am I?"

The fog existed above, below, to every side. I walked and jogged, by turns, desperate to find an entry point. A door, a window, a sign. A horrible picture filled my mind, of a huge, smooth glass jar in which I'd been deposited like an unwary ant. I saw myself running in agitated, endless circles around its confines, a prisoner suspended in time; no matter how much ground I covered, I went nowhere. The surroundings did not alter in any way. My forward motion eventually stalled and I crouched in the exact center of the bright, silent, vacant space, gripping my shoulders in either hand, curving forward. Too terrified to cry, I clutched my torso and begged a refrain of despair. "Help me. Please, help me."

Rain continued falling over the little settlement of Windham, providing a lulling background cadence as Malcolm and I sat together in the rocking chair; my eyes eventually drifted shut. Not quite asleep, I remained peripherally aware of the surroundings; Cole returned downstairs and he and Malcolm talked in hushed voices. The fire in the woodstove crackled, its red heat bathing my half-closed eyes. Intermittent thunder grumbled. The rocker creaked and Malcolm's lithe fingers stroked my hair in a slow, rhythmic caress. My nose rested at the juncture of his collarbones and his pulse beat against my cheek. He smelled exactly like Mathias and in my exhaustion I imagined I was snuggled in my husband's arms, the two of us stealing a moment's rest after finally getting the kids to bed.

Mathias whispered, *Rest, honey. It's been a long day and you're exhausted.*

My heart constricted with a deep and painful yearning.

Thias…

"It's too quiet out there, something ain't right," Cole was muttering.

My legs twitched at this intrusion of sound, chucking me back to reality. I opened my bleary eyes to see Cole positioned at the edge of the window, the curtain drawn aside about an inch as he peered out at the bleak, wet night, rifle cradled in the crook of his arm. He let the faded material fall back into place and took a seat at the table, facing Malcolm and me.

"We'll ride out by morning's light," Malcolm said quietly. "If Patricia and the baby are up to it. What are you thinking, Spicer? You want to push northwest, or head toward Jalesville and your folks?"

Cole passed a hand over his face and I silently noted the physical resemblance between him and Case; both were tall and physically-imposing, with auburn hair and brown eyes. And yet, there was a subtle edge to this man, completely unlike Case; a distinct difference of spirit. Grim and stone-faced, Cole decided, "West. I don't want to risk getting in the Yancys' path if we resume the journey to Minnesota." His gaze held steady as he asked, "What of you two?"

"I don't have an answer for you." Malcolm spoke from behind me, his chest rumbling with the words; instinctively, his arms tightened their grip. "We don't know how much time we've left together."

The words had no sooner cleared his lips when something crashed against the floor directly above us, rattling the walls. Cole was on his feet and halfway up the stairs before I'd bolted from Malcolm's lap; he grabbed his rifle as he leaped to his feet. Frantic and disoriented, I imbibed information in disjointed bursts – Monty crying, Patricia screaming, men shouting – then a gunshot, followed immediately by another. A round pierced the bedroom floor upstairs and splintered the ceiling above the woodstove. Malcolm latched a forearm around my waist and hauled me backward with the force of a tornado.

"Stay down!" he ordered, grabbing the dining table and throwing it on its side, creating a measure of cover. He dragged it against the wall and positioned above it, aiming his rifle at the staircase. I crouched behind his bent legs, shielding my head, stunned at how quickly we'd again become vulnerable. There was a pulse of silence, the absence of sound almost louder than the gunshots.

"Carter! Don't shoot!" Cole hollered seconds later from the top of the steps. "Fallon was here, right in Yancy's room, but they both disappeared. Jesus fucking Christ! I almost didn't believe my own eyes."

Malcolm lowered his rifle. "We're coming up!"

"Derrick disappeared?" Breathless and tense, I clattered up the steps ahead of Malcolm. Cole stood in the hallway with feet widespread and his rifle at the ready, angled so his body blocked the door to Patricia's bedroom. She hovered near the bed holding Monty up over her shoulder, patting his back. She was white with fear and I hurried to her side, gathering both of them in a hug while Malcolm and Cole investigated the room in which Derrick had been resting only minutes ago.

"Fallon was here," Patricia whispered, shivering in her nightgown, her honey-colored hair loose over her shoulders; she appeared no more than about fifteen years old, like a little girl playing house. Much too young for the burdens of marriage and motherhood, and probably exactly the way I'd looked after Millie Jo was born. But I'd handled those responsibilities and so would Patricia – or, so I told myself. She continued, "I woke to a crash and heard Derrick yelp. I fear…" She looked quickly to Cole. "Did Fallon kill him?"

"I don't rightly know. I saw them grappling and then they just…vanished." A man who had faced plenty of danger in his time, Cole still shuddered at the remembrance. "Right before my damn eyes!"

"Who fired?" Malcolm asked, indicating the jagged hole in the wooden planks of the floor.

"Derrick, I think," Cole said, with a note of approval. "He acted quick for someone without a lick of experience."

"It stands to reason that it was Derrick who shot at Fallon," I added, thinking of Ruthie's explanations. "Fallon has this thing, I don't know, like a defense mechanism. When his life is threatened he disappears to another place or time." My thoughts raced. "Let's assume Fallon was just out in Montana and they fought back this time and repelled him…"

"And he appeared here," Malcolm concluded. "And then Derrick fired on him and he disappeared again. But why would Derrick vanish?"

"I don't know about Derrick. But maybe Fallon's losing control." I prayed it was true. "He knows we're on to him and maybe that messes with his ability." My heart lurched as I suddenly considered another angle – what if Derrick had returned home to 2014, leaving me behind in 1882?

Malcolm, watching me, saw fear overtake my face. With no words he asked, *What is it?*

But another voice filled my head before I could respond, inundating my consciousness, commanding my full attention. Urgent with fear, crying my name over and over. I stepped away from Patricia and the baby, pressing hard against my forehead.

Ruthie, I hear you!

Where are you?!

"Camille?" Patricia's high, questioning voice retreated a thousand miles in the space of a heartbeat.

Malcolm was no more than ten steps away, an impassable distance. Sounds fled but my vision did not – *not yet* – and I saw him racing for me in a slow-motion reel; I reached for him, I tried to speak his name. This could not be our last moment together.

"*Camille!*"

Not yet – oh God, please, not yet –

But I was already gone.

Time elapsed.

At least, I assumed it elapsed; I'd been a prisoner in the blank, echoing space for minutes, hours, days, months, centuries…I had no real idea. The passage, or non-passage, in this place reminded me of humid summer days in Landon when clouds knitted themselves together so densely the sky shone blinding-white from dawn to dusk, keeping the sun's hourly angles hidden from view, allowing no sense of time flowing from one minute to the next. Sinister in a passive way, the clouds impervious and expressionless; for all I knew, time had stuttered to a full stop.

The fog surrounding me inspired madness and I huddled in a crouch, ashamed at what seemed like giving up but too terrified to continue moving forward.

I cried out to everyone I thought may have a hope of hearing me – Marshall, Camille, Axton, Aunt Jilly, my mother.

Nothing. Not a flicker, not a breath of response. The fog swirled around my huddled form, utterly devoid of empathy.

Am I dead?

Is this hell?

One thought tortured me, replaying across my mind without letup – Marshall flying backward, struck by a bullet from Fallon's gun. What had taken place in the moments immediately following my disappearance from our bedroom? I imagined Axton and Birdie racing through the door only seconds after I'd vanished, all of them attempting to piece together what had occurred upstairs. I refused to conceive of Marshall as anything but alive. Wounded, but alive. Birdie was probably stitching him up right now. Huddled in a crouch, I bit down on my right forearm with enough force to leave indentations in my chilled skin.

Marshall, Marshall, oh God – be alive. Survive. Please, survive. I need you. Our baby needs you.

A low, keening cry lifted from my throat, swelling to a scream.

"Where the fuck am I?!"

I suddenly realized someone was watching me.

I returned to awareness in the dining room at Shore Leave, late afternoon. Benign sunlight rimming the windows, falling in long, slanting beams across the floor; flat on my back, I blinked and then sat straight with a wailing cry.

Malcolm...

I scrambled to my feet only to pitch forward and stumble, blood draining from my head as I moved too quickly. I grabbed for a chair and clung, letting the dark blotches recede from my vision, inhaling deep breaths as I scanned the familiar space. I let myself believe that we'd done it, that the real timeline had been restored.

"Mom! Tish! *Mathias!*" I gained enough strength to stand and dashed outside, skidding across the icy porch and down the steps, next sprinting across the empty yard. My shouting garnered attention and the door to Aunt Jilly's apartment opened, revealing my sisters. Ravaged, despairing – exactly as I'd left them.

I slammed to a halt as swiftly as if crashing against a brick wall, looking up at their faces in the chilly light of late March. I saw. I realized. And then I went to my knees in the slush.

"*No…*"

᠗᠁

"Ruthann."

I scuttled backward, away from the horror of that abnormally calm voice.

But he advanced through the emptiness, unavoidable as death.

"No one has ever followed me here. It is as I suspected, you are as close to an equal as I will ever have. You are meant for me, Ruthann. Deny it if you wish, but it changes nothing."

There was no hope of retreating. I was naked, alone, without weapons or hope.

I am in hell.

Fallon stopped a few feet away, staring down at me as I hunched with arms wrapped almost double around my body, more helpless than the ant I'd earlier envisioned. Fallon could crush me beneath his boot or keep me trapped in this jar, at his whim; he had maintained the upper hand to the bitter end.

"So much anger. Never mind. You'll move past it." His gaze flickered south and his brows lifted. He crouched so that our faces were on the same level. With obvious astonishment, he observed, "You're pregnant."

My lips parted, primal rage exposing my clenched teeth.

His pale, terrifying eyes held mine as he considered something before speaking. He gripped the lower half of his face as he whispered, "I was wrong. Patricia is not the one who will produce the heir. *You* are." He became at once solicitous, ingratiating. "Come, I'll find clothing for you. No additional harm will come to you."

I blinked, so shocked words refused to take form on my tongue.

Fallon continued thinking aloud. "I've been betrayed in more than one way today, it seems. Things have been kept from me. Dredd's counterpart, for example. Apparently he too is able to jump."

I swallowed, tasting sour bile, limbs frozen in place.

"Come," he ordered, with a growing edge of impatience. "Stand up."

Only my eyes seemed capable of moving, darting like moths entranced by an open flame. Panicked. Out of control. Seconds from becoming ash.

"Get. The. Fuck. *Up.*"

The moths flew upward in an unexpected arc, alerted to rapid movement just beyond Fallon's right shoulder. He must have been startled by the change in my expression because he shifted – but was too late to duck the powerful blow delivered to the back of his skull. I skittered sideways to avoid Fallon's sprawling body, my stunned eyes alighting on a sweating, wild-eyed Derrick Yancy. He gripped a sturdy snow boot – one of his own, I noticed, in a stupor of blank astonishment – the heel of which had just knocked Fallon to his stomach.

"Quick, move!" Derrick ordered, harsh and breathless. "He's not out!"

I obeyed without a word, scrambling away, skittering to my feet as Derrick raised the boot above his head. He would have delivered another solid strike but Fallon rolled to one side and kicked Derrick's legs out from under him.

I moaned.

Oh God oh God…

I can't outrun him. There's nowhere to hide!

Fallon was no stranger to a fight, gliding like a snake to straddle his brother, pinning him by the neck in order to slam white-knuckled punches into Derrick's face.

I hesitated for only a fraction of a second before realizing what I had to do.

Help him!

I figured I might as well die right now, attempting to save us – the alternative included my baby and me existing as Fallon's prisoners.

Flat on his spine, Derrick groaned and struggled. Fallon's back was angled toward me and so I leaped forward, hooking my right arm around his neck, thinking of Aemon Turnbull once doing the same thing to me, long ago in Howardsville. Aemon had kept his head to one side to avoid a backward strike and I did the same, squeezing Fallon's fragile wind-pipe against my elbow. Outrage lent me courage and strength. Fallon released his hold on Derrick, immediately clamping both hands around my forearm, allowing Derrick the seconds he needed to buck free and grab Fallon's wrists. I grunted with the effort to apply more pressure, bent in a half-crouch, fear replaced by pure red fury. This man had caused harm to those I loved for the last fucking time.

"He's disappearing!" Derrick rasped.

Tish raced down the outside steps, clinging to the wooden railing, Ruthann on her heels.

"Milla! Where have you been?"

"What's happened?"

"Is Derrick with you?"

Agony exploded in my chest. I had failed. Nothing had changed here – nothing had been resolved. They were still trapped in the offshoot timeline.

"Take me back," I begged, face upturned to the fading blue sky as I knelt in cold, wet slush. "Take me back there. Take me back…"

Tish had almost reached me, scurrying through the slush in stocking feet.

"Did you find them?!"

I couldn't bear their desperate cries. If I couldn't save us from this timeline I didn't want to continue existing in it; cowardly or not, I couldn't bear the pain. I covered my ears and repeated, *"Take me back…"*

"Don't go!" Ruthie cried, sharp, escalating terror in her voice. *"Don't leave!"*

The violence increased with each passage. My body was hollow, raw, utterly defenseless. Removed from my physical self I watched from a short but impenetrable distance as I hurtled through an endless, narrow corridor of time, racing toward my anchor point – the only security I possessed. I cried out his name and was at once surrounded by a profound and fleeting awareness, perceiving my soul as an entity separate from flesh and blood.

Gentle undulations of pure, transparent energy. No sorrow, no fear. Stars rotated on tiny axis points, flaring across my line of sight in orbits of vibrant color, so impossibly bright I squinted at the glittering brilliance. I saw my children's faces and heard their voices, a thousand and more scenes from their individual existences, flashing with all the radiance of lives fully lived. Of lives brimming with love.

Mathias whispered, *I can't imagine being apart from you for a few days, let alone a lifetime.*

Malcolm spoke next, his voice indistinguishable from Mathias's. *I'll wait right there for you. No matter how long it takes.*

I told them, *Then I will find you there. Nothing will stop me.*

And with those words I was delivered.

Chapter Thirty-Three

"DON'T LET HIM GO!" I SHOUTED, ALREADY KNOWING WE could not stop it. We didn't possess enough power to combat his basic defense mechanism.

Fallon's struggling ceased as he sensed his body losing form and matter.

"*NO!*" I screamed, clenching his throat all the harder.

Seconds later Derrick and I faced each other with nothing between us, alone together in the bright, vacant space.

"Oh my God," he gasped, shrugging immediately from a hooded sweatshirt and wrapping it around me, appalled at my nudity. "You're naked. *Jesus Christ.* Are you hurt? Oh, my God. There's blood on your mouth. You're Ruthann, aren't you? Did he hurt you?"

He helped me into the sweatshirt with the kindness of a father, tugging it as far down my thighs as it would go, both of us struggling to reconcile what had just happened. Fallon had escaped again – we couldn't prevent it. Tears gushed, fury choking out my voice before I could ask any questions, namely how Derrick had come to be here. I couldn't stop crying or shaking, much to my aggravation.

Derrick, however, couldn't stop babbling. "Come here, you must be freezing. Oh Jesus." He gathered me into a loose, awkward hug, cupping my head. "It's all right, I won't leave you here. Where did…how did… you're not the Ruthann I met a few days ago in Landon, are you?"

The taste of bitter defeat filled my mouth. Derrick smelled like horses and sweat, comforting, familiar scents, and I clung to the temporary security of his physical form, even as a wailing cry resounded across my mind.

Fallon got away...

"Where are we?" Derrick wondered aloud. "Do you know? Have you been trapped here? God, I don't know what the hell just happened. Fallon showed up at the foot of my bed and I tried to shoot him. If I'd have moved faster, I might have gotten him. I tried to jump on him but he vanished and I got...I guess I got pulled with him. I don't know how else to explain it. I ended up here, wherever the fuck *here* is, and then I heard him threatening you. God, he's so fucking insane. I'm sorry I didn't kill him. Did he hurt you?"

"How..." I whispered.

"Are you hurt?" he insisted. "Did he attack you?"

"No, not here. But he...he..." I broke down at the thought of Marshall.

"Shit. Oh God. Shit. Here, let's sit down," Derrick invited, helping me to the floor. "I'm so sorry, this is so fucked up. Where were you before you arrived here? Who did Fallon hurt? Did he burn down the Rawleys' house? That's what Camille and I tried to prevent."

I enfolded my legs in the baggy sweatshirt, facing Derrick as he sat cross-legged a few feet away. I hadn't set eyes on this man since the night of Marshall's twenty-ninth birthday, when Derrick had approached Tish and me in the parking lot at The Spoke. He'd tried to warn us about Fallon that very night, but we hadn't understood. His words penetrated my pinwheeling thoughts and I scrubbed tears from my cheeks, whispering, "Burn their house?"

Derrick's lips compressed. "Let me back up a bit."

I returned to the exact moment I'd been ripped from, landing on hands and knees at Patricia's feet. Malcolm almost fell over me, dodging to the side at the last second. He, Cole, and Patricia clustered close, Monty crying, everyone talking at once. Malcolm set aside his rifle so both his arms were free to enfold me; I clung, seeking stability in the flow of time. My head throbbed; I felt trampled, aching all the way down to my bones.

"It hasn't…changed," I gasped, gulping huge breaths. "Nothing… changed."

"You were returned to your home?" Malcolm held me secure, his blood pulsing at a pace to rival mine.

"It's not my home, not like that…" I thought of what I'd been allowed to glimpse on my journey here – stars and lives and souls and brilliant colors – but was unable to articulate the awe, still reeling from my passage through time.

"Camille, you are hurt." Patricia knelt to examine my face. "Come, Malcolm, bring her to the bed."

Malcolm trailed gentle fingertips over the skin beneath my eyes; I allowed myself a moment's respite to lie flat, observing the agony he was trying hard to submerge. I'd vanished and I might never have returned, and we both knew it. I held fast to his free hand, linking our fingers.

Patricia, sitting near my hip on the opposite side of the unmade bed, smoothed hair from my forehead. "Rest for a spell, if you're able. You appear to have been beaten about the eyes, poor thing."

"Do you think Yancy returned to the future, as well?" Cole asked, standing near the foot of the bed, Monty in the crook of his left arm. "Derrick, I mean, not Fallon."

I wagged my head slowly side to side. "I don't know what to think. I suppose if Derrick showed up in the twenty-first century, he may have decided to stay." The more I considered the possibility, the more it struck me as plausible. And a part of me understood his reasoning; would I return to a dangerous, unpredictable century if not forced? Derrick had no vested interest in returning; the offshoot timeline was all he had ever known, at least in this life.

"All we know for sure is that Fallon is not dead yet," Malcolm said, casting a quick glance toward his abandoned rifle. "He's still out there and I believe that's why your future hasn't changed back to what you remember, Camille." My name sounded so sweet on his lips, his soft drawl elongating the vowels.

"You're right," I whispered. "We saved Blythe, we warned Ruthie and Marshall. We have to assume the Rawleys' house didn't burn. But the future timeline hasn't changed. It can only mean Fallon will keep striking at us as long as he's capable. It means nothing changes until he's gone, for good."

"Let that bastard show up here again tonight," Cole muttered, gazing toward the open door at the silent hallway. "I'll fill his rotten hide with lead. Thank the Lord we're the only ones in this place tonight. We'll have to do some fast-talking to explain them bullet holes in the floor."

Thunder rumbled, prompting Monty's crying to escalate. Cole shifted him inexpertly, still cradling his rifle over his other arm, and Patricia rose to retrieve the baby. I thought of what she'd confided about her love for Axton Douglas, recognizing the depth of sacrifice in her courageous, sensitive soul. Cole would never know what she gave up to stay with him and their son, the ultimate surrender of one kind of love for another.

Axton really is Case, I thought, with a shiver of understanding. *Patricia told me she would forget Axton to be with Cole. That guilt must have stuck with her, never fading. That's why Case recognized her right away in the twenty-first century, the night he saw her picture at The Spoke, but why she resisted him for so long. And all along he was all she ever wanted.*

"Here, you should be lying down, too," I told Patricia, indicating the space beside me on the bed; I wanted in that moment to hold her close, maternal and comforting, acknowledging the forfeiture she had made for her child's sake.

She sank to the mattress, feathering her baby's soft hair.

Malcolm leaned close and kissed my lips. Lingering near for a moment, he whispered, "Cole and me will keep watch, don't you worry."

"Fallon changed the entire timeline?" I asked for about the fifth time.

"Yes, like I said, but only your sisters remembered what was right, at least at first. You arrived in 2014 to warn us and the plan was for *you* to come back with me, to 1882 – this was two days ago now – but you weren't allowed to return. Your sister showed up, instead."

It was too much to comprehend in my current state of mind, too overwhelming to grapple with in light of everything else. I couldn't bear to imagine another version of myself existing in the world Derrick had just described and I studied his solemn face without responding; we sat facing each other in our fog-infested prison, two ants in Fallon's glass jar. And then something else occurred to me. "Is this place something that Fallon controls, do you think? It feels like we're almost...*outside* of time. Can he keep us here, indefinitely?" I struggled to remember his words. "He said...he said no one had ever followed him here except me. And now you."

"That's a good question. I don't know. He vanishes when his life is threatened." Derrick reconsidered. "Maybe he vanishes *here*."

"But where is here? It's horrifying," I whispered, casting my gaze in a loose circle. Derrick and I had attempted twice to 'jump' away, to no avail. There was a distinct feeling of stalling in a holding pattern, like an airplane circling the runway without the ability to land. Nor was there a place to seek shelter or conceal ourselves, no solid walls or foundations to guard our backs. We sat in rigid tension, me in a baggy sweatshirt and nothing else, Derrick in dirty jeans and a sweat-stained t-shirt, awaiting Fallon's reappearance armed with nothing more than Derrick's sturdy boots. And our combined resolve.

Derrick nodded agreement. "This place is even worse than the nineteenth century. And I thought *that* was unendurable. Everything stinks there, literally. I've never been exposed to so many terrible smells."

I ignored his slightly pompous tone, concentrating instead on his admirable qualities, of which there were many, no matter what any of us once believed. I persisted, "You were just with my sister and Malcolm? And Patricia? They were all right when you left?"

"They were." He paused for a second. "I know it's none of my business, but isn't your sister married? I only ask because she and Malcolm Carter were all over each other. I mean *all* over."

"Malcolm is her husband in that life," I explained, a small part of me overjoyed by this news. "I know it's probably hard for you to understand..."

"So Malcolm is Mathias Carter in the nineteenth century?"

"Yes, exactly."

"Just like I'm supposedly Dredd Yancy?" Derrick's dark eyebrows knitted so tightly a ridge formed between them. "A man whose brother browbeats him to pitiful submission, whose wife left him and had another man's baby, and who eventually acted on all that bottled-up rage and shot his own father? And then blamed another man because he was too much a coward to take the fall? *That* Dredd Yancy?"

"You aren't him anymore," I said, with as much conviction as I could muster. "It's not too late to move beyond all of that. Leave the past behind, forever." The urge to weep pushed again at my chest. "The past needs to stay in the past, from now on. We don't belong there."

"It's all right," Derrick murmured, patting my arm; inept at offering comfort, he attempted nonetheless. "I know you're worried about your husband. I'm so sorry."

I thumbed tears from my eyes. "I have to believe he survived. I can't lose him now. Not after everything we've been through."

"If we make it out of this place, back to the right timeline, I mean, what if I don't remember any of what happened here?"

Before I could answer, a low-pitched, resonating rumble vibrated through the floor. Startled, we sprang to our feet; Derrick gathered me close in a gesture of protective masculine instinct. But in the next second we were forced to brace against each other in order to remain upright. The rumbling shuddered through our bodies. If there had been plates or glasses on nearby shelves, they would be shattering around our ankles.

"An earthquake?" I shouted.

The fog swirled, an indifferent mass offering no answers. Nothing in sight suggested alarm but the vibrations increased in intensity.

"Come on," Derrick decided, leaning close to be heard. "We can't just stand here!"

Holding tightly to one another, we stumbled forward.

We extinguished the candle lanterns and tried to sleep; in the darkness, our backs lightly touching, Patricia and I lay alongside each other while she nursed Monty and I curled on my right side, facing Malcolm.

He sat on the floor near my side of the bed, angled toward the door and with his rifle braced over his lap; we couldn't bear to stop touching. The late hour and the rain canceled the need for words but our caresses spoke volumes. I stroked his hair, his face, committing its contours to memory; from time to time he gathered my questing hand and kissed my fingers, one by one, or simply placed my palm against his cheek.

Maybe an hour passed – my eyelids drifted closed at last, weighted with near-delirious exhaustion. The thunder eventually rolled east of Windham but the rain continued unabated, weeping over the boarding-house and muffling the sound of someone's passage along the hallway. The furtive steps infiltrated my half-dozing mind, shaping into a blurry gray nightmare. A man crept along only yards from us, rabid eyes fixed on the bedroom door. He wanted us dead with a desire hinging on insanity. He was losing touch with reality, with everything but the need to consume our lives. A small pack of strike-on-the-box matches curled in one hand, a bottle of whiskey in the other. In the dream I hovered along behind him, ghost-like, watching mutely.

My legs jerked beneath the covers.

Wake up…

Camille! Wake up!

My eyelids parted in time to observe our closed door flare with radiant light, sudden and shocking, like a firecracker exploding in an empty black sky. Time skidded to a painful halt, each subsequent moment stumbling forward, one to the next, like an injured runner. Backlit by orange heat, Malcolm and Cole fired their rifles repeatedly at the door – now ablaze – and the adjacent wall, a hail of destruction, the rifle rounds splitting the drywall as though it was tissue paper. Patricia and I huddled together on the bed, Monty wailing between us, unable to blink, unable to process what was happening. Thick smoke swelled inward and long arms of flame encompassed the ceiling beams – and sense suddenly overpowered immobility.

"Get up!" I shouted, grabbing Patricia's elbow, half-dragging her and Monty from the bed. Rain poured over the exterior of the boarding-house but this interior space would be engulfed in less than a minute.

The rain wouldn't save us from burning alive if we remained stationary.

But we're on the second floor!

We can't jump to the ground from up here! What about the baby?!

Of course Fallon had realized all of these things.

"Malcolm!" I screamed. "Cole!"

Smoke billowed, stinging my eyes, closing off my lungs. Heat blistered my skin – a fleeting image of us splayed on a charcoal grill bounced through my mind. Malcolm's pupils reflected the flames, his face bathed in searing red. He threw aside his rifle and clenched hold of my elbow, understanding the necessity of jumping to safety. We couldn't chance a dash through the fire. The entire wall was now overwhelmed – in seconds the floor and ceiling would follow suit. Cole used his rifle to break the window, scraping the stock along the remaining triangle-shaped shards, clearing the way as best he could; cool air rushed inside as he leaned out, sparing precious seconds to scan the ground below.

"The bed!" I cried, pulling free from Malcolm's hold, scrabbling to tear the quilts from its surface before they became ash; their bulk could pad the landing. The floor torched my feet, clad in nothing but dirty socks, as I bunched the blankets against my chest; we could hardly see through the smoke.

"Hurry!" Cole bellowed.

I leaned as far as I dared over the windowsill, letting the blankets tumble directly below. The ground appeared impossibly far away – like the speckled, chlorinated water miles beneath the high dive at the city pool of my youth. There was exactly no time to decide in which order we should exit the room, only that Patricia and the baby could not go first.

Malcolm shouted, "I'll go, then Camille, and we'll catch you, Patricia! Cole, you help her down!" And without another word he shimmied out the window, legs leading the way, letting his body hang down the side of the building while he gripped the sill, therefore minimizing the distance; he let go and I bit through my tongue.

He landed on the blankets, dropped to an inadvertent crouch and fell sideways. But he sprang at once to his feet and hollered, "Come on! I've got you!"

I mimicked his movements, refusing to look down; gripping the sill I beat aside a deep, primal fear of heights and let my body slide downward until I hung like a pair of jeans on a clothesline.

"I've got you!" Malcolm repeated and I trusted him enough to let myself fall.

Patricia was next, Monty enfolded in her arms. Cole helped them out the window and fear clamped my chest in a stranglehold.

"Oh God," I moaned, staring up at them. "*The baby…*"

"We'll catch them," Malcolm said. And to Patricia, "Come on!"

Patricia dropped like a stone but we were there to cushion her fall. The rain whitewashed the sound of my wrist bones breaking; so hopped up on adrenaline at that point, and relief that she and the baby were unharmed, the pain took its time surfacing.

Before he jumped, Cole bellowed, "Look out!" and tossed down the rifles. By the time he hit the ground his clothes were on fire – he landed hard and immediately sprawled flat, rolling on the wet ground to beat out the flames. Not a second to spare; the window above shone orange with deadly light, coils of acrid smoke rolling forth into the storming night. And no respite in sight; Malcolm and Cole were quick to gather up their weapons and hustle us to the safety of the adjacent barn, where they checked on Aces High and Cole's horse, Charger.

"You think we got him?" Cole demanded, the four of us, plus Monty, clustered together near the wide double doors, out of the rain but in view of the burning boardinghouse. "We must have dumped a dozen rounds each."

"I don't know," Malcolm admitted, slightly out of breath. "I pray at least one or two pierced his filthy hide." His observant gaze darted across the street. "We best wake the Lunds, yonder. They ain't gonna be any too happy about all this." He looked down at me, tucked close to his side, and his sweet smile lifted his lips. I would, forever after, remember him exactly that way – suspended in that moment, both of us wet, wounded, dirty and disheveled, but safe in each other's arms; his beautiful dark eyes full of tenderness and love.

Had I sensed the finality rushing toward us?

I must have, at some deep level, because I had the foresight to say, "I love you, Malcolm," before I disappeared.

We could not flee the vibrations and were forced to crouch, huddling together to remain upright. Our jaws clacked, our bones jounced. Talking became impossible. I tipped my chin to my chest, gripping Derrick's forearm in one hand, cupping my belly with the other. I held a picture of Marshall in my mind, imagined him whole and hale and safe, looking my way with his wide, knowing grin. I envisioned him holding our son in his strong arms, nuzzling the baby's cheeks and kissing his downy hair. I added my family, and Marshall's, to the picture; let's say it was December, snowy and bright, and we were all gathered at Clark's to celebrate. Marshall would present me with the little Conestoga wagon carved by his ancestor, the most honorary ornament on the Rawley family Christmas tree.

It's your turn this year, angel.

A hand latched around my bare ankle and I shrieked, recoiling so violently the momentum knocked Derrick and me sideways.

Flat on his belly, Fallon sprawled no more than arms' length away from us.

Derrick lurched to his feet, stumbling to put me behind him. We had neglected to haul along Derrick's boots in our concern over the sudden insubstantiality of our surroundings and so we faced Fallon unarmed.

"He's been shot!" Derrick shouted.

I saw it for myself in the next second; wherever Fallon had materialized after vanishing from our strangling grip had not been a welcoming environment. His clothing was dark with blood. His lips parted, exposing teeth rimmed in red. His pale eyes held mine, flat and unremorseful to the end; he braced with one hand against the vibrating floor while the other clutched a large hole in his side.

"Who shot you?!" I cried, suddenly fearful of the damage Fallon may have inflicted before this incapacitation. "Where did you come from?!"

Derrick knelt, with difficulty, and demanded, "How do we get out of here, Fallon? Tell us!"

"You don't." Fallon's lips twitched in a smile; he was almost inaudible. "You don't. There's no way out."

"Tell us!" I screamed. A rippling swell, like surf crashing upon dry land, knocked me to all fours. "You fucking son of a bitch, *tell us!*"

"This place is self-destructing!" Derrick hollered, unable to find his footing.

Fallon rolled sideways, head lolling.

"It's because he's dying!" I yelled. Something else occurred to me – what if Fallon vanished yet again? Though it seemed impossible, what if he escaped somewhere and was subsequently patched up?

We couldn't chance it.

Derrick realized the same thing and crawled forward, reaching to grasp Fallon's head in both hands. And with a deft movement, before he could reconsider, he snapped Fallon's neck.

Chapter Thirty-Four

MY EYES WERE CLOSED BUT I HEARD MY SISTERS CRYING. Both of them nearby, sobbing and talking fast.

No...

Oh, please no...

I was freezing and ached from head to toes, as if I'd spent a long day waterskiing or jogging, pushing the boundaries of my physical limits.

But you haven't done anything like that lately...

You're pregnant.

I sat up fast, my vision immediately mottled by dense purple spots.

What in the hell...

Camille scrambled to my side from the left, throwing her arms around me and almost taking both of us to the pavement. Because, I realized, sense returning in halting increments, we were sitting on cold, wet pavement between two rows of cars in the parking lot of The Spoke. Music thumped from inside; I was pretty sure I heard Mathias singing. The blacktop beneath us was slushy and my jeans and the back of Case's flannel shirt, which I was wearing, were soaked through. My pregnant belly created a small, smooth swell between my hipbones.

I blinked. Then blinked again. The dizzy spots receded.

"Oh God..." I moaned, eyes locked with my older sister's. Her face was shiny with tears and she was breathing fast. I gripped her sweater, holding as tightly as I could. "Oh, Camille...we just...*we just...*"

"I know," she whispered, hugging me again, squeezing hard, both of us shaking.

To our right, a tall man raced toward the front entrance, waving his arms and shouting, "We need help! This man needs medical attention! He's been shot!"

Derrick Yancy, I realized.

Memories began assaulting, hard and fast.

Case…shot in the stomach in Chicago…

Our real lives erased…

"It's all right, Tish, it's all right." As though I was a little girl, Camille held me close, cupping the back of my head. Her breath fanned my cheek as she whispered, "We're back. We made it back."

"Then who…what…"

"It's Marshall, he's hurt. C'mon," and so saying, Camille stood and helped me to my feet.

Ten paces away Ruthie, clad in nothing but a baggy gray sweatshirt, knelt supporting Marshall's upper body with both arms. He was conscious, clutching his right shoulder; the front of his shirt was covered in blood.

Ruthann and Marshall, here in Jalesville in 2014.

Home. They were home.

Sobs broke like glass in my chest. I fell to my knees to hug Ruthie, to kiss Marshall's face, to touch both of them; it had been so long. And then I heard the front door bang open and my husband shouting my name, brimming with concern, and nothing else mattered. I stumbled to my feet and met him halfway across the lot, crying so hard I couldn't see.

"Baby, what's going on? What's wrong? Who's been shot?!" Case enfolded me in his arms and I threaded mine around him, clinging for dear life, so grateful my knees became jelly.

Home.

Jalesville, Case, our baby…

We had been restored.

"Oh my God, they're back," Case breathed, catching sight of them. Completely floored, he stared with wide eyes, momentarily frozen in place. "Holy *shit!* Marsh! Ruthie!"

I couldn't explain a damn thing, too overcome. The parking lot promptly flooded with people, everyone within The Spoke surging outside from the warm, neon-tinted interior to offer help; Mathias, Garth, Becky, the Heller girls. Ruthie and Marsh were inundated. Everyone talking, babbling, freaking out. I recognized the fact that in almost everyone else's perception Camille and I had only been absent for a few minutes. We would have plenty of time to explain later. For now, I couldn't think beyond Case in my arms, safe, whole, *himself.*

I could never be thankful enough.

"Call Clark!" Becky ordered Garth, on her knees beside Ruthann.

"I already did!" cried Lee Heller, Marshall's cousin; all three Heller girls, Pam, Lee, and Netta, crouched near him and Ruthie, clucking with concern.

"And I called Mom!" Pam added. "They're all on the way."

One arm around Marshall's shoulder and tears on his face, Garth couldn't stop talking, his deep voice ragged with emotion. "Marshall, *you're back.* Oh Jesus, we've missed you, we've been so scared. Dad said they were going to join us for the music so they might be on the way already. They're going to lose it. Marsh, holy shit, where have you two been? We've missed you both so fucking much…"

Pale and drawn, Marshall could only wag his head side to side – *I'll explain later.* He reached with his free hand and Garth gripped it between both of his, squeezing hard.

Sirens sounded, wailing closer.

"Baby, we better call Shore Leave too," Case said. "My phone's in my back pocket…"

I reached up to frame his face with both hands. He couldn't understand in this moment the depth of my gratitude; he didn't realize what I'd endured in the altered timeline – our separation in these past weeks that for him had passed in a matter of minutes. *He had died in my arms on a rainy Chicago sidewalk.* I would never forget the horror of that. But Case recognized my raw emotion, gently gripping my wrists and turning to press kisses to my palms, one after the other.

"I'm here," he murmured, keeping me tucked to his side. "Right here, sweetheart."

Mom answered my call on the first ring by demanding, "What's happened? Jilly just called and said something's happening!"

I choked up all over again; I could hear Blythe and my little brothers, Matthew and Nathaniel, in the background, and pictured them in their cozy kitchen in the cabin Blythe had built for Mom in the woods beyond Shore Leave. Before I could respond a loud truck made a sharp right into the lot and bounced over the curb, slamming to a halt and simultaneously peeling off a parked car's back bumper with a shrill, metallic screech. The local ambulance roared in right behind the truck, which I recognized as Sean Rawley's; he, Quinn, Wy, and Clark left all four doors gaping as they bounded out.

"Ruthie! *Marshall!* Where's my son?" Clark hollered, running full-bore.

Marshall's gaze flew toward the sound of his father's voice and he began sobbing; harsh, chest-heaving sobs. *"Dad…"*

Everyone else backed away to let the Rawleys close to Marsh and Ruthie, and while they were careful of Marshall's injury, it was still pure chaos.

Shouting to be heard, I told Mom, "Ruthie's home!"

Two hours later and well after midnight, we were all gathered in Clark's living room. Every light on the main floor was glowing. Food covered every flat surface, even though it was sustenance enough to know Ruthie and Marsh were in the same county. *In the same century.* Tucked close to Mathias on the leather couch, legs curled beneath me, I sat nursing James, an afghan arranged over his chubby little body. I couldn't bear to let any of them out of my sight and so our tired, wild-eyed kids were running amok, egged on by Wy and Sean, eating brownies and chips and knocking over cans of soda; Clark's sister, Julie Heller, had hauled along enough snacks for the entire county. Ruthie, Clark, Garth, and Becky had stayed in Miles City at the hospital with Marshall, who had required a blood transfusion and would not be allowed home for at least a few days.

Tish and I – and Derrick Yancy – were the only ones who remembered anything about the alternate timeline.

My sister and Case sat on the adjacent couch, Case's arms wrapped almost double around Tish as she snuggled close to him, her head on his shoulder. Because the kids were present we had not related extensive details about what we'd been through; full disclosure could come later, after we'd slept. And…been allowed a little time to heal.

Malcolm, I thought for the countless time, with bittersweet acknowledgment of the tender ache that would, forever after, exist deep in my heart.

I could never thank Malcolm Carter enough, could never hope to repay him for what he'd done to restore my life. I prayed that in return he kept his promise and lived out the remainder of his life seeking happiness rather than running from it; I prayed he had eventually married and become a father. I'd come quickly to recognize that any chance of a child created during our night in Muscatine was an impossibility; with the righting of our timeline my body had been restored to its former condition, the one which had given birth to five babies and was currently nursing the newest. I would not bear Malcolm's baby; the memory of our lovemaking, I decided, would remain sacred, existing between us alone. I would never see Malcolm again and it was the least I could do for him.

Someday, when I was brave enough, I would look for clues. I would search for hints as to Malcolm's later life in old documents, letters, telegrams…

Or…maybe I would not.

Maybe, as Ruthie said, the past was better left in the past.

I cupped my husband's face with my free hand, his thick black beard soft atop the firm line of his solid jaw, and his beautiful eyes, the deep blue of Flickertail beneath summer sunshine, crinkled at the outer corners as he grinned. The sight of his grin caused the next breath to lodge in my chest; the bridge of my nose stung with unshed tears. Malcolm's spirit, his very essence, shone so clearly in Mathias's every movement, his every expression. And I recognized all over again the depth of connection our two souls had shared since time began; in this way, Malcolm would never be far from my side.

"My sweet woman," Mathias murmured, leaning close to steal a quick, soft kiss, tucking wayward curls behind my right ear. "It's been a hell of a night, hasn't it?"

I thought of leaping from a bedroom window into Malcolm's arms; for me, that moment had occurred but hours ago.

"It has," I whispered, edging closer to him, cuddling our baby between us. "A *hell* of a night."

Derrick Yancy, perched on an ottoman between the two couches, looked up from scooping dip onto a handful of chips. A week ago the Rawleys, let alone Tish and Case, would never have welcomed Derrick into their home. But things had changed. Fallon's death had been the catalyst in a series of events that culminated, at least in one immediate way, in a distinct difference in Derrick's persona. He seemed, in fact, almost giddy.

He broke free from his past. He took action and shed his connection to Dredd. And, more importantly, from Fallon, whose natural life should have ended over a century ago.

"It was only a ploy," Derrick had explained earlier, referring to his family's attempt to reclaim the Rawley and Spicer homesteads for themselves. "I don't want this land. I never did, it was only ever for Fallon's sake. I hate Montana, if you want to know the truth. I fucking *hate* nature. I've wanted to move to Manhattan for years now and I told my father so this evening."

"What about Fallon?" Tish whispered. "How will you explain his absence?"

We would not learn until much later exactly what had occurred in the final moments of Fallon's life; Ruthie was unable to speak of it for many months afterward. At that point, I assumed Fallon had died from gunshot wounds inflicted by Malcolm and Cole. Derrick responded quietly, "No one in this century ever has to know, for sure. My father will assume, I suppose, that Fallon reached a point where he was unable to return to the future. Or that he simply died in the past." Derrick's brows drew inward. "He should have died long ago, as it is."

"I think it's a wonderful decision for you, moving to New York. It suits you. You seem different. But in a good way," Tish added hastily. "I mean that."

Derrick looked intently at her for only a second, before sighing and softening his gaze. "It is pretty wonderful, isn't it?" A small smile tipped his lips. "I'd hate to come up against you in a court of law. I wouldn't stand a chance."

Robbie Benson was still alive in this timeline. Tish had called him almost immediately after we'd spoken to Mom and Aunt Jilly, to Grandma and Aunt Ellen – everyone in Landon accounted for, their lives, and therefore ours, blessedly returned to normal; at some point, I would ask Aunt Jilly if she remembered anything. No one else seemed to retain a hint of it, thank goodness, but Robbie had in fact remembered something even more important – Tish's warning to steer clear of all dealings with the Turnbulls. After law school he had gone to work for a small nonprofit and lived in a Chicago suburb along with his wife, a woman he'd met in France while on spring break.

Ruthie called later with the news that Marshall was in stable condition, currently sleeping, and that she and Clark would stay in Miles City until he was discharged; Garth and Becky were on their way back to Jalesville.

"Are you all right? Have you taken a second to sit down?" I demanded. I'd left the living room so there was a chance of hearing her over the din; I sank to sit cross-legged on the carpet in the hallway leading to the back of Clark's house. "You sound like you're ready to collapse. And you're pregnant!"

Ruthie laughed, a soft expulsion of breath. "I'm more than all right. We're home, Marshall is safe." I pictured her sweet, beautiful face bathed in the low-wattage glow of the lights in Marshall's hospital room, surely dimmed for sleeping. After a weighty pause, she whispered, "Camille. Oh, God, *Milla*. There's so much we have to talk about. Not right now… but soon. Promise?"

"I promise." I rested the back of my head on the wall, closing my eyes so no tears would escape. "We'll stay in Montana for a while longer, don't worry. Besides, everyone is flying out here tomorrow, Mom and Blythe and everyone. Be prepared!"

She laughed again, simultaneously clearing her throat; I heard her sniffling and imagined her swiping at tears. "It's just…there's so many things we left unresolved, so much I don't know. And I don't know if I'm brave enough to *ever* know."

I understood on a deep, absolute level.

"What happened to Axton, to Patricia and Cole and the baby? I left them all so quickly, they'll never know what really happened to Marshall and me. Birdie and Celia will be so worried. Ax won't know what to do. *Oh God…*" Ruthie's voice broke.

"I know, honey, I really do."

She sniffled again, with a small, choked gulp. "Derrick told me a little about you and Malcolm. Oh, Camille, I know how that must have been. When I realized who Miles really was…*just before he died…*" Crying now, she was overcome, beyond exhaustion, and I wished I could wrap her in my arms.

"Ruthie, we'll talk when you're ready. I'm here for you, always. I promise."

"Thank you," she managed at last. "I don't know what I would do without you and Tish."

"That's what sisters are for."

Chapter Thirty-Five

Landon, MN - July, 2018

"THIS FEELS SO ILLICIT," MARSHALL WHISPERED, PEERING around as if it was bright midday rather than deep night. Thick with heat and humidity, the summer air felt like juice. Crickets and gray peepers sang in harmony, accompanied by the occasional bullfrog; the stars glittered with no moon to overshadow them, dotting Flickertail's smooth surface with reflected diamonds.

"Hurry, honey, the mosquitoes are going to eat us alive." I giggled, slipping on the dew-damp bank as we scurried toward the water; the dock boards trembled beneath our bare feet. I turned so that my back was angled toward him and ordered, "Untie me, quick, before they carry us away."

"Oh God, with pleasure," he groaned, cupping my breasts from behind, lightly jiggling them against his wide palms before untying my bikini top and slipping the straps from my shoulders. He gently bit my nape, exposed by my pinned-up hair, and then, with a muted roar, leaped from the end of the dock, sending cold droplets arcing over me as he cannonballed into the water.

"You aren't naked!" I yelled in a whisper, hands on hips.

Treading water ten feet out, I saw the bright flash of his teeth as he grinned. "I ain't taking *no* chances," he teased. "Too many fish!"

I stepped delicately from my bottoms and Marshall executed a surface dive, gliding toward me beneath the lake. He reached the dock and rested his elbows on the end board, water pearling from his wide shoulders, catching my ankles in his chilly hands. Wet hair slicked back from his forehead, he offered up a wicked smile. "This is a heavenly view, angel," he murmured, eyes all over my naked flesh.

Our third child and first daughter had joined our family only three months ago – and our sex life had taken a wee bit of a hit since then, to say the least. To indulge in this moment of unhurried and undiluted lust with my husband felt so damn good I didn't even mind the subsequent mosquito bites.

"May I join you?" I asked demurely, the one to cup my breasts this time, gently tracing my thumbs over my distended nipples. Almost immediately my letdown reflex prickled to life, drenching my skin with sticky milk. "Oops…*dammit*…"

"Get in here, woman, right this second. I need you like I've never needed anything in this world." Marsh was giddy with bliss at our secret, skinny-dipping date. "I can't believe how hard I am in this cold water… here, feel, *hurry*…"

Giggling like a teenager I did indeed hurry, joining him with a noisy splash, surfacing to wrap all around his almost-nude body.

"You *are* hard, *you feel so good*…get these stupid trunks off…"

His mouth was too full to respond, his hands too busy to obey my breathless order, and so I made short work of his swimwear, slipping it down just enough to expose the enormous evidence of his desire. Marsh slid both hands along the length of my thighs, sleek and buoyant under the water, drawing them around his hips and deepening our kisses, groaning against my lips. It had been weeks since we'd last managed to sneak in a round of lovemaking and I tore my mouth from his to insist, "Don't come too quick, honey…"

"I can't promise…" And he groaned again, inspiring a new round of giggling, as he slid fully home, grasping my ass in both hands.

"Slow," I demanded in a whisper, licking his lower lip, taking him deep; he was so hard he could probably have pole-vaulted and my giggles dissolved in a wave of pure heat.

"Slow?" he repeated in teasing disbelief. "Holy God, woman, I'm about to explode…"

I ran my fingers repeatedly through his damp hair, which fell past his shoulders when wet. He'd long since shaved his winter beard but his jaws were deliciously stubbled here in the late-night hours as he rubbed his chin against my neck, circling his tongue around my taut nipples until I shivered; biting his earlobe, I met his thrusts with renewed energy.

I'd been so exhausted this past winter, huge with my third pregnancy, that attempting to corral our sweet, busy little boys, Axton Clark, almost four, and Marshall Augustus, Junior, age two, proved almost impossible. Fortunately I didn't have far to walk for help; our back deck was only a stone's throw from Clark's. While Marshall was at work on weekdays – he'd been hired four years ago by Montana Fish and Wildlife – Clark helped me mind Ax and little Marsh. The boys had been so excited for the arrival of their new brother, picking different names for him each day, and hadn't we all been surprised and delighted when a baby girl arrived, instead. We named her Celia Faye.

"*I gotta come…*"

"Not yet!" I slowed our vigorous motion, clinging to his shoulders; the right bore a puckered round scar from the bullet's passage through his body and I put my lips on it, inhaling a deep breath. The lake lapped our waists.

"*Angel…*"

"Now," I gasped at last, shuddering against him, renewed beyond belief.

Marshall kept me wrapped in his arms and ducked us both beneath the surface. We erupted from the lake laughing, soaked and sated, to hear cheering and clapping from the bank; I squeaked and sank to my nose in the water while Marshall remained standing with arms lifted and widespread. He called, "Thank you, I deserve applause for that!"

Case snorted, laughing, already shedding his shirt. "What we saw was about five seconds of performance there, Rawley, nothing to brag about."

"We just got here, we didn't see anything," Tish assured me, shaking out her curls, keeping her swimsuit primly in place until she'd entered the water. She threw it back to shore and then kicked off the lake bottom, swimming underwater until clearing the weeds, surfacing with a happy sigh and smoothing hair from her face.

"Are the kids still sleeping?" I asked, gliding to my sister's side. We'd left the little ones in Aunt Jilly and Uncle Justin's cabin under the watchful eyes of Rae and Millie Jo, who'd both turned fourteen this past winter.

"They were when we snuck out. The big kids are still playing Monopoly."

By 'big kids' she meant Matthew, Nathaniel, Millie Jo, Rae, Brantley, Henry, and Riley. And Wy, who was visiting with Clark; the two of them had ridden from Montana with us, alternating between our truck and Case's. These days the 'little kids' were Zoe, Lorie, and James; my little Axton, Marsh, and baby Celia; and Case and Tish's Annie and Shea. Annie was almost four, same as Ax, while Shea, whose full name was Charles Shea, had just turned one.

"Make *waaaay!*" shouted another voice and five seconds later the dock shuddered as Mathias raced over it and leaped from the end, producing more noise than all of our kids combined. He surfaced with a roar, whooping and splashing, clearly hoping to incite a water fight; Case and Marsh were happy to oblige.

"This was supposed to be a *private date*," I complained, flicking water at them.

Camille perched on the end of the dock and let her toes dangle in the lake, observing us with a smile. Her long hair hung in a loose braid and she wore cut-off jeans over her suit. It was only a matter of time before she joined us; the mosquitoes were atrocious.

"Are Mom and Aunt Jilly coming in?" Tish asked her.

"How come everyone's at Shore Leave? I thought they were at Mom's," I groaned, watching as the cafe windows suddenly glowed with golden light; in the next second I heard Mom and Aunt Jilly laughing as they climbed the porch steps.

"They decided to make margaritas and needed supplies," Camille explained.

I glanced toward my husband, who had Mathias in a headlock, both of them in water up to their armpits; Case leaped and took everyone underwater, displacing about half the lake in the process – and I witnessed my romantic date night disappear over the horizon. I couldn't help but giggle at their roughhousing; the guys tended to revert to teenaged behavior when in each other's company.

"Ruthie, what do you say? You in the mood for a margarita?" Tish swam to my side.

"That sounds great, actually."

Five minutes later, back in our suits and wrapped in beach towels, we followed Camille up the damp shore. I heard the blender before we entered the cafe and hooked my arm through Tish's, taking a moment to count my blessings; I never let a day pass without doing so. Happiness, contentment; the joy of a simple life. I would never again take these things for granted. It had been many years since I'd experienced a cold pulse at the base of my spine, a sickening twinge at the back of my neck – the sense that if I'd turned around a second faster, I would have spied Fallon behind me. Waiting. Biding his time. The first year home I'd suffered panic attacks and intense nightmares; Marshall's love and patience were endless and I'd eventually overcome such anxieties.

Even so, there were still occasional moments when shards of fear pierced my heart and I would have to stop what I was doing and run to find Marshall; times when I would spy him coming my way across our barnyard, silhouetted by the saffron glow of sunset, his wide shoulders and lanky stride, his cowboy hat and easy grace, and gladness would rise so swift and potent in my heart it was half pain. In addition to Arrow and Banjo we kept two mares, Twyla and Tilly, gentle horses upon which Marsh was teaching our boys to ride; Celia, too, once she was old enough. I supposed that one day I would return to work at the law office with Tish, but not anytime soon. I loved being home with my kids and horses; Marsh and I joked about having a dozen of each someday.

The mood inside Shore Leave was one of pure, unbridled summertime joy. All the adults – the *alleged* adults, as Grandma said – were gathered along the bar counter, while Aunt Jilly poured tequila and Mom spun the blender. Clark sat between Dodge and Rich; along with Blythe and Uncle Justin, they were drinking tap beer rather than margaritas. Two relationships of particular magnitude had formed while Marshall and I were away; Grandma explained to me, much later, that they had reconsidered a few things in the face of my disappearance. And so it was that Grandma and Aunt Ellen, the independent daughters of Louisa Davis, raised to rule the roost without men, had finally admitted their feelings for Rich and Dodge. Of course we'd suspected long before that Ellen and Dodge cared for each other, but to witness them openly happy and in love was a blessing to all of us.

Mom, Blythe, Uncle Justin, and Aunt Jilly had undertaken the bulk of running Shore Leave these days. Along with Case and Tish, Jalesville was the place Marshall and I called home these days, but Landon would never be fully displaced in my heart. Every summer Tish and I packed up our busy families, and more often than not Clark and one or two of the Rawley boys, to spend July in Landon. We continued the tradition of celebrating the annual Fourth of July Eve party, watching the parade and fireworks the next day; lounging on the lakeshore during the hot daylight hours and gathering by the fire and listening to Marshall and Case make music as evening faded to night.

My family, I thought, aching with happiness. *My family of women no longer afraid of a curse on them. No longer afraid of the past.*

There were unknowns. Though I thought often of them, I had not yet found the courage to look up any available information on Patricia, Cole, or Axton, the Rawleys or the Davises. A part of me justified this by the fact that their descendents – *us* – were alive and thriving, which assured me that they, too, had continued on long past 1882. Neither had Camille attempted to find Malcolm. One night, two summers ago, she confided in Tish and me, weeping and overcome as she told us about what really took place between her and Malcolm that night in Muscatine; her words were the only secret I had ever, or would ever, keep from Marshall.

Some late nights Marshall and I lay awake in our cabin, speculating about those we'd left behind. Though we both missed all of them intensely, we had decided long ago that we would leave the past alone. Thankfully, neither of us had ever since felt the pull of time on our bodies or spirits.

"We did what we could," Marsh whispered once. "We nearly gave them our *lives,* angel."

But sometimes I thought I heard Patricia's voice, calling to me.

Sometimes I sensed Axton hovering near – his spirit, maybe, or maybe nothing more than my memories of him.

I comforted myself with the knowledge that Axton's soul inhabited Case – he and Patricia finally allowed a life together, after everything they had been through.

I shut out the 'what-ifs' that tried to surface.

"Girls! Just in time. Come have a drink!" Aunt Jilly heralded as Tish, Camille, and I entered from the dining room, raising her margarita glass in a salute.

"Are those the boys I hear roughhousing?" Grandma asked, pretending irritation. "We'll have Charlie Evans out here with all that noise!"

Rich passed Grandma a fresh margarita, kissing her cheek in the process.

"Is our cabin still in one piece?" Uncle Justin asked Tish, with a grin. "I think you and Case were the last to leave."

"Rae and Millie Jo are good baby-sitters," Tish said reassuringly, holding out her mug for Mom to fill with delicious, frothy, citrus slush. "Ooh, *yum.*"

"Wy's still there," I reminded Uncle Justin, hugging Aunt Ellen from behind before accepting a brimming mug. "And he's a very responsible kid." Though, at nineteen, Wy wasn't exactly a kid anymore. It was tough to think of him as a young adult; in most ways, he was still smiley, adorable, adoring Wy. It wasn't lost on me, or Camille, that Millie Jo's gigantic crush on him increased in strength every summer.

Once we each held a fresh drink, Blythe stood and lifted his beer. "I'd like to propose a toast," he said, winking at Mom. He wore a pale blue Shore Leave t-shirt and yellow swim trunks, his long hair in a low ponytail; other than his full beard and mustache, Blythe looked almost no different than the first summer he came into our lives, over fifteen years ago now. Mom, who honestly hadn't changed all that much either, blew him a kiss, which he pretended to catch; then he pressed her kiss to his heart.

"*Awwww*," Aunt Jilly cooed; her blue eyes gleamed with both love and tequila. She hooked one arm around Uncle Justin's neck and planted a smooching kiss on his scarred face, and he laughed, tugging her onto his lap.

Having gained our full attention and adopting a teasing, formal air, Blythe said, "I want to express my deep gratitude at being Joelle's husband and therefore a part of this family. Baby," and he grinned anew at Mom, "I love you. I've never loved anyone more. Thank you for our family and for our lives here together."

Tears and laughter and hearty agreement from everyone. I set down my glass to latch my arms around Camille and Tish, on either side of me, and squeezed them close. My sisters, who I could not get by without. Our men, our children, our extended families. All gathered here in and around Shore Leave and Flickertail Lake, where everything began. We knew how fortunate we were; we understood the blessings of our simple life.

A family of women, no longer afraid to love.

"Thank you," I whispered to the universe, smiling and crying both at once. "Thank you so much."

Printed in the United States
by Baker & Taylor Publisher Services